Warrior Outcast

Book Four of the Dragon Spawn Chronicles

By Dawn Ross

"Prejudice has kept people from helping each other for centuries, with no scientific justification. Even after we met our neighbours in the galaxy, we found new bigotries…"
– Doctor M'Benga from Star Trek: Strange New Worlds

Warrior Outcast

Book Four of the Dragon Spawn Chronicles

by Dawn Ross

Cover
Cyborg art by Jon Stubbington. Spaceship purchased from freestyledesingworks through 123rf.com under their standard license agreement. The starry background is a public domain image from NASA. Images combined by germancreative on fiverr.com.

Special Thanks

I'd like to extend a special thanks to all the beta readers and editors who helped me make this novel shine. And additional thanks to my final editor, Grace Bridges, who has been instrumental in helping me with content and line edits as well as with pointing out opportunities for story improvement.

Reviews for StarFire Dragons

"A thoughtful novel that owes a debt to
Star Trek but works on its own terms."
—*Kirkus Reviews*

"A subtle space opera that explores the ethical
conundrums of intergalactic relations with main
characters who are worth rooting for."
—Becca Saffier, *Reedsy Discovery*

"Fans of epic sci-fi that look for realistic characters and complex
yet believable settings will find *Starfire Dragons*
a powerful introductory story that promises more, yet
nicely concludes its immediate dilemmas."
—D. Donovan, Senior Reviewer, *Midwest Book Review*

Warrior Outcast

Book Four of the Dragon Spawn Chronicles

by Dawn Ross

1
At the Mercy of Enemies

3791:135:14:27. Year 3791, day 135, 14:27 hours, Prontaean time as per the last sync. Jori huffed from the brisk but steady pace as the diagnostic treadmill spooled beneath him. After spending over a quarter of a year recovering from a stab to the heart, he embraced the familiar ache of strenuous exercise. Sweat glazed his skin and his leg muscles burned. It felt so good, he almost forgot he was in the infirmary of an enemy ship.

The colorless composites of the apathetic machines both clashed with and complemented the sterile white walls of the place. Bulky body scanners, nanite healing beds, and other contraptions sat lifelessly in the corners, enhancing the cold atmosphere. Medics in light blue uniforms provided the only vibrancy as they conducted their tasks.

Doctor Gregson leaned over Jori's shoulder, squinting as he reviewed the monitor. "My goodness, young man. You're doing remarkably well for someone recovering from major surgery."

"I heal fast," Jori replied between breaths.

"I should say so. Your new heart works wonderfully. Have you always had this much stamina?"

"Yes."

Commander J.D. Hapker winked at Jori and spoke to the doctor. "He could spend all day in the gymnasium without tiring."

Doctor Gregson's brows shot up. "Really? That's quite a feat, especially for a ten-year-old."

Jori refrained from commenting on the false praise. The doctor meant well.

"He's a remarkable young man," Hapker said.

Jori's emotions swelled at the crooked smile spreading across Hapker's face. A fleeting sensation of warmth incinerated as he remembered why he was here and what he'd left behind. Instead of being in the company of black-garbed warriors with dark, narrow eyes and darker hair, he was surrounded by diversity.

The two men before him exemplified this. Hapker's sandy hair and lighter skin contrasted with the doctor's black hair and darker skin. Even the clothes they wore seemed contradictory—one with a loose white coat and the other with a form-fitting brown uniform.

The differences among all the people here went wider still. The yellow eyes of a medic stood out almost as much as the bright blue ones of another. A different medic on the opposite side of the room had red hair. A doctor he'd met earlier had a tall, thin build while the stout man nearby was shorter than Jori.

The doctor's cheeks rounded as he smiled. "So I've heard, and now I'm seeing the evidence."

Despite the man's easy manner, Jori winced. Not everyone aboard this ship admired his abilities. Whispers of genetical enhancements and cybernetic augmentation abounded.

Neither was the case. He was a warrior, bred to be the best. His greatest strengths—endurance, a strong immune system, intelligence, and excellent muscle memory—were all inherited. He even had a talent for sensing the emotions of others, which he got from his mother. Empathy—his one flaw—prevented him from being the perfect senshi warrior.

A swell of anger surged. His father had always criticized his soft heart. As the son of the Dragon Emperor, he was supposed to be ruthless. Emotions were a weakness, Father would say, but Jori had never been able to suppress them.

Look where they got me, damn it. Thanks to his stupid sentiment, he now lived as a warrior outcast at the mercy of his enemies. He gritted his teeth, trying to shove his feelings aside before they strangled him like some multi-armed sea creature.

Emotion is weakness. Emotion is weakness. Every footfall on the rolling platform kept the beat as he repeated the mantra. Instead of calming him, his temper compounded. In some ways, he regretted his sentiment. A better son wouldn't have saved the enemy. Then again, a good father would have understood.

The doctor's head bobbed as he studied the screen. "Well, everything looks great. How do you feel?"

"Fine." He wasn't fine. Not at all, but that's not what Doctor Gregson had meant.

The doctor patted his shoulder. “I’m glad to hear it. You had us worried for a while.”

“Yes, you did.” Hapker’s hazel eyes turned down, then he smiled. “But you pulled through, stronger than ever.”

Jori’s sixth sense picked up on their sincerity, and it rekindled the festering sorrow that ate at his insides. He’d lost everything. His mother was gone, his brother had sent him away, and his father had nearly killed him.

Dwelling on these losses threatened to suffocate him. He swallowed, forcing the emotions back. An emptiness expanded into a hollowness, like a part of his soul was being scooped out. The irony of escaping his father only to embrace his philosophy was not lost on him, but it was the only way he could get through this. *Emotion is weakness.*

Doctor Gregson turned the machine off. “Alright, that’s enough for now.”

The treadmill slowed, then stopped. Jori stepped down, planting his bare feet on the cold floor. He embraced the distracting tingle and clasped his hands behind him. Hapker stood beside him, cupping his elbow with one hand and his chin in the other as Doctor Gregson swooned over his swift recovery.

The doctor faced Jori with a pleasant expression. “Well, that about covers it. You’ve been a wonderful patient and I’m delighted to see you overcome this terrible injury with such resounding success.”

“Thank you, Doctor,” Jori said flatly. As much as he wanted to feel gratitude, it would have been better if his father had succeeded in killing him.

The commander hugged Jori to his side. “Yes, thank you, Doctor. Truly. You and Doctor Jerome have performed a miracle.”

“Doctor Jerome did all the work with the heart and Jori did all the work with the healing.” Doctor Gregson’s emotions reflected his shy unpretentiousness.

“Don’t be so modest, Doc.” Hapker’s lips curved up, then he faced Jori. “I bet you’re glad to be free of these sterile walls.”

What good is freedom? It wasn’t like the Prontaean Cooperative wanted him here. Well, maybe Hapker. Perhaps Doctor Gregson, too. But Captain Arden and the entire security team weren’t happy about his presence. He was their enemy, after all—a member of the Toradon Nohibito ruling class—or Tredon, as his unwilling allies called it.

Hapker clapped Jori on the back. "We should play wall ball in the gym."

Jori nodded without enthusiasm.

Doctor Gregson smiled, crinkling the skin around his mouth and eyes. "He's got a good heart for it. Have fun, young man."

Jori put up an invisible barrier to block the sensation of the doctor's uplifting spirit lest it penetrate his numbness. He dipped his head, then let Hapker lead him back to his recovery room.

Folded clothes sat by the bed where he'd spent these past several weeks. He grimaced. The material was softer and flimsier than anything he'd ever worn before, and they were the color of dirt, not black. His senshi uniform was no longer appropriate, but these were too different.

"I realize they're not what you're used to," the commander said, "but they're comfortable. I also brought you this." A beaded necklace dangled from his hand. The bright stones layered in varying shades of brown complemented the gold chain.

Jori's vision blurred. The necklace had once belonged to his mother—the one he'd given her—the one she hadn't had time to retrieve before Father exiled her.

His face twisted into a pained frown. It didn't belong here. It was hers. A deep pit of sadness overflowed. He squeezed his eyes shut. Hot tears spilled from them and down his cheeks. He snatched the necklace and clenched it in his fist. The cold metal chain dug into his palm, but he welcomed the discomfort.

"It was in a pocket of your uniform," Hapker added softly. "I'm sorry you can't be with her, but I hope this gives you solace."

Longing twinged through Jori's emotions. "Father probably believes I'm dead. That means I can be with her without putting her in danger."

Hapker knelt to Jori's level. He ran his hand down his face and sighed. "I'm afraid that's not possible."

Jori pulled back. "Why not?"

"We don't have the ability to take you there. If I understand correctly, the planet she's on is at the far end of your father's territory. It's highly unlikely that we'd get through undetected, and it would require more than half a year to travel around. I'm so sorry."

"Half a year isn't that bad."

"That's only the best-case scenario. No single ship will take you the entire way. You'd have to find multiple transports and hope they're not pirates. I'm sorry, but the journey is too dangerous."

Jori lacked the will to argue as tears pooled in his eyes. All was truly lost, then—just like him. "It's not fair."

"No, it isn't." Hapker squeezed Jori's shoulder. "But we'll get through this together."

The commander's attempt to soothe him only heightened his grief. The pain was too much. He inhaled deeply and fought it down.

Hapker grasped his hand. "Listen," he said quietly. "I contacted Sensei Jeruko and told him you were alive. He will let your brother and mother know. They'll be glad you're safe."

The news comforted him—Sensei Jeruko had been more of a father to him—but thinking about how he'd never see him again prodded his anguish. He gripped Hapker's hand but that was the only sentiment he allowed himself.

After regaining his composure, Hapker stepped out of the room and closed the privacy curtain. Jori slipped on the clothes with mind-numbing slowness. The bagginess of the leggings irritated him. Aside from the looseness and ridiculous collar chafing his neck, the shirt fit better.

He jerked the curtain open and sighed. "I hate it."

"You're just not used to civilian clothing. You look good, though."

Jori grimaced. "I look like an idiot."

Hapker smiled in that crooked way of his. "We'll order other clothes from the fabricor later."

"What about the black ones I wore last time?"

Hapker wagged his head. "Sorry. It's best if you wear something less soldier-like."

"I am what I am. I might as well look the part," Jori replied bitterly.

"Not today."

"Why not?"

"Because you need to make a good impression on the council."

"The council?"

Hapker hesitated, emitting a cavernous guilt.

"What is it?" Jori asked. "What's wrong?"

"I didn't think things through." The commander rubbed his forehead. "I'm sorry. I was so desperate to escape your father's ship that I didn't consider the consequences of taking you with me."

"What consequences?" Besides him losing life and his family, but he shoved that thought aside.

Hapker looked away. "The Prontaean Council has reprimanded me for bringing you here. They said it amounts to kidnapping."

Jori tilted his head. "But I came here voluntarily."

"Children can't seek asylum without parental consent."

"My mother would've given it. And Father killed me." Jori's throat rumbled.

"It's more complicated than that. Although I don't doubt your mother would have consented, they're not satisfied with my assumption. And there are far-reaching political implications. If your father finds out you're alive, who knows what he'll do? The council doesn't want to risk a war."

Blood drained from Jori's face. *Will they send me back?* As much as he yearned to return to his old life before Father sent Mother away, he couldn't go home.

"They're upset at me for contacting Sensei Jeruko as well," Hapker continued. "Since he knows you're alive, there's a chance your father could learn of it."

"So what will they do with me?"

"I don't know yet. Me and Captain Arden are working hard to convince them you're not a threat."

Jori scoffed. "Captain Arden, too?"

"The captain, too."

Jori tilted his head, unsure whether Captain Arden would want to help him after what he'd done in their first encounter. He'd awoken from surgery with a foreboding that he shouldn't be back here again. This council seemed to justify that feeling while the captain's unexpected support countered it. His gut roiled as his mind sought stability from a future enshrouded in darkness.

He should never have left home.

No. Staying would have meant Hapker's death.

Tears filled his eyes. If only he'd never met the commander.

Hapker wiped Jori's cheek with his thumb. "I'm so sorry. I never wanted you to suffer. If I had considered all the costs, I wouldn't have allowed you to help me escape."

Jori's mouth contorted as a cry escaped his throat.

The commander pulled him close. "It will be alright."

Jori pulled away from the embrace. "You promised my brother I'd be safe."

Hapker rested his hand on his shoulder. "I will keep my promise. No matter what the council decides, I *won't* let anything happen to you."

The power of his words pushed back Jori's distress. He focused on the hollowness within and put on a hard expression. "When do I speak with them?"

"Soon."

Jori swallowed, then firmed his jaw. He had no idea what to expect, but it hardly mattered anyway. They couldn't make him feel any worse than he already did.

2
The Inquiry

Jori pulled his shoulders back and clasped his fingers behind him. He planted his feet in the same attention stance used when facing his father or Sensei Jeruko—this time standing before the Prontaean Cooperative Council in a virtual meeting room as stark as the white dunes of Jahara.

Hapker patted Jori's arm. "Relax. This will work out."

Jori inhaled and lowered his hands in what he hoped resembled a natural civilian pose.

Nine councilors, each in their own tiled square, filled the giant viewscreen at the front of the conference room. The human diversity intrigued him—Councilor Pham with his elongated head, Councilor Bjorn with his oversized ears, and another councilor with ridges on the side of her face. Their skin colors ranged from pale to dark brown with varying tints of blue, yellow, or red. Their hair color was not as diverse since most were grey. The exceptions were Pham with dark hair similar to Jori's own people, Bjorn with hair a lighter sand color than Hapker's, Councilor Greymore with pure white hair, and Councilor Alvia with no hair at all.

The chairperson, Alvia, wore a smile that deepened the wrinkles by her eyes. "Welcome, Prince Mizuki." Her expression might be sincere, but Jori couldn't sense emotions through a vid-feed.

"Thank you, Councilor Alvia," he said with the same regard. "Please call me Jori. I'm no longer a prince."

Hapker discreetly patted his shoulder. Captain Arden, standing on Jori's other side, broke from his normal stoicism.

What are they so relieved about? Jori could be polite when the situation called for it.

"So you say," Greymore replied with a sour edge. He frowned so deeply that the sides of his chin creased.

Jori furrowed his brow. *What does that mean?* He held his tongue. Hapker had suggested he not take anything the councilors did to heart. "*Be calm and respectful,*" he'd said.

It was good advice. Jori couldn't afford to antagonize the people who'd decide his fate. Besides, emotion was a weakness. Let Councilor Greymore be a jerk if he wanted. Jori could keep a cool head.

Alvia clasped her hands. "Let's begin the inquiry."

"Start with why you're really here, Jori," Greymore cut in.

"I'm here because I betrayed my father, and he killed me for it." Jori winced inwardly at his unintended flippant tone.

"How do we know this isn't some ploy for the emperor to put a spy in our midst?"

Hapker scoffed. "You think his father stabbed him through the heart as part of a ploy?"

Greymore scowled, deepening the wrinkles in his forehead. "The emperor is a brutal despot. I wouldn't put it past him to concoct such a plan."

"That's ridiculous."

Jori agreed, but he remained quiet and masked his annoyance.

"It *is* a bit farfetched," Alvia said.

"Every possibility must be explored," Greymore countered sharply. "We're not talking about some random Tredon. We're talking about—" His jaw tightened. Jori suspected he held back a derogatory remark. "—the Dragon Emperor's son."

Jori balled his fists. "I would never agree to be used like that."

"So you say."

"I don't lie," Jor replied through his teeth.

"So you say."

"I *do* say." Jori bit his tongue to keep from calling the decrepit old man a name.

"Even if he's telling the truth," Greymore said to the other council members, "he could change his mind later. This boy does not belong here. If we have any sense at all—"

"Thank you, Councilor Greymore," Alvia interjected loudly. "We will hear your arguments another time. For now, let's see what Jori has to say."

Jori took in a slow, deep breath. "Where would you like me to start?"

"How about with your hostile seizure of the *Odyssey*," Greymore said regarding Captain Arden's ship.

Jori's calm slipped. The first time he'd met Hapker was after he and his brother had crashed on a Cooperative planet. "You mean when Admiral Zimmer ordered Captain Arden to keep me and my brother hostage?"

Hapker put his hand on Jori's shoulder. "We didn't give him much of a choice, Councilor."

Greymore narrowed his eyes. "Is that why you let them escape?"

Hapker flinched.

"None of this would have happened if you had brought them to us as ordered," the councilor continued.

The commander recovered and hardened his jaw. "And done what with them, exactly?"

Greymore's expression darkened. "We wouldn't have coddled them the way you did. We would've handled them as a threat and prevented this entire fiasco."

Jori heated on the commander's behalf. This wasn't Hapker's fault.

"If I may, Councilor," Captain Arden said. "We did what we felt was best. To be honest, I still think we made the right decision to not treat the children as criminals. They weren't entirely to blame for how things turned out."

Jori glanced at the captain, surprised by his understanding of how he and his brother had fought to escape his ship. Despite the man's stoic demeanor enhanced by his full dark beard and piercing blue eyes, he radiated a serene temperament.

"We had no legal grounds for keeping them against their will," the commander added.

"Yes, we did. They were not authorized to enter our territory."

Captain Arden dipped his head. "I'm sure you are aware of the mitigating circumstances, Councilor."

Jori soaked in the man's equanimity and attempted to match it. "The Grapnes chased us here for no other reason than to take us hostage. We went to the only place we hoped to be safe. Our gamble paid off. Thanks to Captain Arden and the commander, we survived."

Greymore slammed his hand down. "Then you repaid their hospitality by taking over their ship."

"I didn't want to commandeer the *Odyssey*," Jori replied heatedly. "We did what we had to and didn't kill anyone doing it."

"You expect me to believe that was intentional?"

"Of course." *What kind of idiot do you take me for?* "I could've easily switched the phaser to a more powerful setting but didn't."

"Ha! I'm not falling for it. You're no humanitarian."

"Refrain from your opinions, Councilor," Alvia said. "This is an inquiry, not a political arena."

"Just how did you get them to operate, anyway?" Greymore talked over her. "They require biometric authentication."

Jori hesitated. Telling the truth about the nanite implants would probably work against him since the Cooperative eschewed such technology. Yet lying was cowardly.

Greymore's dark eyes turned predatory. "Well?"

"I bypassed them," Jori replied carefully.

"How?"

Jori pressed his lips together.

Greymore leaned forward. "If you don't tell us, we can only assume you will do it again."

"I can't do it that way anymore," Jori said quickly, glad to speak the truth.

"How do we know if you won't say how you did it?" Councilor Bjorn asked.

"Jori," Captain Arden said in a cool tone. "He's right. For us to trust you, you must be completely forthcoming."

"Chusho," Jori cursed under his breath. He swallowed, then jutted his chin. "Father had me injected with nanite functions before our trip."

Greymore's eyes lit up. "So you *are* a MEGA."

"No," Jori replied sharply. "I am not mechanically enhanced *or* genetically altered. The nanites were temporary."

"How did our scanners not detect them?"

"They were in a dormant state, invisible, until your scanners activated them."

"That's not possible."

"Ahem." Councilor Pham dipped his oblong head. "We've recently discovered this technology on the black market."

Greymore grunted. "How can we be sure you don't still have them?"

Jori raised his hand. "When the nanite features were operational, I could access them by pressing here." He pressed his thumb to his palm. "A red light would show up if they worked."

Greymore eased back into his chair and smiled in an irritating way. "So you say."

Jori clenched his teeth at the man's repetition. "I *do* say. Being a MEGA is just as illegal in Toradon as it is in the Cooperative. My father wouldn't risk giving me something permanent. The governing caste would unite against him."

Greymore opened his mouth to argue but Alvia spoke first. "Obviously, we should test the young man further."

Disappointment etched her eyes. Jori sensed it from Captain Arden as well. *So much for having allies.*

"Now, tell us what part you played in the attack on Thendi." Greymore folded his hands and smirked.

A heat flushed over Jori. It drained just as quickly, leaving a biting chill behind. After he and his brother had escaped the *Odyssey*, they encountered it again when Father had attacked the planet Thendi. The friendship he'd formed with Hapker meant it was difficult to take part, but duty had obligated him.

He faced the council despite his wavering confidence. "I assisted my brother at the tactical station during the space battle. Then we went to Thendi and helped my father secure the prisoners."

None of this would be happening if Hapker hadn't been one of them. Without the commander, he wouldn't have cared whether Father killed those captives. No, that wasn't entirely true. He would have cared, but not as much.

"You realize four hundred seventy-two people were killed?" Councilor Bjorn said.

Jori wasn't sure what to think of that. He didn't know them, but they still died because of him. "Soldiers. We lost people as well."

"In a battle you started," Councilor Greymore boomed.

Hapker moved closer to Jori's side. "This line of questioning is outrageous! Jori is just a child with expectations piled onto him greater than any of you can possibly imagine. If his father wanted him at the tactical station, he had no choice."

Jori hated being called a child but appreciated Hapker's point.

"He partook in the battle and that makes him a war criminal," Greymore replied.

Jori's heart sank at the vehement rumbles echoing from the other council members.

Hapker's face turned red. "Under pressure from his father, who is also his commanding officer! But when faced with an opportunity to do the right thing, he sacrificed everything to save me and my fellow officers."

"Who's to say he will choose that again? He's dangerous."

"He deserves a chance to prove otherwise."

"His actions are not the only danger," Councilor Bjorn interjected. "He shouldn't have been brought here to begin with."

"We discussed and concluded this matter already," Councilor Alvia said. Her eyes had dulled as the conversation progressed toward hostility. "Let's talk about the perantium emitter."

Jori shuddered. That damned thing was at the root of all that had transpired.

"Yes, let's discuss the emitter," Greymore said. "Thanks to you, the Thendians have nothing to protect their planet. The device they'd planned to use to alleviate their earthquakes is gone. Thousands will die and their blood is on your hands."

Jori averted his gaze. They were right, even if he couldn't have stopped his father from stealing it.

"And now the Dragon Emperor has something that can be converted into a planet killing weapon," Councilor Bjorn added.

Jori snapped his attention back to them and raised his chin. "I sabotaged it. He won't be able to fix it."

"So you say," Greymore replied, setting Jori's nerves on edge.

"Tell us exactly what you did," Alvia said.

Jori went into a detailed explanation. Only blinking eyes and blank expressions met his technicality.

Greymore darkened. "And you say you're not a MEGA. No one your age is this brilliant without illegal help."

Jori hardened his jaw. The emotions wafting off Hapker indicated similar irritation, though he didn't show it.

Captain Arden smiled. "Not true, Councilor. Genetic coding used for augmentation comes from real people. It's possible Jori's abilities are natural."

"That remains to be seen." Greymore made a face that crinkled his chin.

"Yes, so let's move on," Councilor Alvia said. "Jori, please put everything you did to the emitter in a report."

Greymore glowered. "A report won't confirm that he actually did anything."

Alvia sighed. "Perhaps not. But knowing what he may have done would provide some confidence that the emperor can't repair it."

Greymore huffed.

Alvia's mouth tightened but she didn't comment. The way this council operated confounded him. Although Councilor Alvia was the chairperson, she had little control. If any of his father's advisors ever behaved like Greymore, they'd be expelled from an airlock.

"Commander Hapker," she said. "What are the chances the emperor knows his son is here, alive and well?"

Hapker straightened. "After intentionally stabbing him in the heart?" He shot Jori an apologetic glance. "None. If he suspected anything, we'd know it by now."

"But surely he is aware of our organ regrowth technology," Councilor Bjorn said.

Hapker's mood slumped, but he kept his worry from showing. "I doubt he thinks we'd use it."

"We shouldn't have," Greymore said sharply.

"Excuse me, Councilor," Hapker replied, matching his tone. "Are you saying we shouldn't have saved his life?"

"That's exactly what I'm saying."

"Really? You're advocating that we should've allowed a child to die because we don't like his race? Isn't that contrary to the Prontaean Cooperative's guiding principles? What happened to unity and acceptance? All I'm hearing from you is hate. I expected better."

Jori's jaw dropped. Hapker losing his temper after telling him not to, sent a surge of admiration flowing over him. After everything he'd done with taking over the *Odyssey*, then helping his father kill all those people on Thendi, he didn't deserve such a defense.

Apparently, Greymore didn't think so either. His face turned purple. "Don't you dare sit on your high horse and lecture me, Commander. I have worked my ass off to protect the integrity of our organization. Let's not forget that this is the second time your actions have been called into question."

The muscles in Hapker's jaw twitched. He smoothed the front of his uniform and held his chin up. "I made those choices because I thought they were what the Cooperative stood for. Jori's life was already in danger because he lied to his father to keep us alive. The least I could do was to save him."

"Him being here could trigger a war!"

Hapker huffed. "The emperor doesn't know he survived. If you suspect otherwise, we have a way to find out. Sensei Jeruko—"

"Out of the question!" Greymore struck his desk with his fists. "You never should have contacted him. If it were up to me, you'd be charged with treason."

Jori sensed Hapker's emotions turn cold. His own warmed in response. Any regret he carried for saving this man's life and losing everything because of it melted into a small puddle. He gave the commander a sad smile. Hapker returned the look with calm assurance.

Alvia sighed. "Once again, we've gotten off topic. Jori, let's say your father discovers what's happened to you. What are the chances he'll take the offensive?"

"He doesn't have the means."

Councilor Bjorn cleared his throat. "What can you tell us about your father's military might?"

Jori shifted his weight.

"Well?" Greymore said.

Jori knew the ins-and-outs of all his father's assets, but should he share them? He'd switched sides, but his older brother was still there. Putting him in danger was out of the question. "What do you want it for?"

Greymore smiled, but there was no sincerity in it. "That's not your concern. If you are a part of the Cooperative, you're obligated to divulge that information."

Heat swelled in Jori's chest. "*Am I* a Cooperative citizen now?"

"Maybe not. Returning you to your father is certainly on the table, young man," the councilor said in a sour tone.

Hapker stomped forward. "You can't send him back! His father will kill him."

The councilor ignored him and addressed Jori instead. "If you want us to accept you, cooperate."

Jori's inner heat flickered. "I won't do anything that could bring harm to my brother."

"Do you know what it means to defect?" the councilor said in a higher pitch. "It means you give something in exchange for us taking you in."

"He's given more than enough!" Hapker shouted. "Plus, we shouldn't impose the same expectations on a child as we would an adult defector."

Greymore's eyes darkened. "Him being a child is why you shouldn't have brought him here to begin with."

"Him being a child is why I saved him," Hapker replied in the same hardness.

"I read your report, Commander. You obviously didn't consider the consequences."

"No, Sir. I thought about him and how he willingly made a sacrifice for the sake of my crew and me."

"We've discussed this already," Councilor Alvia said matter-of-factly.

Greymore talked over her. "There's no place for a Tredon prince in Cooperative territory."

"I find it very hard to believe," Captain Arden stated more calmly, "that we're entertaining the idea of returning him to his father. The man relinquished his rights to him, not to mention that doing so would be akin to executing him."

Jori broke into a cold sweat. Although the captain's words were emotive, the council members remained stone-faced. Just because he wished Father had killed him, didn't mean he really wanted to die.

Greymore's eyes hardened. "We should send him back before his presence triggers a war and gets more innocent people slaughtered."

"Enough, Councilor!" Alvia's complexion darkened.

Silence settled until Councilor Bjorn spoke. "Him being here poses a tremendous security risk. What if he contacts his father and shares our secrets?"

"He won't do that," Hapker replied.

Greymore barked a laugh. "You're not exactly known for having a reliable opinion of people."

"Enough." Alvia pinched the bridge of her nose. She folded her hands in front of her and put on a small smile that didn't touch her eyes. "Jori. Sending you back to your father would be unconscionable—and I won't allow it—but if we let you remain here, we're taking many risks, including the risk of war. So if he instigates conflict, are you prepared to tell us more so we can protect ourselves?"

Jori hesitated. Toradon warriors were ruthless, and his insides squirmed at the thought of what they would do to soldiers and innocent people alike. If Father found out he was here, he should return home—even if it meant his death. But if he told the council this, then they might notify his father he was alive just to make it happen.

The corners of Greymore's lips turned up.

"Yes," Jori said to spite him.

"What's the difference, then?" Greymore said. "Why not give it to us now?"

"Because I don't trust you."

Greymore sneered. "The feeling is mutual."

Jori bit down to keep from making a face.

"What about our other people taken prisoner over the years?" Councilor Pham asked. "Do you have information on them?"

"No, Sir," Jori replied with a slow shake of his head. "Slavers don't share details. They simply sell their captives. I will tell you everything I know about who buys slaves and where they take them, though."

"That would be very helpful," Alvia said. "Please include it with your report on the perantium emitter."

"Yes, Si—Councilor," Jori fumbled. What were female leaders called? There were none in Toradon. Some of the most prominent consorts were addressed as *ladyship*, but he doubted the term was appropriate here.

"Does anyone else have any more questions?" Alvia asked.

"I do," Captain Arden said. "Jori, what do *you* want?"

Greymore darkened. "What difference does—"

"Shut up, Councilor," Alvia barked. "Go ahead, Jori."

Jori opened his mouth to speak, but no words came out. When he had planned to help Hapker and the other Cooperative officers escape, he'd assumed he'd stay with the commander. Now he doubted the council would allow it. Nor were they likely to take him to his mother. If he voiced his wishes anyway, Councilor Greymore would probably laugh at him and make some derogatory remark. Jori wouldn't give him the satisfaction.

Tears filled his eyes. "I don't know."

3
Shrouded in Gloom

Jori leaned back on the couch in Hapker's quarters and crossed his arms. He sank into the plush cushion but remained ill at ease. Even though the room had a nice woodsy quality, with its brown and yellow furniture and nature décor, it didn't feel like home—too luxurious compared to the simplicity expected of a soldier.

He was lost here, surrounded by a hostile forest with no path leading out and his loved ones too far away to hear his cry.

Damn it, why can't I go home? He'd risk running into pirates if it meant being able to stay with his mother. Maybe his brother could visit him. Sensei Jeruko too. Come to think of it, perhaps they could find a way to send him to Mother.

His heart constricted. The Cooperative would never let him contact them.

"Hey." Hapker nudged him. "It will be alright. You'll see."

Jori turned away from the false hope. So much had gone wrong. So much could still go wrong.

The vinyl upholstery creaked as Hapker sat beside him. "Don't judge all the councilors by Councilor Greymore. He's pompous and judgmental. I'm willing to bet a few will vote against him for those reasons alone."

"I doubt it. Even Councilor Alvia looked troubled."

"She must appear objective, but don't worry. She's also compassionate. She's the chairperson for a reason. Of all the councilors, she's the most open-minded and level-headed."

"But she could still decide against me. You said there are political considerations."

Hapker raked his fingers through his hair. "Yes, but I'm sure they won't send you back when it means you could die."

Jori harrumphed. "You saw how they were. They couldn't care less about that."

Hapker rested his hand on Jori's shoulder and squeezed. "If they try to do that, I'll lose all faith in them. I won't let them do it. I'll get you out of here—to hell with my career."

Jori blinked away a tear at the commander's earnestness. "You shouldn't have to give up everything for me."

"You gave up everything for me."

Jori's insides cramped.

"Besides," Hapker continued, "it won't come to that. You'll see. It'll all work out."

Jori closed his eyes and strived to hold off the swell of emotions. He wanted to let the commander's warmth put him at ease but allowing himself to feel anything triggered a flood. Whenever he laid a brick of stability, the man's sympathy knocked it down.

Hapker elbowed him. "So tell me more about these nanites that you had."

"They were temporary," Jori replied defensively.

Hapker raised his hands, palms out. "I believe you. It explains a lot, actually. Bypassing the biometric scanners is supposed to be impossible."

"It's not impossible. I didn't want to rely on illegal tech, so I figured out how to do it without."

"Really?" Hapker's tone keyed up. "How?"

"Just break off the grip's cover and bypass the circuitry."

"But doesn't that disable the entire weapon?"

"Not if you do it right."

Hapker's brows lifted. "Huh. That's handy. Can you show me sometime? Not on a real one, of course."

Jori shrugged. "Sure."

The visitor alert dinged. Jori reflexively focused his sensing ability. "Captain Arden and Lieutenant Gresher are here." He swallowed. "They're distressed."

Hapker's features sagged. He helped Jori up, then straightened. "Enter."

Jori struck an attentive military stance as the door slid open. Two joyless faces appeared, and he stiffened even more. Captain Arden's dark brows hooded over his blue eyes. They seemed dull now, as though swathed by rainclouds. The lieutenant's wide mouth turned down. Pity tainted his normally bright expression.

"I have bad news," the captain said.

Hapker's emotions plummeted. "No. They can't send him back, Sir. It's wrong."

"At ease, Commander," Captain Arden replied. "They haven't decided that… Yet." He shifted his feet and pressed his lips together so tightly that they disappeared beneath his beard.

Jori's stomach pinched.

The captain drew in a long breath. "Jori. I'm afraid the council has ordered you to be transferred to the *Defender* for detainment. From there, you will be transported to our headquarters in Asteria to stand trial for the crime of commandeering our ship."

"What!" Hapker's voice pierced Jori's ears. "This is ridiculous! He's a child."

"One they consider dangerous," Captain Arden said without conviction. "I'm terribly sorry. It's out of my hands."

Jori's heart constricted. *They're locking me up?* A quick death would be less painful than having to spend the rest of his life rotting in a Cooperative prison.

Hapker's jaw tightened. "This isn't right, Sir. It goes against our guiding principles."

Jori barely heard him through the pounding in his ears.

"I'm sorry," Captain Arden said. "I tried to convince them."

Jori's knees buckled. Hapker caught him by the arm. "Woah, there. I've got you."

Jori's feet wouldn't hold him. The commander eased him to the floor and held him.

Jori didn't like to expose his emotions, but they came unbidden as tears seared his eyes. "I'm not your enemy."

"I know," Hapker whispered as he rubbed his back. "What are our options, Captain?"

"He's not convicted yet. We will continue to advocate for him."

"They're sending him to a military ship," Hapker said. "Some officers will treat him fairly, but those with too much hate for the Tredons won't keep it to themselves. They'll harass him and who knows what else."

"I have a suggestion," Captain Arden replied. "Use your leave and go with him. You are still his advocate."

Jori sensed some of Hapker's tension deflate.

"I have some leave," Lieutenant Gresher said. "I'll go too."

Jori raised his head from Hapker's shoulder and wiped his tears. "But you don't even know me."

Lieutenant Gresher's smile widened further. "I know enough."

Jori swallowed the lump in his throat. A warmth crept across his body, but the hardness in his gut remained.

"This isn't the final word," Captain Arden said. "The council is still debating on what to do, but you have friends on your side. This will work out."

"Thank you," Jori replied.

Despite all the ugly monsters lurking on the edge of his darkened trajectory, at least he had a trajectory—and Hapker traveled it with him.

*****

Commander J.D. Hapker tried not to bite down so hard as he and Lieutenant Gresher waited for Doctor Gregson to set up the machine that looked more like the gullet of a robotic whale than a scanner. *This is stupid.* The order that Jori be tested for nanites before transferring to the *Defender* was reasonable. The rest was despicable, hateful, and utterly lacking in compassion.

Hapker exhaled noisily. "So what testing are they making you do, Doc?"

The doctor glanced up from the monitor. "Fortunately, something easy. We've already completed several medical diagnostics. The SSHIN scanner will search specifically for nanite traces and other known signs of implants."

Jori's dark narrow eyes reflected indignation. "You won't find anything."

"I'm sorry, young man," Doctor Gregson said. "I can drag this testing out, if you'd like."

Hapker considered it. Given more time, he might think of a way out of this.

"No," Jori replied. "Let's just get it over with." He marched to the scanner.

Hapker stopped him before he reached it. "Remember, no matter what happens, I'll stay by your side."

The boy nodded as he wiped his red-rimmed eyes with the back of his hand. A knot twisted inside Hapker. *This is my fault.* He should've known the Cooperative would treat Jori like this. He stood off to the side and rubbed his forehead while Jori got onto the scanner and Doctor Gregson directed him into the correct position.

Captain Arden stepped beside Hapker with his usual formal bearing. "Saving that child was the right thing, no matter what anyone else says."

"Thank you, Sir. And thank you for defending me." That the captain supported him once again made his throat ache. If not for Captain Arden's earlier passionate speech about the Cooperative's guiding principles and Hapker's moral integrity, he would've been charged with kidnapping.

"And I will continue to do so," the captain said. "I don't know how this will pan out, but I'm hoping you'll return to this ship as my second. I don't want to look for another commander."

"Thank you, Sir." Hapker shifted his feet. "You should know that if they exonerate Jori and let him become a citizen of the Cooperative, I want him to stay with me."

Captain Arden's lips tightened. "I'm not sure how I feel about that. I'm beginning to see what you've seen in him all along, but..."

"It's not easy," Hapker offered. "This is your ship." *I can't imagine how humiliating it was to have it taken over by children.*

"We will discuss this more when you return."

"Yes, Sir." *If I return.* Hapker had meant what he said to Jori about resigning. It would mean giving up his dream of exploring all the wonders of the universe, but so be it. The more he served the Cooperative, the more he recognized their self-importance and hate behind their mask of fairness and tolerance.

Councilor Greymore had stated that this was the second time his actions have been called into question. Hapker viewed it as the second time the Cooperative leaders had disillusioned him. He wouldn't let it happen again.

4
The Defender

Jori seated himself by the window of the shuttle. The resulting whish from the padded recliner was a testament to how pampered the Cooperative was compared to the utilitarian equipment found in a Toradon transport. If not for his destination, he might be grateful for the luxury.

The little vessel parked lengthwise so that his porthole faced the docking bay exit. The vastness of space loomed beyond the open bay doors. A mere energy field was all that separated the shuttle—and him—from the vacuum of utter oblivion.

The *Defender* hovered outside. No lights shone out nearby, so its black silhouette loomed against the tapestry of the universe.

He remembered this ship from the battle at Thendi. Compared to Father's warship, it had a slightly smaller arc drive but more armament. Only the gravity wheel took up more of the ship's bulk than the weapons.

Commander Hapker sat beside him. He wore a blank expression, but Jori detected his unease. He ignored it, having once again managed to quash his emotions. Numbness surrounded him like a force field. Nothing could penetrate it. At least he hoped not.

Lieutenant Gresher entered the shuttle and flashed Jori a smile, white teeth contrasting against his darker skin. His friendliness was genuine, yet his concern wasn't as intense as Hapker's. Even that small amount was more than Jori had expected.

Gresher took a seat opposite them and buckled in. Jori focused on the stars outside, careful not to think about anything other than the mundane constellations. One feature caught his attention—the Shuku Nebula. No bigger than his pinky finger from here, it was large enough to be seen from both his territory and the Cooperative's. *Can Mother see it from where she is?*

The memory of her kind smile struck him like a bolt to the chest. He put his hand over the necklace hidden under his shirt and forced his thoughts to return to the black hole he'd created.

A slight jolt snapped Jori back to the moment. The turntable positioned the shuttle's nose toward the bay aperture. As the vessel moved forward on the conveyor mechanism, Jori's breath hitched. This was it. He was exchanging the hospitality of the Prontaean Colonial Cooperative expedition ship for the hostility of a Prontaean Galactic Force battleship.

"I understand why they hate me," he muttered.

Hapker's emotions spiked. "They're wrong to hate you."

Jori huffed. "I don't belong here, and everyone knows it."

"You don't belong in Tredon, either."

Jori stared ahead as the ship left the dock and gravity eased away. As hard as he tried to concentrate on nothing, moments he'd shared with his mother resurfaced. He hoped she was happy on the insignificant island she'd been exiled to.

At least she's safe from Father. And now Jori was too. Only his situation wasn't better. Being locked up like an animal would be a longer lasting form of torture.

Maybe he deserved it. Although he wanted to do the right things, his warrior training meant he was different—and potentially more dangerous—than these soft people.

He scoffed. Too weak for the Toradons and too forceful for the Cooperative.

Hapker patted his shoulder. "The ones who hate you are the ones who have a problem. The Cooperative is supposed to be about cooperation and acceptance of all cultures. Some just don't know how to do that."

Jori looked away. "How can you or anyone else accept someone like me?" Hapker opened his mouth to speak, but Jori talked over him. "I told you about Gonoro, then there's the Grapnes I killed. After that, me and my brother assaulted you and took over your ship." Hapker rested his hand on his shoulder to calm him, but Jori counted on his fingers, growing more heated. "We helped my father invade Thendi. We took you prisoner and tortured you. And let's not forget that Sergeant Davis' death is my fault."

Hapker pulled back. "How's it your fault? He attacked you."

Jori shook his head. "He was only trying to escape."

"That part is true. I've been telling everyone the same thing regarding you taking over the *Odyssey*. You didn't take anyone's life, though. And when Davis acted out, you didn't kill him either. Your father did."

Hapker went on to defend Jori's other actions. Jori crossed his arms, hearing nothing but excuses. He turned away and focused on the internal void he'd created. He didn't want to have this conversation anymore. Hapker defended him like a zealot no matter what anyone else said. There was no point in arguing.

He rested his head against the portal as much as zero gravity allowed while the shuttle drifted closer to the *Defender*—to the dungeon of the enemy where he belonged.

*****

J.D. Hapker headed down the metal ramp into the expansive, chilly bay, his arm never leaving the boy's shoulder. Six Prontaean Galactic Force officers carrying RR-5 rifles met him with unforgiving expressions. He couldn't sense emotions, but their hate radiated off them like steam from a geothermal spring.

A fire sparked in his core. "He's only ten years old. What the heck are the phaser rifles for?"

"Admiral's orders," Sergeant Banks replied with a smirk. "We won't let him take over our ship the way he took over yours."

Hapker glowered at the overgrown ape with the bald head and wide, squashed nose. He'd served with the sergeant before. Banks was the epitome of everything Hapker had hated about the PG-Force. The man's single-minded attitude left no room for tolerance. And his big, blocky skull lacked a brain to match.

"Watch your mouth, Sergeant," a voice barked.

Hapker and Banks both straightened at the tall and commanding presence of Captain Richforth. The man's brows resembled fuzzy, iron-grey caterpillars and arched down as he glared at the sergeant.

His eyes shifted to something less stern when he turned to him. Hapker resisted the urge to wither. His career had been on the fast track back when he'd served under Captain Richforth on a different ship. It was this man who had promoted him to a lieutenant in the PG-Force and raved about what a great captain he'd make someday. Shortly after that, Hapker had nearly earned a dishonorable discharge and ended up having to take a position on a science vessel.

If Captain Richforth held any disappointment in Hapker's fall from grace, it didn't show. Although he'd encountered the captain a few times through the battle at Thendi and after, he hadn't had a chance to talk with him. His stomach knotted at the prospect of having more opportunities now.

Vice Admiral Belmont entered the bay with a face wrinkled like a raisin. The man's bottom lip stuck out in a perpetual pout. "Why isn't he in handcuffs?"

Hapker frowned, matching the mutual dislike. Admiral Belmont was a sourpuss who shunned anyone who didn't kiss his backside. "He doesn't need them."

"Your doctor may not have found any cybernetic functions, but I'm not taking any chances." Admiral Belmont's eyes hardened. "Why are you here, Commander? I don't recall asking for your services."

Hapker pulled back his shoulders, then stood protectively closer to Jori. "I'm not here as a Cooperative officer, Sir. I'm here as Jori's advocate. Despite these unfair charges, he has not resisted. Handcuffs aren't needed."

"I'll be the judge of that."

"Surely your officers can handle a ten-year-old, Sir." Hapker lifted his chin, glad to see Banks' face turn crimson.

Belmont's bottom lip protruded. "A dangerous one that's probably also a MEGA."

Jori tensed. Hapker tightened his hold around his shoulder to remind him not to react to their hostility.

Lieutenant Gresher cleared his throat. "If I may, Admiral, Captain." He dipped his head to the two highest-ranking individuals. "I understand the bad feelings toward the Tredons, but Jori is just a boy who's been trying to do the right thing. He's done nothing but cooperate. We should give him a chance."

Hapker expanded his chest, glad to have another ally.

"He may be right, Admiral," Banks added with a wicked grin. "Give the child a chance to show us who he really is. Then we can be done with this farce."

"Chima," Jori cursed under his breath. "I won't give you the satisfaction."

"Jori..." Hapker whispered, raising his eyebrow.

The admiral's forehead wrinkled up. "Very well. No handcuffs... For now."

"This way, boy." Banks shot a glare at Hapker and Gresher. "We've got this, Sirs."

"Lead on, Sergeant," Hapker said. "I'm going with him."

"Me as well," Gresher added.

The man's mouth twisted as though he'd bitten into an unripe citrus fruit but didn't comment. The other officers flanked them, leaving no elbow room.

"Watch him, Sergeant," Admiral Belmont said. "Let me know of any mishaps."

"Yes, Admiral."

Admiral Belmont and Captain Richforth stayed behind, talking in low tones. Hapker ignored them, not wanting to hear anything that might provoke him.

Boots clomped as the officers walked in stony silence. Hapker swallowed back a rising pang of bitterness as they passed through the curved halls. Although this wasn't the same ship Richforth had captained before, the *Defender* had a similar design. The walls were cheerless grey. White boxes hung at intervals, some marked with a red cross, others a simplified white wrench. The floor's rubberized epoxy coating muted their footsteps.

Hapker had been overwhelmed his first time stationed on a ship like this. No more distant horizons or expansive blue skies. Just the feeling of being swallowed whole by a massive python.

His mood darkened along with the corridors as they neared their destination below decks. He glanced at Jori. The boy's face held all the expression of someone taking a pedestrian tour.

They reached the brig with its grey walls and dismal atmosphere. Jori's brow twitched, but he didn't comment. Hapker attempted to match his stoic demeanor. At least the air was clean.

When they came upon an empty cell, Hapker's shoulders eased just a little. The room was as clean as it smelled, and it almost resembled the bunk of a lower-ranking officer. Besides the thick-mattressed bed, a lightly padded chair sat in the corner before a mini table. A round rug covered an area of the cold floor and provided some color. A basic yet new-looking food and water dispenser was set into the opposite wall. And beyond a privacy curtain was the bathroom with a clean, white countertop and toilet.

Hapker had spent a lot of time imprisoned on Jori's father's ship. This was a luxury hotel in comparison. Only the wide, transparent door broke the illusion.

Sergeant Banks pressed the keypad and the plasti-glass door clicked. With the press of a button, it opened with a hiss. Banks ushered Jori inside. When Hapker moved to follow, the sergeant stopped him with his arm.

"I'm going in with him," Hapker said. "Order me a cot."

"I wasn't told you'd be in here with the *prisoner*." His last word dripped with disdain.

Hapker's blood pressure rose as he glared at the man's dark eyes. "I'm telling you now, Sergeant."

"I'll need to clear it with Major Esekielu."

"I outrank the major," Hapker replied.

"Not here you don't… Sir."

Hapker puffed out his chest. "I am his advocate. I am responsible for his well-being."

Banks' lips curled into a sneer. He masked it quickly. "I still have to clear it with him, Sir."

"You do that. In the meantime, I'm going in."

Banks hesitated. "Your funeral," he finally said.

Hapker's muscles tensed as he pushed past the man. Jori sat on the neat, pale-colored blankets of the bed with a blank look. Although the boy had a talent for hiding his emotions, Hapker usually saw them reflected in his eyes. Not this time—not even a spark of irritation.

Hapker sighed and sat beside him.

"I will stop by in a bit, Commander," Lieutenant Gresher said. "Perhaps we can take turns."

"A show of solidarity would be nice, Lieutenant. I greatly appreciate it."

Gresher smiled, though he didn't show his teeth the way he usually did.

After he left, Jori scooted his entire body on the bed and turned away. Hapker sighed, wishing he could cheer the boy up.

5
The Admiral

Lieutenant Gottfried Krause's seat creaked as he eased his weight into it. His dark dress slacks tightened around his thighs despite the stretchy material. He preferred something looser, but as the admiral's aide had to wear a crisp uniform. At least he didn't have to keep his beard and hair as well ordered. He had more important things to concern himself with.

He pulled up to his disproportionately small desk. His computer screens remained folded into the surface until he opened them. With one now rolled up, he tapped it awake and accessed Admiral Belmont's schedule. He took in all the upcoming tasks and noted the changes needed to accommodate the man's most recent whim.

Most people would have resented the admiral's fickleness, but Gottfried's logistics talent allowed him to fit right in as his aide. It irked him that the man's idea of organization differed from what was efficient, but Gottfried had learned his quirks and adjusted accordingly. It was his job, after all, to please the man.

The comm at the base of his ear beeped. A few quick taps and he finished up his notations, then answered, "Yes, Admiral."

"Report to my office." The man's voice carried an annoyed tint.

"On my way."

Gottfried left his plain, closet-sized space with mock haste. Despite the admiral's hint of urgency, he wasn't concerned. The man tended to get upset over petty things. He rounded the curved hall and met the beady-eyed Major Esekielu making for the same location from the opposite direction.

The major sighed dramatically and touched the inhibitor hooked over his ear. "With another one like you on this ship, I guess I'll be needing this more often."

Gottfried smiled, grateful that the man's sour mood blinked out. "The young prince can only detect emotions." *Even if he could scan your thoughts, I doubt he'd want to.* No onc wantcd to look inside the head of an egocentric asshole who walked around as though he had a steel pipe reinforcing his backside.

Inhibitors were a recent invention. Although Admiral Belmont trusted Gottfried enough not to care if he read his thoughts, wearing one had become a requirement for certain high-level personnel. Major Esekielu had latched onto the new technology like a...

Gottfried pondered. Despite his memory for details, idioms often escaped him. *Oh well.* It wasn't important.

He resumed walking, ignoring the major's disdainful smile. The office door swished open, revealing Admiral Belmont speaking to someone on the desktop. The admiral's wrinkled face contracted with his well-pressed royal blue uniform. His bottom lip protruded, a natural feature exaggerated by his current mood.

Since he wasn't wearing an inhibitor, Gottfried mentally reached into the man's mind. At first, it was like diving into a pool of muddied colors. Then his thoughts appeared like webs of lightning, allowing him to track down the information he needed.

The admiral was upset about the commander and the Tredon boy, but he couldn't discern much else through the man's clutter.

Admiral Belmont waved them in without removing his gaze from the monitor. Gottfried and Esekielu took their place behind him and greeted the man on Belmont's screen.

Councilor Greymore's discolored age spots and a full head of snowy hair made him look ancient. His wrinkles stretched or deepened as he talked. "Well, Admiral. I see we have a like mind regarding this matter."

"I got that impression too, Councilor."

"Perhaps together we can figure something out. There's too much risk to leave to chance."

"I couldn't agree more," Belmont replied, his dark skin practically glowing with the prospect of being allied with such an influential official. "Does that boy seriously expect us to believe he risked his life to save his enemies?" The admiral shook his head. "How stupid does he think we are?"

Gottfried suppressed an eyeroll. The earlier accusation that the emperor had planned the whole thing was ridiculous. Tredons were known for brute force, not deception.

Greymore grunted. "That's not the only security risk that concerns me. Although I agree this boy should stand trial on Asteria, the *Defender* isn't the right ship to escort him. Putting him on the same vessel as our sensitive cargo is a bad idea."

For once, Gottfried agreed. His plans for the *Defender* had to be altered because of the boy.

"We need more inhibitors," Esekielu said. "We can't let him read us."

Belmont made a face. "Unfortunately, the fabricors here don't have the functionality to produce more. We'll make do with what we have."

Gottfried cleared his throat. "If I may, Sirs. The boy can only sense emotions, not read thoughts."

"So he says," Greymore replied. "Until we have a MEGA Inspection Officer do a full evaluation, we'll assume he's an imperium."

Gottfried's gut soured. As far as he was concerned, these MEGA hunters were no better than the genocidal Tredons. Maybe they didn't *kill* people who deviated from the MEGA Injunction. But they were ruthless in their testing for augmentations and ensured humankind remained in their primitive state.

However, he couldn't voice these dangerous opinions here.

Belmont intertwined his fingers and leaned in. "We must ensure the boy is convicted or sent back. We can't risk him being allowed to stay with the Cooperative where he can funnel information to his tyrant of a father."

Major Esekielu's already rigid posture somehow became more intense. "What if we discreetly let the emperor know he's here? The threat of war might be enough to sway the other council members. They'd have no choice but to return him."

"No," Greymore said. "Although I'd love the opportunity to take down the Dragon Emperor, we can't entirely trust what the boy said about his military limitations. Plus, we can't risk anyone tracing the leak back to us. It would be the end of our careers and make him look innocent."

It hardly mattered what the council decided since someone had other plans for the boy, but Gottfried pretended to be the voice of reason. "If I may, Sirs. Multiple sources have mentioned the prince's intelligence. Do we really want to send him back home? The Dragon Emperor doesn't need that kind of asset."

The admiral emitted opposition. When Greymore tapped his lip, Belmont's emotions changed. Gottfried hid his disdain. *Well, he didn't get this position by* disagreeing *with his superiors.*

"There's also the matter of how we would return him," Gottfried continued. "What will we do? Fly into Tredon territory and hand the boy over? Arrange a meeting at the border and hope that this time the emperor doesn't have a warship waiting? It's an awful lot of risk for one troublesome child."

"I'll tell you who's trouble," Belmont said with a frown. "Captain Arden and his crew. The captain seems to have a soft spot for dissidents, especially that scofflaw, Commander Hapker. Can you believe he's acting as the boy's advocate?" Belmont's face contorted. "If he hadn't been dumb enough to fall for his act, we wouldn't be in this mess."

"Commander Hapker is certainly a problem," Greymore said. "Taking the side of a Tredon is going too far. Why the court let him off the hook for kidnapping is beyond me, but let's move on. I agree that sending the boy back isn't the best option, so we must convince everyone to convict him rather than grant him citizenship."

"Make him a citizen?" Belmont clutched his chest. "They can't seriously consider going that far."

Greymore's upper lip curled. "Councilor Alvia is making a case."

Gottfried warmed to the idea. The boy was in a predicament now, but someday, he'd bridge the gap between two great opposing forces—Gottfried's own kind and ordinary humans. Alvia was an astute woman. Too bad Gottfried's real boss didn't allow him to serve her. Being the aide of this stubborn sycophant admiral could be trying.

"How do we convince everyone?" Esekielu asked.

Belmont drummed the table. "I seem to recall reading about the boy's hostile reaction to an extraho-animi pulling information from him. We have justification to try it again."

Gottfried's breath caught, but he hid his alarm with a fake smile. "We should wait until we get to Asteria."

Greymore made a face. "Why wait? You're an extraho."

Gottfried smiled patiently. "It doesn't take much to resist this ability once one learns to recognize its presence and has a little training—which the boy obviously does. My skills may not be strong enough. Not only that, he needs to believe he has someone besides Commander Hapker on his side. This will make it easier for us to manipulate him."

Esekielu smirked. "You mean to attract more flies with honey rather than vinegar."

Gottfried cocked his head. "What do we want with flies?"

"It means we may get more information out of him with niceness," Belmont said.

Gottfried wasn't interested in getting information. He just wanted an opportunity to show the boy that there were greater humans out there than this primitive bunch.

Greymore stroked his cheek. "Manipulate how?"

"For one, he must have a lawyer," Gottfried said. "It would be in our best interest to allow the attorney here to speak with him rather than let the commander find his own. I don't know Mister Bilsby, but he's served Captain Richforth well."

The councilor nodded. "Good idea. It wouldn't hurt to play this from multiple angles. Now, what else can we do to make sure everyone knows how dangerous he is?"

"Maybe we don't have to do anything," Major Esekielu said in a sarcastic tone. "The child can't hide his true self for long."

Gottfried agreed. He didn't know the prince well enough to determine whether he'd act out. However, he had a little time to learn and pass on his findings to his boss before the *Defender* reached Gideon space station.

He folded his hands in front of him. "To keep from being implicated in any wrongdoing, let's watch and wait for an ideal opportunity. In the meantime, we should order a psychic evaluation. I happen to know that Doctor Mazie Donnel holds a deep prejudice against the Tredons. We should ask her."

Belmont sat back in his chair and grinned. "Oh, Gottfried. You are a genius. Why didn't I think of that?"

Gottfried dipped his head and masked a gloating smile.

"That's settled, then," Belmont said. "Lieutenant Krause, you'll befriend him while we see how the boy behaves. If he doesn't act out, I'm sure we can create situations to entice him."

"We only have a few days before we reach Gideon, Sir," Major Esekielu said. "Will that be enough time?"

Belmont sat back with a smug expression. "Rather than disembark at Gideon, I've decided it would be wiser to stay on board."

Gottfried pressed his lips together. Damn the admiral for changing his mind *again*. This meant finagling the plan once more. "Sir, that will put you more than a month behind schedule. You have a meeting with the Xandu delegation coming up."

"They'll wait."

"True. But, Sir, I'm sure Captain Richforth can handle things."

The admiral harrumphed. "He still believes Commander Hapker is a good officer despite how he got blacklisted from the PG-Force. I don't trust his judgment regarding the prince. Proceed with my schedule changes."

"Yes, Sir."

Although the admiral's fickleness irritated him, he relished the idea of being able to talk to the boy more. Even if it was unlikely that a MEGA hunter would find him to be enhanced, he was undoubtedly a kindred spirit. It would be a delight to recruit him to his cause. As a fellow warrior, Lieutenant Bryce Buckeye would agree.

But first, he had to contact his real boss.

6
Reasons to Celebrate

Sergeant Carletta Ortega weaved through the lounge, around the table of specialists who chatted animatedly, past a pair of laughing sergeants at the bar, and beyond a trio of corporals who observed the crowd with a more subdued merriment. She flashed everyone a polite smile, including the private who gawked at her larger eyes.

Most times, she hid them under sunglasses. Too much light gave her a headache. She didn't need them here where dim lighting fostered a relaxing atmosphere.

A fellow sergeant tapped her arm as she passed. "Love the hair," he said.

"Thanks!" Her smile broadened. Dying the tips of her spiky style a blood red had been a good move.

The back of a woman with her black tresses in a tight bun caught her eye. A handsome young man with a bow-shaped mouth and eyes the color of a jungle forest sat across from her.

Ortega put her finger to her lips to warn him not to give her away, then tiptoed behind Chief Singh. The upbeat music with its high-popping drums and Potaway flute muffled her steps. She wrapped her hands over Singh's eyes, making her flinch.

Singh investigated Ortega's fingers. "I know it's you, Letta. You're late."

Letta Ortega giggled. "But for a good reason." She opened the satchel hanging on her shoulder and pulled out a big brown bottle. With a grunt, she plopped it on the table and grinned. It had taken her months to procure it. She only hoped it was as delicious as promised.

"Happy Birthday!" she and Harley said at the same time.

Singh's hands flew to her mouth. "Wow! Letta, where did you find Shimla sette wine?"

Ortega sat, set her elbows on the table, and leaned forward. "It wasn't easy, let me tell ya. Let's just say it nearly cost me an arm and a leg."

Harley laughed. "She means it literally."

Singh's forehead rolled up.

Ortega shook her head. "Sort of. I actually bought it cheap, but someone attacked me."

Singh's jaw dropped. "For this? The wine is good, but it's not *that* good."

Ortega looked up and sideways. "Well, not because of the wine. I insulted this guy in a bar the night before. Apparently, he didn't like being called a big hairy ball sack."

Singh cackled. "No way!"

Ortega shrugged. "He grabbed my ass. He's lucky I didn't break his teeth in."

"I thought you *did* break his teeth in," Harley said. "You hit him so hard, he fell like a sack of—"

"Balls." Singh giggled.

Ortega flicked her hand, uncomfortable with Harley's praise. "I punched him in the jaw, but I doubt I broke anything other than my knuckles. Humiliated his ass in front of his buddies, though. Then did it again when he cornered me later. Luckily, I saved the wine."

Singh's eyes sparked. "I'm glad you did. Thank you for this wonderful gift." She grasped the bottle and removed the stopper. "Now let's drink."

As the friends drank, talked, and laughed, the rest of the bar disappeared into the background. Harley's laugh carried that exuberant timbre of a young man while Singh's tinkled like bells. Ortega relished these moments.

Taking another sip of the sweet wine, she admired the friend who'd once stood up for her when a guy made fun of her eyes. *"Someone with an excessive flatulence problem should be more concerned about the size of a person's nose,"* Singh had said.

That memory still brought a grin to Ortega's face.

Harley was a new addition. People called him hot-headed Harley. Owners of Harley speedsters had a maverick reputation, but Corporal Harley was more easy-going than that. He could be stupidly cocky, but that was his youth, not his personality. He just needed some guidance and Ortega had become that guide.

She'd initially been attracted to him. His maturity level had changed her mind, though. She still liked him, but more like a little brother.

"Let's make a toast." Singh raised her cup, inspiring the others to do the same. "To an uneventful journey despite the Dragon Prince's presence."

Ortega hated the reminder that she'd been assigned to the child's guard detail, but clinked cups with her friends.

Harley's bowed mouth curved upward just a tad. "It should be alright. He's not so bad, and he seems to look up to Commander Hapker."

Ortega made a derisive noise. "Ugh. Let's not talk about the commander. I don't trust anyone who gets kicked out of the PG-Force, then sides with a Tredon."

"You're being harsh," Singh replied, and Ortega's hackles went up. "He wasn't kicked out. He simply refused to follow an unlawful order. Besides, he's still a part of the Cooperative."

Serving on a science vessel wasn't the same thing, but she stuck to her main point. "He's still allied with a Tredon."

"That's not fair," Harley said quietly as he twiddled his fingers. "If not for his friendship with the boy, I wouldn't be here. I'd still be a prisoner on the emperor's ship—or dead." He looked away with his brow wrinkled in distress.

Ortega couldn't bring herself to argue. He hardly ever stood up for his own opinion. For him to defend this Tredon child might actually mean something. "Maybe you're right," she said.

Harley shrugged. "Yeah. I think he's different."

Singh raised her cup again. "Here's to hoping Harley is right. And not just for our sake—for his. He is only a child, after all."

Ortega joined the cup-clinking. *Hope. It's the only thing we've got.*

Sometime later, the merriment was interrupted when Harley flinched and Singh smiled slyly. Ortega only had a moment to wonder why when a set of big arms wrapped around her. Warm breath brushed against her ear.

"Hey, baby," a husky voice said. "How's my Letta Rosetta Violetta Poinsettia Ortetta doing?"

A sultry heat spread over Ortega's body. She melted into the man's embrace and giggled at his silly reinvention of her long family name. "You're late... Again." She smacked him playfully despite how much his chronic lateness annoyed her.

Lieutenant Bryce Buckeye was a striking figure with his muscular frame, brown-black hair, and striking eyes. He pulled a chair from another table and joined them with a handsome smile. "Sorry, babe. I got held up."

"Give him a break, Letta," Singh said lightly. She poured a drink and handed it to Bryce.

Bryce sipped his wine and smacked his lips. "I have good news."

"Yeah?" Ortega replied. "What's that?"

"I'll be serving on this ship for a while longer. Admiral Belmont wants us to escort the prince to Asteria."

Ortega squealed. "That's great!" She folded her arms around his neck and pecked him on the cheek.

Bryce laughed in a rich bass tone and pulled her close. She soaked in the warmth of his body and scooted onto his leg. A lot of military soldiers didn't like such a display of affection, but the twinkle in Bryce's eyes only held adoration.

"We were just speaking about the prince," Singh said. "What do you think of this situation?"

Bryce shrugged. "I don't know yet. Commander Hapker seems to have a lot of faith in him."

Ortega rolled her eyes. "Because he's foolish."

"Don't be so quick to judge, babe," Bryce replied mildly. "I read the reports. It's more than just the commander who had positive words to say." He gave Harley a meaningful look and the young man responded with a vigorous head nod. "I'm keeping an open mind. So should you."

Ortega relinquished her harsh feelings. Her friends and lover obviously had good judgment, or they wouldn't like her. So if they thought the boy deserved the benefit of the doubt, then she should try to be objective as well.

7
Old Friends

Jori rested on the bed with his hands propped behind his head and studied the ceiling. Dark spots where the paint had flaked off in the corner resembled inverted constellations. A larger blotch had the shape of a deformed space fighter. Another looked like a monstrous face.

This didn't interest him, but nothing did. The hollowness in his chest seemed to weigh him down, but he was too tired to care. Not sleepy-tired either. He merely wanted to sink into the bed and slip into a dreamless state where time didn't exist.

Hapker tried to cheer him up by talking about his homeworld. "The mountains are beautiful. They jut out of the landscape like massive sentinels. They're capped with snow all year around, but we'll want to go skiing in early winter."

"We?" Jori frowned. "You think they'll let me out of here?"

"Yes, I do."

"You have doubts," Jori replied, picking up on the lack of conviction in his tone.

Hapker sighed. "Although I'm disappointed in the behavior of some people, I still have hope that the council will rule based on their guiding principles."

Jori wasn't sure whether the commander's optimism was derived from experience or wishful thinking. He couldn't bring himself to care either way and went back to examining the ceiling.

"Most who enter the Cooperative share these ideals," Hapker said. "It's not always easy to let go of preconceived notions and perceptions, but you can change their minds."

Jori quirked his mouth. "How?"

"By being you." Hapker winked. Jori would've rolled his eyes if he had the energy.

"Seriously, though," the commander said. "You're honest, open to new ideas, have an amazing ability to discern right from wrong—something I attribute to Sensei Jeruko."

Jori both warmed and suffered anguish at the mention of his mentor.

"And you're very mature for your age," Hapker continued. "That means you have the skills to rise above people like Sergeant Banks. When he or anyone else gives you a hard time, keep a cool head. Trust me—the more you do that, the more his words will reflect on him."

Jori considered the interaction with Councilor Greymore and understood. If most of the Cooperative was as open-minded as Hapker believed, then maybe he had a chance. Not that it would make a difference. Being without Sensei Jeruko, his mother, or his brother wouldn't be much of a life.

"I want to rest now," he said, doubting he'd fall asleep.

"Alright." Hapker's chair creaked as he stood. "I'll set up my cot."

"You don't need to stay," Jori replied.

"I'm not leaving you."

"I'll be fine." Jori kept his tone light. Although the prospect of being left alone unsettled him, he also wanted a respite from Hapker's upbeat attitude.

"Are you sure?"

"Yes." When the commander hesitated, Jori urged him more. "I can tell you're not tired. I'll be alright, I promise." He flicked his hand to the guards. "Banks is gone, and I don't get hateful vibes from these people." *Only distrust or indifference.*

Hapker left, his emotions radiating uncertainty but understanding. With the lights out, Jori got under the covers and curled into a ball. At first, his mind remained active as his thoughts flitted from memories to dismal imaginings of his future. At some point, he drifted off.

*****

J.D. Hapker lifted his glass and swirled the clear and amber liquids together. The lounge music frayed his nerves. Too much brass and the wind instrument shrilled like a horny peacock.

Voices of off-duty officers roared above the song, adding to the clamor.

Someone bumped into him from behind. His drink splashed on his hand. Hapker sighed and wiped it with a napkin.

He glanced at the viewscreen above the bar. Karina Klaspil from the Prontaean Cooperative broadcast station spoke with exaggerated facial and arm gestures. As the most dramatic of the newscasters, she had a way of making boring news sound interesting.

"Still nothing about Tredons?" Lieutenant Rik Gresher asked, his bright smile standing out against his darker complexion. The expression touched his eyes, but he seemed more subdued than usual.

"Not a word," Hapker said. "Just a plague of locusts on New Croatia. If the emperor made any moves against us, the news wouldn't be talking about insects."

Gresher glanced at the screen in time to see a close-up of the six-legged creature. "Better them than dragons."

Hapker ran his hand down his face. "Do you think I did the right thing?"

The lieutenant's brows shot up. "Yes. Absolutely."

Hapker pulled back. "That's a stronger response than I expected."

Gresher flashed his teeth. "You and I are more alike than you realize, Commander. We both believe the best about people."

"Some would say that makes us gullible."

"I prefer compassionate." The lieutenant's smile turned sad.

"Is everything alright?"

Gresher leaned on his elbows and inclined his head toward the far wall. "See that guy with the dark red hair, sides shaved?"

Hapker studied the crowd until he found a tall and wiry man fitting the description. "The one laughing?"

"That's him." Gresher's eyes tilted down as though pained.

"What about him?"

"He used to be my best friend. We went to the PG Institute together and served on the same ship and squad for a while." Gresher gulped the rest of his drink and clapped his glass on the counter. "Then I fucked up."

Hapker blinked at the uncharacteristic expletive. "So what happened?"

"In my youth, I was sure I was in the right. If only I had apologized then, we might still be friends. I'm afraid it's too late now."

Hapker reflected on his own old friend. "Some things can't be fixed, but you should try anyway. It may give you both closure."

"Yeah, but not yet. Korbin is obviously having a good time with his friends." Gresher leaned on his elbows. "What about you? How does it feel to be back on a PG-Force ship headed by your previous captain?"

"Let's just say I owe my own fair share of apologies. Haven't had a chance yet, but the night is still young." He took a sip of his drink and let the bite of alcohol mellow out on his tongue before swallowing and glancing around. Would he run into his old friend or any of his other ex-shipmates? He'd seen some during the battle at Thendi, but too much was going on.

Unfamiliar faces consumed most of his view. When a quintuple of people squeezed through the crowd and edged near the bar, his heart leapt at the sight of the fair-skinned blond beauty. Her eyes captured his at the same time and for a split second, they stared dumbly at one another.

"J.D.!" Her mouth spread wide, and she let out a squeal. "I heard you transferred over, but I didn't expect to see you."

Sergeant Chesa Creston threw her arms around him. He returned the hug and drew in the sweet spicy scent of her hair.

When she pulled apart, he felt a tug on his heart. "I'm here for the duration of the trip."

Her lips curved upward as she appraised him. "Mmm. Well, we'll have to do some catching up, won't we?" She waved her friends off. "I'll be with you guys in a bit."

"Yeah right, Firestorm," her tall lanky companion said. "I know that look."

Hapker knew that look, too. Her sassy blue eyes blazed like a fire.

"I *will*," she replied in a long, drawn-out tone that was almost shrill. "I promise. Just get me a volcano, would ya? And make sure it has a double shot of rum."

"Will do." The man winked.

Gresher tapped Hapker's arm. "I'll go see if our young friend is awake yet," he said. "I'll catch up with you later."

Hapker dipped his head. Chesa gave her friends further instructions and returned her sparkling eyes back to him. He studied the curves of her face while she did the same in return.

"So what are you up to lately?" she finally said. "How do you like the *Odyssey*?"

"I like it a lot more than I expected. Good crew. Good captain."

Her eyes rolled up just enough to signal a disagreement. "You sure you don't miss the PG-Force?"

"I'm sure," he replied. He was no explorer or scientist, but serving on Captain Arden's Expedition-class vessel suited him better.

She smacked his arm playfully. "Were we really that bad?"

He laughed. "You know I didn't fit in."

"You fit in well enough to become a lieutenant."

"It was good for the most part. But there were aspects I didn't care for."

"Yeah?"

He shrugged. "It's hard to explain." Especially to a gung-ho fighter like Chesa. If someone told her to shoot, she'd do it without hesitation. He couldn't do that.

"So you don't miss any of us?" she asked with a twinkle in her eyes.

"Sure I do. It's been ages since I've seen Jamal. He's stationed at the Polemos station now. And Carter. He's here on this ship, right?"

Chesa hesitated. "Yes, but… He's still pretty sore at you."

Hapker's shoulders fell. "I was afraid of that."

"You would've made him your second-in-command when you got promoted, so his career stagnated when yours plummeted."

Hapker rubbed his brow. "Darn it. I really owe him. Where might I run into him?"

"He's in charge of the officers guarding the Dragon Prince. I hear you volunteered to act as his advocate," she said with a sourness in her tone.

"I did."

Her mouth twitched. "Many people aren't happy with you about that. *You* are the reason he's here."

"He's the reason I'm *alive*."

She leaned in with a furrowed brow. "So what? That doesn't mean you owe him anything. Let the Cooperative handle him now."

Hapker pulled back. When had she become so unsympathetic? "I want to help him. Besides, it's probably easier for him to be around someone he's familiar with."

Her expression darkened. "That's crazy. Why would you want to help a vicious Tredon? I don't want to smile the wrong way and end up with a knife at my throat."

"Chesa. You're overreacting. Jori's nothing like—"

Her eyes blazed. "I'm overreacting?"

Hapker put up his hands, palms out. "Woah. That's not what I meant."

"It's what you said."

Hapker huffed, remembering the storminess that sometimes struck their relationship. "I didn't mean it that way. I just meant you're assuming the worst without knowing him."

"And I don't want to know him either." Her blond hair swished as her head swiveled.

"Chesa. He saved my life."

She pinched her brow and sighed. "Look. Let's not fight about this. We can talk about something else instead."

"Alright," he said, not wanting their reunion to become an argument. "Well, tell me how you've been?"

"I've been good. I transferred to this ship after Captain Richforth was assigned here."

"Did I hear my name?" a gravelly voice interrupted.

"Yes, Captain." Chesa straightened, then beamed. "We were just talking about you."

Hapker's heart jumped at the sight of the steel-haired man with iron features. "Captain Richforth. It's good to see you again. I've been wanting to catch up with you, but never had a chance."

"Same," the man replied. "I intended to speak with you on your arrival, but decided it was best to wait until you settled in."

Chesa touched Hapker's hand and mouthed, *see you later*. He dipped his head with a smile that she returned.

Captain Richforth sat in the chair beside him and placed a drink order on the stationary tablet. "I didn't expect you to be here. I assumed you'd be with the Tredon boy."

"He's getting some sleep right now."

"So you're here for some leisure time."

Hapker rubbed his chin. "Not just that. I thought it would be nice to reconnect with some old friends." He waited for a response. None came. Hapker cleared the awkwardness from his throat. "Are we making any stops other than the rendezvous with the Gideon station on our way to Asteria?"

"The admiral has decided to stay with us through the entire trip. So far, no detours are planned, but he could change his mind."

Hapker recognized a hint of irritation in his tone. "He's staying? Didn't he have another assignment?"

"He thinks we need extra protection, considering our two consignments."

Hapker's drink soured on his tongue. It sounded like something Admiral Belmont would do. Captain Richforth was a competent captain. He could easily handle the secret cargo that everyone assumed he didn't know about, as well as Jori's security. But the admiral didn't seem to trust anyone who wasn't a part of his own personal circle.

"He's been on your ship awhile," Hapker said.

"Five damned months." Captain Richforth took a gulp of his drink and pulled a face. "Sorry. That was unprofessional of me. To be honest, the admiral isn't so bad. It's his nosy little aide that gets on my nerves."

"The roundish man with black curly hair? I don't recall his name."

"Lieutenant Gottfried Krause. He's friendly enough, though."

Hapker remembered meeting him before the battle at Thendi. He found his constant smile odd. "I only spoke to him twice."

"Well, you'll speak to him more, I'm sure. He'll probably be looking in on that boy you brought us."

Hapker detected an edge to his tone. He dipped his head apologetically. "Jori won't be a problem, Sir."

The captain's eyes turned stony. "There's some worry that your defense of the Tredon prince means you're scheming with him and his father."

Hapker's jaw dropped. "What? That's ridiculous. Why would I collaborate with a tyrant and murderer?"

"I don't believe it, but many people are asking why you allied with his son. They see you as a security risk."

"You read the report, Sir," Hapker replied in a defensive tone. "You know why."

"I did and I do, but your decision was poorly considered."

Hapker agreed. He wished he had come up with a better solution—one that would have protected Jori without getting him killed by his father or arrested by the Cooperative. "I've had many people tell me what I should've done, but none of them were there. I did the only thing I could think of to save everyone, including Jori."

"You've always had a way of taking on other people's problems. Your mindfulness is one reason I promoted you. But this was beyond your obligations."

Hapker wagged his head. "He put his life at risk to free me and my crew. I couldn't abandon him to his fate. Even his brother and the sensei thought it was the best option."

Captain Richforth huffed. "Of course they did. Now they have their own personal connection to the Cooperative."

Hapker poked his tongue into his cheek. "Not to be disagreeable, Sir, but Jori won't have access to sensitive information. Besides, him being here could mean future peace between our peoples."

"I understand there are no easy answers." The captain's tone indicated disagreement, but it wasn't as strong as expected. "You acting as this boy's advocate could hurt your career further, you know."

"Yes, I'm aware."

"I mean, it's not like you haven't gone against authorities before."

Hapker winced. He'd been dreading this conversation. It needed to happen, though. He'd served as Captain Richforth's lieutenant on another ship where he'd received a commendation for saving lives. It also earned him a commanding position under Admiral Zimmer. The irony that the self-sacrificing determination to do the right thing under Richforth had backfired with Zimmer wasn't lost on him.

He met the man's eyes. "I'm sorry I let you down, Sir. I can't say that I would've done things differently if I could do it over, but I regret disappointing you."

Captain Richforth set down his empty glass and stood. "I know you believe you did the right thing, and maybe you did, but… The universe isn't as simple as we'd like it to be." He clapped Hapker on the shoulder. "I harbor you no ill will and truly wish you the best."

A flat smile conveyed the captain's disappointment, making Hapker's shoulders hunch. "Thank you, Sir."

The captain dipped his head, then froze. His eyes squeezed shut.

Hapker hopped off his stool. "Sir? Are you alright?"

Captain Richforth doubled over, clutching his chest.

Hapker grabbed his arm as he slumped to the floor. He tapped the comm behind his ear. "I need a medic here now!" He focused back on the captain. "What's happening, Sir? Tell me what to do."

"Chest…" the man gasped. "Hurts."

An officer knelt beside him and assessed the situation. "He's having a heart attack!" she yelled out. "Someone get me an AED!"

Hapker's own chest hitched from a mixture of confusion, worry, and helplessness.

Captain Richforth stopped breathing. An officer handed the woman the AED and Hapker got out of the way. She set up the device with perfect efficiency and used it.

Medics rushed in. One performed the ministrations while another injected a hypospray into the captain's neck. Hapker held his breath. Signs on their scanner showed erratic beats, then nothing. The scene turned surreal as the medics continued working—every moment like both an eternity and an eye-blink.

After a prolonged flatline, the medics gave up. Hapker saw their mouths moving but didn't hear them. He stood in frozen shock as they loaded him on a gurney and wheeled him out.

This couldn't be real. The captain wasn't that much older than him and took his health seriously.

He watched their backs long after they'd gone.

"What happened?"

Hapker blinked. "Wha—"

Major Esekielu glared at him with the fury of a wild animal. "I said, *what happened*?"

Hapker drew back, unsure if the major intended to sound accusatory. "I-I don't know."

"You were the last one to talk to him. How did he seem? Was he upset? Angry? Were you arguing?"

Hapker put up his hands and scanned the disgruntled crowd that had gathered. "We were just talking. A normal conversation."

Major Esekielu snorted. "I suggest you get back to your little dragon, Commander, before someone jumps to conclusions."

"I had nothing to do with it!"

The major shook his head, condemnation still etched his features. Hapker glanced about, feeling ill at ease with all the stares and whispers.

This can't be good.

8
Imperium

Gottfried Krause entered the cozy sitting area and reclined on the padded bench against the wall. A giant viewscreen on the opposite side showed a woodsy scene. The speakers emitting sounds of birds, insects, and trickling water complemented the artificial setting.

He accessed the controls on the table beside him and flicked through the options. Lakeside, beachfront, and other nature scenes scrolled by. From the main menu, he selected *viewport* and the display changed to camera view from outside. Traveling via the arc drive distorted the constellations, but not enough for the average person to notice.

Since no sound accompanied this mode, he chose something from the *instrumental music* section and turned it up—not too loud, but enough to mask his conversation.

A few minutes later, a tall, dark-haired man in a PG-Force uniform approached. The accompanying grey armor fit him well, accentuating his perfect physique. Lieutenant Bryce Buckeye was the most exemplary specimen to come from his boss' genetic experiments.

If only the man also had implants. Then Gottfried could communicate with him better.

He waved the lieutenant over with a smile. After Buckeye sat, Gottfried turned serious. "I contacted you-know-who and received new orders. Since we're staying here, you'll oversee the welfare of the Dragon Prince. I want him to look to you as an ally."

"I will make sure one of our friends is on every watch."

"No. Don't interfere to that extent. I want our enemies to antagonize him. All you will do is step in when you see it."

"Done."

Gottfried grinned. Although he hadn't assisted his boss in the experiments, he was aware of the complexity involved in making the perfect soldier. Buckeye still wasn't as good as a Tredon or Rabnoshk warrior, but he fit in well with these Cooperative soldiers. His personable qualities helped. So was the fact that he wasn't *too* skilled. Society had a way of keeping down those who were better, which was why Jori was likely to have problems here and why he needed exceptional friends.

"What are people saying about our most recent development?" Gottfried asked.

"Thanks to Major Esekielu, there are whispers the commander had something to do with it."

"Perfect. That was an unexpected result, but perfect."

"Do you want me to question him—give life to the rumors?"

Gottfried suppressed a sigh. Buckeye was an outstanding soldier but lacked a mind for strategy. "No. Do nothing to the commander. If the boy finds out, he'll see you as the enemy rather than a friend."

"Yes, Sir."

"Let me know if you hear more at the memorial services." Gottfried stood, signaling the meeting's end. "We'll talk again."

The lieutenant returned to his duties. Gottfried went back to the bench and checked the guard schedule on his tablet. Two officers appeared to be promising targets. Sergeant Banks would come on duty the soonest. He should catch him beforehand.

He closed his eyes and focused his sensing ability. Banks' lifeforce had a distinctive sour flavor but finding him among the hundreds of other people on this ship was a challenge. He finally caught his essence in the gym. That wasn't the place for a private conversation, so he kept tabs on him.

Thank goodness they didn't have enough inhibitors to pass out. If Gottfried did this right, Banks wouldn't recall any of it.

A broad smile spread unbidden across his face. With Richforth dead and the admiral predictably taking charge, his plan was officially underway. Next step, drop hints about the Indore space station.

*****

The hall ended at a T. Gottfried Krause turned left and adjusted his pace accordingly. Using his special ability, he sent out a suggestive tendril. Reactive people like Banks didn't have the best mental self-awareness, so slipping in was easy.

Gottfried passed four officers before the corridor cleared and Sergeant Banks appeared. As usual, his lifeforce reeked of vinegar and moldy cheese. The brow of his bald, blocky head wrinkled in a permanent scowl while the nostrils of his wide flat nose flared.

"Sergeant Banks," Gottfried said with a smile. "How are you today?"

Banks halted and frowned. "Not so great. It's my turn to watch the stupid Tredon brat."

Gottfried's expression lifted at how easily he'd induced the man to volunteer his thoughts. "So you don't like him here either?"

Banks' face reddened. "Absolutely not."

"I can't believe we're permitting the son of a murderous tyrant to be here," Gottfried said, exaggerating his mock-dismay. "And to think you must watch out for *his* safety."

"You're telling me."

The man's temper slammed into Gottfried's senses, an emotion he didn't need his imperium abilities to evoke. He tilted his head with mock sympathy. "I never had the chance to tell you how sorry I was to learn of Sergeant Davis' death."

Banks snarled. "Davis was a good man, and that dragon spawn got him killed."

Gottfried clicked his tongue to the roof of his mouth. "I wish there was something we could do to get justice." He shot his brows upward. "I have an idea. You're in the perfect position to bring out the boy's violent tendencies. All it will take is a little verbal antagonization on your part."

Banks scowled. "I can't do that without getting myself in trouble. I hate the brat, but not enough to fuck up my career."

Gottfried pressed his imperium ability. The tendrils of his will weaved through Banks' brain, snapping some lines of thought while building new ones. The man's narrow-minded simplicity made it easy. "You will antagonize the boy every chance you get."

Banks blinked and rubbed his forehead. "Of courth," he slurred.

Gottfried smiled. He pushed a little harder to make certain and repeated the command.

Sweat beaded on Banks' brow. He shook his head as though he'd just stepped into a spider web. Only a slight pushback resisted Gottfried's intrusion before he succumbed.

"You will be careful not to get caught," Gottfried continued. "If you're discovered, you'll tell them you did the Cooperative a service. You won't remember this conversation."

Banks' eyelids hung over his eyes. He nodded slowly.

Gottfried pulled his ability away. "I hope your day improves, Sergeant."

Banks shuddered, then returned to normal. "Thank you, Lieutenant."

They parted ways. Gottfried sensed the man's emotions stew, and his own steps grew lighter. There was no better way to get the boy on his side than to make sure he had sufficient enemies.

Now to get in contact with the other officer—a man with a distinctive nose that curved up so much that his nostrils faced outward rather than down.

9
Services

Jori bolted upright. The world exploded with color and light. A chill swept over him. He glanced about, trying to gain his bearings. His heart burst with every beat as he gulped for air.

Pieces of his dream flittered through his head. He'd been on his ship searching for someone—anyone. All he found were empty corridors, an oppressive heat, and a feeling that something in the shadows hunted him. When the monster revealed itself, it had his father's face. A raging inferno glowed in his eyes and his teeth bared in a canine snarl. His knife-like claws stabbed into his chest and Jori had woken with a start.

Blinking away the nightmare, he faced new monsters now. With Hapker and Gresher at Captain Richforth's memorial service, Sergeant Banks sneered at him from the other side of his prison door.

Jori pulled the blanket over his head. A small lump in his bed dug into his shoulder, but he endured it. His hand groped for the necklace. Relief at touching the cold chain was quickly replaced by a sadness that threatened to drown him.

He scrunched his eyes, clutching the last remnants of her to his breast and wishing she could comfort him the way she usually did after a nightmare. If only he could've gone with her rather than come here.

They would live on a planet instead of a spaceship. There'd be a surrounding forest full of promising adventures—hiking rugged terrain, swimming in crystal-clear waters, observing the wild fauna. And even though they'd be on a remote island, they'd be free.

A surge of hate emanated from one of his four guards. Peeking from under his blanket, Jori recognized two. The heavy eyebrows curving over bright green eyes marked the youngest as Corporal

Harley. Jori remembered his hostility when he'd been a prisoner on Father's ship, but not a hint of dark qualities tainted his aura. Oddly, both confidence and insecurity dominated his lifeforce.

Sergeant Banks was the other and he wore his loathing like a uniform. His essence matched his looks, echoing some of the most brutal senshi warriors back home.

"I can't believe that commander brought him here thinking he'd be free to just waltz around," said an officer with a long upward-pointing nose.

Corporal Lengen's aura reminded Jori of those sneaky little animals that would somehow find their way onto ships and get into the food. His essence reflected this, plus a smidge of darkness that held more self-righteousness than hate.

Banks snorted with derision. "That brat won't be taking over *our* ship."

"Knock it off," another sergeant—this one a woman—cut in. It no longer surprised him that the Cooperative allowed women to become soldiers. However, he wondered why two equally ranked officers were on the same team. Perhaps all the deaths from the battle at Thendi had disrupted the organizational structure.

Guilt mingled with his sorrow, so he diverted his attention by scrutinizing the woman. Sergeant Ortega intrigued him. It wasn't just her unusual color-spiked hair. Large eyes were barely discernible through her shaded visor. Was she from one of those subterranean worlds he'd read about? Her skin was darker than he'd expected from someone living underground, but it had a grey tint to it, as though darkness had somehow leached out some of the color.

"What, are you on his side or something, bug-eyes?"

"Screw you," she replied. "This isn't about sides. It's about following the rules."

"You always were a suck-up."

"I don't suck up. I do my job. You should try it sometime, dickwad."

The emotions she emitted spiked through Jori's own. Her overall essence revealed a fearless personality peppered with positivity and fierce loyalties. However, she soured whenever she looked his way. At least she wasn't filled with blackness like Banks was.

Jori gripped the necklace tighter. He had to get out of this place and back to his mother. Maybe if Sensei Jeruko or his brother realized his current predicament, they'd come to rescue him. If only he could contact them.

Thanks to the rigorous training imposed by his father, he knew the layouts of nearly every spaceship owned by his enemies, including this one. Getting out of the prison cell and away from his guards would be tricky, though. And although their low-power stun weapons wouldn't cause any lasting harm, his situation would worsen if they caught him.

"Fuck you, Ortega," Banks said. "Justice would be better served if we jettisoned him out into space *with* a space suit."

"That would be a mercy," Lengen replied.

Banks chuckled. "You're right. Put him out there with a suit on and let him drift. Either he'll run out of air, or the heater will give way and he'll slowly freeze to death."

"Oh, yeah. I'm with you."

Ortega shifted her stance. "Listen. I don't like that he's here either, but he's just a boy."

"Yeah, a boy," Harley said.

Jori silently cheered.

Banks' lip curled. "Exactly what I'd expect from a woman and a wussy corporal. He's our enemy, plain and simple. And any soldier who doesn't see that doesn't deserve to be here."

Ortega's emotions blasted Jori's senses like combustion from a freighter. He hoped she'd punch him in the face. Her jaw tightened but a bubble of self-doubt held her back.

"No one wants him here," Lengen said.

Harley made a noise. "No one wants him *anywhere*."

Ortega shot Harley a glare. The corporal responded by looking at the floor and emitting guilt.

Jori attempted to suppress the burn in his sinuses by gnashing his teeth. A spew of curses hovered behind his lips, but he stuck with Hapker's advice and hoped Banks' behavior would reflect on himself. Besides, he wouldn't let these chimas know how much their hailstorm of words hurt him.

Their time would come, though. When he escaped here, he wouldn't make the same mistake twice. He'd kill every single one of them, especially Banks.

A resounding hiss indicated the main door into the brig had opened. Jori sensed the despondent emotions of two new officers.

"How was the service?" Sergeant Ortega asked them.

"It was nice," one said. "They did a great job setting up the lounge. There's stuff about the captain that goes all the way back to when he was a baby."

A pang spread through Jori. He didn't know Captain Richforth, but Hapker's sorrow magnified his own grief. The mood from most of his guards did the same.

Banks' temper increased. "If that commander hadn't stressed him out, he'd still be alive."

Huh? Now Banks was directing his irrational hostility at Hapker? The stupid sergeant wasn't much different from Jori's father.

Ortega scoffed. "That's ridiculous."

"Is it? The captain was perfectly fine less than an hour before."

"You're so dumb," Ortega said. "Cancer caused his heart to give out. It could've happened anytime, regardless of the commander."

"Shut-up, bug-eyes." Banks shot her a glare. "Shouldn't you be leaving now, anyway?"

"Yeah. Let's go, Harley. We've got our respects to pay."

The main door swished. Ortega and Harley's emotions dwindled away until he lost them. He drifted off, trying to avoid thinking about anything that would remind him of his misery.

Time ebbed and flowed until a blaring alarm jolted him to full consciousness. Living on a spaceship his entire life caused him to react instinctively despite these sirens being more of a wail than a beep. Normally, he'd go straight to the nearest emergency section of his father's ship, but he couldn't do that now.

As he eased into a sitting position, a twinge ran through his skull. Apparently, his brain didn't like being disturbed after resting for so long. He planted his bare feet on the rug at his bed and waited for the hateful apes to open his prison door and escort him to a safety depot.

*****

The gloom that permeated the temporarily restructured lounge bored into J.D. Hapker's entire being. They'd brightened the lights and cleared a space for all the people to gather in the center, but doleful murmurs replaced the cheery buzz.

This was supposed to be a celebration of life, but all the lives that had already been lost in the recent battle seemed to cast a pall over everyone. Richforth's unexpected demise was another reminder of their own mortality.

Glowers flickered through the glumness as people noticed Hapker. He didn't bring his dress uniform so only wore a plain brown shirt and black slacks, but that wasn't why they stared.

Ignoring their whispers, he browsed the remembrances, studying every photograph, viewing all the videos, and reading each tribute. He stopped at one image where a much younger Richforth beamed as he stood atop a mountain. A crisp blue sky hovered behind him and a board as tall as him propped up in the crook of his arm. *Hmm. I didn't know he enjoyed snowboarding.*

"He was a local champion, you know?"

Hapker startled at the sturdy middle-aged woman standing beside him. "Really? He never mentioned it."

First Lieutenant Suarana's eyes turned doleful. "When I found this photo a few months ago, I asked him about it. He seemed embarrassed but told me how much he loved racing down mountains. It had been his dream to enter the Prontaean Games, but his parents talked him out of it. Said the career wouldn't last and he'd be left with few options afterward."

"He didn't seem to have any regrets." A lump formed in Hapker's throat at the reminder of how Richforth's exemplary leadership had propelled his own career.

"I can't believe he's gone." She brushed her finger along the side of the frame. "It's unreal, isn't it? He had a full physical less than nine months ago. Surely we should've detected the cancer."

Hapker's mind reeled. Cancer was generally curable.

She sighed heavily, then gave him a small, awkward smile before moving on. Hapker remained there, staring at the picture without really seeing it.

Gresher stepped beside him. "He seemed like such a strong man."

"Yeah. He was. Strong, firm but fair-minded, and brilliant. Much like Captain Arden, but more personable."

"I'll take stoic over nitpicky any day." Gresher tilted his head at Admiral Belmont and his beady-eyed lackey. Nitpicky described them perfectly, but in different ways. Where the admiral brooded over details, Major Esekielu warred over them.

Hapker shook his head. "Commander Ramgarhia should be in charge." Admirals rarely took over the day-to-day duties of ship captains, but this seemed to be Belmont's habit.

"I agree, but Ramgarhia only has four years of experience as a commander. It makes some sense to defer to the admiral's expertise."

"I doubt he deferred," Hapker replied bitterly and changed the subject. "Have you spoken to your friend yet?"

"No. You?"

Hapker glanced at Sergeant Andres Carter. The man's pointed chin hid beneath a short beard. His usually full lips and small mouth spread into a somber smile as he spoke to a junior officer. "No. This is the first I've seen of him since arriving, and now isn't the right time."

"Agreed. I had a chance to talk to Korbin yesterday but found an excuse to weasel out."

"It's easy to find excuses, isn't it?"

"Maybe we can have a contest?"

Hapker tilted his head. "A contest to see who can come up with the most excuses?"

Gresher's lips curved upward. "No," he said, drawing out the vowel. "The first one to attempt to make amends wins."

Hapker couldn't help but smile in return. It was almost like he was back in school engaging in silly little competitions with his friends. "Since winning might entail losing, the prize should be worth it."

Gresher put his finger to his chin and looked up. "Hmm. I hear you like outdoor adventures, so how about next time we're planetside, the winner chooses the sport while the loser carries all the gear?"

Hapker chuckled. "Deal."

As they shook on it, Gresher's wide and bright smile returned. "I hope you enjoy snowboarding." He pointed to the photo.

"As a matter of fact, I do." If only he'd known Richforth's interest before.

His sullen mood resurfaced—a bit of guilt as well, for allowing himself that moment of cheerfulness. He stepped over to the next memorabilia—a video of Richforth receiving his certificate from the PG Institute.

Gresher accompanied him. "So tell me more about your experience serving this great man. Something good. This is supposed to be a celebration of life, remember?"

Hapker drew in a deep breath and reminisced. There'd been the short skirmish with the Grapnes that had hardly been a fight at all since they surrendered at Richforth's warning shot. Another time, Richforth outsmarted a smuggler by letting the man believe he didn't know about the stolen foodstuffs. Then there was the miraculous save of a damaged transport vessel that had nearly fallen into a planet's atmosphere. But those were things he had done. They didn't reflect who he was.

"Alright," Hapker finally said. "On my first day as lieutenant, the captain sent me a huge file document and quizzed me on its contents. The questions were weird. I can't even remember the—oh, yeah. One was about Kimurian ceremonial wear. Another asked the name of Councilor Alvia's dog. It's Cuddles, by the way. As he fired off question after question, I stammered, trying to answer while also questioning why I needed to know these things."

Gresher covered the bottom half of his face and shook with silent laughter.

"Everyone on the bridge bore such stern expressions. I thought he was serious until someone let out a snicker when he asked whether Lady Gretchen wore a wig."

Mirthful tears formed as he and Gresher laughed without trying to be too loud. People looked at them, but he didn't care. The lieutenant was right. This was a celebration of life, not a time to dwell on regrets.

He dried the rims of his eyes and let out a contented sigh. "Ah, he was such a prankster. He certainly kept us on our toes."

"Sounds like a good man." Gresher's expression sobered. "I wish I had known him."

"You would've liked him."

The two perused other remembrances in mournful silence before Gresher excused himself to return to Jori. Hapker moved on, stopping at a video of Richforth receiving a commendation for his rescue of the transport vessel. He'd already seen it a dozen times.

After graduating from the PG Institute, Hapker had received several requests to serve on vessels from both the PG-Force and the PCC. The service aspect of the PCC had its appeal. Helping broken-down ships, providing transportation to people from various cultures, and getting to visit exotic worlds promised the exploratory adventures he'd always yearned for. But his youthful self also wanted to be in on the action of the Cooperative's policing side. This video had decided him, and he'd signed on with Captain Richforth of the PG-Force.

"Funny how things turn out," Hapker mumbled. Not only was he better suited to the PCC as Captain Arden's first commander, but he'd also found more life-threatening action there. And now here he was, back on a PG-Force ship that had once belonged to the late Captain Richforth.

A blaring alarm sounded. Hapker glanced at the MM tablet on his wrist, expecting orders. The red text on his display ordered him to a safety depot, so he headed to the exit with calm haste.

"What do you think is going on?" someone asked.

"Probably a drill," another person said.

Hapker frowned. *It's an odd time for a drill.* The admiral was a self-important control-freak, but he wouldn't be so callous as to schedule one during the service. Something else must be happening. He rubbed the prickling from the back of his neck and hoped Jori would be alright.

10
Zero Gravity

Maintaining a sorrowful expression through the service had been difficult but Gottfried Krause had force himself. Now that the alarm sounded, trying to pretend concern while also suppressing a smile proved tougher. His glee came unbidden as people filed out of the room to their pre-assigned emergency positions.

The attack arrived right on schedule. His boss' ability to reconstruct the plan on such short notice was astounding. If all went well, the admiral would need to make a stop to get more officers. And not just any officers, either. Two special squads had been formed within the Cooperative ranks and were waiting for their day to serve MEGA-Man.

A passing officer ran into him. "Sorry, Sir."

"It's alright." Gottfried's smile almost slipped out, so he continued down the corridor with a forced frown.

A minuscule vibration issued through the floor. Weapon's discharge. The admiral and the major quickened their steps. Gottfried hurried to keep up, reaching the conveyor just behind them. As they waited for the car, Major Esekielu shot him a sour, baffled look. Technically, an aide was non-essential and should've been getting into a safety depot. Instead, he stuck out his chin and dared the major to protest. The prickly man turned away, having learned long ago not to subvert Gottfried's importance as the admiral's trusted advisor.

They entered the conveyor where the major dominated the conversation. "Acting-captain Ramgarhia reports that a Rhinian mercenary ship suddenly appeared."

A conspiratorial giddiness bubbled in Gottfried's throat. The Rhinians had probably been hired by MEGA-Man.

"What do they want?" Admiral Belmont asked.

Esekielu made a face as though to say *I'm getting to it*. "They didn't explain. They simply attacked."

"Attacked? Why am I only hearing about this now?"

Esekielu's jaw twitched. Gottfried's mouth quirked with amusement. How someone as intolerant as the major managed to serve someone like the admiral for so long was beyond him.

"This just happened, Sir," the major replied, barely keeping his irritation out of his tone. "Ramgarhia raised the shields in time and is now returning fire."

"Let's hurry," the admiral said.

Gottfried refrained from rolling his eyes. The conveyor could only go so fast and Ramgarhia was perfectly capable of handling this situation on his own.

They exited the car to the command deck. Belmont and Esekielu took long, swift strides and Gottfried huffed to keep up. Once they entered the bridge, he sat at the back and buckled in.

The massive viewscreen at the front of the command center displayed a vector image of the battle. Red text labeled the red dot of the enemy. Red lines representing missiles emerged from it while yellow ones represented the *Defender*.

"Report!" the admiral barked as he motioned for Ramgarhia to exit the captain's chair.

Major Esekielu did the same to the major at the tactical station.

Major Kozlov bristled but she stepped aside and gave her report. "Our shields average at eighty-nine percent. We estimate the Rhinian ship at sixty-two percent. Our plan of action just shifted from defense-sequence sigma to offense-action eta."

The admiral's bottom lips stuck out as though upset that he couldn't find fault with Ramgarhia's tactics. "Has anyone heard from the Rhinians? What do they want?"

"They're not responding to our hail, Sir," the communications officer said.

"Sir!" Major Esekielu called out. "Three hundred stealth missiles just appeared on our radar!"

"Evasive action!" Belmont gripped the arm of his chair. "They must be using their entire arsenal of ballistics in one go," he said to himself.

Three hundred? Gottfried's insides squirmed. The *Defender*'s shields worked best against lightspeed energy weapons, which couldn't fire as often. The slower yet more numerous projectiles had rapidly changing frequencies that could often penetrate an energy shield. However, they were usually destroyed by anti-missile turrets. It was rare for one to get through. But not even a ship as advanced as the *Defender* could stop that many at once. What were the Rhinians doing? This was just supposed to be a ruse, not an outright attack.

The *Defender* quaked. Gottfried's teeth rattled. Then his stomach wobbled. An odd sensation took over his body. He was no longer anchored to his seat.

"We're hit! The gravity wheel is damaged!" an operations officer shouted.

Gottfried's breath caught as he noted the diagram in the bottom right corner of the viewscreen. That section of the wheel was close to the brig. This shouldn't be happening. Jori wasn't supposed to be hurt in this attack.

Those damned overambitious Rhinians.

*****

Jori waited with mock patience as Banks muttered and reentered the door code. The deception emanating from him suggested he only pretended to forget it.

The floor tremored, which Jori assumed meant weapon deployment.

Banks sneered. "A real emergency, then. Well, that figures."

The main cellblock entrance hissed open, startling the guards. Banks drew back, his emotions spiking like a criminal caught in the act.

Coward.

Lieutenant Gresher appeared, making Jori breathe easy even though a part of him wished everyone would just leave him alone.

Gresher's forehead wrinkled up, then down as he regarded the guards. "Why haven't you taken him to a safety depot yet?"

Banks cleared his throat. "Sorry, Sir. I was having trouble with the door code."

Gresher gave him a dubious look but didn't call him out on the lie. "Do you think you've got it now or should I contact your superior?"

"I've got it, Sir." Banks gave a flat smile.

The big ape's lips curled as he entered the code and glowered at Jori. When the door opened, Jori resisted the urge to step back from the man as he flashed his teeth.

"Good. Then let's go," Gresher snapped.

When Banks reached for him, he shifted his shoulder and swept past. Gresher fell in beside him. Jori didn't know him as well as the commander but appreciated his presence. The consistent evenness and mild nature of the lieutenant's lifeforce helped.

Instead of taking the left to the cellblock exit, they turned right. A long hallway led to eleven other cells, all empty, and a safety depot at the end.

Banks marched with haste. He either finally believed the alarm wasn't a drill or hoped Jori wouldn't keep up so he could drag him. The man's growling emotions made him suspect the latter.

The floor lurched. A quake rattled Jori's bones, making him slam into someone, backward into a wall, then onto the floor. A strike to the side of his head sent a flash of blackness through his vision.

When the shuddering subsided, he found himself floating. Droplets of blood hovered in the air in front of him, but he didn't know if it was his or someone else's. A piercing ring infiltrated all six of his senses, making his body throb and his head spin.

He gasped. A pang gripped his chest. Maybe a cracked rib? As he attempted to control the depth and duration of his breathing, the internal ringing sensation subsided.

Jori took in his surroundings. He hovered above the floor, too far for his feet to touch. A smear of blood bubbled there, the liquid undulating in irregular globs. To his left, two officers floated face-down with their arms and legs at varying angles. Another slowly rotated above and in front of him. Gresher drifted face up on his other side. His eyes were closed, and his head tilted at an uncomfortable angle.

Using his senses, Jori determined they were all unconscious. He let out a sigh of relief. Although he despised at least one of these people, he'd never been comfortable around death. The inertial dampeners must've done their job, otherwise they'd be pancaked all over the walls.

Jori reached for Gresher's boot, touching it with the tip of his finger but not able to get a hold on it. While he searched for something to use as leverage, he caught a stab of fury from Sergeant Banks. Twisting his neck and shoulders around brought him face-to-face with a raging squall.

Banks hovered above him. His deadpan expression turned Jori's blood to ice as large hands grabbed the front of his shirt.

Damn the loose civilian clothing. Jori chopped at the man's wrist to no avail. His heartrate picked up as a devious smile spread across the sergeant's face. Jori flailed, trying to find something, anything, to help him against this madman.

Banks pulled him close. The sour smell of his heated breath kicked Jori's adrenaline into overdrive. He jabbed upward with his palm, striking the man under the chin. Banks' teeth snapped. Jori took advantage of his split-second disorientation and wheeled his arms backward. Two fingers struck Gresher's boot at the same time as a sharp twinge radiated from his ribs. He tried again in frantic movements, ignoring his pain and hoping his momentum wouldn't send the man out of his reach.

Corporal Lengen woke. He shook his head, then flapped his own arms as he realized his situation.

"Help me!" Jori called out as Banks' big arm came toward his neck.

The pounding in Jori's chest spiked through his ribcage as he scrambled to keep the sergeant from getting him into a hold. He planted his hands against Banks' forearm and pushed himself down. His head slipped between the crook of his elbow. With the floor now within reach, he bent his legs into it, then sprang over to Gresher.

He reached the man's calf and grasped on for dear life. "Wake up! He's trying to hurt me!"

"Hurt you?" Banks gave Lengen a conspiratorial look. "I would never do that. You attacked me."

The menace in his emotions prickled Jori's skin. He pulled himself over Gresher until he was face-to-face. He smacked his cheek, softy at first, then harder when he didn't react. "Wake up, damn it!"

"Help me restrain him before he hurts someone, will you?" Banks asked.

"You got it, Sir," Lengen said with a feral grin.

Jori's breath hitched. He shoved himself away from Gresher in time to avoid the corporal's grasp. The opposing force made Gresher's body roll in the way. Jori's foot found purchase on the floor, and he thrust himself further back.

Gresher's head jerked. Then his body. His eyes snapped open. "Huh?"

"Gresher! Lieutenant Gresher!" Jori fumbled for one of the emergency handholds along the wall.

The lieutenant righted himself as much as zero gravity allowed. He touched a dark lump on his forehead. "What... Is everyone alright?"

Banks pointed at the two unconscious officers. "I haven't had a chance to check them yet. I've been trying to get that boy back in custody, but he attacked me."

"You were about to hurt me," Jori blurted with the heat of an engine blast.

"I was attempting to restrain you."

"Liar!" Jori latched onto an emergency handle. The buzz of his adrenaline wore off now that he was safe, but anger still roiled inside him. "Only cowards lie."

Banks growled. "I'll show you—"

Gresher waved his hands. "Alright! Stop! We can work this out later. Right now, I need everyone to get to the safety depot. You—" He pointed at Banks, then to an unconscious officer. "Help him. You," he said to Lengen. "Help her. Jori. Get yourself to the depot, grab a first aid kit and send it over, then strap in."

Jori glowered at Banks as he pulled himself down the wall just out of reach. Banks wasn't likely to try anything with Gresher awake, but he wasn't taking any chances.

After he passed him, his nerves calmed enough for him to realize that he'd forgotten something—someone. *Where's Hapker?* He used his senses to forage through the ship. His emotional connection to the man made it easy to find him. Concern dotted the commander's emotions, but there was no sensation of injury. Enough relief washed over Jori that he no longer cared about the animosity that rolled off the two malevolent guards.

So long as he had Hapker, he had hope.

11
Blind

Carletta Ortega cradled her throbbing head in one hand and gripped an emergency handle on the wall with the other. Measured breaths helped dull the pain. She suspected the lack of gravity helped too, since it didn't pull her brain down.

She eased open her eyes. Spiderweb cracks distorted the scene before her like a kaleidoscope of nonsense. Thank goodness her sunglasses hadn't completely shattered.

She removed them with care, trying not to exacerbate the ache in her skull. The only light came from the red flashing alarm further down the corridor, yet her excellent vision allowed her to see everything with perfect precision—every emergency hand and foothold, the corners where the walls met the floor and ceiling, even the writing on the tool and first aid boxes.

The empty hall meant she was the only person who hadn't made it to a safety depot. They were all over the ship, so she cursed her stupidity. The one time she thought it was just a drill was the one time it wasn't.

She'd been giving Harley a stern lecture about the importance of not letting those bullies influence his opinions when the alarms sounded. After accompanying him to a safety depot, she'd headed back to her quarters to make sure little Matro, her pet lemur, was alright.

Dummy. The rules were there for a reason. Although she'd worried Matro might get hurt, she never should've taken the risk. After all, she had an emergency protection unit that would've activated—unless the booger got out of his cage again.

The lights flickered back on. Ortega squeezed her eyes shut. It wasn't enough. The brightness still stabbed into her like daggers. With a grunt, she smacked her palm over her eyes. *This won't do.* She needed both hands to pull herself down the corridor to the safety depot. If she pushed off and floated while blind, she might miss the door and drift.

She felt around with her foot until she found an emergency divot in the wall and jammed her toes into it. With her body somewhat stabilized, she let go of the handle. Swallowing her pride, she tapped the comm behind her ear. "This is Sergeant Ortega. I'm on deck six, section D and need assistance getting to a safety depot."

In less than a minute, door hydraulics sounded. She didn't need her eyes to know it came from her targeted safety depot. Her ears told her someone emerged, followed by the door shutting behind them.

"Ortega!" a familiar woman's voice boomed. "You alright?"

"Sergeant Fenyvesi, thank goodness! Yes. I'm alright, but I can't see."

"Oh, shit." Rustling indicated Feny hastily pulled herself along the handholds.

"Don't worry. It's just temporary," Ortega replied. "My sunglasses broke and the light hurts."

"Whew! That's not so bad, then. Okay. I've got you."

The woman's heavy breathing crept closer until a tug at Ortega's waist followed by a snap told her Feny had attached a tether to her belt. Ortega let go of the handhold and allowed herself to be tugged. She kept one arm out, occasionally touching the wall and gently pushing herself away from it so that she drifted down the center of the corridor.

"What the hell are you doing out here, anyway?" Feny asked in a harsh tone.

Ortega winced. *Damn it*. She could lie but fessed up instead. "I made a lapse in judgment. I assumed it was a drill, so decided to check on my trouble-making pet."

Feny tsked. "Girl, that's a serious breach of protocol."

Ortega agreed. "I'm sorry."

"Sorry won't cut it if I get hurt too."

Shame burned Ortega's cheeks. Another apology wouldn't undo what she'd done, so she remained silent.

"We're almost there," Feny said in a kinder tone.

"Yeah, I can hear people talking."

"You can hear that? I can't."

"My hearing is as acute as my eyesight—that is, when the lights aren't so bright."

"Huh. I guess that makes sense. I read that some of your people can use something like echolocation. Can you do that?"

Ortega laughed off her embarrassment. "Very few can. My grandmother could make supersonic yells, but I've never tried it myself."

"Supersonic yells, too? That's interesting. I wouldn't mind having your enhanced eyesight and hearing either. Amazing."

Ortega didn't know about that. Most often, her abilities caused people to be wary of her. It was stupid since the Cooperative was full of humans with unique qualities, but that was just the way things were. At least Feny didn't judge her.

Once secured in the safety depot, Feny wrapped something around her eyes. Ortega smiled. She'd deserved the earlier rebuke—and the forthcoming writeup—but Feny didn't hold a grudge.

*****

The once smallish conference room made for a nice-sized office. It had space for a prodigious desk designed to look like real wood, and a kitchenette complete with an elegant bar cabinet where a bottle of fine Henthean brandy waited for a special occasion.

Gottfried Krause eyed the luxurious ivory couch placed against the wall as he stood before the admiral, waiting for him to review the information. The man had made the right decision in not pursuing the fleeing Rhinian ship earlier. Pointing out that the Rhinians tended to set traps almost hadn't been enough. Gottfried had to remind him of the *Defender*'s original mission—to transport the database with instructions on building a new perantium emitter to Asteria.

Convincing the admiral they needed more PG-Force officers had been easier. The *Defender* was grossly understaffed. With Jori alive and well—thank goodness—and with the fear that the Rhinians might know about the database and attack again, they'd need a force strong enough to fight off a ship incursion.

Now to convince Admiral Belmont to acquire these soldiers from Indore station.

The wide monitor on the admiral's desk flicked from available officers on Shashti station to the ones on Indore. Gottfried didn't point out which option he preferred. He'd misrepresented reports so the admiral would make the obvious choice.

"Their records are exemplary." Major Esekielu scanned the list of their accomplishments with his hungry, beady eyes. "Their fight with the Kraykians required immense discipline and fortitude. We could use people like that here."

Belmont leaned forward in his chair. With the gravity now fixed, the major stood in his usual inflexible pose at his left shoulder. Gottfried waited on his right.

"And two full squads are available," the admiral said.

"There are more at Shashti," Gottfried offered, boosting the man's ego by providing an idea he would shut down.

"But their qualifications are mixed," the admiral replied, exactly as predicted.

Esekielu dipped his head. "Agreed, Sir. We don't need technicians and engineers. We need battle-hardened troops."

Gottfried refrained from bouncing on his toes. The crew here wouldn't stand a chance against these special soldiers. *As if kittens could defeat tigers.*

For once, Belmont's pout ticked up in a smile. "And Indore station isn't too far. It will only add three days to our trip."

"Shall I give the order, Sir?" Gottfried asked, keeping his glee from coming out in his voice.

The admiral tapped his desk and sat back. "Do it. Major, tell the helms officer to change course."

"Yes, Sir," the major snapped. Gottfried opted to bow instead. Belmont dismissed them both. Gottfried left with a spring in his step while Esekielu marched out with a rigid gait.

Once out of sight, Gottfried let a broad grin spread across his face. MEGA-Man would be pleased.

12
Defense

After contacting the two squads at Indore and updating MEGA-Man, Gottfried Krause headed out to fulfill his next task. When he entered the cellblock, he nodded to the four guards. “Let me in.”

“Sir?” Sergeant Banks replied with a scowl. He emitted disbelief and a touch of outrage. Behind it was an everlasting loathing that tainted everything he did, even before Gottfried’s influence.

“Let me in,” he repeated. “I wish to speak to the young man face-to-face.”

“Sir, we have orders.”

Gottfried raised his eyebrows. “I know. I was there when they were given. Do not concern yourself, Sergeant. Commander Hapker and Lieutenant Gresher are here. I’m sure the three of us can handle things. And if not, I’ll take responsibility.”

“Yes, Sir.” Resignation wafted from the officer as he unlocked the door. A shot of his hatred spiked as he scowled at the boy.

Another guard made a similar face. Gottfried assessed the essence of the corporal with the upturned nose. Having also used his imperium ability to influence this one’s will, it hadn’t darkened as much as the sergeant’s—but it was enough. The more animosity directed at Jori, the more likely he’d see Gottfried as an ally.

As the thick plasti-glass hissed aside, Gottfried took in the emotions of the three occupants as they played a board game with small, round, colored pieces. The animated men had no effect on the boy’s joylessness. Nor did his mood change when he looked Gottfried’s way.

He needs to be with his own kind. Superior people would bring out his potential far more than these feeble-minded Neanderthals.

A sourness swirled inside him. He analyzed it and realized it was jealousy. Interesting. It made sense, though. He wanted Jori on his side, but the child seemed more at ease with this commander. *I'll turn him soon enough.*

Hmm. What if he implanted his will into Commander Hapker and turned him against Jori? Then again, he needed to earn the boy's trust. Befriending this man might help.

He considered his options. His imperium-animi ability might not be powerful enough. The commander seemed like a strong-minded person and his feelings for the boy were stronger still. Manipulating him might backfire.

No, it was smarter to make friends with both Jori and the commander, then eliminate the man later. After all, Commander Hapker was part of the institution that rejected Gottfried's kind.

"Are you going in or not, Sir?" Banks asked.

Gottfried startled. He must be more careful. Processing information made him freeze, which unsettled people.

He put on a smile and entered. "What have we here? Is that Corners you're playing?"

"Sure is." Lieutenant Gresher smiled. His perfectly straight teeth formed a primate grin that took up almost the entire width of his face.

Jori rose and planted himself in a soldier's stance.

"I seem to recall reading you like schemster," Gottfried said.

"I do." Jori maintained solid eye-contact as he spoke, demonstrating both fortitude and self-assurance.

Gottfried attempted to read the essence wafting off the boy. A mental shield blocked him. He could use his extraho abilities to poke inside, but Jori might sense the intrusion. *He'll let his guard down once we're friends.* "I like Galactic Dominions, myself."

"I've never played it."

"Perhaps I can teach you and we can play sometime."

The boy only reacted with an abrupt bob of his head.

"Wonderful. My name is Lieutenant Gottfried Krause, or just Gottfried. It's nice to meet you." He extended his open hand. "I'm here to make sure you're well cared for."

Jori took it without enthusiasm.

Gottfried didn't need to detect his emotions to know why. He tapped the device placed behind his ear. "This is an inhibitor. It blocks people from reading me. I don't want to hide anything from you, but the admiral ordered me to wear it."

Jori expelled a sourness, but quickly masked it.

"You're sentio-animi," Gottfried said without accusation. "I am required to tell you I'm a level higher—extraho-animi." Imperium-animi actually, but not something he could reveal without risking his freedom.

While some people disliked those with sentio abilities, that skill didn't require getting into someone's head, only sensing what a person emitted. Extrahos and imperiums were a different matter. They could invade minds and so roused fear. No one here reacted, though. The commander and lieutenant probably already knew. The boy either didn't care or had remarkable self-restraint. *Impressive.*

"Don't worry," Gottfried said. "I'm not here to violate your privacy."

Jori's face remained blank.

"I hear you have other skills as well," Gottfried continued. "A level nine combat fighting skill is astonishing. People train for years before they get to this point, and you've accomplished it at the age of ten."

The boy dipped his head but still didn't reply. Frustration vibrated through Gottfried's emotions, but he maintained an outward friendliness.

The boy's brow twitched as an awkward silence settled. The sound of the main cellblock door opening provided a relief. A lanky man with a mustache and goatee appeared, his essence full of business-like purpose.

"Ah, here he is," Gottfried said. "Mister Bilsby can help you with this unfortunate dilemma."

Banks opened the cell. Bilsby told him to activate the privacy setting, then came in wearing a weak smile.

Jori kept a straight face as an inexplicable annoyance escaped him. "I don't need help."

Gottfried hid his confusion. "Don't be so quick to dismiss him. He's an excellent lawyer."

Jori's mouth tilted. "Lawyer?"

"You need someone to defend your case."

"Why? I'm guilty. I took over the *Odyssey* and I attacked Thendi."

Gottfried pulled back.

Bilsby stepped forward. "Yes, but your reasons for doing so are defendable."

"But why would you defend *me*?"

"I've read all the reports," Gottfried replied. "It's obvious you want to change your situation for the good, and I would like to give you that chance."

Jori's eyes narrowed. Hapker crossed his arms and faced Gottfried. "What's the catch?"

"No catch."

Jori returned to his wooden expression and pointed his question at the lawyer. "Will you be working for me or the admiral?"

"I'm a public defender," Bilsby said. "Although I'm compensated by the Cooperative, it's against my code of ethics to play politics. I'll fight for you and for you alone."

Gottfried nodded, pleased at the man's forthcoming attitude. Putting someone on the boy's side almost contradicted his plans for an alliance, but he couldn't risk offering a less determined lawyer. The more Gottfried assisted the boy, the greater the Prontaean Cooperative council's betrayal would be when they passed their judgment.

"I've inspected your file," Bilsby continued. "There are some concerns, but I believe that giving the Cooperative a little information about your father's military holdings will sway them and earn you your freedom."

Jori's mouth hard-lined. Commander Hapker touched his shoulder. "Hasn't he done enough to prove himself?"

"And I've already told the council I'm not giving them that," Jori added.

"I'm sure we can figure out something," Gottfried said. "You agreed to divulge all the changes you made to the emitter, plus the information on slave traders."

"Are you still willing to provide those?" Bilsby asked.

"Yes," Jori said with a firm face.

"Well, let's get started then." Bilsby handed the boy a tablet.

"He hasn't agreed to let you be his lawyer," the commander said.

Jori frowned. "I have a choice?"

"Yes." Commander Hapker put his arm over the boy's shoulder.

Gottfried pushed away his jealousy and smiled instead. "Bilsby's first loyalty is to his profession. He has the same choice regarding whether to represent you and it's in his best interest to do the best job possible." He motioned to Bilsby, who didn't have an inhibitor. "Tell him."

Bilsby faced Jori with a solid conviction. "I will do everything I can to free you of these charges. However, I need your help to do that."

A wary sensation wafted off the commander. "I want to believe you, but you'll have to prove it."

"Of course." Bilsby swept out his hand as though making an offer. "What would you like me to do?"

"Well." The commander stroked his chin. "Jori is a very active young man, and I imagine he's feeling restless in here. Is there a way he can get some activity in the gym?"

Bilsby's brows shot up. "Actually, I think free time is a requirement. I know it's a security risk, but for them to keep you here when your case hasn't been decided is counter to the rules of our justice system. I'm sure I can get you this."

Jori sucked in a breath as a glimmer of hope escaped his mental shield. If the admiral permitted this, it'd alter Gottfried's plans a bit but in a good way.

Hapker dipped his head. "Thank you."

"Since you're looking out for me," Jori said, "shouldn't I be allowed to contact my mother?"

While Gottfried considered the possibility, Bilsby answered. "By Cooperative law, you should. But those laws apply to Cooperative citizens. I'm not sure if the importance of their security will outweigh your rights, but I'll present the matter and push it as far as they'll allow."

Jori's eyes lit up.

Gottfried relished the breach of defenses and clasped his hands in thanks. "We will speak to the admiral right away and get back to you."

Jori subtly bounced on his toes. A pleasant tingling sensation expanded from Gottfried's core. Making friends with the boy would be easier than expected.

*****

Gottfried Krause stood before the desk. Feigning self-restraint. Admiral Belmont liked these games of pretending he was too engaged in his work to acknowledge him. Gottfried played along. Let the admiral keep his sense of power for now. His delusions would be shattered soon enough.

Belmont finally looked up. His bottom lip protruded in annoyance. "What can I help you two with?"

Bilsby stepped forward with a friendly expression that was as much of a forgery as Gottfried's patience. "It's regarding the Tredon child."

"You mean the son of the dragon?" the admiral asked with admonishment in his tone.

Bilsby bowed, but no contriteness emanated from his emotions. "Yes. As his legal representative, I'm obliged to remind you of his right to be allowed out of his cell from time—"

"Absolutely not!" Belmont slapped his hand on his desk. "I don't want him taking over this ship like he did on the *Odyssey*."

"By law, he should have at least two hours of exercise daily."

"He can exercise in his cell," Belmont said sourly. "There's plenty of room to run in place or do aerobics."

Although Bilsby presented calm, Gottfried sensed his irritation. An inhibitor blocked Belmont's emotions but reading his features was easy. The man was as predictable as a sunset.

"Legally, it's not enough," Bilsby replied with a tight expression.

"It is when it comes to MEGAs," Belmont said.

Gottfried ground his teeth. The arrogance of some people. Just because someone was more talented didn't mean they had augmentations.

Saying this would get him nowhere, so he tried another tactic that would appeal to this small-minded man. "If I may, Admiral. Remember that discussion we had with the councilor? This could provide the perfect opportunity."

Belmont cocked his head. The creases in his forehead smoothed and Gottfried could almost see realization sinking in.

"He will be guarded, of course," Gottfried said. "And we can add more if you wish."

The admiral eased back into his ridiculously big chair. "Very well. Two hours a day. No more. And double his guard detail during that time."

"Thank you, Admiral. I'm sure this will serve our interests."

Belmont nodded and dismissed them. Gottfried suppressed a self-satisfied expression.

13
Martial Training

The gymnasium bustled with activity. Jori glanced about, surprised at how it differed from the *Odyssey* where the most common exercises were anaerobic, jogging, or sports. Many activities here reminded him of home. Three separate groups practiced varying forms of martial arts. Several holo-systems designated for virtual sparring occupied a corner. Two obstacle courses with climbing, jumping, running, and agility challenges took up much of the central area.

The major difference was this place had more weight machines. Strength training was just as important to senshi warriors, but they preferred to build their muscle with nonstationary activities.

Hapker clapped his back. "How about a game of wall ball?" He pointed to a series of partitioned courts.

Jori wasn't sure he wanted to do anything. Although acclimated to daily vigorous exercise, the thought of staying in bed all day held a new appeal. At least there he could drift in and out of slumber and let his mind meander at a snail's pace.

"It'll be alright," Hapker said. "No one will give you a hard time while I'm here."

"It's not that," Jori replied.

"Is it Lieutenant Krause and the lawyer? Did they seem off to you?"

Jori shook his head. "I couldn't get a read on Gottfried because of that inhibitor, but he seemed genuine. And Bilsby spoke truthfully."

"He *did* come through for you, but I'm worried they might have a hidden agenda."

Jori didn't comment. Their intentions hardly mattered since nearly everyone was against him anyway.

"So what is it, then?" The commander asked.

Jori shrugged.

Hapker put his arm over him. "It'll get better. I promise."

Jori replied by pulling away. Not that he didn't appreciate the friendliness, he just wasn't used to it. The only person who'd ever shown him this kind of warmth was his mother.

The commander nudged him with a playful smile. "Come on. Let's see if you can beat me."

"Yes, Sir." Jori forced himself to take a step.

"Hey. Call me J.D., alright. I'm not your father or your superior officer. I'm your friend."

Jori's cheeks warmed. "Sorry. Habit."

They walked by the courts and found them all occupied. Hapker scanned the gym. "Well, how about something else, then?"

Jori eyed the holo-machines. It would mean working out by himself rather than with Hapker—J.D.—but being alone complemented his current frame of mind. "I want to do that." He pointed.

"Are you sure you don't want to do something together?"

"Yes. I'll be fine. I'm just not in the mood for fun today."

Hapker emitted a hurt and reluctance. "Alright. I'll take a run and check on you every lap."

Jori ambled over to the holo-machine as his eight guards took posts nearby. Hapker watched him with growing concern before heading to the track that circled the gym. The departure of his comforting essence left Jori feeling hollow, but he set the program parameters and willed himself to do something other than dwell on his losses.

*****

Jori chopped at his opponent and missed. The holo-man blocked his counterstrike and punched in rapid succession. The blur of the virtual fist erupted before reaching Jori's left eye. An annoying buzzer sounded, signifying that he'd lost—again.

Chusho. He couldn't beat level eight today. His heart just wasn't in it. No matter how hard, fast, or focused he strived to be, his hurt smothered and ate at him with no sign of abating.

He had to get to his mother. Being with her would make everything better.

An idea popped into his head. He paused the program and the haptic image disappeared. Jori stepped off the platform and considered his options. Free time was good, but what if he could use it for something else—like getting to a communications room?

He was familiar with the layout of this kind of ship. There was one near here. Weaving between the exercise machines that crowded the gym might slow him down but could also hinder any pursuers. His agility training would give him an edge, though. And the equipment would provide cover from their stun weapons.

He only had one shot at this. He almost went for it, but a taut readiness lurked in the stances of the guards. There'd likely be some physical confrontation before he got away. Corporal Harley would be easy enough to handle, but there were seven more to contend with.

Most seemed to have indifferent attitudes toward him, but Sergeant Banks and Corporal Lengen harbored an intense dislike. They'd be the first to go after him if he ran, and neither would play nice when they caught him.

Perhaps he could find something to use as a weapon. *No. No weapons*. Killing someone just to call his mother didn't sit well.

He returned to the holo-program and set up another challenge. A new holo-man appeared. He jabbed, kicked, and blocked, relishing the physical aches in his body. With each passing level, his melancholy retreated.

Sergeant Banks made a disparaging sound. "Looks who wants to be like his father."

"Just what the universe needs," Corporal Lengen said in the same snide tone.

"Another damned dragon," Banks added.

A spark of bravery ignited in Harley. "Sir, we shouldn't talk like that. We were told—"

"I know how to do my job, so mind your business, soldier."

Harley's emotions cowered. Jori winced. Banks' bullying reminded him of his father while Harley's reaction evoked his own feeling of helplessness.

"Is everything okay here?"

Jori ignored Gresher's arrival and continued to attack his virtual opponent, pretending it was the fat-headed Banks.

"Other than a criminal being allowed out of the brig, it's fine, Lieutenant," Banks said.

Jori punched the holo-man in the nose and wished the program showed blood. Even hearing the crunch of cartilage would've been nice, but all he got was a mechanical voice telling him he reached the next level.

"He gets free time, part of the same rights everyone gets." Gresher's tone carried a smile. "Are you familiar with article seven-point-eight-three of the Cooperative code of conduct, Sergeant?"

A spark of annoyance reverberated through Banks' emotions, but he didn't reply.

Jori fought on but threw sidelong glances as Gresher squared himself before the sergeant.

"We must treat prisoners with human decency," Gresher said while wearing his usual friendly grin. "They are to be protected against violence, intimidation, and insults. Any breach of these duties diminishes the higher calling of the Prontaean Cooperative and undermines its mission to unite humanity in peace. Did they not teach you this at the institute?"

Hapker jogged up with a hard expression. "Everything alright here, Lieutenant?"

"Just reminding them of their sworn duties, Sir."

Jori snuck a look while circling his virtual opponent and silently cheered as Banks clamped his mouth shut.

Gresher's eyes tilted in sympathy. "I get that we lost friends because of this boy's father. Tensions are high. But we have a responsibility to rise above hate and anger."

Banks and Lengen looked away in resentment. At least Corporal Harley and the others had the decency to radiate shame.

"Keep your words civil, Sergeant," Hapker said. "That's an order."

Jori didn't hear Banks' reply. He swung, ducked, blocked, and blocked again. With a power grip, he clutched the back of the holo-man's wrist with his left hand, sidestepped, and jammed his right palm into the point of the elbow. Had it been a real person, the arm would have cracked at the joint.

"Level seven," the machine's voice chimed.

The holo-man disappeared and a taller one took its place. Jori tensed, ready to attack. The program blinked out and he halted mid-strike.

"What the hell do you think you're doing, boy?"

Jori whirled around and found Vice Admiral Belmont. The man's furrowed eyebrows protruded almost as much as his bottom lip. His nose flared wider than a snorting blackbeast.

Hapker and Gresher hastened to Jori's side. "Admiral?" Hapker said, confusion etching his features.

"I asked him what he's doing."

Jori's stomach fluttered. His mind raced. Had he done something wrong? Despite also wanting to match this man's hostility, Hapker's presence inspired him to be civil. He went into an at-ease stance and gave the admiral his full attention. "I'm exercising, Sir."

"Exercising? Is that what you call it?"

Jori's brows drew together, sensing the ire but not understanding why it was so intense. "Yes, Sir."

"It looks terribly brutal for *just an exercise*." The admiral practically spit the last words.

"That's unfair, Sir," Hapker said with a firm yet controlled tone while a wildfire raged through his essence.

Gresher's emotions and countenance remained calm. "Others use this program all the time, Admiral. It doesn't make them brutal."

Belmont huffed. "*Their* intent is defense. I doubt it's the same for this boy." He faced Banks. "Sergeant, whose idea was it to allow this?"

"The commander's, Sir." Banks smirked at Hapker.

The admiral shook his head. "Figures. No wonder he got demoted."

A spark of indignation burst in Jori's chest. "If we're so horrible, why are you the one being an asshole?"

Belmont took two giant steps forward and towered over him. Jori held his ground and arched his neck upward to hold the man's fiery gaze.

Internally, Jori faltered. The admiral's expression matched one Father gave before turning violent. Anticipation danced inside him.

Fear reared its ugly head, but he kept it from taking over—like Sensei Jeruko had taught him. He remained rigid and braced himself for a blow.

Hapker swept between them. "Admiral," he said in a low, menacing tone. "What exactly is *your* intent?"

Belmont glowered. "Back off, Commander. I wouldn't harm a child, but I won't tolerate disrespect from one either."

"Admiral Belmont, Sir." Gresher spoke in a calm voice as he placed himself beside Hapker, acting as a barrier against the admiral's hostility. "Perhaps we should have this conversation in your office. I'm sure we can work this out in a more agreeable manner."

Belmont seemed to waver between caving to the lieutenant's reasonable offer and his own confrontational inclinations. He recovered by yanking the hem of his workout shirt down and jutting his chin. "No more martial training. Is that clear?"

Hapker's jawline twitched but he responded. "Yes, Sir."

"If you can't make wise decisions, Commander," the admiral said, "I'll see that you're demoted again."

The glowing ember in Jori's core ignited. A slew of insults sprang to mind, but a hand on his shoulder didn't let them reach his lips.

As Hapker and Belmont glared at one another, Gresher whispered in Jori's ear. "Don't give him the satisfaction of reacting."

Jori's internal fire dwindled but didn't disappear.

Belmont stepped backward and glowered at both men. "Find something else to do."

Gresher smiled. "Certainly, Sir."

Jori locked eyes with the brooding admiral again and held it long enough to show he wasn't cowed. When the man finally left, both Hapker and the lieutenant led him away.

"I think he means to aggravate you," Hapker said. "It's like he's trying to push you into doing something."

Jori soured. "Chima."

"I know. I know." Gresher patted Jori's shoulder, then glanced at Hapker. "But perhaps he has a point. Maybe it's a good idea to avoid the holo-man for a while."

Jori curled his lips at the thought of giving in to that chima.

"Not only because of the admiral," Gresher said. "Things are a bit precarious right now. Although normally it wouldn't matter that you're a warrior, I think it's important to present a low-key image."

Hapker ran his hand down his face and sighed. "He's right."

Jori considered digging in his heels, but the lieutenant's quietude eased his own temper.

"If you'd like," Gresher added, "you and I can practice something else. It won't be as intense as the holo-device, but I promise it will be as challenging."

One side of Jori's mouth tilted up and the other down. He was supposed to be breaking out of here. His insides squirmed at the thought of doing it with Gresher and Hapker around. He could always try tomorrow. "What is it?"

"Changdu."

Changdu. Sensei Jeruko had taught some. "The art of least-force. Or as I've also heard it, the art of not fighting."

Gresher smiled. "It's the art of *control.* Fight words with words. Fists with fists. Weapons with weapons. But only to the extent necessary to dispel a situation. Never more."

"So don't punch a man in the face just because he pisses you off."

Gresher barked a laugh. "Definitely not. But there's more to it than that. And I must warn you—learning control is tougher than you think."

Jori raised an eyebrow at the prospect of a challenge. "Alright. Teach me."

Gresher smiled, showing his snow-white teeth, and Jori forgot all about his grief.

14
Mechanically Enhanced

Gottfried Krause lingered in an alcove of a narrow corridor. A nearby light flickered in the throes of death, confusing his optics. It was unlikely to be fixed anytime soon, but having few visitors meant this was the best spot for a private exchange.

If only Glastra's implant hadn't stopped working when he beamed onto the ship from Thendi. Meeting like this could raise questions if someone saw them, but he had little choice. Communicating via electronic channels risked discovery.

A smallish man with a crown of grey hair turned the corner and locked eyes with Gottfried. He neither smiled nor spoke. He merely held out his hand as he passed. Gottfried gave him a data transfer device carrying encrypted instructions, then the two moved on in separate ways.

Soon after, Gottfried reported to the admiral. Instead of his usual game of pointless delays, Belmont met him with barely contained displeasure.

"Admiral," Gottfried said as he inclined his head.

Admiral Belmont released his clenched hands and indicated the chair in front of his desk. "Have a seat, Lieutenant."

Gottfried settled and faked concern. "It's the boy, isn't it?"

Belmont drummed his fingers. "And Commander Hapker. Can you believe he allowed him to use the holo-machine to practice his killing skills? You should have seen how brutal that child was."

"Unbelievable, Sir." Gottfried widened his eyes, validating the admiral's unrealistic dismay. "Surely the council will never agree to let the boy stay here."

"Dear god, I hope not. How did he seem when you met him?"

"He is understandably suspicious."

"Was he hostile?"

Gottfried lifted a brow. "Surprisingly, no."

Belmont rapped his fingers on the desk in a mindless rhythm. "Hmm. I need you to spend a little more time with him. Gain his trust and see if you can find out anything incriminating."

Gottfried hid his smile as he bowed. Having permission would make his task much easier.

"I also want him tested—soon. Check if the Indore station has any MEGA Inspectors there."

"They don't, Sir." Gottfried swallowed his distaste. "It's only a small military outpost."

Belmont exhaled noisily. "Fine. We'll have our doctors do it."

Gottfried's resentment settled in his gut as he added a note to his MM. Doctor Fritz had his own special testing methods. There was nothing wrong with being mechanically enhanced or genetically altered. It was the future of humanity, but the weakest members of society were so afraid of being outdone that such testing continued.

Not for long, though. One day, MEGA-Man's followers would infiltrate the many governments throughout the galaxy. These fruitless restrictions would meet a swift end.

He smiled to himself at the name, MEGA-Man. MEGA—mechanically enhanced, genetically altered—was an acronym the Prontaean Cooperative used to describe anyone who chose to evolve. So Gottfried's boss, the most advanced being in the known universe, adopted the moniker for simplicity's sake.

The admiral here had never heard of him, but he would soon enough. And he had no clue that Gottfried was one of them. *Fool.*

"The doctors are a little overwhelmed right now," Gottfried said, "but I can get the boy in for more testing shortly after we pick up the soldiers from Indore."

"Very well. That's only two days away."

"What if we can't find any enhancements?" Gottfried asked, just to rile him.

The admiral grunted. "Impossible."

Gottfried held back an eyeroll. *What an egotistical, weak-minded idiot.*

"Once he warms up to you," Belmont said, "perhaps you can glean more about where his abilities come from."

Gottfried assented, though he already suspected the answer. The young prince was undoubtedly bred, his skills grandfathered in from the time prior to the MEGA Injunction which prohibited anyone with augmentations to hold a position of power. Enough generations had passed that the genetic markers wouldn't show up in DNA testing.

In truth, it didn't matter if Jori was enhanced or not. That he had multiple exceptional abilities gave the Cooperative plenty of reasons to hate and fear him. While the Cooperative shunned him, Gottfried's own people would welcome him. Let Admiral Belmont and Councilor Greymore persecute him. It would only turn the boy against them.

"What about the psych evaluation?" Belmont asked.

"I'm afraid the doctors are already overbooked. We have several officers still coping with the attack on Thendi, plus the handful who'd spent time on the Dragon Emperor's ship."

"Have them fit the boy in as soon as possible."

Gottfried smiled, and it was genuine. Doctor Donnel would undoubtedly turn Jori further away from the Cooperative. She wouldn't be available for several days, but he could wait.

15
The Squads

Carletta Ortega often forgot that she lived on a ship. Being in a docking bay reminded her, especially this smaller single-point entry one where an eternal void lay just beyond the hatch. Sure, the reinforced space between the inner and outer hull was wider than she was tall, but the connecting skywalk didn't have the same protection.

This didn't frighten her so much as remind her of how fragile they all were.

The docking hatch hissed as pressure equalized. Ortega adjusted her new sunglasses and waited for the arrivals with her feet at shoulder width and her hands clasped behind her back. She prepared a neutral expression, thankful it wasn't custom to give a joyous welcome.

It would be nice to have more officers to fill the gaps in the roster, but she didn't relish the influx of so many new faces. There was always that awkwardness of discovering what strangers were like—their pet peeves, what set off their tempers, whether they were lazy or complained a lot. And of course, new people might comment on her eyes—some in a hurtful way.

This hadn't been Ortega's original assignment but putting Feny in danger had earned her extra duty hours. It could have been worse. It turned out everyone was okay, including her pet.

The hatch lifted, triggering a slight discomfort in her ears. She and her fellow officers straightened their postures. The heavy tromps of dozens of boots battered down the walkway in perfect rhythm. She almost rolled her eyes at how elite troops liked to make a dramatic entrance.

The first soldier to cross the threshold onto the *Defender* made Ortega's chest hitch. She wasn't sure why. He was short compared to Bryce, with a wider build. The average features of his square-jawed face wouldn't stand out in a crowd. But there was something about his ice-blue eyes.

While Ortega and her fellows wore the standard steel-grey PG-Force uniform, these two squads had added smoke-colored armor fittings. Even without the enhanced protective gear, the way they solidly carried themselves while maintaining stony expressions named them an elite outfit.

Bryce met them with a snap of his fist to his chest. They returned it, all keeping their eyes straight ahead like robots.

"Welcome to the *Defender*. My name is Lieutenant Buckeye. This is Sergeant Carter." Bryce indicated the dark-skinned man with the trim beard and mustache standing beside him.

Carter dipped his head and licked his lips. Did that blue-eyed man make him nervous as well?

Ortega glanced at her crewmates. Korbin's throat bobbed. Wide-eyed alarm replaced Sergeant Chesa Creston's usual stormy expression. If not for Ortega's own discomfort, she would've found the woman's uneasiness funny. Creston, aka Firestorm, liked to pretend she was a badass. But really, she was just a Firebitch. Not when it came to soldiers with stares that practically stabbed into the soul, apparently.

Only Bryce seemed unaffected. The way he stood with his shoulders back and his chin held high made Ortega's skin tingle with warmth. Nothing intimidated him.

He introduced Ortega and the other officers. When the blue-eyed man stared at her, she locked up. She couldn't even nod her head. Introductions were given from the other side, but Ortega didn't catch a single name. When it came time to escort the two squads, someone had to nudge her to get her moving.

"Sir?" Korbin leaned in toward Bryce's ear. "Didn't the admiral order that we carry stun weapons only?"

Foreboding crept into Ortega's bones at the sight of the deadly Power-K sidearms the soldiers carried. Although those midsized weapons had multiple energy and projectile settings, none were stun. They were versatile and lethal—and generally only reserved for the most intense combat situations.

"I noticed that and will bring it up with the admiral," Bryce said. "They'll be protecting the database, so a stronger deterrent would be useful."

"Will I get one, then?" Korbin asked.

"If they carry them, you should too, but I don't know. These guys are in a class all their own."

Korbin shook his head. Ortega shared his disbelief and planned to ask Bryce about it later. It made some sense to give an elite force some special leeway, but Power-Ks?

The soldiers kept their eyes forward as they traversed the ship. She was careful to do the same. Her misgiving abated until Korbin attempted to engage a soldier in conversation and got zero reaction.

No one spoke another word until they reached their destination. "L-let us kn-know if you n-need anything," Creston said.

Ortega forced herself to smile but dared not open her mouth and end up stuttering like a fool, too.

As soon as she was allowed to leave, she rushed away as though fleeing from a rumbling cave. What the hell was it about those men that scared her so much? She stopped short. They were all men, weren't they? Not a single woman among them. Why was that? Maybe there wasn't one willing to be around them long enough to integrate with their team.

She shivered. When she finally caught her breath, she berated herself for being such a coward. *What the hell is wrong with me? They're just soldiers!*

With a curse, she vowed not to let them intimidate her the next time she saw them.

16
MEGA Discussion

Two dozen enemy battalions blockaded the planet Gramosh. With no cargo ships being allowed to leave or enter, the inhabitants couldn't get the support needed to defend their cities from the invading Edenshire. Jori followed the paths of all his options. He must come up with an idea to save the Gramoshians or they were doomed.

A tingling spread from his core all the way to his restless limbs. This game took all his attention, helping him forget about his distressing situation. He leaned toward the playing board, speculating on his opponent's responses.

Galactic Dominions was far more complex than schemster. At setup, each player received different resources. The opponents knew some while others remained hidden. Plus, they gained assets along the way, providing millions of options—too many to memorize.

Hapker clapped him on the shoulder. "I'm getting lunch. Will you be alright here for a little while?"

"I don't know," Jori replied while narrowing his eyes at his opponent's flat smile. "I can't tell anything when he wears that inhibitor."

Gottfried Krause's smile spread, and he removed the device. "All I intend to do is win."

Jori attempted to draw in his essence but came up with nothing. "You're still hiding something."

Gottfried cocked his head. "I'm not, but what makes you think so?"

"You're blocking me."

"Ah." The man's smile returned. "Not intentionally. It's a habit, I'm afraid. I've had my mental wall up for so long that it takes effort to bring it down."

A trickle of truth came through, but Jori remained suspicious. Despite his misgiving, he dipped his head to Hapker—J.D. He should remember to think of him as J.D. in honor of their friendship. "I'll be alright."

J.D. glanced sideways at the admiral's aide. "You sure? I can have something brought in."

Jori wanted him to stay, but the boredom seeping from his friend contributed to his own despondent mood. Besides, Gottfried's chubby physique didn't present much of a threat. "I'm sure."

"Alright. Call me if you need me." Hapker indicated the communications panel inside the door. Generally, the comm was only for contacting security in an emergency, but Bilsby had convinced the admiral to add extra channels.

After Hapker left, Jori entered the instructions on the game console, which included a diversion tactic. The plasma laser projection went into motion. Gottfried took his turn. He destroyed Jori's lead vessel and sat back with a grin that might have been smug, except it was too flat to hint at his emotions.

Several moves later and Gottfried's blockade held. Jori was down to ten vessels. Time for desperate measures. His heartrate pattered as he programmed his next action.

Two remained hidden in the orbital debris while the rest of his ships attempted to break through the siege. Gottfried gave chase but one escaped. Just one was all Jori needed to turn the tides of battle.

The admiral's aide sat back and reviewed the stats on his game display. His eyes roved the screen, then glazed over. Not a single muscle twitched. It was like he'd become stone.

A minute passed. Jori fidgeted in his seat. "Gottfried?" The man didn't respond, not in voice or movement. "Gottfried?" Nothing. Jori stood and shook his shoulder. "Gottfried!"

Still no reaction. Panic swelled in his chest. Was the man having a seizure? A worker back home had occasional seizures where he'd stare off into space for a few moments, but this lasted too long.

He glanced around for help. Hapker—he still couldn't think of him as J.D.—and Gresher had gone out. The guards weren't paying any attention. If he yelled, they wouldn't hear him since Gottfried had activated the privacy setting. Jori considered alerting the officers by waving, but they might think this was his doing. He had a comm panel in his room programmed for emergency use only, but the same problem of him being accused kept him from using it.

He jostled the heavy man even harder. “Gottfried!”

The man blinked as though surprised to see Jori standing there. “I’m sorry, I was thinking,” he said with a smile. “I hope I didn’t frighten you.”

Jori eased into his seat. His worry turned to confusion as Gottfried took his turn like nothing had happened.

Weird. No one with this medical problem was allowed to hold such a prominent position back home, but perhaps the Cooperative made exceptions. Jori narrowed his eyes, wishing he could make out the man’s emotions.

“Why do you need to keep your mental wall up?” he asked. “People who can read your thoughts are rare.”

“That is quite true. Very astute.” Gottfried leaned in and whispered, “I’m actually imperium-animi.”

Jori’s jaw dropped. Several questions ran through his head. His mother, who was also an imperium, had trained him so he should be able to defend himself against this man. But if Gottfried intended to use this skill on him, why tell him about it?

Gottfried’s mouth widened into something more genuine. “Oh yes. It’s true.”

Jori glanced about, wondering whether anyone could hear.

“Don’t worry, it’s illegal to put listening devices in cells,” Gottfried replied as though he’d read Jori’s thoughts. “And you know I initiated the privacy settings before I came in. We should keep our voices down anyway.”

Despite his uncertainty, Jori dipped his head.

Gottfried continued in a hushed tone. “My almost permanent mental wall is in case there’s another with my skills around. I can’t afford to be discovered.”

Jori frowned. From what Hapker had told him, the Cooperative didn’t regulate those with sentio-animi abilities like his. Anyone with acute observation could read emotions. Sensing them involved a little more than that, but not in the same way as extrahos and imperiums who invaded minds.

“You reported you’re an extraho-animi, right?”

“Correct.”

"So why not just register this ability as well? Why keep this secret?"

Gottfried folded his hands and leaned back. "People don't like extrahos reading their minds, but they have more to fear from imperiums. I wouldn't have this job if they believed I could put thoughts into people's heads."

The hairs on Jori's head prickled. "Like the admiral's?"

"No, no." Gottfried flicked his hand. "You misunderstand me. My talent isn't powerful enough to work on the strong-minded. I haven't reported it because if I did, the Cooperative would put *even more* restrictions on me. I'd be judged more harshly. You know what that's like—people being afraid of you just because you can do something they can't."

Jori nodded, remembering all the times Cooperative officers had misjudged him. Even Hapker once.

"Please don't tell anyone." The aide emitted a hint of fear. "Not even the commander."

Jori's gut fluttered. Of course he wouldn't tell the Cooperative, but Hapker was his friend. When he didn't answer, the man issued nervousness.

"Please," Gottfried said. "I know you trust him, but I can't take the risk."

Jori crossed his arms and studied the man. This could be a ploy to either test him or get him to reveal his own secrets. Even if the act was innocent, he remained reluctant. "*Don't make promises you can't keep, boy,*" Sensei Jeruko had once warned him.

He placed his palm over the necklace hanging beneath his shirt. "Do you swear not to use your ability on me?"

"Of course."

The training from his mother meant he'd sense it if he tried, but what about Hapker? Gottfried had said he couldn't use it on someone with a strong mind, but he must make sure. "Or Hapker?"

Gottfried raised his hand. "I swear."

Jori sensed what he hoped was a genuineness in his reply. "So long as you keep your promise, then you have my word that I won't tell anyone."

A smile spread across Gottfried's face. "I appreciate that." He returned his attention to the game and made a move that thwarted the plan Jori had laid. "Another reason I hide my abilities is because it tends to provoke jealousy and hatred in others. People can be cruel to those who are different. That's something you've experienced, is it not?"

Jori's head swelled with understanding. For a moment, he saw the man in a new light—like a friend who understood him almost as well as Hapker.

"It seems like no matter what you do, people are against you," Gottfried said.

A bitterness filled Jori's mouth. "Everyone hates me because of my heritage."

"They have strong feelings about your abilities, too, I imagine."

"Yes. The admiral berated me for using the holo-machine."

"Yes, he told me about it. He also made some serious accusations about you being a MEGA."

Jori huffed. "It's just one of many he's made against me."

"Yes, and it's very unfair." Gottfried leaned in. "Between you and me, is there a possibility that you might be a MEGA?"

Jori scowled. *So that's his angle. Build trust, then ask personal questions.*

Gottfried waved his hand. "Don't worry. I won't share your answer with anyone. I want you to succeed. You can sense the truth of my words, yes?"

"Why are you asking me this?" Jori asked, still heated.

"I'm curious, is all."

"Well, I'm not a MEGA. I was bred. The only reason my father procreated with my mother was because her genes had a good chance of complementing his."

Gottfried's head bobbed. "That's what I thought, and you seem confident that your father didn't cheat."

"He can't cheat. It would be too risky."

"Oh?"

Jori clenched his fists.

Gottfried waved his palm back and forth. "I'm not trying to pry information from you. I genuinely wish to understand."

The man spoke honestly, and it cost nothing for Jori to tell the truth, so he filled his lungs and answered. "The Toradon lords insist on testing. Every time we visit a territory, they look at our DNA, compare it to our parents, then make sure we don't have cybernetic implants."

"But your father is emperor. Why does he need to subject himself to this?"

It sounded like something his father would say. "He gets to test them as well. Plus, my father is strong…" He bit back the bitterness that came whenever he thought about him. "But not strong enough if they all band together. There are certain laws in place that he can't do away with without alienating his supporters."

"Ah. I see." Gottfried's forehead folded up, then down. "Let's say you *were* genetically enhanced. How would you feel if the Cooperative kept restrictions on you? If they wouldn't let you take certain jobs or do the things you are so obviously good at just because of something your father did?"

"What do they do to people who are enhanced, besides that?"

"Since they are barred from political offices or positions of power, the rest of society shuns them. Most employers won't hire them, even if their ability has nothing to do with their job descriptions. Some go into business for themselves. That's not regulated. But most end up homeless because they can't find jobs. And many of those take up lawlessness to survive."

Jori screwed up his face. "Why don't they just find another place to live?"

"There aren't many places they can go. And it would cost them money. If they can't work, how do they make money?"

"That doesn't seem fair."

Gottfried smiled the most genuine smile Jori had ever seen from him. His emotions matched the sensation. Jori narrowed his eyes, wondering why the man was so happy at his response.

"No, it's not," Gottfried said. "At least *I* don't think it is. Do you realize that even if the Cooperative releases you, you will always be watched and possibly held back simply because of your chance birth?"

Jori stewed. How stupid of him to keep hoping that just because Hapker cared about him that the Cooperative would too. His shoulders slumped. "There's nothing I can do about it."

Except contact Sensei Jeruko. Next time he went to the gym, he'd have to find a way. He only had one shot at it. If they caught him, they'd tighten security.

"That's too bad." Gottfried's external sensations seemed crestfallen, but his internal ones felt oddly satisfied. Yet, Jori still wasn't sure. It was as though a pillow covered the man's emotions.

Although most of Jori's suspicions had fallen away, a niggling piece resided in the back of his mind. The man was up to something. He just didn't know what.

17
Testing

J.D. Hapker sat across from Jori and eyed the schemster game illuminated on the table between them. Most of his key pieces remained while Jori's had dwindled down to only a few. The boy propped his chin in his hand and slumped over the board. As he picked up his colonel and moved it, a disinterested haze clouded over his eyes.

Hapker suppressed a sigh as he slid one of his soldiers over and took Jori's colonel. The boy wasn't putting much effort into this game—or anything else, for that matter. He still wore his night clothes, his bed wasn't made, and his meal sat untouched on another table.

Hapker reached out to give him some encouragement, then changed his mind. *He just needs a little time. He'll be alright.*

The cellblock door swished open. The guards' uniforms rustled as they jumped to attention.

"At ease."

Hapker took in the man that used to be a good friend. Sergeant First Class Andres Carter looked much the same as before except he now wore an anchor-shaped beard and a thin mustache.

Carter entered the cell and snapped a salute. "Commander Hapker."

"At ease," Hapker repeated with a smile.

Carter's mouth curled up as well but lacked the geniality Hapker had hoped for. At least he didn't seem disagreeable.

"It's good to see you again, Sergeant."

"You too, Commander. I'm not here for pleasantries, though. I've been ordered to escort the Tredon child to sick bay."

"What for?"

"The admiral wants him to undergo MEGA testing."

Again? Hapker bit the inside of his cheek. *Will this persecution ever end?*

Carter directed his attention to Jori, who stood with matching formality. "I'm told that I can trust you to come peacefully."

"Yes, Sir," Jori replied.

Carter dipped his head, then swept out his arm for the boy to go ahead. Jori marched out. Sergeant Ortega and Corporal Lengen took the lead. Sergeant Banks grabbed Jori by the elbow and jerked him into place behind them.

"Hey!" Hapker pushed between them and glowered. "No need for that, Sergeant."

"Just making sure he doesn't go anywhere, Sir."

"You can do it without being rough."

"Yes, Sir. Whatever you say, Sir."

Hapker bristled. He was about to call the man out for his flippancy when a look from Carter stopped him short.

"So it's true," Carter said.

"What's true?" Hapker asked.

"You're more than just his advocate."

"Yes, I'm also his friend." Hapker put his hand on Jori's shoulder. This time, the boy inched closer rather than pulled away.

Carter kept a straight face, but Banks' eyes bored into Hapker, and his tight lips curled at Jori.

"Traitor," Banks mumbled as they exited the cellblock where four more officers waited.

A spout of fire burst in Hapker's chest. "Keep your attitude in check, Sergeant. Regardless of how you feel about me or the boy, you are expected to behave professionally. If that's too difficult for you, perhaps you should be reassigned to something you can handle."

Banks halted with a scowl that could've cowed a lion. Hapker squared up nose-to nose with the man.

"Sergeant!" Carter snapped. "Stand down. You will respect your superiors, even if they're off duty."

Banks put on a mocking smile but stepped back. "Yes, Sir."

Hapker clenched his teeth hard enough to cause pain in his neck. "And keep your hate to yourself. If you so much as lay a finger on this boy, I will make sure you have a cell right next to him. Do I make myself clear?"

Sergeant Banks' hostility didn't leave his face. "Yes, Sir."

The trek through the ship crackled with silence. Hapker's fury threatened to bubble over until he noticed Jori looking at him. Though the boy carried himself with the precision of a soldier, his expression had softened and there was a glow in his eyes.

Hapker gave him a small smile, which Jori returned.

The cluster of soldiers tightened as they passed a bot working on an info console in the corridor. With a hum, the machine plugged its proboscis-like appendage into a port. Its eyeless, domed head and many arms did other work. What was a basic service bot doing here?

The bot did something to the components inside. Hapker frowned. Bots did this sort of thing all the time, but he'd never seen one move so fast. They generally operated more carefully. *Maybe it has an upgrade.*

Not knowing much about robots, he put it out of his mind and moved on.

After riding and exiting the conveyor, a doctor with messy dark hair and cobalt eyes met them in the lobby. "This way, please," he said without enthusiasm.

The officers spread out, guarding all the exits. Carter stayed close to Banks, who crowded Jori like a lion with its kill.

The doctor swept his hand over a scanning bed. "Put him up here."

When Banks moved to grab Jori, Hapker shouldered him back. "He can get up on his own."

Banks smirked but said nothing. Hapker cocked his eyebrow. *What the hell is wrong with him?* The man was a sergeant. He should know better.

Jori got on. His expression remained blank as he lay down, but Hapker noted a dangerous glint in his eyes. The doctor pressed a button and a giant scanner above glided along the track.

"What does this do?" Hapker asked as a mechanical arm moved in over Jori's head.

"This will verify he has cybernetic enhancements," the doctor said.

Hapker grimaced. Everyone wanted to find a reason to depress this boy. His faith in the Cooperative had cracked after the incident that caused him to leave the PG-Force. Captain Arden had repaired it. Now the actions of the council and the people here threatened to shatter and destroy it. What happened to the Cooperative's ideals of bringing everyone together in peace?

"He'll be alright," Carter said. "The machine won't hurt him."

That's not what I'm worried about, he considered saying. "I know."

An awkward silence settled as Hapker struggled for the right words to make amends with his friend. Everything that came to mind sounded lame, but he should say something.

He drew in a great breath. "So, how have you been?"

Carter shrugged. "Been doing alright. Can't complain."

"I see you've been promoted. Sergeant First Class carries some weight."

"It's not lieutenant, though."

Hapker's gut took a plunge. "No. I'm sorry about that. Our friendship probably didn't help your career after I got in trouble."

Carter made a noise as he exhaled through his nose. "It is what it is. I'm not upset about it anymore. You did what you thought was right."

Hapker would have felt relieved if Carter hadn't been looking at some distant nothing instead of meeting his eyes. *Darn it*. Chesa hadn't exaggerated Carter's unhappiness with him.

"Well, I'm sorry regardless. You were always a good friend."

Carter wore a tight-lipped smile that indicated they'd never be that close again. Hapker suppressed the urge to swallow. He almost said he wished he could go back and do things differently, but that would be a lie. Sometimes, doing the right thing wasn't easy.

"Hey!" Banks lunged forward, snapping Hapker from his thoughts. "Get back here!"

The room erupted with activity. Hapker followed the guards as they all merged into a pursuit.

Darn it, Jori. What are you doing?

Carter touched the comm behind his ear. "The dragon is loose. Deck eight, hall seventeen-a. All hands be on the lookout."

His dark eyes flashed as he gave Hapker an accusatory look. He was right to. Hapker had distracted him and now Jori had slipped away. Dread lumped in his middle. This wouldn't end well.

They jetted down the hall. Elbows jostled at first, but then they spread out. Everyone held a tight expression as they ran through the corridors. Hapker's heart raced, and he imagined theirs did too. He hoped their surging adrenaline didn't cause them to act out against Jori when they caught him. If only he actually had a chance to get away.

They turned a corner and stopped short.

"It's alright!" someone shouted. "He's with me."

Hapker pushed through, expecting Jori had been tackled. Instead, he found Lieutenant Buckeye with his hands on his shoulders. His grip was tight but didn't look painfully so. Jori's jaw twitched but he seemed more annoyed than angry.

Banks stormed forward, his face a bright red and his eyes full of murder. "I'll take him, Sir."

"That's alright, Sergeant. I've got him," Buckeye said casually. "You lead the way to his cell, and we'll follow."

Banks' mouth opened as if to argue, but he obeyed.

Hapker dipped his head to Buckeye, who smiled in return. His friendliness caught him off guard, but he appreciated it.

After verifying the examination complete, they returned to the cell. Hapker sat beside him and whispered, "What were you thinking? You're on a ship in the middle of nowhere."

Jori glowered. "I wasn't trying to leave the ship."

"What were you doing?"

"I had a plan to reach the communication room that's supposed to be on this level. I almost made it too."

Hapker slumped forward and dropped his head in his palm. "Ah. You want to contact Sensei Jeruko."

Jori's eyes turned sad, then angry. "I thought maybe he could come get me off this damned ship away from these horrible people."

Crap. That was a good reason. It explained his desperate and ill-conceived actions. But no one else here would understand. He ran his hand down his face and sighed. What a mess this all was.

18
Accidental Death

Carletta Ortega stepped away from the sonic shower, feeling fresh despite it being ultrasonic vibrations rather than water. Although she'd give anything to take a bath in a mountainside spring, this method had a way of revitalizing her. The fifteen-watt light was bright to her eyes, but it also helped wake her up in the morning. Much brighter than that and it'd give her a headache.

She stepped to the mirror. Grabbing the biodegradable gel, she squeezed a pinky-nail sized drop onto her palm and ran it through her hair. A pinch and a twist here and there, and she had prickly, red-tipped spikes.

She tilted her head, studying herself from different angles. *How about a bright blue?* Last time she'd done that, Singh had said it made her sizzle like an electric fire. Bryce had complimented the red color, though. He'd told her she looked deliciously fierce.

A smile spread across her face. As much as she loved his praises, she needed a change. Besides, Bryce was never short on flattery.

"Blue it is," she said to herself. *But a frosty blue.*

Once done and dressed, she fed Matro and perused her messages. An updated alert flashed red at the top, making her groan. Despite the Tredon child's stunt yesterday, he would still get two hours in the gym each day. Rumor was, Lieutenant Krause had somehow convinced the admiral to allow the boy's little stunt to go unpunished. *Weird.*

According to the schedule, she'd be on duty during that time. Worse, she'd share her shift with Sergeant Banks again. She huffed and dropped her head onto the back of the couch. The prospect of having to confront the sergeant on the boy's behalf made her insides clench. She should ask Bryce to switch her.

No, she wouldn't use their relationship to get special favors. It would just give Banks an excuse to criticize her more. Ass kissing was for wimps, he'd say. Then again, so was not speaking up against dickwads like him—even when a Tredon was involved.

A beep sounded from her MM. She turned off the alarm, donned her sunglasses, and headed out the door. Minutes later, she entered the cafeteria. The nutty odor of brewed coffee filled her nostrils. A sweet scent mixed with something warm and buttery followed, making her mouth water. *Cinnamon rolls?*

Sure enough, on the counter were plates of white frosted gooey confections. God, she loved fresh food day.

She grabbed the biggest roll, then beelined for the coffee machine. After filling her cup and adding just a touch of cream and sugar, she made her way to where Singh and Harley waited.

With a grin, she plopped onto the padded chair in the corner. Harley had the one against the wall to her right while Singh had her back to the room. She wasn't military, so that kind of vulnerable exposure didn't bother her.

"Good morning," Corporal Harley said with his usual youthful, charming smile. Ortega returned it.

"Hey, girl." Singh winked. "You look awfully happy."

Ortega lifted her cinnamon roll. "If not for this beautiful, sweet, mouthwatering thing, I wouldn't have anything to be happy about."

"Yeah? Why not? Please don't tell me it's man trouble."

"No, not at all." Ortega waved the idea away. "It's about the Tredon boy."

Sergeant Banks leaned over from the table nearby. "You mean that fucking dragon spawn?"

Ortega glowered. "No need to be an asshole about it, Sergeant."

Banks huffed. "Someone's got to speak out. What I don't get is why I'm the only one."

"No one else is stupid enough to go against the code of conduct, and in front of a commander, no less," Ortega said.

"The commander's a wuss."

Ortega wasn't sure about that, but the way he took their enemy's side gave her plenty of other things to say. She didn't reply, though. Feeding Banks' attitude was a bad idea. Or maybe she was just being a chicken again. Why the hell did this man intimidate her so much?

"And so is your pet corporal here," Banks added.

Harley looked away.

"Fuck off, Banks," Ortega snapped.

"Don't be an ass," Singh said at the same time.

Banks rolled his eyes. "No real soldier would defend that little shit."

"Nobody's running off to join the Tredons," Singh replied.

"He's just a kid," Harley mumbled.

Banks laughed humorlessly. "Speak up, coward."

Harley's throat bobbed, but he remained quiet.

Singh turned all the way in her chair and scowled. "Go fuck yourself, you giant turd."

Ortega beamed at her friend. Singh wasn't a soldier, but she had a strong personality. Harley could use some of her spunk. So could she.

She gave the corporal a nudge. "Don't be afraid to share your opinion," she said in a tone too low for Banks to hear. Then louder, "Unlike the big dickhead over there, your friends won't hold it against you."

"Thanks," Harley replied, saying nothing more.

Ortega wanted to smack a little fire into him. Not really, but she wished he'd find some confidence. It might help her with her own against that asshole.

Banks towered over their table. Ortega tensed, ready to face off with the bastard if he made the wrong move.

The man smirked and turned away. Ortega growled. "I hate that fucking jerk."

"Agreed," Singh said. "You know, him being such a dick about this child might tell us something."

"What? Certainly not that we should be like him. I don't want the emperor's son here, but I won't be belligerent about it."

"No." Singh leaned in. "That he's wrong. Not just in his behavior but about our young guest as well." She pointed at the corporal. "Harley here is a good person. Maybe he has the right of it."

Ortega frowned. "I don't know. I've seen him in the gym. He's a fierce fighter."

"So are you. And so is Buckeye."

"So is Banks," Ortega said.

"Well, there you have it, Letta. Just because someone can fight doesn't mean they're *good or bad.* It depends on the person." Singh thumbed the area Banks had vacated. "You get any hints this child is like our jackass buddy?"

Ortega looked up in thought. "No, not that I've seen. He's determined, intense even, but he doesn't seem like an arrogant bully. He kinda keeps to himself."

"Definitely not like Banks," Harley said.

Silence lingered as they returned to their breakfast. Ortega took the opportunity to savor her roll's sweetness, something she'd never experienced in her underground home where luxury crops such as sugarcane didn't exist. She followed it with coffee, almost regretting washing away the flavor, but loving how the flavors melded.

Singh wiped the corner of her mouth with a napkin. "Did you hear about Vavich?"

"Who's Vavich?" Ortega asked.

"He's that tall skinny guy with the long mustache that I work with."

"Oh, yeah. What about him?"

"He's dead."

Ortega spurted her coffee all over the table. "What?"

Harley gasped. "How?"

Singh shrugged. "We're not sure. A console gave him a big jolt of electricity while he was working on it, which makes no sense since he's practically a genius with those things."

"That's crazy," Ortega said. "We haven't had a mishap like that on this ship for… Like forever."

"I've been here five years," Singh replied, "and the only person we've lost to an accident was because of their own stupidity."

"Do you have any guesses?"

"None. I have an investigation team on it, though. Hopefully, I'll find out something soon."

Ortega shook her head. "Shit."

Haven't they lost enough people in the battle at Thendi? Was the boy responsible for this too? He did run off yesterday, but surely didn't have the time to sabotage a console without anyone noticing. *No, it must've just been an accident.*

*****

J.D. Hapker leaned back in his chair and grinned. Chesa stood, returning the smile with a glint in her eyes.

"I'll see you again later," he said.

She twiddled her fingers in a cute goodbye gesture and winked. "Damn right you will."

Hapker rested his elbows on the cafeteria table as a warm lightness fell over him. While Lieutenant Gresher had stayed over with Jori, he met Chesa in the lounge. It had gone much better this time, and they ended up at her quarters. Being with her again brought back so many exciting memories.

He stirred his coffee. It was cold now, and his cinnamon roll remained untouched. They'd been so engaged in a conversation that he'd forgotten all about his breakfast.

He bit into the roll and glanced at the viewscreen on the far wall. It played clips from some tournament that had happened in the city of New Bristol on Aeneas over a week ago.

He shook his head. People there sure took their sports seriously. This game called football had been revived from Earth history and garnered a devout fanbase. Who would have thought kicking around a black and white ball would inspire such diehard loyalty? If they enjoyed it so much, why not play it themselves?

Although he liked active activities, he'd never gotten into team sports. Give him a rough trail in the mountains, and he'd spend days hiking and climbing. Better yet, skiing.

He rubbed his jaw, daydreaming about the trip he and Chesa had once taken during a shore leave. The white-capped peaks, the crisp air, the bright snow. They'd skied from sunup to sundown on that first day. Later they'd enjoyed conversations and cocoa spiked with a sweet, fermented milk.

There was nothing like spending a nature excursion with another nature lover. It would be nice if he could take Jori to it someday. If things went well with Chesa, she'd be there too. The three of them would have grand adventures together.

Someone spitting brought him out of his musings.

"What?" a woman said with incredulity in her voice.

Hapker bit into his roll, not wanting to eavesdrop. He focused on the internal sound of his chewing, then slurped his coffee. A few words still caught his attention.

A console shocked somebody? An accident? Hapker turned his ear, capturing snippets of their conversation. *They died?*

Curiosity got the better of him. He swiveled in his chair, taking in the three people in the corner. He recognized Sergeant Ortega with her spiked hair and sunglasses. Corporal Harley was there too. The tanned woman with black hair in a tight bun didn't look familiar, though.

He left his table and approached them, giving Harley a friendly smile.

Harley's mouth stretched in return. "Hey, Commander."

"How are you doing, Corporal?"

Harley shrugged. "Okay, I guess."

Hapker cleared his throat. "I'm sorry I haven't spoken to you sooner, Corporal. I considered it, but also wanted to give you some space."

"I understand, Commander," Harley replied with a sheepish smile. "It's been kinda weird since then."

Since being held prisoner by Jori's father. "It sure has." Hapker shifted his weight. "I must be honest, though. I only just realized you were here—in the cafeteria, I mean. And I overheard you talking." He regarded the two women.

The woman with a bun blinked. "Sorry, Commander. I didn't realize we shouldn't be discussing this."

Hapker waved his hand. "No, that's not it. I wasn't intentionally listening in, but you said something about an accident and someone dying?"

"Yeah," the woman said. "His name is Vavich. He's one of my engineers."

"What happened?"

"They didn't tell you, Sir?" Ortega asked with an inexplicable edge. "Well, I suppose they wouldn't, all things considered."

"No one told me," he replied with a tight smile and a hard gaze that he hoped would warn her about her tone.

The other woman shot Ortega a scowl and faced Hapker with an open expression. "A terminal in Recreation Hall C sent a surge of electricity through him as he worked on it."

"Recreation Hall C? I thought I saw a bot fixing it just yesterday. How did this happen?"

She shrugged. "I don't know yet."

"I've never heard of a console sending out enough electricity to kill someone," he said. "Have you?"

"It has several electrical components, so it could technically happen." She put up her hands. "But it'd have to be some crazy fluke."

"Well, thanks for filling me in. And again, I apologize for intruding." He gave them a disarming smile. The woman and Harley returned it, but Ortega gave him a stony expression and a sharp nod.

"Good seeing you, Corporal," he added.

He retreated to his table, finished his breakfast, then headed out. On the way, he passed a smile to the trio. Ortega raised two fingers in a gesture of farewell, but nothing more.

He entered the conveyor and directed it to security. The car glided into an almost indiscernible movement. It stopped shortly after it had started, and its door slid open. Hapker stepped out and met the admiral's aide.

"Lieutenant Krause," he greeted.

"Commander," Krause said. "What brings you here?"

"I heard about the accident in the Recreation Hall."

"Ah, yes. Very tragic."

"Indeed," Hapker said. "I saw something yesterday, which I thought I should report."

"Oh?" Krause's tone indicated curiosity, but as always, his expression seemed simulated.

Hapker shook off the weird feeling the odd aide generally gave him. "I saw a service bot working on it rather than a maintenance bot. I think it was the same console that killed a crew member."

Krause tilted his head as though in thought. It seemed practiced as well, but that was true for all the man's features. "I doubt it was a service bot. They don't have the right tools."

"Did the bot make a mistake?"

Krause let out a hollow laugh. “If it did, it was because of a human programming error. The technicians are looking into what happened.”

“I should report it to security anyway.”

“Of course.” Gottfried dipped his head. “I’ll leave you to it, Commander.” Krause stepped around him into the conveyor.

Hapker moved on. His mind wagged back and forth between suspicion and accepting that someone made an error. Why the suspicion, though? Mistakes happened. It was just such a shame that a man died because of it. But that totaled two deaths since this journey began. What if people used them as opportunities to blame Jori?

19
Nails

Gottfried Krause didn't need to use his sentio ability to know how the admiral and major felt. As they read the report on the doctor's findings, Admiral Belmont's bottom lip jutted out more than usual and Major Esekielu's beady eyes narrowed to mere slits.

Gottfried mimicked concern. A part of him had hoped the tests would confirm Jori was like him. It would make it so much easier to convince the boy to side with his cause.

The inconclusive results had a benefit, though. Jori's natural skills made the Cooperative's restrictions on augmentations pointless. Humanity still evolved. If the rest of society didn't keep up, they'd get left behind.

Admiral Belmont glowered. "There has got to be something we're missing."

Major Esekielu's mouth contorted to match his sour disposition. "It's impossible for this boy to be so advanced and not be a MEGA."

"The doctor's results are sound." Gottfried put up his hand to forestall the admiral's temper. "He's requesting retesting. He has a personal lab where he's researching new ways to detect and neutralize implants." This last part made him want to spit. He despised Doctor Fritz and his obnoxious anti-MEGA attitudes. "I'm sure he wants to find something as badly as we do."

"The results will probably be the same, but I don't trust our ability to catch everything," the admiral said. "We try to keep up with the changing technology, but it's a game of cat and mouse."

Gottfried cocked his head. "Sir? What do mammals have to do with it?"

"It's an expression. It means every time we upgrade our detection methods, others find ways to circumvent them."

"That's an odd way to put it."

Belmont waved his hand. "I'm not sure of its origin. You can look it up later."

Gottfried filed it away.

"For now," the admiral continued, "get that psych evaluation scheduled. If they're booked out for more than a couple of days, have the boy take a psychological questionnaire. This will give us something to start with until a doctor is free. I also want you to contact the MEGA Inspections Office at the Kishimer outpost. Tell them we need a MEGA hunter here."

Gottfried cringed inwardly at the nickname. He agreed with the term but hated the people. While some members of humanity wanted to become something better, these hunters condemned them and held them back.

Stupid MEGA Injunction. No one should be persecuted for their life choices.

Gottfried kept his ill feelings from showing. "Certainly, Admiral," he said with a smile. "If I may inquire, however, why not leave the testing to authorities on Asteria?"

"If he's a MEGA, it will be one more nail in his coffin."

Gottfried frowned. "Another strange idiom. Why would anyone put nails in a coffin?"

Major Esekielu rolled his eyes as Belmont answered. "It's an old Earth practice, back when coffins were made of wood."

"Ah. Nails for closing the coffin, meaning you're hoping to find something in this boy that will tilt the council's favor against him—a death sentence, so to speak."

He mentally shook his head. *People and their dumb idioms.* It seemed he'd been too quick to delete that information from his memory chip. Making room for more important things had been necessary, but he couldn't afford to have his superiors think there was something wrong with him either. He made a mental note to re-upload it.

"Exactly," the admiral replied. "I've said it before, and I'll say it again. That boy doesn't belong here."

"No, he doesn't," Gottfried said truthfully. Even if Jori hadn't been augmented, he belonged with those who matched his intellect. Gottfried's kind would benefit from the boy in return. They'd use his pedigree to spread their ideology to the Tredons and his DNA to enhance more soldiers—ones better than

Lieutenant Buckeye and the elite soldiers. A mere blood sample wouldn't be enough. Too many things could go wrong. Samples could get lost or contaminated. They needed Jori in person.

Belmont massaged his temple. "Did you find out why that boy ran from the medical bay?"

"No, Sir." Gottfried suspected the answer but gave a different one instead. "Perhaps it's because he doesn't enjoy being locked up."

"What, getting free time isn't enough for him?" Belmont shot an accusatory glare. "No thanks to that confounded lawyer."

Gottfried smiled in mock patience. "If we don't allow it, it will make us look bad." *As you well know*. "Is there anything else you need from me before I contact the Kishimer outpost?"

"Yes. What's the status of the accident investigation?"

"The acting captain has been very cooperative. Everyone is keeping me posted, but nothing significant has been found yet. Don't worry, I have some people I trust working on it."

"Very good," Belmont said.

"Is that all, Sir?"

"Yes. Just keep me apprised."

Gottfried dipped his head, then left. He should put a hold on the accidents lest the admiral make another rash decision. The one set up for the first lieutenant might be too late to stop, but it shouldn't raise any suspicions.

Contacting Kishimer was easy enough. He needed to tweak his plan to accommodate the stopover, though. Fortunately, having a MEGA hunter here wouldn't interfere with it too much. It might even improve things—figuratively put a nail in the admiral's own coffin.

He added another item to his task list. Per MEGA-Man's instructions, he must let the boy contact Sensei Jeruko. With any luck, the *Dragon* warship would also be near a communication hub and allow for a quick reply. The sooner Jori found out Sensei Jeruko and his brother were dead, the sooner he'd realize there was no place for him in his galaxy—other than with MEGA-Man, of course.

The thought made Gottfried's insides tingle with excitement.

20
Friends and Foes

Jori swung the racket, hitting the rubber ball with enthusiasm. It flew to the wall and bounced back, its dark blue color standing out against the white room with its faux wood floor. Hapker struck the projectile with the same spiritedness. Back and forth they went, with their scores often tied. Their intensity increased with the match point close at hand.

Jori dived, barely hitting the ball in time. Hapker returned it, sending it too wide to be reached.

"Yes!" Hapker raised his arms in triumph, revealing circles of sweat under his armpits.

Jori smiled, remembering the times they'd played wall ball on the *Odyssey*. Their competitions had been fierce, but only from their determination. The challenge of trying to best one another brought more satisfaction than contention, even in the beginning when they hadn't been sure of each other yet.

He remained uncertain about his situation, but he was sure about Hapker. The way he'd defended him against Banks gave him hope. He still had to contact Sensei Jeruko, but at least Hapker had understood why and didn't criticize or lecture him about it.

Eight guards stood watch outside the enclosed court. Sergeant Ortega, with her hair now spiked blue, glowered at him through the wide plasti-glass door. No way would he be able to slip past her or the others again unless something distracted them.

His shoulders fell as he thought about home. He'd never played games like this with his brother, but they'd compete on the shooting range and in battle simulations all the time. Their rivalry had been as intense and as friendly, though his brother would sometimes brood after losing.

He touched the necklace hidden under his shirt. Its warmth kept him from falling into the coldness of despair. Perhaps he should ask Hapker to help him contact Sensei Jeruko.

He wagged his head to rid himself of the thought. Getting the man in trouble with that hateful council again didn't sit well. There must be another way.

Hapker doubled over and caught his breath. "That was quite a game. You almost had me there." He straightened and beamed. "Want a rematch?"

The man's cheerfulness helped Jori to put aside his worries. "Why are you in such a good mood?"

"This." Hapker spread out his arms, displaying the wall ball court. "Aren't you having fun?"

"Yeah, but it's more than that."

"You got me." Hapker's crooked smile curved even more. "I met an old friend here." He shrugged. "She's more than a friend. Things are going well."

"Is that why Gresher stayed with me last night?"

A hint of guilt dripped into Hapker's emotions. "Yep. Don't worry, though. I didn't forget about you."

"I know. You don't need to be with me the entire time," Jori said to ease the man's conscience. "I'm glad you're happy." *It seems there's always one thing or another to make one of us miserable.*

"Perhaps you can meet her sometime."

Jori gave him a sidelong glance. "I doubt she'd want to meet me."

A pained expression crossed Hapker's face. "I realize people are being judgmental, but things will change once they get to know you."

Jori looked away without answering. Countering Hapker's optimism was pointless.

Sergeant Ortega poked her head through the clear plasti-glass door. "Times up."

"Well, so much for a rematch. Tomorrow?" Hapker's eyes twinkled. "If you think you can handle it, that is."

Jori suppressed a smile. "Maybe I'll let you win again."

Hapker laughed and threw his arm over Jori's shoulder. Together, they left the court and entered the expanse of the gymnasium. The eight guards closed in. Jori sighed inwardly.

*****

J.D. Hapker didn't let the over-the-top security measures bother him. Things were looking up. Jori seemed to be in a better mood. He and Chesa were having a great time together. And even though Carter hadn't fully forgiven him, he was glad he'd had the opportunity to express his regret.

"It feels a little early, Sergeant," Hapker said to Sergeant Ortega. "You sure it's been two hours?"

"Sorry, Commander. There's been an incident."

"An incident? What kind—"

"There you are." A man with a strict demeanor cut in. Major Esekielu's perfectly pressed grey uniform enhanced his severity as he glowered at Jori with a predatory grimace. "If you hadn't been in here, I would have assumed *you* had something to do with all this."

Jori pulled back with a twist of his mouth.

Hapker put his arm over him. "What development? What happened?"

The major somehow stiffened his posture even more, looking like a cobra ready to strike. Disdain crawled across his face. "Apparently, Commander, the death of Captain Richforth has set off a chain of events. You were there, were you not?"

"You know I was," Hapker replied through gritted teeth. "And you know I had nothing to do with it."

Major Esekielu grunted. "Well, something is going on here. Until then, there will be no more free time for this…"

His lips curled obnoxiously. Jori returned the expression.

Hapker suppressed the urge to do the same. "Unless we are suspects, you have no right."

Esekielu bared his teeth. "People are dying, Commander."

"I get that, but you can't take away his rights just because you don't like him."

"Security overrides his rights."

"Is everyone else being confined?"

"No," the major replied as though Hapker was daft.

"Then unless you think Jori magically escaped his cell and bypassed his guards, you have no grounds."

"He did that once already."

"He didn't have enough time to do anything, and you know it."

Jori nudged Hapker's arm. "Can we ask my lawyer?"

Hapker continued to train his glower on Esekielu. "Darn right we can. We'll return for now, but you'll be hearing from his lawyer."

The major harrumphed. "A lawyer won't do much good once the MEGA hunters find out what you really are." He faced Jori with a viperous smile. "We'll be making a stop soon and put this nonsense to bed once and for all."

Hapker bristled. Jori went taut. Hapker held him firmly to make sure he didn't react.

Major Esekielu stormed off. Some of Hapker's anger tapered off, but not all of it. By the scowl on Jori's face, his day had been ruined as well.

Why does everyone have to be so nasty?

He gave Jori a distressing look, then turned to Sergeant Ortega. "Who died?"

"First Lieutenant Suarana."

Hapker had only spoken to her a few times, but regret replaced a little of his ill temper. "How'd she die?"

"She choked."

Hapker's heart skipped a beat. "Natural causes or someone choked her?"

"It appears she choked on some food."

"Appears?"

"By all accounts, it looks like an accident. But losing three high ranking officers right after…"

She didn't look down at Jori, but he got the sense that she was about to say after he came on board.

He let out a long exhale. *What the hell is going on?*

21
Major Problem

Carletta Ortega strode down the corridor, humming. The familiar melody tickled her memory but no matter how many times she sang it, she couldn't pinpoint where she'd heard it before.

Maybe Bryce would know. She'd be seeing him tonight. Possibly staying over in his quarters as well. Warmth filled her. What better way to spend this crap mission.

She made it to the engineering room without running into Singh, which meant her friend was working late again. Nothing new there. Ortega always rushed off after her boring guard shift was over, while Singh tended to get caught up in her tasks.

"Hey, Ortega," said an engineer seated at the primary operations workstation.

"Hey Chance. How's it going today?"

"It's going." He thumbed behind him. "You'll find the chief back there. I'd wait a minute, though. I think she's in trouble with Mister stick-up-his-ass."

Ortega groaned inwardly. Ever since Captain Richforth died, Major Esekielu had taken it upon himself to interfere with other people's jobs. Technically, Commander Ramgarhia should be running things. Rumor had it that the admiral put him on limited duty so he could process his grief. It made some sense, but she suspected Belmont preferred his own people.

He found Major Esekielu talking to her friend and hovered at a distance within her acute hearing range. Singh stood casually with her hands clasped while the major took a ridiculously stiff stance.

The three-deck tall cylindrical arc reactor rose above them like a billion-year-old stalagmite. It was even the same color. A narrow metal staircase wound around it, stopping at a platform every few meters. Each had a different setup. One was an observation station with gauges and readouts while others had computer access.

"Chief Singh," the major said. "I told you to have this conduit fixed by oh-two-hundred."

"Yes, Sir," she replied matter-of-factly.

Ortega held back a smile. The man undoubtedly expected her to apologize profusely under his scrutiny, like many others.

Esekielu's beady eyes blazed. "Well, why didn't you?"

"If you recall, Sir, I also told you it couldn't be done by then."

Esekielu glared up at her, standing a half-head short. "When I give an order, I expect it to be obeyed. And if I'm not, I'll find someone else to do it."

Singh's eyebrow lifted. "If you must, Sir, but I doubt anyone can meet unrealistic expectations."

Ortega's jaw dropped at how she'd told the man off without saying anything to get her in trouble.

Major Esekielu sputtered. "It's a simple conduit!"

"With surrounding applications that are also damaged. Replacing the conduit is easy enough but if the items around it aren't fixed, you'll still have an inoperable ventilator."

"If more needed repairs, you should have assigned more technicians to it."

Singh sighed heavily. "Only so many people will fit in that small space, Sir. And the admiral put a priority on the accident investigation. Most of my team, including myself, have been working on that."

"We have plenty of other workers—"

"With all due respect, Sir. I know what I'm doing and I'm damn good at my job. If I say it can't be done by then, I'm not lying or making excuses. I'm telling you the simple truth. I apologize if you don't like the answer."

Ortega's breath caught. Surely Singh would be in trouble now.

The major's face tightened. Singh maintained a firm but nonconfrontational posture as he seemed to waver between exploding and defusing. "How much longer?" he finally said.

"One-and-a-half hours, Sir. I guarantee it."

"Then get it done."

Singh firmed her jaw. "Yes, Sir."

Ortega withheld a smirk as the major passed, walking in the way that earned him his nickname. After he disappeared, she let her smile spread across her face and approached her friend. "Damn, I love it when you do that."

Singh smiled. If Esekielu had irked her, it didn't reflect in her cheerful tone. "Do what?"

"Put arrogant little pricks—emphasis on the *little prick* part—in their place without getting yourself in trouble."

They laughed, Singh's tinkling voice ringing throughout the room. Ortega took her arm and they headed to the cafeteria for lunch.

She appreciated the darker paint in this corridor. Why engineering was the only area that had coffee-colored walls was beyond her.

"So how was your shift with the Tredon child?" Singh asked.

"Your friend made an ass of himself there, too. You heard about Lieutenant Suarana?"

"Yeah," Singh replied in a drawn-out tone, undoubtedly wondering who she meant by *friend.*

"Well, Major Esekielu decided the boy shouldn't get his free time anymore because of it."

"Why? He had nothing to do with it."

"Because he wants to be an asshole. He claimed it was for security reasons, but the commander spoke out and threatened to involve the lawyer."

They dodged a trio of engineers too engaged in their heated discussion to look where they were going. Their maroon uniforms were the same color as Singh's, though hers had two indigo stripes down the front and a pair of indigo epaulettes.

"Good for him."

Ortega didn't have her friend's conviction but had enjoyed watching Commander Hapker stand up to that little prick.

"So what did the child say about it?" Singh asked.

"He didn't say much at all. Just let the commander handle it."

"That's interesting. You'd think he'd get angry and try to fight it."

Ortega gave her friend a side-eyed *I know what you're doing* look.

Singh raised her palms. "All I'm saying is you should be objective."

"Yeah, yeah, yeah. Base my opinions on his words and deeds and not on stereotypes."

A dome-headed bot passed them, zipping along a little faster than usual. Singh frowned as it retreated. She turned back to Ortega and elbowed her. "So…"

"So what?"

"So what have you observed objectively?"

Ortega sighed. "Well, Lieutenant Gresher is training him."

"Lieutenant Gresher? That good-looking man with a fantastic smile?"

"That's the one."

Singh opened the MM on her wrist. "Sorry. Let me check on what that bot is up to." When she was done, she shook her head, then gave Ortega her full attention. "What's he teaching him?"

"Changdu."

"Really? That sounds beneficial. And it went well?"

"Yeah, the boy was eager to learn. He listened to instructions and seemed determined to do it right. No sign of the arrogance or bullying behaviors I mentioned."

"None at all?"

"I didn't see any when he played wall ball with the commander, either. Same terrifying focus, though."

"Terrifying?" Singh's brows drew together. "Don't most good soldiers take their training seriously?"

"Yeah, but he's just a child. He should be laughing and playing—or at least smiling a little. Lieutenant Gresher seems to be a very upbeat guy, but none of it rubbed off on the boy. It's like he has no emotions, like some robot or something."

Singh shrugged. "Well, he doesn't have a reason to smile nowadays."

A sinking sensation weighed Ortega down. She'd thought the child might be a budding psychopath, and here Singh was giving a reasonable explanation. *Damn her.*

"Remember when you first came to this ship?" Singh continued. "You didn't smile much either."

Ortega's stomach rolled. Their situations weren't the same, but she caught Singh's point. People had seen her as an outsider and that's what Jori was, too. "You may be right."

Singh winked. "Just keep an open mind."

"Don't I always?" she replied, knowing very well that she sometimes didn't. But that's why she appreciated Singh.

22
News

The main cellblock entrance hissed open, but Jori hadn't detected anyone coming. He continued reading his MDS tablet, suspecting who it was and too engrossed to care.

This academic study on machine-learning algorithms proposed some interesting concepts. A few applications were still in the testing phase, but Jori's insides hummed with the possibilities. Even as his prison door opened, he ignored the intruder and focused on the article.

"Activate the privacy settings, Sergeant," Gottfried said to a guard. When the door slid shut, he spoke to the man sitting near Jori and reading his own MDS. "Greetings, Commander Hapker."

"Lieutenant Krause. I'm glad you're here. Did you get the dispute about Jori's free time straightened out?"

Jori tightened his jaw at their distracting conversation and reread the last two sentences.

"Most certainly." Gottfried replied. "Bilsby pointed out a few lines of law and the major had no choice but to concede."

"That's good."

Hapker's mood elevated along with Jori's. After completing that painfully boring questionnaire this morning instead of exercising in his room, he could use some activity.

"What are you reading, Jori?" Gottfried asked as he bent low.

Jori put up his hand and continued studying. Thankfully, silence followed. He soaked up the information until finally reaching the concluding paragraph.

He set down his MDS, masking his annoyance at not having the opportunity to ponder on what he'd read. A frown came unbidden when he noticed Gottfried not wearing an inhibitor. He should've been able to sense him.

Rather than ask about it, he stood and clasped his hands behind his back. "It's an academic journal on machine learning."

Gottfried acknowledged Jori's response with raised brows. "That's an interesting topic, and it has many applications. Do you plan on entering that field someday?"

Jori thought about it. "It's fascinating, but I'm not sure…" Would the Cooperative even let him have a future?

"Don't worry," the admiral's aide said. "Everything will work out."

Jori didn't reply to the meaningless encouragement.

Gottfried turned to Hapker. "Would you mind giving us a little privacy, Commander?"

The uncertainty emanating from Hapker mingled with Jori's own, but probably for a different reason. He still wasn't sure what to think about the last private conversation he'd had with the aide. And he didn't want to be put in another uncomfortable position where he had to keep secrets. "Hapker can stay."

If Gottfried was disappointed with his response, he didn't show it. His bland smile remained. "Certainly. I wasn't trying to exclude him. I just want to get to know you better."

Jori narrowed his eyes, wondering whether he'd spoken the truth.

"How did that questionnaire go?" Gottfried asked.

"It's done." That damned questionnaire had required serious introspection. Nobody had told him what it was about, but it didn't take long for him to realize they could use the answers against him. He'd considered blowing it off and putting half-assed responses, but the training Sensei Jeruko had instilled in him about being honest wouldn't let him.

"Good," Gottfried replied.

"Since you're here," Hapker said, "I have some questions."

"Of course. I'm happy to help."

"What came of that console incident that killed the engineer?"

Gottfried's ever-present smile flattened. "It seems the bot you saw *did* make an error. But it was done by the programmer. Specialist Nedell has been reprimanded."

"Ah," Hapker replied. "I know Nedell. He's a good officer. I can't imagine how he feels right now."

"It's a shame for both officers." Gottfried's eyes tilted almost sadly, but it was difficult to tell whether he actually cared.

"And what about the most recent death? An accident?"

"Most certainly. Lieutenant Suarana was alone in her quarters at the time."

A deep misgiving emanated from Hapker. Jori shared it, mostly because the aide continued to block his emotions.

Gottfried faced Jori with a smile that didn't touch his eyes. "Well, you have the good news. I'm sure you're looking forward to having more free time at the gym. But now for the bad news."

Jori didn't react. Getting bad news had become the norm.

"Your MEGA testing with the doctor came up negative, so Admiral Belmont has called for a MEGA hunter to test you further."

Jori twitched at the term Major Esekielu had also used the day before.

Hapker put his hand on Jori's shoulder. Exasperation infused his emotions. "MEGA Inspectors aren't supposed to test children."

Gottfried raised his palms and shrugged. "There's no law that says they can't. I had Bilsby check. I'm afraid I can't prevent it."

"What's a MEGA hunter?" Jori asked even though he had his suspicions.

"It's someone from the MEGA Inspections Office. They're tasked with tracking down people suspected of having enhancements and testing them with their own special equipment."

A trickle of distaste broke through the aide's emotions, making Jori want to spit. "I'm not a MEGA, so let them test me."

"Getting tested by a MEGA hunter carries a stigma," Gottfried said. "They will note it on your record where everyone can see it, and many will make their own assumptions about you regardless of the results."

"It's a political move, then." Hapker's naturally crooked mouth twisted further.

"I'm afraid so. Plus, I should warn you. Their tests are more invasive."

Jori swallowed. They wouldn't find anything, but what would they try next?

"May I?" Gottfried asked as he indicated the chair Jori had vacated.

Jori dipped his head.

The admiral's aide barely fit on the smaller seat. His features sagged. "Although I'm hoping the council rules in your favor, I'm worried that you will never escape who you are. They'll always see you as the son of their enemy and as a possible MEGA."

"So my life is over," Jori replied with a croak.

"Not necessarily."

Jori grunted. "I can't go home and if I stay here, I can't do anything worthwhile."

The aide made a pitying expression. "I believe there are places you can go where you will flourish, where people won't mistreat you just because you're better."

Hapker cocked his head. Jori narrowed his eyes. "Where?"

Gottfried waved his hand. "Oh, there are many societal niches. I can give you some ideas later if you like. Rest assured, I will help you no matter what. You're not alone."

Jori should be grateful, but he couldn't sense if the man was genuine.

Gottfried leaned in. "In fact, I can do something for your now," he whispered, moving closer. "The request you made to contact someone back home…"

"The one the admiral denied?" Hapker asked.

"That one." Gottfried licked his lips in what seemed an uncharacteristic gesture. "Maybe I can do it."

Jori's eyes widened. He held his breath as the warmth of his mother's necklace burned against his chest. "You would do that?"

Gottfried leaned back and smiled. "What good is it to have such a prominent position and not use it to help my friends?"

Jori tried to wet his mouth. He didn't consider Gottfried a friend, but anything was possible if the man let him talk to Sensei Jeruko. Then again, what if this was a trap? His mentor had often warned him about people giving things without asking for something in return.

"Why would you do that?" Skepticism radiated off Hapker like the exhaust of a ship at full thrust.

"Don't you agree it's the right thing to do?"

Jori tensed at Gottfried's accusatory tone.

"Of course I do," Hapker said. "But you're talking about violating orders, orders that the admiral and those higher up believe are in place for our safety."

Jori's jaw tightened. He finally had an opportunity to contact Sensei Jeruko and Hapker was trying to stop it? Whose side was he on?

"But you know our safety isn't at risk. Surely, you've already considered it."

"I have." A touch of guilt flicked through Hapker's emotions. "But it's complicated."

"I understand the position it would put you in, Commander," Gottfried said. "But not to worry. This is a risk *I* am willing to take."

Hapker's emotions went on the defense. Jori caught the aide's accusation. Part of him did the same, but the other part wanted to be indignant on Hapker's behalf. The prospect of speaking to his mentor made his heart pound, but what if Gottfried was setting him up?

Gottfried rose. "We'll talk more about it later."

Although Jori couldn't sense anything from him, the back of his neck prickled.

23
Robots

J.D. Hapker ran his hand through his hair. Why would Lieutenant Krause allow Jori to contact Sensei Jeruko when the council had forbidden it? Not that he wasn't grateful. He'd considered doing it himself. It didn't sit well that an admiral's aide would risk his career for someone he hardly knew.

The corridors bustled with normal activity. Disquietude droned under the surface, tightening the knot in his gut. There was more to worry about—such as losing three people in such a short time.

A few officers shot him a dark look as they walked by. Rumors that he had something to do with Richforth's death had probably grown to include the other two. This rekindled his own suspicions about the deadly console. Lieutenant Krause's explanation made no sense.

As he meandered through the hallways, he noted every robot he passed. It didn't surprise him that the *Defender* still needed work, but he couldn't help but wonder what the machines were really up to.

By the time he reached engineering, he'd seen eight robots.

Several workstations lined either side of the main workroom. All but three had an officer seated before it, working at various monitoring or maintenance tasks while the hum of the arc drive carried from the area further back.

"His interference is making my job harder," a technician said.

The dark-haired woman Hapker had met in the cafeteria rubbed her brow. "I know, and I understand. I really do. But he's the major and I can't do anything about it. Just do the best you can."

"Yes, ma'am," the officer replied with a shake of his head.

After he left, the woman noticed Hapker there and approached. "Welcome, Commander. It's good to see you again." Despite the fatigue that weighed down her expression, her smile seemed genuine. “I haven’t properly introduced myself. I’m Chief Singh.”

Hapker cleared his throat. “Sorry about that abrupt encounter. The death of Vavich threw me for a loop.”

“You and me both, Sir.”

“I apologize for interrupting, but I’m hoping you can give me an update on the investigation.”

“Are you helping?”

The uptick in her tone suggested she didn’t like the idea. Considering the conversation he’d overheard, he wasn’t surprised. He raised his palm and kept his smile. “I have no intention of interfering, I promise. I’m just curious. Plus, I have a question about the maintenance bots.”

Her shoulders sagged as though relieved. “Certainly. I could use a break. Would you step into my office?” She waved her hand to a room with an open door and allowed Hapker to take the lead.

He entered an office that looked more like a workshop. The long table against the wall held a disassembled combustion engine. A plasti-glass case covered it so that parts wouldn’t go flying during emergency maneuvers. A wide desk sat in the middle of the room. On the corner appeared to be another work in progress, also encased. This one was a model of a Santerian space fighter. Various three-dimensional puzzles from cultures all around the known galaxy were crowded on the shelf to the right. He noted the larger cubic one in the center. “You have a Cambiner puzzle.”

Her face lifted. “You’re familiar?”

He smiled. “My father had one. It took him eight months to solve.”

She gave a small laugh. “I completed it in a little less time but only because I was obsessed with it. My father had to keep reminding me to eat and sleep. I’m surprised I made it through my studies.”

Hapker warmed at the story. “Rumor is you solved that puzzle when you were twelve.”

“You heard about that? I’ve heard rumors about you as well.” Her hand sprang up. “Good things. About how you used to be a Pholatian Protector.”

“That’s right. But not for long. I wanted to see the galaxy, so I signed up with the Cooperative.”

"I have a lot of appreciation for the Protectors. It also explains your desire to help our young guest."

Hapker almost became defensive, but her smile put him at ease. "Most people don't like me for that."

She shrugged. "I prefer to give people the benefit of the doubt.

"Yeah? Me too."

"Besides, he can't be all that bad if he has you as a friend."

"Thanks." He blushed, hoping his awkwardness from the compliment didn't show. "So tell me more about the defective console."

She explained what she'd found. Everything sounded plausible but something in her voice indicated that she also harbored suspicions.

Hapker cupped his elbow with one hand and his chin with the other. "Do you find any of this odd?"

"Specialist Nedell was good at his job. I can't imagine him making this sort of mistake."

"I find it hard to believe anyone could make it. Were you told that I saw the robot that'd been working on it? It was a service bot, not a maintenance bot."

She cocked her head and brought up the MM on her wrist. The creases in her forehead deepened after every tap. "No. It says here it was a maintenance bot."

"I don't know a lot about those machines, but it looked like a service bot. They have the domed heads, right?"

"Yeah, but so do some maintenance bots." She tapped the screen again. "Wait. Hold on. This says the machine Nedell programmed wasn't one of those. Let me see if any others worked on that console." She shook her head. "Nope. Maybe you saw a different one in a different location?"

The lilt in her voice caught his attention. "You don't sound certain."

"I recently spotted a bot that wasn't where it belonged," she said. "By the time I verified this on the schedule, it was gone. I never did track it down."

Hapker's spine tingled. "So I'm not the only one who thinks something is off."

"Definitely not, but all I have is a feeling—no evidence."

"Alright." Hapker shifted his feet. "Can you tell me about the robots I saw on the way here? I counted eight."

He told her which corridors he'd seen them in and what kind he thought they were. She scrolled through the information on her MM tablet, dipping her head now and then.

After a few minutes, she looked up. "They're all accounted for, Commander."

He relaxed. "That's good. I don't want this to be more than an accident."

"Me either, Sir. But I swear something's up."

"Well, a lot about our current situation is unusual. Me being here, for one."

"That must be it." She waved her hand. "Not the part about you. The admiral and his people are the ones who've upset the flow here."

Oh, yeah. The meddlesome admiral and his irksome team. "How much has Major Esekielu been in on the investigation?"

"None. The major has been keeping tabs on all the engineering aspects while Lieutenant Krause heads the investigation."

Another prickle zipped down Hapker's backbone. "Do you double-check his work?"

Her brows rose. "I do. You think something is off about him too?"

"Yes, but I can't pinpoint why." *Other than him risking his career for someone he doesn't know.* "What have you noticed about him?"

"Nothing concrete. It's just that weird smile of his. And Glastra…" She rubbed her arm as though chilled.

"Glastra?"

"He's one of my engineers. He's also been helping with the investigation, usually assisting the lieutenant. There's nothing unusual about that, but they both have this mechanical way about them that…"

"That?"

"It's not my place to say," she said. "It feels too much like gossip."

"I'm not a fan of gossip either, but maybe this is important."

She leaned in. “Glastra’s nickname is Glastrabot. He’s called that because how he moves and talks is so *precise*, for lack of a better word.”

Hapker’s chest swelled with understanding. “Yes, I’ve noticed. Krause hardly ever gestures, and his posture is so rigid. And when he *does* move, it seems awkward, unnatural even.”

“Not a good reason to be suspicious, though,” she said.

Hapker frowned. “No. Just a strange feeling.”

“Agreed, but he’s friendly enough. He’s always polite and offering to help.”

“Yes, there’s that,” Hapker said. “And he’s helping Jori.”

“He’s helping him? I would’ve thought with the admiral’s attitude that he’d be against him.”

“I expected that too, but he got Jori the lawyer and helped convince the admiral to allow him free time.” *And will commit treason if he goes behind the council’s back.*

“That’s a good thing.”

“Yeah, but I can’t help but think he has an ulterior motive.”

“Like what?”

“I don’t know. I just don’t trust him.”

“Well,” Singh said. “Rest assured, Commander, that I’m keeping an eye on him—on everyone here, actually.”

“Let’s hope it’s all in our heads and that everything is fine. Will you let me know if you find out anything?”

“Sure thing.”

“It was nice meeting you, by the way,” Hapker said.

“You as well. We should chat under better circumstances next time.”

Hapker agreed, but only to a point. He wasn’t sure if that was a purely friendly invitation or if she was interested in him. If not for Chesa, he’d consider the latter.

24
Antagonizers

The prison door hissed open. Jori shoved the necklace back under his shirt, slid off the bed, and rose to his feet.

Sergeant Banks' expression twisted. "Time for undeserved free time."

The level of hate spewing from the man's essence gave him pause but he dared not give this chima the satisfaction of letting it show. Emotion was a weakness, and the last thing he wanted was to react like a blackbeast's prey. "It's not for another half hour."

The sergeant snatched his arm and yanked forward. "You go now, or you don't go at all."

Jori resisted, but he might as well have been a mouse struggling against a blackbeast with the ease that Banks pulled him along. *Where are Hapker and Gresher?* They didn't leave him alone often. Banks' timing was suspicious.

The man thrust him through the main exit. Jori stumbled, then grit his teeth to hold back a curse. Corporal Harley's guilt spiked, but he said nothing. Jori shot him a distressed look, but the corporal turned away.

Jori swallowed the rising dread. He didn't resist as Banks grabbed him again and swiftly marched him through the corridors.

He managed to keep up without running and without allowing the ugly man to jerk him onward. Then a guard behind him stepped on his heel. Jori pitched forward. Banks let go. Jori fell to his hands and knees with a stifled grunt. *Stupid chima.*

Banks yanked him up. "Get going, damn it. I don't have all day."

"Sir?" Harley said, his emotions emitting hesitance. "Is this really necessary?"

The sergeant halted and planted in front of the corporal. The corporal stepped backward. His throat bobbed. Banks sneered. "Just who the fuck's side are you on?"

Harley glanced at the floor, then raised his chin. "We should follow the code of conduct, Sir."

The ugly sergeant squared his shoulders and leaned in, making Harley back up more. "It's only us here, Corporal. And unless you say something, no one's gonna know."

Harley's throat bobbed again, his guilt bombarding Jori's senses.

Banks turned away, dragging Jori with him. "Hot-headed Harley, huh? What a joke. You're a fucking wimp."

Jori's nerves tingled with both foreboding and annoyance. Just because Harley was a coward didn't mean he deserved to be bullied. He considered kicking Banks in the shin or ramming him into the wall, but Gresher's advice against fighting over words echoed in his head. Did it count that this chima gripped him like the claw of a salvage ship?

As they ushered him onward, the guard behind him stepped on him again. Jori stumbled. He nearly regained his feet when Banks added a shove. Jori fell with a resounding smack.

"Sir!" Harley stepped in between. "Stop it!"

Banks bared his teeth and palmed Harley in the chest. "You got something to say, Corporal?"

"That's enough!" came a woman's voice from further down the hall.

Jori barely heard it through his own exploding emotions. He twisted his torso and kicked out his leg. It smacked into the weak spot behind Banks' knee. The man dropped like a sack of rocks. Jori elbowed him in the nose with a resounding crunch.

Banks roared and pounced. Jori bounded out of his reach. Two officers lunged for him. He dodged. Another swung at him. He ducked. Banks dove for him. Jori twisted behind him but ran into another officer. Corporal Lengen struck his cheekbone. Jori toppled to the side but found his footing in time to catch his balance.

The move put him against the wall where Banks and Lengen moved in too close for him to maneuver. He covered his head, blocking two ramming fists. Lengen forced his arms away.

"You fucking cowards!" Jori shouted.

He kneed the closest attacker but was too small to faze them. Lengen pressed his arm against Jori's neck, cutting off his air. Banks struck him in the mouth. Wetness sprang from his lip.

"Enough!" Sergeant Ortega's chest heaved as she raced down the hall. Her greyish-brown skin was rouge. "What in the fucking hell is wrong with you, Banks?"

The weight pressing against Jori released. He doubled over and choked in air. No more strikes came at him. His vision returned, his breathing eased, and his senses recovered.

He pulled himself upright and took in the situation. Three officers aimed stun weapons at his head, their bodies tense. Jori glared at each one, wishing they'd exposed some sort of weakness so he could get the hell way from here.

Banks glowered at Ortega. Her lips curled in return, as though daring him to strike her next. Harley, reeking of fear, stood beside her with creased brows.

"What the fuck is wrong with *you*?" Banks replied. "Since when do you care about what happens to this brat?"

"There's a code of conduct, you *ass*."

"There's also a code about taking care of our own. People died because of him. So what are you gonna do? Are you taking the little traitor's side in this or are you gonna go about your business and let us do our fucking job?"

Her emotions warred. He got the sense that she wanted to fight him on this, but something held her back. Perhaps the soldiers here had the same unspoken code to not rat out your teammates.

"What's going on?" A familiar officer with the epaulette of a lieutenant arrived. His dark eyes hardened as they bored into the officers as well as Jori. His emotions were cool, however, and they radiated purpose.

If Jori had any chance at all, it was with him. He met the lieutenant's glare. "They kept tripping me, making me fall. I was told I'd be treated fairly, yet they took advantage of me because they thought I couldn't fight back."

The lieutenant's features darkened but his emotions remained level. "Put your weapons down."

The guards obeyed.

Lieutenant Buckeye planted his feet in front of Banks. "Is what the boy said true, Sergeant?"

"No, Sir."

The lieutenant glanced at another officer. "No, Sir," the man replied.

Neither seemed ashamed of their lie. The fire in Jori's chest reignited. Code or not, if their actions were so righteous, they should be honest.

Buckeye looked at Harley, whose throat bobbed. His eyes darted between Jori, Sergeant Ortega, and Banks. "No, Sir."

"Cowards!" Jori yelled. "First you hurt me because you think I'm helpless, and now you're too afraid to tell the truth!"

Sergeant Banks faced him with the menace of a blackbeast. "You started this, you little shit."

Lieutenant Buckeye moved between them. "Sergeant! If you can't keep your attitude under control, I will remove you from duty."

Banks straightened and masked the hatred in his face. It remained in his emotions, though.

Buckeye stepped back. He eyed Jori, then gave the same intense scowl to all the officers. "Everyone is to wear a body cam from now on. If I find out anyone—" He looked pointedly at Jori and Banks. "—is instigating trouble, there will be severe consequences. Is that understood?"

Banks and the others barked out a yes, sir. Jori met the man's eyes and refused to reply.

The lieutenant squared up to him. "Is that understood?"

Jori held his glower. "I didn't come here to fight but I won't be pushed around, either. If they leave me alone, I'll leave them alone."

Buckeye held his look a moment longer, then nodded. "Get him to sick bay. Make sure there's no further incident."

"Yes, Sir," the officers chimed.

Banks moved to grab his arm. Jori jerked away. "Don't touch me. I know the way. I don't need you dragging me there."

Banks sneered and tried again.

"Sergeant!" the lieutenant said. "Keep your hands off unless he makes it necessary. And once you get him there, take care of yourself and report to my office."

"Yes, Sir," he replied contemptuously, wiping the blood from under his nostrils.

Jori puffed out his chest and marched forward. Banks matched his gait and the other officers fell in behind.

When they reached the infirmary, Banks turned to him and leaned in. The fiery specks in his brown eyes didn't waver. "One wrong move and you're mine."

"Will you wait until I'm helpless like the coward you are?" Jori said through gritted teeth.

"Keep up the smart mouth, you brat. Remember, the only thing stopping me from beating the shit out of you is a lieutenant who is no longer here."

Jori ignored his rising fear and raised his lip. "I'm not afraid of you. You're just like my father, but I'm still not afraid."

Indignation swelled from the sergeant and widened into fury. He didn't strike out or retort, though. He turned away, indicating for the others to take guard positions while he went to get his cracked nose taken care of. Two officers sneered or made faces at him, but Harley refused to look at him. The corporal's emotions remained conflicted, but Jori didn't care. These Cooperative people were all cowards in one way or another.

25
Lovers and Haters

Carletta Ortega glowered at Banks' back as he escorted the boy. Her heart pounded like a jackhammer. A fight with him would come sooner or later. She wished he'd swung at her so it'd be sooner and she could get this stupid fear of him out of her system.

"So what happened here?" Lieutenant Bryce Buckeye asked her.

She snapped her attention to him, taking a military stance. Here, he was her superior officer, not her lover. "Banks started it, Sir. I saw the whole thing but was too far away to do anything until it was too late."

Bryce crossed his arms, indicating a switch in formalities. "That's not what the others say."

"You think I'm lying?"

Bryce's eyes tilted apologetically. "Of course not. But keep departing and you'll find yourself at odds with them."

Ortega pulled back. "I should keep my mouth shut?"

"Listen, Letta." Bryce cupped her upper arm and drew in almost close enough to kiss. "I just don't want you to deal with the same harassment you dealt with at the institute."

Ortega withered. She'd told him how hard it had been to fit in. Somehow, she'd gotten on the wrong side of the instructors and the most prominent students. After that, many others either turned against her or avoided her—except Singh.

"So I shouldn't say anything?" she asked again.

"I think you should be careful, especially when it comes to this child. Things were bound to turn ugly and I'd rather you not get caught up in it."

She swallowed. "Maybe you're right."

"Don't worry. I'll give Banks a proper dressing down."

Ortega gave him a small smile. “Thank you,” she said, though she wasn’t sure what to be thankful for.

Bryce’s eyes lit up as he grinned. “Of course. Anything for my Letta Rosetta Violetta Poinsettia Ortetta.”

She giggled and smacked his arm playfully.

He winked. “See you tonight?”

“You know it.”

They parted ways. The toasty feeling he’d given her evaporated quickly as the intensity of Banks’ violence rushed back in. The brutality of it curdled her insides and made her hate that man even more.

“Shit.” *This is fucked up.* Banks shouldn’t have done that, but Bryce was right. Siding with the Tredon was a bad idea.

*****

J.D. Hapker stroked Chesa’s luxurious hair as she lay in the crook of his arm. Her spicy yet sweet scent reached his nostrils, making his toes curl. A velvety peace enveloped him.

She stretched her neck and met his lips. “See. I told you it would be alright.”

“It was more than alright,” he said, glad he had made this impromptu visit.

“It doesn’t have to be over,” she whispered as she traced her finger along the contours of his jaw. “I have a bottle of Primitivo. We can order creamy pastries, lounge around, talk about old times.”

“That sounds wonderful.”

She slid out of bed with the grace of a Loushian cat. He crossed his hands behind his head and admired her soft curves as she retrieved the wine.

An annoying buzz broke his trance. With a heavy sigh, he tapped his comm. “Hapker here.”

“Sir.”

Lieutenant Gresher’s tone made Hapker bolt upright. “Is everything alright?”

“There’s been some trouble between Jori and the guards.”

Hapker threw off his covers. “Is Jori alright?”

"What?" Chesa plopped the bottle onto the table and rushed over. "What's wrong?"

"For the most part," Gresher said.

He sprang out of bed and scrambled for his clothes.

"*J.D.* What's going on?" Chesa asked, her tone laced with irritation.

He donned his pants. "Jori's in trouble."

"So?"

Hapker ignored her and spoke to Gresher. "Where is he?"

"Sick bay."

Crap. "I'll be right there." He cut the comm and pulled his shirt over his head.

"What?" Chesa yelled. "I thought we were staying in and having wine."

"Sorry, but I've got to go."

Her eyes ignited. "Let someone else handle it."

He tugged on his shoes. "Jori needs *me*."

She put her fists on her hips. "I can't believe you're abandoning me for him!"

Hapker huffed. "I'm not abandoning you. I'll be back, alright?"

"Who says I'll want to see you?"

He groaned inwardly. There was no point in arguing with her when she was fired up like an angry bear, so he headed to the door. "Sorry, I've got to go. We'll talk later. I promise."

"Fuck you, you bastard."

He left with an exasperated sigh. Why did she hate Jori so much? He remembered her fiery temper, but this was worse. Maybe after she calmed down, they could have a heart-to-heart. If he understood her reasons, perhaps he'd change her mind. For now, he had to get to Jori.

The swift trek through the ship was a blur. By the time he arrived at the medical bay, his forehead was beaded with sweat. He scanned the room, locating the guards first. Sergeant Banks sat on a cot on one side while the doctor ran a thera-pen over his nose. A stream of dried blood indicated Jori had done more than a little damage.

Banks undoubtedly deserved it, but the man wasn't the type to let this go. More trouble would come.

Hapker beelined to the other end where two officers guarded a hall leading to the private recovery rooms. His heart capered at what that might mean.

An officer sneered as he passed. Hapker glowered back but was too rushed to speak. He approached two more officers guarding a recovery room. Neither met his eyes as they snapped to attention.

Hapker pulled the curtain open, the rings running along the rod with a metallic zing. Two more guards moved aside, revealing a sight that sent Hapker's temper into a boil. Jori sat on the healing bed. His upper lip had swollen to the size of a cherry and blood crusted under his nose.

Hapker planted his hands on his hips and shot the officers his most thunderous glower. "What the hell did you all do?"

Only Corporal Harley had the decency to show some remorse as he hung his head.

"He made the first move," Corporal Lengen said with a bitter hook to his mouth.

"He's lying." Jori gritted his teeth and scowled at the guards.

Hapker knew him well enough to know he'd spoken truthfully. He stared at Harley and hoped he'd confirm it. The corporal's eyes shifted to the other officers. His throat bobbed, but he didn't speak.

Hapker held a glare that could melt steel. Still, Harley remained quiet.

What the hell? He understood the soldiers' unwritten code to have each other's backs, but this went too far. He kept his hands behind his back to hide his fists but let every other part of him show his ire. "If Jori was giving you trouble, you should have restrained him or used the stunner. This—" He pointed at Jori's face. "—is pure savagery. You think you're better than Tredons, yet you did this to a ten-year-old child!"

"We tried to restrain him, Sir," Lengen replied as though he had swallowed a lemon.

"So Banks could hit me, you coward," Jori snapped in a garbled voice caused by his injured lip.

"Enough!" Hapker yelled. "I'm sure you'll all be spoken to individually about this. And I hope…" He cast a challenging look at Harley. "I hope some of you will be more forthcoming about what really happened."

Harley kept his eyes on the floor. Hapker sent them all out and yanked the privacy curtain shut.

He faced Jori and ran his hand down his face. "I believe you," he said more sharply than intended, making Jori flinch. He sucked in some air and let it out slowly. "And I'm sorry for leaving you alone with them. It won't happen again."

Jori didn't reply. The sparks in his eyes indicated he had more to say, though. Hapker wasn't sure whether to be relieved at the boy's self-control or worried his simmering anger would explode later.

He hoped for the former.

26
Lawyers and Doctors

Gottfried Krause practically glided down the bright hall. Despite Sergeant Banks' susceptibility to the imperium influence, no one—other than that annoying commander—suspected he'd been the instigator. Even with Commander Hapker acting as advocate, Jori was bound to develop an unredeemable hate toward the Cooperative. The plan was coming together nicely.

The boy appeared from around the hall's curve with his guards in tow. Commander Hapker and the lawyer came too. Gottfried hid his glee and met them at the entrance to the admiral's office.

"My dear, Jori," he said. "I'm so sorry about what happened. I'm glad to see you're alright."

The boy's mouth took a hard turn down. Gottfried caught a whiff of his outrage before the emotions cut off. He made sure his own mental wall firmed in place as elation swelled inside him.

With a press to the side panel, the door opened, revealing a man with an expression more dour than usual. Admiral Belmont leaned on his elbows, his hands clutched into a knot.

Jori planted himself before him with severity. The admiral removed his inhibitor. A fury that rivaled the boy's crashed into Gottfried's senses. No doubt, the admiral wanted Jori to sense it and be intimidated. Gottfried almost laughed. If anything, it converted his emotions from an ember into a full-blown wildfire. He hid it from his features well, though.

"Your actions are completely out of line, young man!" the admiral said. "I don't know what you hoped to—"

"They started it!" Jori's teeth flashed like a wild animal.

Belmont matched his anger, though his showed up more in his crumpled brows. "That's not what any of the reports say, and I trust my people a lot more than I trust you."

"Sir!" Commander Hapker barked. "You haven't heard his side of it. Considering the level of hate everyone here seems to have, we should be more objective."

"I heartily agree, Admiral," Bilsby said. "The boy's story has a ring of truth to it."

Belmont jabbed his finger on his desk. "I have *four* officers saying he started it. Four! No one else has come forward with anything different. If you expect me to take the word of one child who has already escaped from his guards, you're sorely mistaken."

"With all due respect, Admiral," the commander said in a tone too loud to be respectful. "This attack has hate written all over it. You've seen the medical report. What they did to him was totally uncalled for. It reeks of the brutal behavior you ascribe to Tredons."

Admiral Belmont stood, leaning on his knuckles. "I know how well that boy can fight, so when the officers tell me they needed to subdue him, I believe them."

"That's ludicrous! If they got close enough to punch him in the face, then they were close enough to restrain him."

"Again, I concur, Admiral," Bilsby said. "The severity of the injuries inflicted on my young client makes you obligated to investigate this further."

"That he's a child compounds the seriousness of this situation," Hapker added.

Belmont darkened. "We all know he's no mere child. He can fight better than just about everyone here."

Gottfried's heart danced with the sizzling energy that filled the room. This was an amazing moment. Not only was the admiral not the least bit swayed, but the force of Jori's emotions had demolished his mental block.

"Yes, he can fight," the commander admitted. "But his size and strength should have made it easy for the officers to restrain him."

"*I've* seen him, Commander! That boy moves like a whirlwind and hits like a hammer."

"Be that as it may," Bilsby said, "you are obligated by law to evaluate this situation further."

"How in the *hell* am I supposed to do that? It wasn't recorded—"

"Well, that's convenient," the commander muttered.

Belmont jabbed his finger at Jori. "—and all witnesses say *that boy* started it."

"Sergeant Ortega saw some of it," Jori said. "And so did a lieutenant."

"Lieutenant Buckeye," Gottfried offered.

Belmont shook his head. "I have both their reports. Ortega says she arrived just as you knocked Banks over and Lieutenant Buckeye said he didn't get there until it was already over."

"All of you are nothing but a bunch of cowardly liars!" Jori stamped forward with his nostrils flared.

The commander's swift hand grabbed him by the shoulder.

Gottfried wanted to rub his hands together in greedy anticipation. Jori would be wholly on his side in no time.

"No matter who started it, Admiral," Bilsby said, "we should look into the way the officers handled it. At the very least, put everyone involved on suspension and—"

"Don't tell me how to do my job." The admiral's forehead wrinkled, making his brow stick out almost as much as his bottom lip.

"If I may, Sir," Gottfried said.

Belmont snapped to him with the same anger.

Gottfried smiled. "We are obligated *by law* to investigate this further. And if we don't, it will reflect poorly on us."

The admiral's expression turned murderous. Gottfried relished in it. Pointing out when the man was about to make an unwise decision was the best part about his job. Plus, it bolstered his standing with the boy.

"Fine." The admiral straightened and tugged at the hem of his uniform. "I'll have someone interview all those involved—"

"Someone who isn't biased," Bilsby put in.

"And," Belmont said in a rising tone, "remove the officers from duty until this is resolved. But!" He paused and puffed out his chest. "No free time until then. And if he ever needs to leave his cell, he will be handcuffed."

Bilsby raised his palm. "Admiral, you can't—"

"I will not put the safety of this crew at stake! He will remain confined unless I say otherwise."

Bilsby dipped his head in resignation while anger and scorn radiated off Jori and the commander. Gottfried studied the pair.

Perhaps their closeness could win the man to his side as well. There was the stigma around augmentations the Cooperative had instilled in their people, but surely Commander Hapker would realize that Jori's abilities put him in the same category. He filed that thought away for further analysis.

"Dismissed!" The admiral plopped back in his chair and pointedly ignored them.

After everyone except Gottfried had gone, Belmont turned to him with a twisted glower that matched his emotions. "Who the hell's side are you on, damn it?"

"Yours, of course, Sir."

"Then why did you agree with the lawyer?"

"If we don't uphold the law, it might garner sympathy for the boy. I'm sure we don't want that."

Belmont's mood deflated. Of course, the man hadn't considered that. He was too obtuse to think ahead. If it wasn't for his schmoozing, he never would've gotten this far in his career.

He's a bootlicker, that's what he is. Gottfried refrained from laughing at the image that popped into his head. He'd forgotten how funny some idioms could be.

The stoic emotions of someone outside the admiral's door brushed Gottfried's senses. *Right on time.* "I have Doctor Donnel waiting to speak with you, Sir."

Belmont folded his hands before him, though not as tight as before. "Enter."

Doctor Donnel marched into the office with the rigidness of a soldier. Her pinched expression tightened even more at the sight of Gottfried. The dislike was mutual, but she suited his purposes.

Eager anticipation danced through the admiral's emotions. "Tell me what you've found, Doctor."

"Nothing concerning, Admiral."

Belmont startled. "You're joking?"

Her mouth puckered as though the concept of joking repulsed her. "No, Sir."

"Doesn't that surprise you?"

She smartly folded her hands before her and reset her shoulders into its inflexible stiffness. "Anyone can pass these tests if they know the right answers."

The admiral's chin jutted in superiority. "You mean he gave the answers he thought would help him?"

"He *could have*," Doctor Donnel said in a matter-of-fact tone. "I find it difficult to believe that a child surrounded by so much violence, and who has already taken lives himself, doesn't have more psychological concerns."

Belmont drummed his fingers on the desk. "So what's next?"

"Someone will need to do a one-on-one evaluation."

"Agreed. Can you do it?"

She reviewed the MM on her wrist, her eagerness to find an opening penetrating Gottfried's senses. After a few taps on her screen, she returned to her militaristic bearing. "I can squeeze him in later today. Note that this will take more than one session."

"How many?"

"Without meeting him, it's hard to say. I will rearrange my schedule and try to get him in every other day."

"Do it. I want the evaluation report completed before we reach Asteria."

"Yes, Admiral."

Belmont made a sharp nod. "Thank you, Doctor. This will help tremendously."

When he dismissed her, she expeditiously took her leave.

Gottfried faced the admiral with a more leisurely demeanor. "I'm sure this will go well, Sir."

Belmont harrumphed and a sourness emanated from him. "Your help notwithstanding."

Rather than call out the admiral's ungrateful attitude, Gottfried merely smiled. This thankless ignoramus would get what he deserved soon enough. So would everyone else who was too short-sighted to see their own shortcomings.

27
Doubts

An odd sort of music wafted from the speakers. A whiny electrical instrument fluctuated from a high-pitched wail to a dismal toll. J.D. Hapker glanced around the lounge, wondering if anyone else found the sound grating.

Being here after what had happened with Captain Richforth depressed him. It was like waiting for the heavy clouds to drop a torrent of rain. The recent violence made it worse. Hapker rubbed his temple. Jori was fine—physically—but Banks' lies had spread like wildfire and would inspire more trouble.

If his old friend hadn't agreed to meet him, he never would have come here where too many people whispered behind his back or shot him dirty looks. He could practically feel their burning displeasure.

He hated leaving Jori alone again, but the admiral insisted he speak to the ship's psychiatrist in private. Although the boy could use therapy, Doctor Donnel's sour expression had made him certain that she wasn't doing this with his best interest in mind.

Hapker set his worries aside to take advantage of the good company. Taking a sip of his drink, he listened as Andres Carter talked about his recent visit to Triptolemos where people lived in huts.

"They make their clothes by hand," Carter said as he leaned into the cushions of the half-circular couch with one arm lounged on the back. "Not a single machine in sight unless you count the handcrafted spinning wheels and looms."

"Really?" Hapker smiled at how well their conversation progressed. There was still some aloofness, but this was a good start. *Thank you, Gresher, for making amends with your friend and inspiring me to do the same.* "Sounds like a challenging yet satisfying lifestyle."

Carter laughed genuinely. "Somehow, I knew you'd say that."

"You know me. I love nature. I'm not sure about working the land and making my own clothes. A month-long visit would be interesting, though."

"Yeah, I could get in on that." Carter raised his cup. "Here's to many more adventures."

They clinked cups and drank. The bite of the fermented tea tricked Hapker's tastebuds into thinking it was alcoholic. Sweet yet tangy, and all natural. He had to convince someone on the *Odyssey* to make this stuff. Assuming he ever got to return.

A hollowness expanded inside him at the possibility that Captain Arden wouldn't allow Jori to live on his ship. He set that thought aside, preferring to focus on his friend.

He changed the subject to general matters about work, being careful to keep the conversation away from the database Carter guarded.

"For the most part, we've got a good crew," Carter said.

"For the most part?" Hapker asked, wondering if he had the same antipathy toward Banks.

"Yeah, I'm not too sure about those soldiers we picked up from the Indore station."

"Two elite squads, if I remember right."

Carter huffed. "E*lite* and *offbeat*—kinda goes hand-in-hand with these guys."

"How so?"

"They're just different. I never quite understood the mentality of those hard-core soldiers, but they take it to a whole new level—like machines or something."

Hapker's heart skipped a beat. Although his investigation of the death-by-console had ended due to lack of evidence, he still couldn't shake the feeling that it hadn't been an accident. Any mention of machine-like people made his hairs stand on end.

"Chesa called them mindless drones."

"That's about right, though I'm sure Firestorm didn't quite state it so nicely."

Hapker laughed. "No, she most certainly didn't."

"How's it going between you two, by the way?"

Hapker hesitated. Not too long ago, he would've said *great*. The more he spent time with her, the more he remembered how turbulent their relationship had been. Add in her attitude toward Jori, and he wasn't sure how he felt. "About the same as before."

Carter chuckled. "Like dodging trees as you're skiing down the slopes, right?"

"At least in skiing, I have some control. This is more like parachuting without steering lines." Hapker swallowed the last of his drink and ordered another through the tablet set into the tabletop.

"She doesn't have a good opinion of that boy."

Hapker's insides did a flip. The intensity of Carter's eyes made his stance clear. Not wanting to argue, Hapker didn't reply.

"You know," Carter said as he eased from his casual slouch to a more closed-in posture. "I agree our officers didn't handle that situation well, but you're not making any friends siding with the Dragon Emperor's son."

Hapker forced his jaw to relax. "Jori didn't start that. It was Banks."

Carter grimaced. "See. That's what I mean. You believe a Tredon child over our own people."

Hapker leaned in and tried not to sound defensive. "Jori doesn't lie, even if he knows the truth could be used against him."

"He's a child. Children tell fibs sometimes, especially when the truth will get them in trouble."

Hapker shook his head. "Not all children. Jori could've lied about a lot of things, but he hasn't. He considers it cowardly and dishonorable." A bot set Hapker's drink on the table. He took a sip and used the moment to settle his temper. "What about Sergeant Banks? You work with him. Can you honestly say there's no chance he started this?"

Carter lowered and wagged his head. "No. I can't." He flicked his hand and sighed. "Banks can be a jackass even on his best days. But…" He looked upward as though in thought. "I don't know. It just seems more likely to be the other way around."

"It *does* seem unlikely that any person would intentionally harm a child, but Banks wouldn't be the first to take his hate too far. We had an officer on the *Odyssey* who did something similar."

Carter didn't look convinced. "Maybe."

"Listen. I don't expect you to change your mind. Just try to remain objective about it. Fair?"

"Fair enough." Carter sat back, almost in an amenable pose except the downturn of his features suggested it was closer to tolerance. "I get you want to do the right thing, I really do. But where is this going? Even if the boy is exonerated, what's next? I doubt the Cooperative will allow him on our ships. What will you do then? Are you willing to set aside your career for him?"

Hapker's gut dropped. This wasn't the conversation he wanted to have, but talking about it might help him sort his thoughts.

He rubbed his chin and sighed. He would help Jori no matter what, which meant he might have to resign his commission. Until now, he hadn't pondered this in depth. Did he really want to leave? Not even after having to move to the PCC side of the Cooperative had he wanted to give up. Now he was happy serving Captain Arden. But he'd quit before he abandoned Jori.

"You would, wouldn't you?" Carter shook his head as though disappointed. "You never were very good at doing your duty."

Hapker bristled. *And you always did everything so by the book that you left no room for compromise.* Rather than say it, he released a heavy sigh. "Sometimes doing the right thing is our duty."

Carter nodded, but not in agreement. "That, my friend, is where you and I went wrong. You're a subordinate officer. It's not your place to decide what the right thing is."

The conversation faltered from there. Even after changing the subject, the gap between them widened until there was nothing else to say. Hapker finished his drink and left with a dispirited weight.

Am I the one who's wrong? As he walked the corridors and passed officers who either avoided his eyes or frowned at him, his confidence wavered. If this many people disagreed with his actions, then perhaps he was. He still couldn't imagine abandoning Jori, but the prospect of giving up his career gave him a sensation of wading through a sludge of regrets and depressing options.

28
The Session

The incense wafting from the decorative burner tweaked Jori's nostrils. It was too sweet and contrasted too sharply with the brown-patterned furniture and matching abstract art. Few other decorations adorned this space—an uninteresting vase with zigzags, a bronze sculpture that could've been a snake but was too angular, a simple lamp with a cream shade.

Jori forced his jaw to relax as the guard clamped his wrists to the chair. The padded seat was comfortable enough, but the situation was unbearable.

His sinuses burned, but he'd cried so much already he doubted he had any more tears left. Long, steady inhales and exhales eventually moved his emotions to the back corner of his brain.

By the time his guards had stepped out, he reached a state of precarious calm. The woman introduced to him as a therapist pulled back her shoulders and intertwined her fingers. The expression on her face matched her tightly pulled back hair. Except for her bangs, she wore her blond hair in a ponytail. The style Jori had only seen on little girls did not detract from her austere bearing.

"I'm Doctor Mazie Donnel. It's a pleasure to meet you."

She spoke the truth, but her bland emotions conveyed formality rather than sincerity.

"You as well," Jori replied with the same coolness.

"Jori. Is that the name you prefer to go by?"

"Yes."

She tapped the screen of her tablet with a stylus. "Alright. Now, why don't you tell me a little about yourself?"

Jori furrowed his brow. "You know already."

"Yes. But I'd like to hear your perspective."

He sensed some interest from her emotions, but only in the way that a mechanic took interest in his work. His insides tensed. "I am the youngest son of Emperor Mizuki."

"The youngest of how many?" she asked dispassionately.

"Several, but I only ever met three of my brothers."

"Really? Why is that?"

"Because the others died before I was born."

"Do you think about them?"

Jori's stomach twitched but he maintained his neutrality. "No."

"Really?" She frowned. "Not even to wonder why you've lost so many?"

The room seemed to close in around him. There was only one brother he ever cared about, but it was none of her business. "It's the way things are."

"I see." She tapped her MM tablet. "Tell me of the brothers you knew."

"One died in battle, one was killed because he was whiny and incompetent, one is still with my father." A swell of sadness threatened to choke him at the last brother, but he kept his face neutral.

"Killed how?"

"Killed by my father."

Her eyebrows lifted. "You saw this?"

"Yes." That day had horrified him, but he didn't dare let her see it. Perhaps the saying about emotion being a weakness didn't apply with Hapker, but here she'd undoubtedly exploit it.

"That must've been traumatic. It helps to talk about these things. Perhaps you can share more, tell me how you feel when you think about it."

Jori pressed his lips together. His choice was between sharing his emotions or lying. Both were out of the question.

"Were you afraid you could be next?" Doctor Donnel pushed with a penetrating stare.

Despite the urge to fidget under her scrutiny, Jori refused to answer.

"Most people would be afraid," she said. "I would be."

Jori remained still. This topic was too painful and he didn't want her to see him hurt.

Irritation skipped through her emotions, but she didn't show it. "Perhaps we should come to an understanding before we go further." She set down her tablet and rested her hands on her lap. "I'm here to help you."

She'd spoken with a hint of truth, but her underlying misgiving countered it.

"If you say nothing," she continued, "I can't evaluate you properly."

I knew it. The Cooperative wanted to find a reason to hate him even more. Well, he'd be damned if he'd give them one. He jutted his chin but still refused to speak.

Her emotions sparked with exasperation. "Do you want me to make assumptions?"

"That's what everyone else is doing." Jori's own annoyance came through in his tone.

"I'm giving you a chance to prove me wrong."

Again, her words didn't have enough honesty to persuade him. "You *are* wrong, but I doubt there's anything I can say that will convince you since you've already made up your mind."

Her lips compressed. She leaned back and flattened her hands on her thighs. Her silence pressed around. After slowly filling her lungs, she spoke. "I've decided nothing yet, and I promise to be fair."

Jori narrowed his eyes. Her candor held no hint of deceit, but what was her definition of fair? Her emotions shifted from an attempt at patience to barely concealed edginess.

"You say you'll be fair," he said, "but you distrust me as much as I distrust you. I'm not a fool. You're only talking to me because the admiral wants you to. I won't give either of you more ammunition to use against me."

Her mouth quirked as though she'd just snared him. "You think that by speaking to me, you'll give us something to use against you?"

Jori clenched his teeth and flexed against his restraints. "It doesn't matter what I say. When I tell the truth and it doesn't coincide with what you believe, you'll just assume I'm lying. This entire interview is pointless."

Her indignation slammed into his senses. After a bout of hard stillness, her poise relaxed. "You're right. The admiral wants me to find something wrong, though I doubt he understands the complexity involved. And I am likely biased." She intertwined her fingers. "Perhaps we should adjourn until a later time. You've given me something to think about, and I hope I've done the same. Maybe with some time to reflect, we can see eye to eye a little better."

Her sincerity rang true, but it was still forced. He conceded, but only to the part about postponing. The meeting ended with resolute detachment on both sides. When the guards returned to remove his restraints, however, something inside him broke.

Even though he'd maintained an outward compliance, his insides rebelled. Fury clashed with despair. Indignation fought against surrender. And through it all, hope twisted and crumbled like a spider sprayed with pesticide.

29
Suspicions and Confessions

Carletta Ortega entered the engineering room with a heavy gait. The air pressed around her as though she waded through sludge. Today had not gone well.

She loved that Bryce wanted to protect her from her peers. The unwritten code was real. If she spoke up, her life would be more difficult. It could even affect her career. Still, she couldn't let go of what had happened with the Tredon boy. Banks had been out of control.

Seeing Singh at her station should've lifted her spirits. But the way her friend's face pulled down told her she wasn't having the best day either.

"Hey," Ortega said to her.

Singh snapped her eyes up from her terminal and blinked. "Hey, Letta. Is it that time already?"

"Yeah," Ortega replied in a drawn-out tone. "You're working too hard again."

"I've been distracted."

"By what?"

Singh inclined her head to the side. Ortega peered over to the rear area but didn't see anything.

"Lieutenant Krause," Singh said. "For some reason, he's back there talking to Glastra."

"Glastrabot?"

"Shh" Singh hissed. "Don't let anyone hear you calling him that."

Ortega hid a smile. "Sorry. What do you think it's about?"

"I have no idea. It's just strange. We've completed our investigation of the console, so why would the admiral's aide speak to my specialist and not me?"

"Maybe they're friends," Ortega said. "They both have an oddness to them. Two weird little peas in a pod, ya know?"

Singh almost smiled. "Perhaps. I just don't like—"

She cut off as the aide appeared from around the corner wearing his usual idiotic grin.

He caught Ortega staring at him and his mouth curled up a tad further. "Sergeant, Chief."

Singh put on a friendly expression just as fake as his. "Lieutenant. Is everything alright?"

Krause halted and his brows drew in. "Of course. Why wouldn't it be?"

"You had a pretty long conversation with my specialist."

The man flicked his hand. "Oh, that. It was nothing. Not business related at all."

"Oh," Singh said.

Krause dipped his head, then swept past them. Ortega watched him waddle out, then returned to her friend.

"See." Singh's brow rose. "Weird, right?"

"Yeah, but it kinda makes sense, too, doesn't it?"

"It does. Glastra has always given me the willies but seeing those two together makes it worse."

"You think they're up to something?"

"Probably just my imagination," Singh said. "Maybe I don't like that Krause is here."

"I hear ya. You ready to go?"

Singh pushed away from the terminal. "Give me a sec."

Ortega hid her impatience. This anxiety was killing her. If she didn't talk about what had happened soon, her stomach would twist itself into knots.

She followed her friend to the rear area but hung back.

Singh stood over a balding man who knelt before an open conduit. "Glastra, what's your status?"

He continued working without response.

"Glastra!" She touched his shoulder, but he still didn't react. She nudged him. "Glastra!"

The man's eyes rolled up. "Yes, Chief."

Ortega's skin prickled at the mechanical way he moved and spoke.

Singh planted her fists on her hips. "I asked you, *what's your status*?"

"Working."

Singh's eyebrow twitched. "When will you be done?"

"Ten minutes, thirty-two seconds, if I don't get any interruptions."

Singh frowned. "You gave me a different timeframe earlier today."

"Yes, ma'am. That was before I realized there was something wrong with the AV sensors."

Singh rubbed her forehead. "Did you notify me of this issue—"

"Yes."

"—in person, like I asked?"

"You were working. I assumed notating it in my work order was appropriate."

"You *need* to tell me in person. Or at least in an IM."

The specialist didn't react. His face held the same lackluster expression it always did. "I don't understand. All incidents must be documented. It seems illogical to provide a verbal or instant message when everything is in a work order."

Singh huffed. "Damn it, Glastra. I told you I can't watch those reports real-time. If a work order takes longer than expected, I need an immediate update so I can readjust the schedule."

"Of course, Chief."

He returned to his work without waiting for a response. Singh wheeled away and mimed a strangling gesture. Her mouth narrowed into a tight line.

She grabbed Ortega by the crook of her arm, and they marched out. As soon as they were out of earshot, Singh growled. "I don't get why he won't listen."

"Didn't you say he was good at his job?"

"He *is*. But when he is told to do something that he doesn't agree with, he has a way of ignoring me and doing what he wants anyway. It pisses me off."

"So write him up."

"I tried that. The asshole pointed out that he did exactly as regulations stated."

"Ah. So he's not a team player," Ortega said.

"No. He's so one hundred percent by the book that he can't understand how doing something a little different can help other people do their jobs better."

Ortega let her friend stew for a bit, knowing she didn't need her agreement or sympathy.

By the time they reached the leisure deck, her friend's steps lightened.

The hall split. Singh led her to the left, but Ortega pulled her in the other direction. "We're meeting in the B-Lounge today."

"Hmm," Singh said. "So you've had a bad day, too."

"You have no idea."

They came to a small quiet alcove with a wide viewscreen displaying an ocean scene. Harley was there, sitting at the tiny central table. His hunched shoulders straightened when he saw them, but it seemed more in relief than in welcome.

Ortega's gut somersaulted as she took the chair facing the entrance. She shared a nervous glance with Harley.

Singh settled in, her eyes drifting back and forth between them. "Alright. What happened? Tell me everything."

Ortega drew in a long breath, then unloaded the earlier events in a rush. Harley nodded along, throwing in tidbits from his perspective.

When she got to Bryce's advice, liquid built on her lower lashes. "I don't want to alienate my team, but I don't think I can let this go either."

Singh squeezed her hand. "You can't let this go, dear."

Ortega drew her finger under her sunglasses and swept away the wetness. "But what about what Bryce said? He's right, you know."

"Oh, I don't doubt that certain people will give you a hard time. But this is different from when you were at the institute. You have more friends here who believe in you."

"Not everyone. Jakes, Sadalge, Venezuela. They'll make my life miserable. They'll say that since I turned on one of my own, I can't be trusted."

Singh grasped her hand in both of hers. "Forgive me for saying this, my dear, but who gives *a fuck* about those jack holes. If you let Banks get away with this, you're basically giving everyone else permission to do the same thing."

Ortega sucked in the strength that her friend exuded. Harley straightened as though he'd received the same confidence.

"You are better than that," Singh continued. She took Harley's hand. "You both are. Don't let the mentality of a few close-minded dickwads turn you into someone you don't want to be. I know it will be tough, but no one ever said doing the right thing would be easy. Be strong because your real friends will stand with you no matter what."

Ortega's sinuses burned as her pride swelled. "You're right. Thank you."

Singh dipped her head.

"You with me, Harley?" Ortega asked.

He held out his hand and she took it. "I'm with you," he said.

Ortega sniffled, then tightened her grip in resolve. "Banks is going down."

30
Reports

Acid ate at Gottfried Krause's insides as he listened to the two officers give their report. This wasn't how it was supposed to go. His analytics hadn't predicted this. Somehow, he'd miscalculated.

He'd suspected Corporal Harley would side with the boy but didn't expect anyone else to. This Sergeant Carletta Ortega surprised him. She'd seem so eager to prove herself to her peers that he didn't think to use his ability on her.

"This will go on your record, Sergeant!" Belmont bellowed at her. "If I can't trust your initial report, what can I trust?"

A sense of contrition seeped from her, but the firmness of her jaw indicated she didn't regret coming forward.

While the admiral continued to berate her and the corporal, Gottfried considered his options. These two were not on his list for elimination, but perhaps they should be. Should he wait until they picked up the MEGA hunters or could he do away with her before then? Lieutenant Buckeye might have an idea.

"I take full responsibility for my initial judgment, Admiral." Sergeant Ortega stood tall. "I *will* amend my report, however. What Sergeant Banks did was wrong."

The admiral's temper soared. Although his skin turned maroon, he refrained from his usual foolish outbursts. The silence crackled as he regarded the sergeant's firm demeanor.

"Fine," he finally said. "Now get the hell out of my office."

They left with haste. The admiral stewed for a few moments before turning to Gottfried with a penetrating glower. "Were they telling the truth?"

Gottfried forecasted the results of each reply. Saying they'd lied would set his plan right, but what if the boy found out? He couldn't risk alienating him. "I'm afraid so, Sir."

Belmont smacked the top of the desk. "Damn it! What the hell was Sergeant Banks thinking?"

"Remember, we wanted this to happen."

Belmont's dark eyes flared. "We wanted it to look like the boy started it."

Gottfried nodded. He'd told Banks not to be obvious, but his ability only influenced so much of a person's own inclinations. "What now, Sir? We should obviously suspend Sergeant Banks but I'm not sure about the others. The boy claimed someone stepped on his heel to make him trip, but it might have been an accident."

"Fine," the admiral said. "I'll charge Sergeant Banks with misconduct. Everyone else will resume their normal duties."

"Yes, Sir." Gottfried typed a message to Lieutenant Buckeye, explaining what had happened and asking him to handle the reprimand.

With that done, he reviewed the list of officers who could take Banks' place. Only one stood out. Sergeant Chesa Creston's connections to the commander and dislike for the boy made her a great candidate, but he wasn't sure how easy she'd be to manipulate. Plus, he'd have to be more careful with his imperium ability.

"What did you think of Doctor Donnel's report?" Belmont asked.

Gottfried's irritation spiked. He'd used his ability on her, but it didn't work as well as he'd hoped. "She cited a possibility of antisocial personality disorder but refuted it at the same time. The superficial politeness we saw when he spoke to the council might be self-control. He seems to have self-confidence rather than arrogance. She mentioned that deceit and aggression are also symptoms but didn't see evidence. This recent confession from our officers means we've only seen him defend himself."

Belmont's glower deepened. "What about the level of violence he exhibits when he uses the holo-program?"

"I doubt it qualifies, since it's a simulation."

The admiral's annoyance expanded. "And his criminal history?"

"She asked him about his violent past and said he showed no sign of emotion. However, she suggests it's because he's holding back. She needs to have more sessions with him before she can determine whether he lacks empathy or has a disregard for right and wrong."

Belmont's face scrunched, matching the displeasure he exuded. Gottfried's own emotions were piqued. The boy must experience the full prejudice of the Cooperative, but making it happen was harder than he'd expected. Perhaps he'd have better luck with Sergeant Creston.

*****

Carletta Ortega strolled down the corridor. Smiling at everyone she passed elicited more smiles, which heightened her mood even more. She hadn't realized how much weight she'd been carrying until after confessing. Getting the truth out felt good. The reprimand seemed a small price to pay.

She approached the same sitting area where she'd spent time with Singh and Harley earlier today, finding Bryce pacing at the entrance.

"Hey!" she called out cheerfully.

Bryce turned to her and crossed his arms. The hardness of his features stopped her short.

"I suspended Sergeant Banks," he said.

She exhaled and deflated at the same time. "Oh, thank goodness."

"Letta, what did you do?" he asked with severity.

Ortega blinked, taking in the downturn of his face. "I know you told me not to say anything, but I had to do the right thing."

"Damn it, Letta. You shouldn't have done that."

"Look, I appreciate you looking out for me, but I can handle the repercussions."

He rubbed his brow and shook his head. She shifted her feet. She'd never seen him like this. *What's he so upset about?*

"What Banks did was wrong," she said through the tense silence.

"Yes, he's an asshole," Bryce finally replied with an unexpected exasperation. "But you shouldn't have said anything."

"I told you I can handle—"

"That's not it. There is more at stake and you siding with that boy won't help."

"I didn't side with the boy. I just reported the truth about what Banks did."

"You shouldn't have done it," he snapped. "There are things you don't know about."

She pulled back. "If you're talking about the database for the perantium emitter, everyone knows about that. I don't see what Banks has to—"

Bryce flipped up his palms. "Forget it. What's done is done."

"I'm sorry, alright?" She took a step toward him. "I just did what I thought was right. I had no idea you'd be so upset about it."

"Of course I'm upset. I told you not to say anything and you did it anyway. You should have trusted me."

The pit of her stomach shriveled as she realized why he was mad. "Sorry. I didn't think about it like that."

He waved her off with a sharp flick. "Well, like I said. What's done is done. Can't undo it now."

He turned away and stormed off. Her heart leapt after him, but her feet stayed put. Her mouth hung open in stunned disbelief as she tried to process what had just happened. She'd expected some of her crewmates to be pissed, but not him.

A part of her wanted to rebel against his anger, but another part was crushed. She so wished for him to be the one. Until now, she was sure he had been.

Don't be stupid. She was overthinking it. One fight didn't change how much she loved him. Knowing him, they'd make up soon.

31
Betrayed

The white ceramic ball rocketed to the center of the blue-felted table and cracked into the colored ones. Jori analyzed all sixteen balls as they spread out. A solid red one dropped into the hole at the side, which Hapker called a pocket. According to the rules, the solid balls were now his and he must hit them all into the pockets.

Easy. He leaned over the table, holding his stick the way Hapker had shown him. Lining up the white ball so it hit the blue one just right required only a little geometry. A quick jerk, and the rubber tip of his stick, or cue, struck the ceramic ball and sent the blue one off at a thirty-five-degree angle into the corner pocket.

"You sure he should have that stick?" his new guard asked, eliciting a grunt from another officer. Sergeant Creston's blond hair and pretty face contrasted with the absent Sergeant Banks' ugly head, but her disposition was similar.

"He's fine, Chesa," Hapker replied.

Calling Sergeant Creston by her informal name indicated how much he liked her. This alone had made Jori eager to meet her. He expected her to be cheerful like Hapker and sweet like his mother. She was neither. Her aura reminded him of a red-hot pepper people back home enjoyed, only laced with more acid.

She wagged her head, making a pfft sound.

Hapker quirked his brow at her but said nothing. Jori shot him a glower, then aimed for the purple ball. If he concentrated hard enough, her sour emotions wouldn't bother him.

Thwack! The balls clashed. The purple one banked off the edge and soared into the side pocket.

Hapker whistled. "You said you never played this before."

"I haven't, but it's like another game I used to play with—" He shoved the memories of his brother aside. A lump remained in his throat as he shot a yellow ball, then a green one in.

The sensation wafting off Hapker signified he'd caught onto the sensitive topic, but took Jori's lead and ignored it. He quirked his lips, making them more crooked than usual. "Will I get a turn?" he asked in a jesting tone.

Jori allowed a small smile, then aimed for the maroon ball.

"What do you expect from a MEGA?" Chesa muttered.

Hapker's mouth tilted the other way. "Keep your comments to yourself, Sergeant."

"Yes, Sir," she said with fake seriousness.

Jori gripped his cue and glowered. Her blue eyes sharpened onto him, and her upper lip curled. It twisted into a snarl when Hapker's attention returned to the game table.

Jori ground his teeth. *What the hell does he see in her?*

He struck the white ball harder than intended, making it crash into the orange one. It still went in.

Hapker tried a joke, but it seemed forced. He didn't have an ability to sense emotions, but undoubtedly felt the tension Chesa caused. He rested his hand on Jori's shoulder. "It's alright," he whispered. "Just ignore her."

Jori wanted to snap at him. Why was he giving him a warning and not her? She was the one making snotty comments.

Rather than argue, he did his best to pretend she wasn't there. He couldn't hear what she mumbled to the other guards, but the derision in her voice told him enough.

He finished the game in short order. When Hapker congratulated him, Jori's usual sense of pride didn't come.

Chesa and the others chuckled.

"Is something funny?" Hapker asked with an edge.

"Oh, nothing, Commander," Chesa said. "Just a joke between comrades."

Jori threw her a dark look. She gave it back as soon as Hapker turned away.

"Come on." Hapker stretched his arm over Jori's shoulder. "Let's play something else."

Hapker described the other games as they wandered around the recreation room. Darts might be fun, but the point of coming here instead of the gym was to appear less violent while everyone calmed down from the incident with Banks. Jori hated catering to this nonsense. Others could use the holo-program or throw darts. Yet when he did it, he was a monster. *Stupid Cooperative chimas.*

"How about this one?" Hapker asked. "It's called candlepins."

Jori eyed the aisle leading to a cluster of cylinders set in a recess. "How does it work?"

Hapker held up a ball larger than his palm. "Roll this into the pins. The more you knock over, the greater your score."

"Seems easy."

Hapker's eyes twinkled. "Not if I put the setting on *expert*."

"What will that do?"

"It'll spread the pins out and make them move at random."

Jori considered the challenge and smiled.

"Just pretend those pins are people," Chesa said with snark, "and you got this, kid."

Jori's cheeks heated.

Hapker threw her a scathing look. "Sergeant, can I have a word?"

"Of course, Commander."

They stepped aside. Jori fumed and hoped Hapker would reprimand her the way he'd done with others who harassed him.

Chesa stood in a haughty, attentive stance. Hapker expelled a frustrated sigh and said something. She responded by setting her hands on her hips and speaking in a condescending tone. Hapker rubbed his brow, then made a pleading gesture with his arms. She threw up her palms in return. Her argumentative voice carried, but not enough for Jori to catch the words.

Hapker scowled. Whatever he said caused her lips to turn white. She spoke again, this time bringing about guilt in Hapker's emotions.

Jori edged closer as Hapker's remorse grew.

"—believe this is part of your job," she said. "He supposedly saved you and so you feel obligated."

Jori's emotions took a tumble. *Is he really only helping me because he feels obligated?*

Hapker sighed. "Come on, Chesa. I can't leave him with some stranger who doesn't know him like I do."

"I don't see why not. He was a stranger when you took him in the first time. Now he's a criminal and you're still taking care of him."

Hapker ran the other down to his chin. "Listen. It's only for a short while."

Jori's entire body constricted as though he were being bound and shoved into a small box. "What do you mean, *only for a short while?*"

Hapker's eyes bulged. Chesa crossed her arms and smirked.

The clash of Hapker's self-reproach with her smugness made Jori stagger. Now the guilty feelings made sense. "What do you mean?" he shouted.

Hapker reached out to him. "Jori, I didn't mean it like that. I just meant this situation."

"This situation that *you* put me in?" The air pressed around him. He couldn't breathe. His peripheral vision blurred and all he saw before him was betrayal.

"I'm sorry. You know I am," Hapker said in a pleading tone. "I only wanted to help you."

"Yeah, help me, then abandon me, you mean. Leave me to these blackbeasts who are no better than my father."

Hapker approached. Jori backed up. "Stay away from me."

"Come on, Jori. I'm sorry. I didn't mean it that way."

Hapker's soft and desperate words didn't quell the storm in Jori's head. It both hurt and angered him that all his sacrifice had meant nothing. He'd lost everyone he'd ever cared about to help this man. The commander had been the only one who made him want to keep going. Now he didn't even have that.

Hapker reached out to take his shoulder. "I'm sorry."

Jori jerked away. "Leave me alone!"

"Jori, I—"

"This is your fault! I never should have let you bring me to this horrible place."

"Jori—"

Jori threw his whole body into stomping his foot. "I said, leave me alone!" His throat ripped out the words as tears spewed from his eyes.

"Alright," Hapker replied with reluctance laced through his tone.

His hurt gave Jori vindication.

"I'll leave you for a bit. Then we'll talk." Hapker pressed the comm behind his ear. "Lieutenant Gresher? Would you mind—"

"Forget it." Jori's jaw quivered as he struggled to pull back the flood. "Take me to my prison cell," he said to the guards.

Chesa's chin pushed out. "Of course."

Her emotions made his insides squirm, but he allowed her and the guards to escort him out. Hapker's lifeforce weakened as they separated. That was fine. Jori couldn't stand his pity anyway.

Chesa's growing self-satisfaction was no better. Every step away from the commander heightened the sensations coming from her and made him feel more alone.

Betrayed. Abandoned. An outcast in a hostile world.

*****

A black abyss swirled behind Jori's eyes. A deep ache throbbed in his head. He sweated under the blankets but embraced the sweltering darkness.

Sleep teased him as he clutched his mother's necklace. Vague images floated around in his mind. None of his thoughts stuck. He couldn't even create the mental void that kept his emotions at bay.

"Open it," a voice said, disturbing Jori's peace. "And activate the privacy settings."

No sensations accompanied the newcomer, as usual, which nettled Jori more. He threw the covers off and sat up. A curse nearly flew, but a wave of dizziness stifled it. *Chusho*. Dehydration from the loss of too many tears had made him weak.

Gottfried swept in. "Oh my. I heard what happened. I'm so sorry, young one. You must be so disappointed."

Although the words sounded sincere, Jori grated at not being able to tell for sure. Gottfried attempted to pull him into a hug, but Jori pulled back.

"You still don't trust me," Gottfried said. "After everything you've been through, I understand. But maybe I have something here to help you change your mind about me."

Jori frowned.

Gottfried brought out his tablet. For once, his smile seemed genuine. "How would you like to contact Sensei Jeruko?"

Jori's breath hitched. He regarded the man with pure gratitude.

"I'm sorry it took so long to get back to you about this," Gottfried continued, "but I had to wait until we were in range of a communication hub. Let's hope your friend is near one too so you can receive a quick reply."

Jori swallowed. He slowly reached for the tablet, hardly believing this was real. His hand shook as he entered the private address Sensei Jeruko had set up.

He depressed the record button and wet his mouth. "Sensei. I need your help. Things aren't going as well as the commander promised…"

32
Nightmare

Darkness. This corridor shouldn't be so full of shadows. Jori's footsteps echoed despite his cautious movements. His heartbeat pulsated in his ears. One step for every six beats.

No one was around. Normally, senshi warriors traversed this hall. Their dour faces and black uniforms would enhance the murkiness of the dark metallic walls and tread-worn floors. But like the rest of the ship, a hollow emptiness consumed this place.

Urgency filled him. He must find his brother before it was too late.

As he progressed, a sense of familiarity ghosted through him. He'd searched through these same gloomy halls before. He should know what awaited, but his mind kept slipping. All he could do was keep going.

He passed through an entrance. A cold, dark void pressed around him. He blinked until little pinpoints of light coalesced. As the room brightened, the controls of the cloaking and shielding machines became clear. Still no people.

Fear gripped him by the throat. He forced one foot in front of the other and made his way to the dim corner.

"Is anyone here?"

A stifled noise pricked his ears and sent a chill down his spine.

"Hello?"

He rounded the machinery. A towering figure stopped him short. It had its back to him, but he'd recognize those broad shoulders anywhere.

"Father?"

The figure turned. Jori's heart clenched.

The man's eyes burned with a hatred that bored into his soul. He snarled like a raging blackbeast. "You!"

Jori's feet refused to move. His father's hand rose. A glint of light reflected from the blade of his dagger.

Jori managed a step backward, but it was too late to run.

The jagged knife came down. His arms flew up to deflect it. A stinging pain struck his forearm. He flailed, hitting nothing. Another stab. Everything blurred. He struggled to fend off his attacker, but it was like fighting a phantom.

Father's eyes blackened with madness, compounding Jori's agony like a crippling electrical current.

"Jori?" The new voice muffled as though spoken through a wall.

Jori's panic prevented recognition. He fought off his father's dagger, swinging with furious desperation.

"Jori, stop!" The alarm in the stranger's tone heightened his terror. "Stop! It's me!"

His knuckles smashed into something hard. He punched again. The vision of his father skidded, almost like a distorted video.

He had no time to contemplate it as another face appeared. They gripped his shoulder, making him scream. More pinches dug into his body. An arm wrapped around his neck. Something plummeted into his gut, ejecting the air from his lungs.

He roared. A quick twist and he broke from the grip and crashed to the floor. His vision blurred. He fluttered his eyes. Strange faces appeared. His chest tightened with renewed panic. *What the hell is going on?*

A fist dove for his face. He ducked and kicked out at the same time.

"Damn you!" They kicked back, their boot cracking into Jori's temple.

A burst of white eclipsed his sight as he dropped. Hands grasped his arms and legs. He fought but they held him firm. He hyperventilated as either sweat, blood, or both poured down his face.

Someone twisted him around and clamped cold metal onto his wrists. That same person jabbed their elbow into his spine. He gritted his teeth and struggled. The futility of it made him stop.

He forced his breathing to even out as he attempted to gain his bearings. A blanket. No, a sheet. They pressed him onto a bed—his bed, but not the one at home. He couldn't see the attackers at this angle but sensed his Cooperative guards.

Someone lay sprawled on the floor. Blood splattered his face, but his lopsided mouth gave Jori pause.

He gasped as realization slapped him back to reality. He was on the *Defender*. If he hadn't been fighting his father, who then?

Hapker! His body flushed with a prickling freeze. He desperately reached out his senses to check Hapker, but his own emotions pressed around him.

Before he could detect the man's lifeforce, the officer shoved his arm up, sending a sharp pain through his shoulder. A profusion of apologies formed on Jori's lips, but the guard pushed him down hard enough to keep him from taking in air.

"You little shit," a man said. "I knew you'd do something like this."

"No!" Jori managed. A different hurt welled up inside him. He forced in a shallow breath. "It was an accident."

He tried to focus on Hapker but couldn't concentrate through his strangling fear. "Please? Is he alright?" His voice was barely audible.

"Shut up," Corporal Lengen said. "Even in your sleep, you're a menace."

Lengen jerked Jori to his feet. Jori glanced over to check on Hapker, but the other guards blocked his view. The corporal let go of his arm and grabbed the back of his neck instead.

Tears rolled down Jori's face. His chin quivered and his insides churned like ungreased ball bearings. *What have I done?*

Medics rushed in. Hapker groaned. They lifted him unsteadily to his feet and walked him out.

Lengen pinched him in a vice grip that stung his neck muscles, then pushed him forward. They moved briskly down the hall, almost racing after the medics. Jori stumbled from the momentum. He kept extending his ability, but every jarring movement from Lengen pulled him back within himself.

The medics entered the conveyor. Jori attempted to get a sense of Hapker's lifeforce again but failed. The doors slid shut, as though cutting him off forever.

His dread swirled with a hurricane of emotions as they waited for the car to return. The question of where they were taking him disintegrated when he realized it didn't matter. He deserved whatever came.

The conveyor doors opened, revealing a cold, empty space. Lengen shoved him inside. Jori stumbled and hit the back wall. Before he could right himself, the corporal reached out to grab him again.

Sergeant Ortega shouldered in. "I'll handle this, Corporal."

Lengen's lip curled. "Going against your own team? Not surprising."

"What Banks did was wrong," she barked. Jori couldn't see through her sunglasses but imagined her sparking eyes. "If you keep pushing him around like that, I'll report you too."

Lengen jabbed his finger at Jori's face. "You saw what he did. How can you defend him?"

"He was having a nightmare!" Her tone inched up. "The commander tried to wake him. He probably thought he was still in the dreamworld."

Lengen huffed. "He was probably dreaming of murdering someone."

"It doesn't matter. You can't just push him around like that. We have a code of conduct to follow."

"Yes, Sergeant," Lengen replied in a strained, contemptuous tone.

"I'm only doing my job," Ortega replied with chagrin.

"Of course you are, *Sir*."

Ortega's shaded eyes deflected from his and turned onto Jori. An accusatory distaste emanated from her, as though this was his fault. He didn't have the strength to contest it. Nor was he sure he should. Lengen was right. He'd hurt his only friend. A new flood of tears broke out.

The guards escorted him out of the conveyor. Jori halted, surprised to be at the infirmary and not an airlock.

Admiral Belmont confronted him. "What in the hell happened here?"

Jori sniffled. He couldn't wipe the mucus with his hands behind his back, so he left it to drip. "It was an accident. I had a bad dream."

Belmont's forehead drew into folds. "A bad dream? You put someone in the medical bay!"

"I didn't mean to." Jori's voice came out weak. "Is Hapker alright?"

Belmont jutted his chin and pressed his mouth together into as much of a thin line as his fat bottom lip allowed. "You better hope so."

Jori swallowed the lump in his throat and looked down at the floor. "I'm sorry."

Doctor Donnel leaned forward, her head cocked. "Are you?"

"This is the violence we feared," Belmont said.

Jori's eyes burned. He couldn't hold back the tears. His chin quivered and his face flushed. "It was an accident. I swear. I would never purposely hurt Hapker Not ever."

"And why is that?" the doctor asked, her voice surprisingly soft.

"Because he's my friend."

Doctor Donnel shifted her stance. "Friend? Hmm. Can you tell me why?"

Jori replayed all the moments he'd spent with Hapker. He could say Hapker was kind, understanding, helpful, and a slew of other positive things. But those sounded rather lame and didn't convey what he felt. He swallowed hard, realizing the one thing he'd appreciated from the beginning had just been shattered by his actions.

"I trust him," he croaked.

"And look where that trust got him," the admiral replied.

Jori wanted to apologize again, but a silent sob gripped his throat.

*****

Gottfried Krause hugged the wall as the space before the admiral's desk shrunk. Corporal Lengen entered first, then Sergeant Ortega. Doctor Donnel followed in last, her stoic demeanor countered by her concern.

Gottfried absorbed the overwhelming hostility permeating the room, letting it fill his veins with the excitement of a plan coming to fruition. No way would the Cooperative accept the boy now. And with what Jori was about to learn regarding his brother and

Jeruko, he'd realize he had nowhere else to go except to MEGA-Man.

Commander Hapker arrived last. Although Gottfried didn't care for how much influence this man had on the young prince, he admired how self-assurance radiated off him.

Admiral Belmont folded his hands. "Commander, you start."

Commander Hapker pulled his shoulders back. "Jori was having a nightmare. I'm sure you all know how dream and reality can intermingle. I should've known better than to wake him like that."

"So it was truly an accident?" Doctor Donnel asked.

"Yes."

Belmont fixed his gaze on the other officers. "What did you see?"

"That boy was hitting the commander," Corporal Lengen said. "When we tried to stop him, he fought us too. We have the marks to prove it, Sir."

Sergeant Ortega firmed her jaw. "I saw what had transpired before that, Sir."

A heat rose from Gottfried's core. Damn this woman for taking the boy's side again. If he didn't do something about her soon, she'd mess up all his plans.

"And?" Belmont asked.

She cleared her throat. "The boy thrashed in his sleep, like he'd been having a nightmare."

"Could he have been pretending?"

Ortega hesitated. "I doubt it, Admiral. It looked real."

"Traitor," Corporal Lengen mumbled.

The sergeant ignored him, but her emotions swirled with guilt. Gottfried analyzed it. She didn't want to side with the boy but seemed obligated to be honest. Why, though? What compelled her to put the truth above her hate and over her allegiance to her peers?

Belmont darkened. Gottfried wavered between satisfaction that someone had countered the admiral's prejudices once again, and annoyance that the prince had another Cooperative officer sympathizing with him.

"I've known Jori to have intense nightmares before," Hapker said.

The admiral shot him a look, then faced the psychiatrist. "Doctor. What do you think?"

She hesitated. Her eyebrows squished together. "It sounds like he had a terrible dream and that he didn't intend to hurt anyone."

Belmont's emotions exploded as he lurched forward. "You seriously believe the boy did this on accident?"

The commander radiated indignation, but he kept it from showing.

"He expressed genuine regret and shame afterward," Doctor Donnel said.

The admiral huffed. "Because he got caught."

She shook her head. "He'd have to be one hell of an actor to be so convincing."

"Since when did we stop believing he's capable of deceit?"

"Jori doesn't lie," Hapker interjected.

"I'm fairly certain it was real," Doctor Donnel said. "Between him and the commander, I'm quite convinced they're *both* telling the truth."

The admiral directed his glower at Gottfried. The doctor and the officers fidgeted, knowing very well that he could probe them using his extraho ability.

Gottfried considered lying. However, if any of these people told Jori about it, their trust would crumble. "She's right."

Belmont's frown deepened. "You had better be sure of your opinion, Doctor. If you're saying it was an accident, then I have no choice but to let a psychopath on the loose."

The commander turned red. "Jori is not a psychopath."

Doctor Donnel pursed her lips at the admiral. "The correct terminology is ASPD, and I no longer believe that's the appropriate diagnosis. If anything, it's PTSD—something just about every PG-Force officer on this ship has a touch of."

Gottfried smiled inwardly as Belmont's emotions swirled into a storm. Although his plans hit a bump, nothing pleased him more than to see the insufferable man not get his way.

"One violent incident and you change your mind?" the admiral asked.

The doctor straightened her shoulders and kept her eyes fixed to his. "I witnessed his remorse and his raw emotions. He has sympathy, which means he doesn't have ASPD tendencies."

Belmont spoke but she ran over his words. "My findings were preliminary and based on *two* meetings. I've revaluated his records and reviewed our conversations and concluded the reason he was so standoffish was because he didn't trust me."

Her emotions blasted Gottfried like a gust of wind. He suppressed the urge to shudder as another ordinary, yet influential, person defended the boy. This couldn't go on. He must stop this. He needed to up his game and do it soon.

It wouldn't be easy, but accidents happened all the time on this ship. He'd think of something.

33
Forgiveness

J.D. Hapker should have felt more serene in this isolated sitting area. The scenic displays and real flowering plants reminded him of his mother's office in the city back home. Soft musical notes enhanced with sounds of wildlife matched the music she had played, filling him with nostalgia. The modified temperatures and false breeze complemented their corresponding nature scenes. The padded chairs and couches were different colors and styles than hers, but invited the same comfort.

In his youth, he'd clicked through her collection of scenery, his eyes glued to the screen with each new vista. As a tour guide, she knew all the great places to travel both on-world and off. If she wasn't busy, she'd tell him about them. Her voice had conveyed a wonder that inspired his dreams to leave home and become a part of something grander.

Sometimes he wished he hadn't. The Cooperative had been one disappointment after another. First when he'd gotten into trouble with the PG-Force. Then with how Jori had been treated on the *Odyssey*. And now here.

The rainy scene he selected matched his gloomy mood and permeated his voice. "You should have seen it, Rik," he said to Lieutenant Gresher over the backdrop of a thundering shower. "Yeah, Doctor Donnel defended what Jori had done, but I still can't get past that she'd initially considered him a sociopath."

"Her mistake makes some sense, though," Gresher replied with an apologetic tilt to his eyes. "Jori has a way of masking his emotions."

Gresher's lack of a smile depressed Hapker even more. "I doubt she made it because of that. Haven't you noticed how much everyone wants him to fail? The Cooperative is supposed to be enlightened, but it seems people here, including the admiral, can't let go of their bigotry. Jori deserves better."

"I agree on all counts. But not everybody is like you and me."

"They should be. Why else would the Cooperative include the sentiments of acceptance in their guiding principles?"

"They established those with good intentions," Gresher said. "I believe most people *want* to uphold them, but not everyone has the mentality to do it. Humanity has always had a disconnect between what they know they *should* do and what they *actually* do. It's our fatal flaw."

Hapker concurred, but not just about humanity—about himself. He shouldn't have hesitated in doing right by Jori. Yet he'd failed miserably. Jori no longer trusted him because he'd let his doubts about the Cooperative show through.

It wasn't the broken trust that hurt Hapker the most. Every time he thought about how alone Jori must feel, guilt writhed through his guts like maggots in a corpse.

"So what do we do?" Hapker asked. "If so many of us are this flawed, how can we help them see differently? Show them Jori isn't a Tredon stereotype?"

"You're looking at this from too dark of a corner."

Hapker frowned, not understanding.

"Stop looking at the negatives," Gresher said. "Let's look at the positives." He held up a fist and raised his fingers one by one. "Captain Arden agrees with you. I agree with you. Corporal Harley and Sergeant Ortega spoke up on Jori's behalf. And Doctor Donnel readjusted her viewpoint."

Realization made Hapker blink, but he still wasn't convinced. "You're right, but Jori shouldn't have to work so hard to change their minds."

"Maybe it will be different after he's exonerated."

"You really believe that'll happen?"

"Yes."

Hapker sighed. "Well, your faith is stronger than mine. You should've seen how upset the admiral was that the doctor didn't give the diagnosis he wanted."

Gresher smiled for the first time since they'd met here. "Again, you're looking at this all wrong. If Admiral Belmont continues to hold a negative opinion despite the evidence, that makes *him* look bad, not Jori. Think about it. He has nothing to base his prejudice on. Not a single thing."

"Except what Jori did to me," Hapker said. "Don't misunderstand. The fault lies entirely with me. I'm afraid most people won't see it that way, though."

"Of course they will. PTSD is well documented. Even those who haven't experienced the power of trauma-induced nightmares can't refute their reality."

Hapker exhaled slowly. "Thanks, Rik. You're right. I just need to adjust my perspective."

"Sure thing. Whatever I can do." Gresher gave a small but hope-inspiring smile.

Hapker rose from the overly soft couch and stretched, his body much lighter now.

"You heading back over?" Gresher asked.

"Yeah. I want to be there when Jori wakes so I can apologize for what I said." Hapker doubted Jori wanted to talk to him, but he had to try.

"He'll understand."

"Ever the optimist." Hapker clapped Gresher on the shoulder and left. His steps seemed almost weightless now. He and Jori would get through this. *Whatever it takes.*

*****

Jori took the cup of water from the fabricor. The liquid touched his tongue and sent a revitalizing tingle down his throat. He gulped it all and embraced the smooth, refreshing taste. If he concentrated on it hard enough, all the heavy emotions lurking on the fringes stayed where they were.

He plopped back onto the bed and avoided looking at the empty chairs in his prison. He hadn't expected anyone to be here when he awoke anyway. Not after what he'd done.

He sat motionless and concentrated on the functions of his body. His heart thumped steadily, matching his even breaths. The rhythm soothed him, and each intake of air expanded the void he'd created.

A familiar sensation prodded through his sensing ability. He clutched the nothingness and built a mental wall to keep it out.

When it came closer, his wall crumbled. Jori's throat tightened at the sturdiness and warmth of Hapker's lifeforce.

What's he doing here?

He gulped the saliva that filled his mouth and examined the man's essence. It held no anger, nor a hint of condemnation. *He must be holding back.*

The main entrance swished open. Jori braced himself for a torrid rebuke as the commander ordered the guards to let him in. They questioned, then warned him, but he remained firm.

Hapker entered with a caution borne of concern rather than fear. Jori kept his head down, not daring to meet his eyes. A warm hand rested on his shoulder, making him flinch.

Hapker knelt to Jori's level. "Hey. How are you doing?"

Jori lifted his chin, then glanced away from the man's softness.

"I'm sorry," he managed to say despite the sudden dryness in his mouth.

"I know. You had a bad dream. I should've known better than to wake you like that."

Although it was true Jori hadn't hurt him on purpose, shame still filled him. "I don't blame you for not wanting to take care of me."

Hapker squeezed his shoulder, emitting emotions that spread warmth over Jori's entire body like a soft blanket. "When I said that to Chesa, it wasn't because I planned on giving up on you."

"What then?"

Hapker sighed.

A spark ignited through Jori's temper. "What?" he snapped. "I can sense that you're hiding something."

Hapker ran his hand down his face and stroked his chin. "It's complicated."

Jori huffed.

"Everything that's happened these past several months," Hapker said, "has shaken me."

Jori's throat hardened. "Because of me."

"Not in the way you think." Hapker sat beside Jori and put his arm over his shoulder. "I joined the Cooperative to serve a higher purpose and lately I'm finding that they're not what they've promised."

Jori's brows twitched with uncertainty.

"I'm disappointed," Hapker continued. "Not just in them, but in myself. I had all these expectations and they've fallen short at every turn. I'm not sure whether to declare myself a fool or be angry that they deceived me."

"Because of me?" Jori repeated, asking this time.

Hapker's eyes penetrated his, but in a way that made Jori feel secure. "Their treatment of you has rattled me. If they don't see you for the good person you are, I will do what I promised and continue to look after you. Never doubt that. I'm still sad about it, though. Not because I wouldn't want to leave them, but because they've let me down. Does that make sense?"

Jori examined the emotions that accompanied the man's words and found no hint of deceit. And what he'd said resonated. He'd felt something similar when he went against his father to save the Cooperative officers. It had been the right thing to do, but it meant losing people he cared about. Hapker might not be giving up a mother, brother, or father-like mentor, but he'd lose things that were important to him.

"I'm sorry," Jori said. "I should've thought of that."

Hapker hugged him close. "It's not your burden to bear. You've sacrificed more than I in all this. It's not right and it's not fair. But if I had to do it all again, I wouldn't change helping you."

"Me either," Jori replied and meant it. "Except maybe do the same things without having the same consequences."

Hapker grunted in agreement. "I'd probably change how I guilted you into rescuing me and my crew. If you hadn't saved us, you wouldn't be in this predicament."

"I don't regret that," Jori said. "If I hadn't helped you, I would have helped someone else somewhere down the road. My father would've ended up killing me anyway. You—Captain Arden and the doctors—saved me."

"Out of the frying pan and into the fire," Hapker replied.

Jori cocked his head.

"Basically, you're alive but no better off. That will change, though. One way or the other."

He pulled Jori close. Jori closed his eyes and sank into his warmth.

"Although we're not supposed to contact you-know-who," Hapker whispered, "we'll find a way. I'll help you however I can."

Jori straightened. Whether in surprise or remembrance, he wasn't sure. "Gottfried has already allowed me."

Hapker raised an eyebrow. "That's great, but…"

"I know," Jori said. "I don't trust him either, but I couldn't let the opportunity slip by."

"No. I suppose not, but I'm worried there are strings attached."

"Probably, but I thought you didn't want…"

Hapker embraced him, not letting him complete his thought about abandonment. It spilled out anyway, but as tears. He wasn't alone after all.

34
Darkness

If not for the lighting, the narrow meandering halls would've made Carletta Ortega feel right at home. The way voices echoed, the extra moisture, and the stagnant air resembled the caves she'd lived in as a youth. She used to love exploring the caverns. There were places her parents had told her not to go, but she'd do it anyway. The challenge of climbing or descending into deep spaces, squeezing through small crevasses, or swimming through underground rivers was too much of an adventure to pass up.

A part of her missed home. She'd never return to a skyless lifestyle, though. Bypassing the conveyor to walk through the subdued lower decks was enough to satisfy her nostalgia.

It also gave her time to think. Watching the boy and the commander make amends shifted her perspective. Before, she'd assumed that Jori being the son of a monster made him one too. But now she understood what it meant for him to be the son of a monster. The things he must've seen and endured caused her insides to squirm. The way the commander comforted him changed her mind about him as well. He wasn't siding with the enemy. He sympathized with a child who'd been through hell.

More than ever, she was convinced that reporting Banks had been the right thing to do. She just needed to explain her reasons to Bryce. He'd understand.

She stopped in a low traffic corridor where Bryce would come once his shift guarding the database ended. By seeing him in person rather than leaving a vid message, he'd be more apt to hear her perspective.

So why did her insides feel like a whirlpool?

She adjusted the chafing of her uniform for the hundredth time and paced. When footsteps finally echoed near, her breath hitched. Her nerves jittered as she waited with an uncertain smile.

Two soldiers appeared and her shoulders fell. She opened her mouth to greet them only to get tongue tied by the blue-eyed man. Her heartrate spiked as he passed, making her flush. *Damn.* Why did it seem those eyes bored into her?

After they'd moved on, the temperature seemed to return to normal. She peeked around the opposite corner hoping to see Bryce. *Where the hell is he?* Disappointment turned into anticipation and back again as she resumed pacing.

She reached the corner once more and took a glance. Whack! A painful blow struck the back of her head, blindsiding her. She pitched forward. Her chin struck the floor and she bit her tongue. Blood pooled in her mouth. She gasped as a rough, black fabric was pulled over her eyes.

Someone grabbed her hand and pinned it behind her, preventing her from removing the blindfold. Her heart danced into a frenzy. She cried out, only to have her yell cut short by another blow to the head. Spots dazzled through the pitch. She struggled as fists pummeled her body. Her ears caught grunts and heavy breathing, but she couldn't tell who made them.

"Stop!" She gasped for air. A strike to her temple knocked her senseless. A moan escaped her lips as her mind clawed for consciousness. Wholly blind, reality collapsed around her until nothing remained.

*****

Carletta Ortega floated through an abyss. Something. Nothing. A brush of sensation, then nothing again. *What?* An urgency. A stabbing headache made her jerk. Her head hung back. She tried to lift it, but the movement sent a spike of pain that shot down through her spine and to all her extremities.

The sultry air clung to her throat and smothered her body. Somewhere beyond the blackness, machines hummed. *Where am I?*

Something jostled her arms and legs and realization struck her. At least two people carried her. One had her arms and the other her feet. She still couldn't see. Whatever they'd put over her head blocked all light. Her body tensed, then she yanked, wrenched, and kicked with all her might. Her captors tightened their grips. Their deep grunts suggested they were male and there were three of them.

A faint glow glinted through the cloth. She made out the shape of the one carrying her feet. He had a short and stocky torso and a head shaped like a block. It wasn't Banks, though. The image of the soldier with the square jaw and ice-blue eyes popped into her mind, triggering a flooding panic.

"Let go of me! You sons of bitches!" She thrashed her body and roared. A hand lost its grip on her leg and so she kicked. A thump followed by a guttural oof indicated she'd done some damage. She flung her foot over and twisted her hips. The front of her ankle slammed into the man who held onto her other leg. His grip slipped and now both were free.

With both feet on the floor, she pushed off and spun. The person holding her arms lost his hold. She dropped but didn't stay down. She lunged. The top of her head struck armor. He was either a guard or a soldier. Her neck bones protested from the impact, but the adrenaline surging through her veins dispelled the pain.

A hand grasped her upper arm. She jerked out of the hold and flung herself away. Her back smacked the wall. She rebounded off it and bounded in a direction she hoped was escape. Bootsteps clomped after her. She tried ripping off the cover over her head, but her shaking hands made it difficult. Somehow, she turned a corner at the right time.

Hoping this next hall was longer, she broke into a sprint. She removed the covering and glanced over her shoulder. Nothing. Her pursuers were gone. She rounded another corner and ran into someone.

Panic seized her as she bounced back. A split second later, recognition flooded through her. "Bryce!" She sprang to her feet. "I've been attacked!"

His expression was pure fury. "What the hell, Letta!"

She flinched. She'd expected him to be angry at whoever did the attacking, but he directed his fiery eyes at her.

She pointed behind her. "At least three men ambushed me. I didn't get a chance to see who they were."

"I told you this would happen!"

She pulled back. "What?"

"This!" He flicked his hand at her face. "You snitched on one of your own and now they're teaching you a lesson."

Her jaw dropped. She couldn't believe this. "Teaching me a lesson? Are you fucking kidding me right now? This isn't some petty squabble. They attacked me and were carrying me to who knows where to do who knows what."

"Damn it, Letta! This is *your* fault." He stepped toward her. The inferno in his expression made her step back.

"Hey!" someone from down the hall called out.

Ortega glanced over Bryce's shoulder. Seeing Sergeant Fenyvesi should've been a relief, but Bryce left her on shaky ground.

Feny marched up, the crease in her brow deepening with every footfall. "What the hell happened? Are you okay?"

Ortega wiped the wetness from under her nose. Blood, and lots of it. "At least three men attacked me."

"Who?"

"I don't know. They put something over my head."

"Oh, fuck!" Feny shot Bryce a scowl. "Did you do this?"

Bryce's brows shot up. "What? No."

"Then what are you yelling at her for?"

Bryce raised his palms. "I'm not. I'm just upset at the situation."

Liar! He was angry with *her*, but she couldn't understand why. *What's wrong with him?*

Feny turned back to Ortega. "Where did this happen?"

Bryce's sudden change and Feny's concern helped Ortega calm. A tingling sensation vibrated through her body as the adrenaline wore off. She pointed behind her. "This way."

Feny stormed ahead with a determined expression. Bryce's features tightened but he followed. Ortega swallowed, unsure of what to think about his behavior—or herself for not wanting to smack him upside the head.

They reached an intersection and turned right. Everything had happened so fast, but she was almost certain of the way. However, rounding the next curve made her heart stop. The waste incinerator loomed ahead. *They brought me here?*

While Feny searched the area, Ortega remained frozen in her spot as a bone-aching chill settled over her.

Feny returned. “Whoever they were, they’re gone. Did they say anything?”

“N-no,” Ortega said.

“They were probably trying to scare her,” Bryce replied.

Feny nodded. “Many people are upset.”

Ortega deflated with an agonizing sigh. “But I did nothing wrong!”

Feny’s features softened. “Come on. I’ll take you to sick bay.”

Bryce stayed behind to investigate while Feny led her away. After some distance, she spoke. “You’ve got to be careful. Ratting out your peers is serious business, especially for us women. We have it hard enough as it is.”

“It shouldn’t be that way.”

“Nope, but it is.” Feny shared a look. “For what it’s worth, I think you did the right thing.”

“Really?”

“Yeah. That Banks is one big asshole. Someone’s got to put a leash on him or he’ll go ballistic, kill a bunch of folk, and call it justice.”

“He’s as bad as most Tredons.”

Feny let out a short laugh that had nothing to do with humor. “Yeah. Ironic, isn’t it? And the jerk can’t even see it.”

Ortega replayed the incident in her head. If all they’d intended to do was teach her a lesson, why not take her to a nearer secluded area?

She swallowed the dryness in her throat. “I think they were going to do more than just hurt me.”

“What do you mean?”

“I was in section C when they attacked,” Ortega said. “Yet they took me all the way to the waste incinerator.”

“Are you saying they wanted to kill you?”

“Maybe. I don’t know.”

“They probably just wanted to scare you.”

“Yeah. I guess so.” Ortega wasn’t convinced and the creases in Feny’s forehead indicated she wasn’t either.

Killing her for telling seemed beyond excessive, but she couldn’t shake the feeling that she’d barely escaped death.

35
Dinner

J.D. Hapker rubbed his chin as his nerves jittered.

Jori jumped over three of his red pieces, making them disappear from the board. "Don't worry. I'll be respectful."

"I know," Hapker said. He wasn't worried about Jori acting out. His mood was too subdued, and a different concern altogether.

He was more nervous about Chesa. She'd apologized profusely, stating that she didn't mean to act like that. She'd been so sincere, and he remembered the woman she used to be. Giving her the benefit of the doubt seemed the right thing but now he second-guessed himself.

He tapped a flat, cylindrical piece and moved it without thinking. One side of Jori's face quirked as he took his turn, eliminating a king and soldier.

Hapker rubbed his jaw and sighed. "Sorry. My mind is elsewhere."

"That's alright," Jori said. "She's almost here anyway."

Hapker's foot stilled. The tension in his shoulders loosened, but the tightness in his gut remained.

The main door opened just as they switched off the virtual game. Hapker sprang to his feet and met Chesa at the entrance with a grin. "Come in, beautiful," he said as the guard tapped in the door code.

The dimples in her cheeks deepened as she smiled back. When she glanced at Jori, her expression flattened. Hapker gave her an entreating look, and she swept in with forced pleasantness.

Great. Jori will see through that, but at least she's trying.

Jori removed the tray covers, revealing three steaming dishes. Hapker waved his hand over one. "I ordered your favorite, Andulan sausage."

She touched his cheek. "Thank you. It smells perfect."

Hapker beamed. He pulled out her chair. She demurely sat, her eyes twinkling at him but sparking when she looked at Jori.

The boy took a formal stance with his hands clasped behind him. Hapker indicated him with a sweep of his arm. "Chesa, this is Jori."

She dipped her head. Her smile was flat, but at least she tried.

"Jori, Chesa," Hapker finished.

"Hello," Jori said.

Hapker clapped him on the shoulder, hoping to ease the tension, then settled in his seat. Jori took the chair beside him. An awkward silence fell over them as they served their portions.

The pressure in the room seemed to increase as utensils scraped plates. The sounds of their chewing amplified to a grating obtrusiveness. Ideas for conversation starters ran through an assembly line in Hapker's head, only to be discarded because he worried either Jori or Chesa would turn the topic into one of contention.

"So, Jori," she said, rupturing the deafening quietude. "What do you like to do for fun besides playing board games?"

"Exercising."

"What kind of exercising?"

"Martial arts, obstacle courses, agility."

"So basically, anything to do with combat training." Her tone sounded surprised, but Hapker suspected an accusation lay underneath. "You should consider lower-level recreations. Children in the Cooperative play nice games."

Hapker stiffened. "It's not that he likes those things because they're violent. He enjoys the physical challenges."

"Oh. I know." She laid her hand on his arm. "I'm just saying he doesn't need those kinds of challenges here. It might send the wrong message."

Hapker scowled at her. She glanced away and cleared her throat.

Jori remained silent as he ate dolefully. Hapker had expected him to retort, but he still hadn't forgiven himself for the nightmare incident. Lately, he'd either been too quiet or too eager to please. As glad as Hapker was that he didn't react to Chesa's depreciating remarks, he wished he'd perk up.

Chesa asked Jori more questions. The boy answered with as few words as possible and didn't reciprocate.

"Hey." Hapker nudged him. "She's trying," he whispered.

Jori inclined his head. His eyes reflected understanding but lacked faith.

"Chesa," Hapker said. "Why don't you tell him about your homeworld."

She went on to describe the city she'd grown up in. With Hapker's prompting, she told them about her family.

"She had the warmest smile," Chesa said regarding her mother.

Hapker elbowed Jori.

The boy blinked. Hapker tipped his head to Chesa, hinting he should reply.

Jori cleared his throat. "Mine, too."

"So you *do* have a mother," she said.

"Yes."

"Really? I had no idea. Didn't you live on a warship?"

"Yes, I did."

She set her fork down. "And your mother lives there too?"

"Lived. She's been exiled."

"Oh, that's right. I heard. So when she was there, what did she do? What was her job?"

"She didn't do anything."

She touched her hand to her chest. "Oh yeah. I forgot. She must have lived in a harem then."

"Chesa…" Hapker said in a drawn-out warning tone.

Jori's face turned hot pink. "I don't want to talk about her anymore."

"Why ever not?"

The boy's eyes ignited with the intensity of a blowtorch. "Because I'll never see her again."

A pang pierced Hapker's chest. When Chesa opened her mouth to speak, he put his hand on her arm. "Let's talk about something else."

She flung her napkin onto her plate. "What's the point? It's not like he's listening."

"He's listening. He just needs to warm up to you, is all."

She pushed away from the table, her chair scraping the floor with a screech. "I can't do this. I'm not having a one-sided conversation with him."

Hapker's jaw tightened. "Come on, Chesa. Your questions aren't exactly geared toward learning more about him."

"Sure they are," she replied with a defensive bite.

Hapker pressed his lips. "You didn't forget about women in Tredon culture."

"Well, excuse me for wanting him to understand that the way his people treat us is unacceptable."

"He can learn that without being shamed." Hapker glowered. "You said you'd be nice."

"I'm trying," she replied with the same hot temper."

"Chesa," he said in what he hoped was a calmer tone. "Look at him. If he's not being responsive, it's because he's hurting. He doesn't need our judgment. He needs our kindness and understanding."

She crossed her arms and looked away. After a stretch of silence, she replied, "I really did come with good intentions, but I can't stand being here."

That's harsh. "Why not? Why is it so hard?"

"I don't know. It just is." She rose to leave. "I'm sorry. I can't do this right now."

Hapker blinked. She'd always had strong opinions about things, but not without an explanation.

She signaled the guards. Hapker didn't stop her as she rushed out. He ran his hand down his face and sighed.

"She doesn't like me," Jori said.

"I know. She seemed determined to make amends. I thought I could…" Hapker rubbed his temple. "This was a bad idea. I'm so sorry."

"You like her."

Hapker cupped his chin. Yes, he liked her a lot. Her confidence and boldness had attracted him from the start. And she was fun, always eager for an adventure. Plus, she was stunningly beautiful. Sometimes her headstrong attitude wore on him, but this seemed different—more forceful without any logic behind it.

"You should go talk to her."

Hapker's brows shot up. "Why do you say that?"

"I can tell you want to."

He considered it. "I do, but only so I can find out what's really wrong. She has no reason to dislike you."

"She doesn't have a reason to *like* me, either. No one does—except you and Lieutenant Gresher."

"It's just taking people time. Sergeant Ortega and Corporal Harley changed their minds." Hapker shook his head. "I wish Chesa would too."

"Maybe she will. It's alright if you go talk to her."

Hapker studied the boy's eyes. The sincerity they held touched him. He made up his mind and stood. "I'll do that. But again, only so I can find out what's wrong."

After exiting the cellblock, he activated his com. "Chesa, can I speak to you—privately?"

The comm was open but she didn't answer right away. "Fine," she replied at last. "I'll be in my quarters."

The walk through the ship rushed by in a blur. His anxiousness returned, making his stomach grumble. It intensified after he rang and she opened her door. The taut expression that twisted her eyes and mouth didn't bode well, but she let him in.

Hapker expanded his chest. "Hey."

"Hey," she said. "Come on in." She waved him to a chair at the small dining table and brought him a cup of coffee.

He smiled and thanked her. She undoubtedly made it the way he liked it, but it didn't appeal to him right now.

She sat across from him and folded her hands. "I'm sorry for being rude to him. I really didn't mean to."

He lifted his eyebrows, surprised at her apology.

"But," she continued, "every time I'm around him, I get so angry."

"Why? Where is this coming from?"

"Maybe it's because he's a child capable of killing. I can't get it out of my mind."

The hair on Hapker's arms stood on end. Something about the way she said it made him think of a parasite.

She huffed. "What's keeping him from turning on us?"

Hapker frowned at her exaggeration. "Jori wouldn't do that."

She threw up her hands. "How do you know?"

"Because I've been around him," he replied in the same exasperated tone.

"How can you not see it? He practices combat skills almost every single day. And if he's taken lives before, he can do it again."

"He acted in self-defense."

Chesa harrumphed. "What if it's another boy his age? Will he kill him in *self-defense*?"

"Of course not." Hapker scooted closer to her. "Forget about who his father is and consider what he's done to help our own people."

"Children are very impressionable, and he's been brought up with nothing but violence. How can you just assume he won't resort to the only thing he understands?"

"Jori hasn't been raised with nothing but violence. He spent the first few years of his life with his mother."

"In a harem," she said.

"He didn't understand what that was. All he knew was his mother's love."

"That doesn't mean he didn't also have bad influences."

"I'm not saying he hasn't. I'm saying he's not inherently violent. You've met him. You've seen it for himself. He hasn't given you any reason to worry about what he *might* do."

She massaged her brow.

He placed his hand over her fidgety cold one. "Chesa. I care about you a great deal. There's no reason for this to come between us."

She shook her head. "How can it not? You plan on taking this boy in, after all."

"There's so much more to him than you give him credit for. If you just give him—"

She glowered and pointed at him. "If you say give him a chance one more time, I'm kicking you out of here and never speaking to you again."

Hapker's mouth fell open and he snapped it back shut. *Why is she being so stubborn?*

"Listen," she said before he could reply. "I can't help how I feel. The truth is, I don't want to give him a chance. Nor should I have to. You need to make a choice."

He tensed. "A choice about what?"

"I don't want to be with you if that boy's around."

Hapker put up his hands. "I'm not leaving him to the wolves."

Chesa shook her head and then pinched the bridge of her nose. "I get that." She looked back up and her face seemed somewhat calmer. "You're a good man and want to do what you think is right. But I can't be with you if you choose him over me."

Hapker pulled away. "I'm not choosing him over you. There's no reason why—"

"There are plenty of reasons!" She let out a huff of air as tears welled in her eyes. "Let's see how things play out. We don't even know if he'll get to stay in Cooperative territory. When the council takes him off your hands, we can be together."

When the council takes him off my hands? She made Jori sound like a burden. Sure, the situation was complicated right now, but that wasn't Jori's fault. It was everyone else making this hard.

He dropped his forehead in his hand. "I'm not choosing one of you over the other. I'll continue to care for him because I want to and because it's the right thing to do. If you decide not to be with me because of it, that's your choice, not mine."

She clicked her tongue and let out an exasperated sigh. "Fine. You don't need to choose until after the council decides. I'll play along in the meantime. I love you, J.D. I want us to be together—but just us." She squeezed his hand. "Just think about our future, alright?"

His head spun. He thought he wanted a future with her, but abandoning Jori was out of the question. When she smiled, his heart tugged one way. When he remembered her disparaging remarks about Jori, it yanked another.

Rather than debate the matter with her further, he nodded and left. Numbness fell over him as he forced away any thoughts that their relationship might be over.

36
Disquietude

Deep breath in. Hold. Deep breath out. Despite the rhythm, Jori's thoughts continued to jump and twist like a live wire. They flitted from Banks' violence to the unexpected rescue by Sergeant Ortega.

His feelings about Sergeant Creston were even more confusing. Distaste wriggled through him whenever he thought of her, yet he'd done far worse and Hapker still stuck by his side. Besides, Hapker deserved to be happy. He didn't deserve to lose his career or his girlfriend over some criminal.

The unlocking click of his prison door broke him from his meditation. He'd been so immersed that he hadn't heard anyone come through the main entrance. That he hadn't detected them either didn't surprise him when he opened his eyes.

Gottfried entered with his usual emotionless smile. The tablet he clutched made Jori's heart skip a beat. Did he have word back already?

He eased his legs out from underneath him, trying not to appear eager, and rose to an attentive stance.

Gottfried waved him down. "No need for such formality. I have news and you'll want to be sitting for it."

Jori perched on the edge of his bed, his heart hammering so hard that it hurt.

"Would you excuse us, Lieutenant?" Gottfried said to Gresher.

Gresher asked Jori with a head tilt. Jori snapped a nod, not wanting the man to be culpable.

After Gresher left, Gottfried pulled a chair from the corner and sat before him. His brows curled in with an almost distressed manner. "Word has come back from your ship. I'm afraid I have bad tidings."

Jori snatched the tablet and pressed the play button on the video already displayed. The face of a senshi popped up. Not one he knew well, but still someone familiar.

The tall man in a black armored uniform wore an anguished expression that looked more real than Gottfried's. "I'm sorry to inform you, my Lord, that Sensei Jeruko and your brother are dead."

Jori sucked in a sharp breath and clutched the necklace hiding under his shirt. Icy tendrils zipped through his body. This couldn't be right. There must be some mistake.

His focus tightened on the video as the man explained. "The perantium emitter exploded while it was being fitted to the new ship. The emperor suspects sabotage."

Suffocating horror clutched Jori like an attacking blackbeast. He was the one who'd sabotaged that damned thing. This was his doing. They were dead because of him.

He gripped the tablet with a shaky hand. *This can't be real.* Yes, he'd made alterations. Only one could've triggered a reaction, but it shouldn't have had enough power to kill anyone. Did the Cooperative prisoners do something? No. He'd double-checked their work.

He squeezed his eyes shut and dropped his head into his palm. This was all his fault.

"Do you know him?" Gottfried asked.

A gush of tears fell. Sobs racked his throat, but he couldn't get in enough air to make a sound.

"It might be a lie," Gottfried said.

Jori considered it, but his emotions smothered his ability to think.

"So do you know him?" Gottfried prodded again. "We sent our message to Mister Jeruko, but the reply is from this man. Who is he?"

A twang of irritation pierced through Jori's grief at the title of mister. The correct honorific was sensei. Mister made him sound like some minor functionary. Sensei Jeruko was so much more than that. He hadn't just been his father's closest confidant. He'd been Jori's mentor. His friend, even. More like what a father should be. *And now he's dead.* Why couldn't it have been his real father instead?

That flash of anger allowed him to consider the source. The senshi warrior stood tall, but he didn't have as much bulk as most other senshi. His specialty lay in programming. He worked with the primary ship's programmer, but Jori's distress didn't allow him to remember his name. He knew him enough to know he tended to be an honest man.

The video had reached the end and he'd missed most of it. He hit play again.

"I'm sorry to inform you, my Lord, that Sensei Jeruko and your brother are dead." The man's bushy black brows titled with sincerity. Every aspect of his body remained still, but not tight, so he likely spoke truthfully. "The perantium emitter exploded while it was being fitted to the new ship. We suspect sabotage." He paused and glanced down, hinting that this troubled him. "The damage was severe, leaving few survivors."

The senshi shifted his stance and glanced away. It might mean he was lying or about to lie, but it could also be nervousness or discomfort. "I'm happy to discover you're alive, my Lord, but you shouldn't return. Your father has gone mad and there's no telling what he will do if he finds out about you. You should know that I found your message when your father ordered me to investigate Colonel Jeruko's communications. I didn't report my findings and I purged it from the system. No one here will learn about you. I'm sorry if it's not going well with the Cooperative. Trust me when I say you're better off right now. Be well, my Lord. Maybe I'll see you again someday."

Tears dripped from Jori's quivering chin. He didn't doubt the man's words since nothing else made sense. Sensei Jeruko and his brother were gone forever.

What would his mother think if she learned he'd killed her other son? She'd pity him, sure. But she'd also be heartbroken and perhaps resentful. Even if he had a way to get back to her, it was out of the question now.

"He sent an attachment showing the damaged ship," Gottfried said. "It looks real. There's no indication that the image is fake."

A dark loneliness crept over Jori's thoughts. He returned the tablet to Gottfried. "I don't want to see it."

The aide patted Jori's shoulder awkwardly. "I'm sorry, young one. I truly am. But you're not alone. You have the commander. And if something ever happens to him, you also have me."

Jori pulled back. "Happen to him? What do you mean?'

"*If.* I said *if.*"

That's an odd thing to say right now. If only he could sense Gottfried's emotions and determine if he had ulterior motives. As grateful as he was for the help, suspicion fluttered through him.

It disappeared as quickly as it had come, submerged under his mounting grief. All the friends and allies in the world wouldn't make up for his loss.

He buried his face in his hands and wept.

*****

Gottfried Krause suppressed the exuberance that kept tickling him. MEGA-Man was a true master. A few snags had diverted the original plan. However, he'd cleverly altered the schemes to get him both the database and the boy's allegiance.

As Jori cried, Gottfried took stock of all the changes. The admiral staying on the *Defender* had given the opportunity to win the boy over to their cause. Doctor Donnel didn't do as expected, but the admiral's attitude still left the desired effect on Jori's perception of the Cooperative.

The attack on Sergeant Ortega hadn't worked, but Lieutenant Buckeye would assuage her suspicions and keep her from becoming Jori's ally. Gottfried had used a little of his imperium ability on her to make sure. She wasn't as susceptible as Banks or Lengen, but perhaps enough to make her second-guess herself.

This video message was his best plan-alteration of all. With nowhere else to go, Jori would soon realize where he really belonged.

Gottfried absently patted Jori's shoulder. It was difficult to pretend compassion. If only the boy understood the glories awaiting him.

"I know you're hurting," he said. "Things will get better. You'll see. Remember when I told you about the places you can flourish?"

Jori's curiosity sparked. Misgiving quickly rolled back in, though.

Gottfried frowned. "You still don't trust me?"

Jori slammed his imaginary wall in place so hard that it left an emotionless vacuum. Even his sadness was gone. *No, not gone. Hidden.*

"I'm not sure I understand why," Gottfried continued. "I swear the admiral knows nothing about what I've done to help you."

The boy didn't react, not with a flicker of his eye or a twitch of his brow.

Gottfried gripped Jori's shoulder the way he'd seen the commander do. "And I'll keep helping you."

"Why?" Jori asked in a gravely tone.

"Because I am your friend, and I want the best for you."

"You don't know me. Why risk your career for me?"

"Because you not being allowed to contact your family is wrong. Plus, I can tell you're special. You and I are a lot alike. More than you realize."

Though no emotions seeped out, Jori eased away, his eyes shifting with uncertainty. "How so?"

"Well, have you noticed how the Cooperative spouts ideals about bringing humanity together, yet they seem to condemn certain people for being different? Especially those who are more talented than they are?"

"How does that make you like me? They accept you."

"They limit me," Gottfried said. "If they knew everything about me, they'd put more restrictions on me. If the council accepts you, it won't be without limitations. They will always watch you and they might even suppress you by not allowing you to do the same things other ordinary Cooperative citizens are allowed to do."

The boy still didn't emit any sensations, but his silence indicated consideration.

Gottfried shoved down the buoyancy that once again threatened to bubble up. "But there's a place you can go where you will be embraced for all that you are."

"Where?" Jori asked warily.

"Someplace that truly accepts all of humanity and its desire to evolve." Gottfried grinned eagerly and leaned in. "The Cooperative doesn't allow us to grow. They only embrace humankind if they're like them—average. You and I aren't average. We're different. Better. And we could become even more than what we are now if they weren't holding us back. Aren't you tired of that?"

A flash of indignation escaped through the boy's wariness. "So where is this *magical* place?"

Gottfried refrained from rubbing his palms together with glee. "It's a system deep in the Kanivian sector. A place you may have heard of, dubbed Cybernation."

Jori's eyes bulged.

Gottfried forced his hands to still and slanted closer. "That's right. I am a MEGA. And I'm proud to be one, too. If I had to follow the Cooperative's rules, I'd be nothing."

The boy's mouth hung open, but his thoughts remained hidden. Gottfried pressed on. "If the Cooperative found out, I wouldn't be allowed to serve here. And all because my parents made a choice for me. It's not my fault, yet the Cooperative would punish me for it by labeling me and by making sure I am excluded from participating in my own society."

The freedom of being able to voice the injustice inspired Gottfried to keep speaking. "Although the Cooperative disdains people like me, I strive for a galaxy where everyone can be free to be anything they want to be. Cybernation is just the beginning of our liberation."

When the boy's throat bobbed, Gottfried wondered what it meant. "I know it's overwhelming, but don't you see how alike we are now?"

"I'm not a MEGA," the boy replied defensively.

"True, but we are both being held back for the circumstances of our birth. I can't help that I am genetically enhanced or an imperium, and you can't help that you're a Tredon warrior, bred to be superior."

A trickle of suspicion leaked out from the boy, but so did acceptance. Gottfried had never been good at reading expressions, but he swore he saw hope in the Jori's eyes. "The Cooperative is against you because you're different and better than they are. They say they want equality, but they treat you like a criminal despite all you've sacrificed for them. They don't deserve you."

Jori's mental wall fell away. Not a hint of distrust remained, just sadness and a touch of anger.

Gottfried smiled inwardly. Jori was his.

*****

Carletta Ortega glanced over her shoulder and shuddered. *What the hell is going on with those two?* The extreme reactions of the boy combined with Lieutenant Krause's cheeriness made her skin crawl. Where all the man's emotions seemed fake, Jori transitioned from grief to nothing to suspicion. None made any sense. What was he sad about? Who was he suspicious of? The lieutenant? The commander? Her?

She edged closer to the door despite herself, hoping her acute hearing would pick up the conversation through the privacy setting. Garbled sounds reached her ears only, making her grind her teeth.

"What do you think they're talking about?" Harley whispered so Lengen and the other guard down the hall wouldn't hear.

Ortega stole another peek. Lieutenant Krause's wide grin made the hairs on her neck stand up. "I don't know, but I don't like it."

"It must be serious for Jori to cry like that."

"Did you see the way his face went completely blank after? It was as though someone had turned off a robot that'd gone haywire. And now he's angry, but it doesn't seem to be directed at the lieutenant. Maybe they're scheming."

Harley shot her a doubtful look. "The admiral's aide and the Tredon boy in cahoots? That makes no sense at all."

Ortega shook her head, remembering what Singh had said about the man and Glastra. "Something is off."

"A lot of strange stuff's happening around here. So what did Lieutenant Buckeye find out?"

Her chest tightened. "Nothing."

"Nothing?"

"Not a single clue." Ortega pulled in a deep breath and let it out with an involuntary shiver. "He said he questioned everyone he found down there. No one showed any evidence of being in a scuffle and none fit the physique I'd described to him. And…" She sighed. "He doubts anyone was trying to kill me. He says it was probably just some officers getting revenge because I ratted them out."

"What?" Harley made a face. "If that's true, it's rather extreme, isn't it?"

"It happens, though," she said. "You've seen it at the institute. You misalign with the team, they put you back in line."

She swallowed the lump in her throat as an unpleasant memory flashed through her brain. She'd been reckless, playing a prank that almost caused harm. After that, a group of schoolmates cornered her in a hall and beat the crap out of her.

One man had been rather vicious about it, wailing on her like a madman. His ferocity had terrified her. She'd only suffered a few cuts and bruises, but became wary of men with hateful attitudes. Even her boyfriend made her nervous now.

"Still," Harley said, "you'd think Bryce would take it more seriously. You two are back together, right?"

"Yes," she replied despite the doubt wriggling inside her. Bryce had forgiven her, but she didn't feel that she'd needed forgiveness. A heavy disquietude fell over her whenever she thought of him now. He seemed different, but she couldn't pinpoint how.

"Nothing about this entire situation feels right," she said.

"You know what's not right?" Lengen called out. "People who turn on their own."

The sting of his words burned Ortega's cheeks. "If anyone turned on anyone, it's the assholes who violated the Code of Conduct."

The man's mouth slanted with a steepness that matched the slope of his nose. Ortega imagined herself punching it.

Apparently, the lack of support from the other guards was enough to silence the corporal. He looked away, his jaw working about as much as Ortega's. Her bitterness turned to hurt, though. Bryce had forgiven her, but he still kept her at arm's length. Any attempt she'd made to get together was met with a brisk *I'm busy.* Perhaps he really was. She hoped so, but deep down she knew it would never be the same between them.

A beep sounded in her comm, making her jump.

"Sergeant," Lieutenant Krause said. "I'm ready."

She snuck a look at Harley and the others to see if they noticed her flinch, then opened the cell. The aide left with a lightness to his gait that made her uneasy. She peered at the boy. His dark eyes hinted at something smoldering beneath, but they also reflected a pain that almost matched her own.

Hers was short-lived. His, however, was deeper and her heart ached.

She shook her head, scattering her thoughts before they took too strong of a hold. With a jab to the panel, she shut the cell door and turned her back in a huff. What the hell was wrong with her? She shouldn't be pitying him. He was the enemy. Maybe Lengen and Bryce were right. She was a traitor.

37
The Hyena

Every grate and scrape of the guest ship attaching to the *Defender* made Gottfried Krause's jaw twitch. He waited with his hands clasped behind his back, presenting an outward calm despite his disdain and dread. Normally, he had little room for emotions, but he hated these people with a passion.

Who were they to decide how he should live his life? Even if he'd had the misfortune of being average, they'd still be no better than him. They clung to their mediocrity with fanaticism. Like hunters, they shot down perceived threats, hoping to make their primitive asses look supreme.

Admiral Belmont maintained a businesslike mien. For an older man, he poised himself well. Not too surprising. After decades of fooling others into believing he had control, he'd duped even himself.

Gottfried almost laughed. Three deaths and an attempt on an officer's life would have put most people on high alert. Not Belmont. A few carefully chosen words and the admiral believed those incidents were just accidents. And a casually given report by Lieutenant Buckeye convinced him the attack on Sergeant Ortega had been nothing more than hazing.

So predictable.

The only challenge to the admiral's delusion of control had come from the MEGA hunters. The initial assumption had been that they'd pick up the hunters and leave. However, the MEGA Inspectors insisted on running a few of the most specialized tests here on the station first. Although Gottfried didn't mind the delay since they'd still travel with them, the admiral had made a fuss that would've put a petulant child to shame.

Even now, the man pouted. He'd never liked waiting, especially not for those with an inflated self-importance. Gottfried suppressed the urge to chuckle. At least he despised the hunters because they hunted him. Belmont didn't like that their egos were bigger than his own.

The airlock safety light turned from red to yellow and finally to green. Gottfried, the admiral, and a contingent of officers stepped through the now open hatch. Their footsteps echoed as they made their way down the long, reinforced tube.

Three old men and a younger one met them at a station terminal for a formal introduction. Gottfried's mouth curled with distaste, but he quickly masked it with a smile. "Greetings, Doctor Menger," he said to the oldest man with wrinkled skin. "I present, Vice Admiral Belmont."

The admiral jutted his chin. Doctor Menger stepped forward without offering a handshake. Gottfried ground his teeth. This man, nicknamed the Hyena, resembled his namesake by both his physical traits and reputation. He had an elongated upper body that sat on short legs, his big round ears stuck out from the side of his head, and he had a wide mouth with distinctive yellow canines. Like the animal, he was a hunter, a scavenger, and a thief. He freeloaded off other people's success and degraded their identities by slapping a MEGA label on them.

"It's a pleasure, Admiral," Doctor Menger said with no hint of pleasantness. "I understand you have someone you want me to test."

"Yes, Doctor," Belmont replied in the same to-the-point manner. "He's ten years old and has several above-average abilities."

"So you stated in your report," the Hyena said with a superior tone. "Your own testing found nothing, which isn't surprising. These MEGAs are getting sneakier by the day."

Gottfried corrected the twist in his lips. "The boy says the abilities were bred into him. My understanding of the upper Tredon warrior caste is that breeding is common."

Doctor Menger raised his chin and sniffed. "I find it very difficult to believe that animi abilities, intelligence, stamina, and all the other things you listed can be bred into one person. Rest assured, I will figure out where he gets them from and make sure he's marked for life."

A fire ignited in Gottfried's gut.

"That upsets you, Lieutenant?" a doctor with age spots all over his bald head asked.

Gottfried straightened his face and put on a fake smile. "I'm upset that this boy might be hiding something."

Doctor Menger raised his pointed nose to the air. "Depending on how long these formalities take, it won't stay hidden much longer. When can I expect to have him?"

"He's already on the way," Belmont said. "I'll leave you with my aide. He and a handful of our guards will accompany the boy."

A sickly smile crossed the Hyena's face. It crimped downward after the admiral left. Gottfried waited with him and the other hunters. Three wore inhibitors but Doctor Menger didn't, and his aura reeked of arrogance. It took everything Gottfried had not to grab the old man by the throat and squeeze until he turned blue.

Jori arrived with a concrete expression. Only his red-rimmed eyes hinted at the emotions hiding behind his mental wall.

Gottfried held back a smile and tilted his brows in what he hoped conveyed sympathy. "It's alright, young one. I will stay with you."

"If you're not a MEGA, you have nothing to fear, boy," Doctor Menger said.

Jori's lip curled. "I'm not afraid of you."

The Hyena sneered. "Let us be on our way, then."

Doctor Menger led them through a maze of narrow, unpainted corridors. The dark metal walls pressed in, making Gottfried's skin prickle. They soon reached a stark white room crammed with diagnostic machines. Situated in the center was a broad bed that looked like an operating table. "Is this a surgical room?"

The doctor shuffled over to a monitor. "Not quite. We don't need to cut him open to look inside him. He'll remain conscious through these first procedures."

Gottfried's blood kindled to a boil. "What other sorts of tests will you do?"

Doctor Menger named several, counting on his fingers. Gottfried's muscles tightened in increments. This was outrageous and unnecessary. People shouldn't have to endure such rigorous examinations by the likes of these self-important men.

He bit his tongue and forced a tight smile. If he wasn't careful, they'd realize how much he despised them. He couldn't endure these tests himself.

"Now move aside and tell your soldiers to bring the child," the Hyena said.

Gottfried reluctantly stepped over. "I'm so sorry, young one," he whispered as Jori passed.

The boy walked in without a hint of concern. With his emotions blocked, Gottfried couldn't determine whether he was scared, angry, or both. It hardly mattered, though. Despite the atrocity of what these animals were about to do, at least it would bring Jori closer to his side.

*****

Jori eased onto the operating table. He'd kept his fear from showing outwardly, but it became evident the moment they hooked him up to the machines. The jagged waves on the heart monitor raced by, his blood pressure shot up, and the machine detected his increased adrenaline.

If only they'd allowed Hapker to be here. Something about the hardiness of the man's lifeforce gave him strength.

He closed his eyes and took in deep, steady breaths. While the doctors prepped their equipment, he distracted himself with reevaluating all that he'd done to the emitter. He'd examined this a dozen times already but digging deeper might help him figure out what had happened.

One thing kept resurfacing. Sensei Jeruko used to tell him that first instincts were usually correct, so Jori picked at that memory, evaluating all angles from everything to what he saw to what he felt, and even what he smelled.

A garlic-like metallic scent had permeated the auxiliary bay as shokukin workers welded the structures that would hold the emitter pieces during transport. The bay had increased in temperature, making it easier for him to work. He'd rerouted circuits, removed others, and rewrote the program to make his alterations appear correct. After that, he'd reset the warning parameters so it wouldn't alert anyone when operations went off target.

"Janelle," Doctor Menger said, his tone conveying his annoyance as much as his emotions. "I thought I told you to put the H.A.R.K. testing before the Barker test."

"I did, Doctor. I swear."

"Then why is the Barker test listed first?"

Jori's eyes remained shut, but he could practically see the man's sour expression. Gottfried had called him the Hyena, but Jori thought of him more like a giant hissing lizard.

Someone cleared their throat. "Sorry, Doctor. That's my fault. Since we usually start with that test, I thought it was a mistake."

Those words struck a chord. Jori grasped onto them, trying to see how they related to the emitter.

"You're just a damn medic," the doctor said, his voice rasping with an old man's rage. "Keep to your own duties and quit meddling in others."

Jori sensed the younger medic's smoldering indignation and thrust it aside. *He thought it was a mistake.* The shokukin must've noticed what he'd done and tried to repair it, only they'd worsened it because they barely understood what they were doing.

They're the ones who made that part unstable. It was their fault his brother and Sensei Jeruko were dead.

No. The blame still fell on him. If only he hadn't messed with it, the people he cared about would still be alive.

His sinuses burned with grief and guilt. He'd been so ashamed that he hadn't told Hapker yet. He'd cried on the man's shoulder but couldn't bring himself to speak.

A whirring yanked him back to the present problem. He snapped his eyes open and forced himself to remain steady as a robotic arm advanced with a long needle. He lay flat, unable to move. A thick strap pressed against his forehead, causing his neck to ache. Thinner straps cinched into his wrists and ankles. Two longer straps lay over his chest and thighs.

"Be very still," Doctor Menger said.

Jori's heart pulsated like an overworked arc drive. His breath hitched as the sting of the needle stabbed behind his ear. A grinding pang followed as the probe crawled around inside.

He managed the pain well, just as his jintal teacher had taught. His muscles relaxed and his respiration returned to normal. Not even the slight pinch afterward took him out of his detached state. The needle pulled out.

Another robot arm came down over his torso. This larger needle gleamed menacingly as the scanner of the upper part of the machine flicked lights over his naked abdomen. Fortunately, they'd only lifted his shirt and so his mother's necklace remained unseen.

"This one will hurt, but you must not move," the doctor said.

"Shouldn't you put him under for this type of thing?" Gottfried asked.

"Mind your business or leave," the Hyena replied.

Gottfried's sudden emotions struck Jori with a force he'd never sensed from the man before—almost like a glitch. Well, he was a MEGA after all, both mechanically enhanced and genetically altered. A true cyborg and one who stood amid his worst enemies. Had he come for Jori's sake, or because the admiral ordered him to? Jori hoped it was the former.

That Gottfried was part machine put odd pieces of his puzzle together. It explained the strange way the man had seemed to freeze that day they'd played Galactic Dominions.

Then there was his subdued lifeforce. It had been the same with the cyborgs Jori had met back home. If they had brain implants near the limbic system, their limited ability to feel made sense.

Jori shivered. He'd always been told emotion was a weakness. Somehow, the thought of putting something in his head to take away his feelings frightened him more than the large needle sliding toward him.

He suppressed his trembling and prepared his mind to endure the pain. The arm made a mechanical whirring sound as it positioned over his left side. Jori couldn't see the needle move in from this angle, but the piercing pinch told him enough. His insides burned, followed by a gnawing, as though some sharp-toothed parasite ate him from the inside out.

A stab exploded from the area of his pancreas. He sucked in a breath but forced it back out again. Each intake of air increased his agony, but Master Bunmi's teachings helped him endure.

"Hmm," Doctor Menger said. "Doctor Wood, please indicate in the report that this young man has diminished pain receptors."

"I can feel the pain just fine," Jori croaked.

Menger leaned over him. "This is not the reaction I usually get."

"I've had jintal training."

"Really?" the Hyena drawled in disbelief.

"My father commissioned—" He swallowed. "—a jintal master—to teach me. He did far worse."

"Hmm. I've never heard of a jintal master training a child."

"He had no choice."

Doctor Menger turned away. "Varma, is he telling the truth?"

"Yes. I can sense his pain, too. He's very good at not reacting to it, but it's there."

The doctor harrumphed. "See what else you can find in his head. The admiral wants to know everything this boy knows."

When the ugly man with the sallow face fixated on Jori, a probing sensation pressed into his skull. *Another extraho.* At least Gottfried hadn't tried anything. Jori pushed back and glowered at the man as best as he could from this position.

"This is illegal!" Gottfried's pink cheeks turned red.

"This is part of the testing," Doctor Menger replied testily.

"Testing for what?" the aide asked.

"If his body won't divulge whether he's a MEGA, then a mind probe will do the trick."

Jori clenched his jaw, partly from the pain of the machine, partly from the exertion of fighting off the intrusion, and partly from annoyance. "I'm not a MEGA."

"We shall see," the Hyena said, adding a chill to the other sensations teeming through Jori's body.

The needle pulled out. Jori's chest fell from the sudden release, but he kept his mental wall in place. The purple vein in Varma's forehead indicated his effort to get in was more difficult than Jori's struggle to keep him out.

Jori turned away, hoping to convey his disregard for the continued prodding. "Why can't Hapker or Gresher be here?" he asked Gottfried, just to show the sallow-faced man he could carry on a conversation while still maintaining his mental block. "Hapker is my advocate and Bilsby said it's his right to accompany me wherever I go."

"I'm afraid these MEGA hunters are above the law."

The Hyena's mouth twisted. Either he didn't like being called a hunter instead of an inspector, or he resented the implication that he acted lawlessly.

A prune-faced woman entered. Her burnt orange dress complemented her dark complexion, but that was the only complementary thing about her. Where Doctor Menger's lifeforce reeked of undeserved pomposity, hers blistered with scathing disdain.

Varma grinned wickedly. His cheeks rounded, cracking his dry skin. Jori braced himself against the new assault from the orange-dressed woman.

"Tell me about your father's military might," she demanded both vocally and internally with a force of a ship accelerating at nine g's.

Jori gritted his teeth and glowered. Every ounce of energy he had went into keeping her out. It'd be easier to stop a moon from orbiting its planet.

"They call Doctor Menger *the Hyena*. Do you know what they call me?"

Jori didn't answer. He couldn't afford to be distracted with the effort of making words.

"I'm *the Lamprey*."

Goosebumps formed on Jori's arms and ran to his face and head.

"It's a bloodsucker. I'm an extraho, far more powerful than these two put together." She flicked her wrist at Gottfried and Varma. "You resist me, make me angry, I might extract so much information from you that there will be nothing left. Just an empty husk."

All the water in Jori's mouth evaporated, leaving a granular feeling. He bit down harder, gathering his will as her attack intensified to a painful buzz.

Sweat broke out over his entire body. The Lamprey's persistence showed no sign of weakening. Jori wasn't sure how much longer he could hold out.

The buzzing turned into a grinding saw, then into a drill. An ache grew in Jori's head. At first, just a pounding throb. But then it deepened, searing through his skull like a laser torch. He forced himself to keep breathing and endure.

The woman's face darkened. Jori trembled with effort, but his imaginary wall remained firm. The Lamprey clenched her jaw. Her eyes bulged as she marshalled another shove against Jori's unrelenting determination.

"Impossible!" Her attempted break-in faltered then crumbled. "How are you doing this?"

Jori puffed. The pressure was gone but the pain lingered. He was sure his head had swelled to ten times its size. Every vibration of his shaking body felt like a million tiny razors cutting through him.

"I guess he's stronger than you." Gottfried smiled, this time appearing genuine.

"Proving he's a MEGA," Doctor Menger said.

Gottfried smirked. "That's not proof of him being a MEGA. That's proof of evolution."

"Bah!" Doctor Menger said. "Only a MEGA can fend off such a powerful extraho."

The sharpness of Jori's pain subsided.

"Anyone can learn to protect themselves," Gottfried replied. "Even *you*, apparently."

The doctor sniffed and looked away, not liking the comparison.

"I inherited my sentio-animi abilities from my mother." Jori didn't add that she was an imperium-animi, the highest level of readers. It wouldn't convince them and would only get him labeled and restricted like Gottfried. "Someone had trained her to fend off extrahos and imperiums, and she passed that knowledge on to me, my father, and other high-ranking senshi warriors."

"Impossible," the Lamprey muttered. "I don't believe a mere child can do such a thing."

Gottfried waved at Jori. "Didn't you sense him? He's not blocking us now and I can tell that every word he spoke is true."

The woman's jaw muscles worked. Varma looked away. Doctor Menger flicked his eyes back and forth between them, probably hoping one would refute Gottfried's claim.

When they didn't, he slammed down whatever metal object he'd been holding. "On to the next test."

Jori's gratitude for Gottfried swelled. Hapker couldn't be here, but at least this man was here to challenge these false accusations.

38
Depart

The gold chain glittered as Jori fingered his mother's necklace. The glint sparkled even more as tears filled his eyes. He unclasped it, tugged it away from his neck, and settled it in his palm. The brown stones reminded him of his mother's eyes, as if she judged him. "*You killed my son,*" her voice echoed in his head.

"I didn't mean to," Jori whimpered.

He stifled a sob, not caring whether the guards heard him. This group tended to ignore him anyway, which was fine since it meant they also didn't harass him. He had his grief—and his shame—all to himself.

Hapker would undoubtedly tell him it was alright, that it wasn't his fault. But those words wouldn't help. Most likely, the commander would put some blame on himself for insisting on damaging the perantium device. That part was true, but Jori had gone along with it. The responsibility lay with him and him alone.

Mother was probably devastated that she'd lost both her sons. His heart ached at the thought. She might rejoice if she found out Jori was alive, but only for a moment. Learning who was responsible for her other son's death would devastate her all over again. She would forgive him, but she'd never forget. The truth would hang between them forever.

Jori rose and went to the food recycler chute. He stood there staring it. If he dropped the jewelry inside, the separators would catch it and send it off to the proper recycling unit—forever casting away the reminder of what he'd done.

He pressed the button. The covering swirled open, and a sucking sound filled the room. He dangled the necklace over it. The chain oscillated, the beads dazzled, unaware of their pending doom. All he had to do was say goodbye and let go. It was that simple.

Only his fingers wouldn't move. His entire body froze, including his lungs and probably his heart too. *Let go. Let go!*

The sensation of Hapker returning from the cafeteria prompted him into motion. Only instead of releasing it, he closed the chute. Rather than put it back on, he shoved it beneath his mattress. The compromise allowed him to separate without getting rid of it.

Hapker entered with a smile that fell almost as soon as it'd formed. "You alright?" He swept in, his righteous anger expanding like a dying star. "What did they do to you?"

Jori wiped the wetness from his eyes. "It's not about them." *Not right now, anyway.*

Concern replaced Hapker's outrage as he set the tray of fresh food on the table. "Are you sure? Did they hurt you? Do something else? What happened?"

"They ran some tests." Jori sniffled. "Nothing terrible."

"What is it then? Why are you crying?"

Jori wagged his head.

Hapker's mouth slanted, making it more crooked than usual. "It's Lieutenant Krause, isn't it? You still haven't told me what he said that made you so upset."

"It's not Gottfried either," Jori managed to reply.

"You sure? Because you've been even more out of sorts since his last visit."

"I'm sure."

Hapker ran his hand down his face and released an empathetic sigh. "Whatever it's about, you can tell me. I'm here for you."

Jori nodded but couldn't bring himself to confess that he'd killed his own brother. This shame was his alone to bear.

*****

The buffet spread across the conference table. A seasoned protein-mix shaped like a giant roasted bird sat in the center. Bowls of fresh fruits and vegetables mingled with the dizzying selection of cooked dishes—spicy noodles, hot rolls, steaming bean stew, a cheesy casserole. A dozen empty plates rounded the edges, waiting to be filled.

Gottfried Krause took in the savory scents. A part of him wished he had a chip to identify each odor, but that luxury was out of reach. Someday he'd have more tech—maybe even be as advanced as MEGA-Man.

He smiled as he sat and watched the *Defender* depart the station. The feed on the wall monitor was for Major Esekielu's benefit. Important stats either displayed in the corner or scrolled along the bottom. Any deviation from protocol, and the major had an excuse to escape the tedium of this gathering.

Gottfried almost envied him. He regarded the guests with a bitter eye. Doctor Menger's lip curled as though this lavish display wasn't good enough for him. Varma frowned at the desert fountain. The woman who called herself the Lamprey looked like she'd rather eat a lemon than be here. The others displayed only a little more politeness.

He hated having them here, but they'd be gone soon. The nudge he'd given Doctor Fritz earlier should set his plan back into motion. *And I can kill two birds with one stone.* The ancient idiom almost made him laugh out loud.

He piled his plate with various delicacies, not caring if he looked like a glutton. If he had to endure all this idle talk, then he'd enjoy himself another way.

"What do you think, Lieutenant Krause?"

"Hmm?" Gottfried replied through a mouthful of liangpi. He quickly replayed the scene in his head, holding up a finger for a pause. After dabbing his lips with a napkin, he answered. "I think that if he's not a MEGA, he might as well be. Perhaps the emperor didn't alter his genetics or give him permanent enhancements, but he certainly made sure the boy received the right genes."

"You seemed rather keen on defending him," Doctor Menger said.

"That was for his benefit." Gottfried allowed his emotions to leak so the readers would sense his truth. "I assure you, I want him to be a MEGA just as much as you do."

The doctor harrumphed.

Since this conversation turned interesting, the man's sourness didn't bother him. "How many more tests will you run, Doctor?"

"As many as it takes."

"You know," the admiral said as he wiped sauce from his chin, "if the tests still come up inconclusive, you can always—" He flicked his hand. "—fudge the results."

Gottfried almost choked. *Fudge the results!* How dare they. The admiral's remark shouldn't surprise him, though. These Cooperative oppressors would do anything to keep their betters down.

"That goes against our policies." A wicked smile spread over Doctor Menger's face. "However, it is my sworn duty to weed out cheaters."

Heat flushed over Gottfried's body. Evolution wasn't cheating.

"Speaking of MEGA testing," Doctor Fritz said. "I'm doing some promising research in my private lab. You should come take a look."

Gottfried's temper cooled somewhat. The nudge had worked. However, Doctor Menger's mouth puckered. Luckily, Gottfried had the perfect argument lined up. "You should check it out. One of Doctor Fritz's experiments shows promising results in locating protein-based enhancements."

"You mean like the ones the boy said he had when he was on the *Odyssey*?" Esekielu asked.

"Exactly like that," Doctor Fritz said with the enthusiasm of a child showing off his new trick. His face brightened as he explained it in greater detail.

A swelling joy filled Gottfried as Doctor Menger leaned in with rapt attention. "Well. That *does* sound interesting. Perhaps we'll find the time."

"There's no rush regarding your testing, Doctor. It's a long way to Asteria," Gottfried replied. "I can set up the tour for you tomorrow."

Doctor Menger bobbed his head while chewing his food. After swallowing, he said, "Tomorrow, after I've completed one of the tests."

Doctor Fritz beamed. Gottfried refrained from doing the same as elation tickled his insides. *Perfect. Absolutely perfect.*

Next step, convince Major Esekielu and a few other key officers to go too, while also making sure the admiral didn't. He couldn't lose Belmont, but the universe had no more use for the rest.

39
Breakup

J.D. Hapker's patience wore thin. Chesa's rank afforded her a nice room of her own. Colorful artwork from her homeworld adorned the walls. Brightly painted figurines stood in an encased shelf. The vivid patterns on the cushioned chairs dazzled the eye. All this lively décor usually lifted his mood. Today it clashed with it.

She'd convinced him she didn't mean to give him an ultimatum and, like a fool, he'd fallen for it. Everything had been fine when he first came over. As soon as he mentioned his worry over Jori undergoing another day of tests, she flipped.

She threw her hands in the air. "I can't believe you're choosing that boy over me."

"I'm not choosing him over you," he said, trying to keep his irritation from showing through his tone. "I already told you, I'm not putting either of you above the other."

Her brows knitted in the way he'd grown to dread. "You're leaving me to go back to *him*."

Hapker coughed out a half-laugh. "I'm not leaving you. I'm only heading to another part of the ship."

"That's called leaving!"

He pinched the bridge of his nose. "This *isn't* a contest, Chesa."

"It is when you put everything else above me."

"That's not what I'm doing." He strived to keep his voice calm, but the fruitlessness of this discussion grated on his nerves.

"Oh please. We had a good thing going until your fluffed-up ideals got you kicked out of the PG-Force. Now those same ideals are coming between us."

A fire ignited in Hapker's chest. "Fluffed-up ideals? Are you kidding me? They ordered me to do something that wasn't just illegal, but immoral."

"Whatever. My point is, this won't work. I'm a soldier and I fight the enemy, not coddle them. And I can't be with someone who does."

Hapker inhaled, filling his lungs to stretch out the tightness building within. She was right. Not about the coddling part but about it not working. She'd always had a bit of a temper. How had he forgotten about that? People called her Firestorm for a reason. Jori didn't need to be around someone like that.

He ran his hand down his face and stroked his chin. "Alright. I guess we're done," he said calmly, surprised at the sudden sense of liberation. *I guess I* am *choosing Jori over her.*

Her ivory skin turned rouge. "You bastard. I can't believe this."

Hapker rose and headed out.

Her scream pierced his eardrum. "Damn you, J.D.! You're not doing this to me again!"

He didn't respond as the door swished closed.

"You fucking asshole!" her voice carried through.

Hapker ignored the darting glances of two officers passing by. He turned the corner and sighed. Exasperation fell away, but a gloom fell over him. He still cared about her, but her hateful attitude was too much. Ending things made his heart heavy, but it was for the best.

*****

Jori eased off the recovery bed and clutched his aching stomach. There'd been no lasting effects from the days of testing, but the constant struggle to endure all the discomfort and occasional pain had taken its toll. Everything hurt, not just his midsection. He still felt the straps pushing onto his skull and digging into his wrists. His head throbbed from lack of sleep. And he couldn't gather enough spit in his mouth to get rid of the pasty medicine taste.

As achy as he was, though, he didn't want to rest. He had to break up this tension by doing something else. It didn't need to be anything strenuous.

"Can I go to the gym now since I missed my usual time?" he asked Lieutenant Gresher.

The man smiled, revealing his sympathy. "Sure. I'm headed that way myself." He turned to Sergeant Ortega. "That should be okay, right?"

The woman shrugged. Her despondent mood indicated more of a *whatever* attitude than a *why not* one. Hapker had mentioned that someone attacked her. She'd stood up for him and paid an unfair price. He wanted to tell her he was sorry, but Hapker had said he shouldn't apologize for somebody else's actions.

Still, he wished he hadn't been the reason for it.

His guards shepherded him through the infirmary. When they exited, Jori expected Hapker to be there but found an empty corridor instead. He reached out his senses, finding the man's distinctive aura right away despite his location in a distant part of the ship.

Hapker's lifeforce was a soup of negative emotions. A little more prodding and Jori recognized the source. The sensations from Chesa had the same intensity, though outrage dominated her rather than frustration.

Gresher touched the comm he wore behind his ear. "Hey. You on the way?"

Jori perked up, knowing Hapker was on the other side of that communication. Maybe they could play wall ball today.

"Sure, no problem," Gresher replied, then tapped out. He placed his hand on Jori's shoulder. "The commander will be a little late."

"He's fighting with his girlfriend."

Gresher emitted a mild surprise at his insight. "He said they had a dispute and that he'd like to visit the lounge for a half hour or so to cool down."

It made sense, and Jori was grateful in a way. He didn't want their bad moods to feed on each other. "You'll stay with me?"

Gresher flashed his teeth with a broad grin. "You bet. Would you like another changdu lesson?"

Jori perked up. His body ached, but the challenge was too good to pass up. “Sure.”

“Great! You can train with Korbin and I.”

“Korbin?”

“A very good friend. You’ll like him.”

Jori’s enthusiasm waned. *But he probably won’t like me.*

40
Explosions

Jori stuck by Gresher's side as he beelined over to a tall, wiry man with bold red hair. The two smacked palms and grasped forearms. Then Gresher wrapped his arm around the man's shoulder and brought him to Jori. Broad grins spread from the pair, Gresher's the wider by far, but both still showing a line of perfect white teeth.

"This is Jori," Gresher said. "Jori, my friend, Korbin."

Jori took in the man's amiable lifeforce and liked him right away. The red hair combined with his essence reminded him of a tangy tomato. Like Hapker and Gresher's essences, his had a good-natured strength.

"Nice to meet you."

Korbin extended his hand. "Nice to meet you as well."

Jori shook it, noting the firmness of his grip despite his leaner frame.

"You don't mind if he trains with us today, do you?" Gresher asked.

"Not at all," Korbin replied truthfully.

Jori smiled, glad that Gresher's friend was a much better match for his personality than Chesa was with Hapker's.

"Sir?" one guard said hesitantly. "Didn't the admiral express concern about him learning to fight?"

"Just what I was about to ask," Corporal Lengen muttered.

"I'm not teaching him to fight," Gresher said. "He already knows how to do that. I'm teaching him control—a much harder lesson."

Sergeant Ortega's mouth quirked with uncertainty. "I suppose that makes sense, Sir, but you're not making any friends this way."

Gresher shrugged. "I'm not worried about that. I just do what I think is right."

Ortega's emotions tilted, but she quickly returned to her somber mood. Jori's own took a turn downward at the reminder of his own decision to do what was right, only to have detrimental consequences.

Twenty minutes later, the immersion into his studies dispersed all the stress from earlier. He punched the accelerometer. Twelve point six. Still off. He punched again, lighter this time. Eleven point nine. Too soft. Again. Twelve point two. Close.

He paused to analyze how each hit had felt, then struck again. Twelve even.

"Good," Lieutenant Gresher said. "Now do it some more—until you can hit at a consistent twelve-force."

Jori struck the accelerometer bag. At first, he did it with care. As the knowledge took hold, he moved more quickly.

"Hey," an authoritative voice interrupted. Jori turned. Lieutenant Buckeye planted his hands on his hips. "What are you doing here?"

For some reason, Sergeant Ortega's emotions took a dip.

"He missed his normal time because of the tests," Gresher said.

Buckeye glanced between them, exuding concern. "Well, let's wrap it up."

Gresher made an apologetic noise. "We just got started. He gets two hours, right?"

"Yeah, but..." Buckeye's brows curled inward. "This isn't the time we designated, so hurry it up."

Jori frowned. *What's he worried about?*

"Sure thing," Gresher said.

Buckeye left, a consternation wafting behind him. Jori shook off his unease and continued his practice. After about ten minutes, Gresher directed him to hit at a thirteen force. Sweat poured from Jori's brow, but he kept up the tedious exercise.

A deafening bang penetrated his ear drums. With a jolt, he launched into the air. His head smacked the accelerometer and he crashed to the floor. Agony burst from his tailbone and up his spine. A rolling vibration rattled his eyesight. He moved into a crouch and focused his sensing ability. The pain of death struck him, and he gasped. Not just one death—many.

The trembling of the ship subsided, but those hurting overwhelmed his senses.

"Are you alright?" Gresher asked as he helped Jori to his feet.

Jori nodded and took in his surroundings. Several people rose from the floor, some quicker than others. A few didn't get up at all. Blood pooled by one man's head. A woman's body draped over an exercise machine, her neck bent awkwardly. Neither had a lifeforce.

BREACH. DECK FOURTEEN. BREACH. ALL PERSONNEL TO THE SAFETY DEPOTS.

The trepidation that permeated everyone's emotions hovered just below hysteria as people hustled to the safety centers. Some were helped, either hoisted over a shoulder or carried. Jori looked on in shock.

Gresher dipped his head to Korbin. "Help them. I'll take Jori."

Korbin took off, his red hair sticking out like a torch.

The message repeated. Jori let Gresher lead them to their guards. Two seemed shaken, but fine. Ortega's blue-spiked hair above her right ear was splotched with blood. She glanced about with heightened alertness, though. Lengen appeared to have no injuries, but Jori determined he had an ache somewhere.

Gresher rested his hand on Jori's shoulder. "Let's get to a safety depot."

"Shit" Corporal Lengen glowered at Jori. "We could be helping folks."

A heaviness swelled in Jori's middle. Gresher's emotions shot up but dropped back down. "Go on. I'll take care of him."

"And leave my post?"

"The circumstances allow for an exception. Go."

Three officers moved to leave but Lengen turned to Ortega. "You coming?"

She scanned the room, her hesitance wafting from her. "We have orders."

"You want to help *him*?"

She jutted her chin. "One of us should. It might as well be me."

Jori admired her defiance even as he worried what others would think of her for sticking with him once more.

"Figures." Lengen shook his head and left.

Gresher escorted Jori out of the gym while Ortega stayed at his back. He scanned for Hapker before remembering he wasn't here. Despite the chaotic emotions around him, his ability reached out and located him. Jori blew out a breath, relieved that he wasn't hurt.

They passed several depots before finding one that had a few seats left. Jori jumped into the small, round room after Gresher, then took the chair beside him. Ortega sat on his other side, and they all buckled in.

"Fuck," Ortega said. "Singh, are you alright?"

Jori glanced at the woman she spoke to. Half her black hair was tied back while the other half stuck out in a crazy nest of curls. Blood oozed from her left cheekbone.

Singh dipped her head. "You?"

Ortega nodded. "Do you know what happened?"

"No clue. I was on my way to the gym to take a jog when the shit hit the f—"

The ship quaked. Jori bit his tongue. The door to the safety depot slid shut, locking them in.

Jori's heart raced. The auto-close meant the explosion threatened their section. Whether by smoke, fire, or radiation, he wasn't sure. Again, he extended his ability and found Hapker's distressed lifeforce. And again, no indication of injuries.

He forced himself to focus on his present situation. The round space of the depot enabled him to observe everyone around him. Most of the officers wore a stony expression, but he picked up on their anxiety. That they kept it from showing spoke to their courage.

Jori matched their external calm and soaked in the lifeforces of those sharing this small space with him. A bulky officer to the left of him had the darkest essence, while most others seemed lighter. The one called Singh eyed him, but her emotions were more curious than hateful. She had facial features similar to those he saw most often on Tredon, but he doubted she was from there. Perhaps she was Tavandish or Vadomese. Either way, her attributes triggered a pang of homesickness.

A console rose from the center of their circular enclosure. A holographic image of text formed above it. Before he could read it, a rapid beep sounded and masks dropped from compartments above their heads. Jori's heart jumped into a pitter-patter that matched the alarm. He grabbed for his mask and put it over his face. His first breath stung, making him fling off the mask and cough. Those around him did the same.

"What the hell?" Ortega said.

"Shit!" someone else cried.

Jori covered his mouth and nose. The masks had fallen because something dangerous was in the air. But the emergency air was tainted too.

Gresher yanked off his harness and turned about. With the press of a button, the compartment behind him opened with a hiss.

Jori took his lead and unsecured his straps as well.

"Oh no you don't," Ortega said. "You keep your ass in that seat."

Gresher handed Jori a new mask, then retrieved the one from Jori's compartment for himself. It was bulkier with its own air tank. Jori pulled it over his head and wrapped the straps around to the back. Others did the same.

"Mine is out of air," Singh said.

"How can it be out of air?" Ortega responded. "These things are inspected every thirty days."

"I don't know," she replied. "But I'm telling you, it's empty."

Gresher stretched out his hand. She handed him the mask. The lieutenant's brows pinched between his eyes as he examined it.

Ortega pointed at the information on the hologram. "The air in here is contaminated. Don't breathe too much of this stuff."

Singh's emotions spiked, but she merely dipped her head. Jori's heart thumped as he studied the toxicity indicated on the holographic display. How long could she go without losing consciousness?

His insides twisted. Although he didn't know her, he detected her decency. Someone like her wouldn't get their own brother and mentor killed. She didn't deserve to die.

"Scheisse." Gresher tossed the mask aside. "Check to see if you have an extra one."

Everyone but Jori searched. Frantic rustling filled the small space of the depot.

Ortega searched her compartment, then double-checked the others. She turned to them with her palms out. "There's no more."

Singh clapped her hand over her mouth but maintained a straight face. Her panic seared through Jori's senses. "I'll be alright. They'll get this fixed in time."

Jori swallowed the lump in his throat. The others clearly didn't believe her. Whatever had happened with the ship, many people were dead or dying. The pain of death was more distant than this woman's fear, but it still thrust into Jori's senses like a stabbing knife.

He removed his mask and held it out to her. "Here."

Her dark brows folded in. "Don't you need it?"

Jori shrugged. He didn't want to die, but he didn't like the idea of her dying either. Besides, what difference would his death make? No one wanted him here anyway. No one would miss him.

Singh hesitantly reached out her hand, then pulled it back.

"It's alright," Jori said. "Take it."

She glanced around at the others, then shook her head. "I can't. You keep it."

Jori tossed it in her lap. Her eyes widened and her mouth formed an o.

"Take it," Gresher said. "We'll each have a turn. One-minute intervals."

Singh nodded. Relief emanated from her and Ortega as she put on the mask. Most other officers seemed relieved to have a workable solution, but three gave Jori a dirty look. Jori pressed his lips together. *Why are they upset?* He'd helped one of theirs. Shouldn't they be glad?

"SD-fifty-six, status," a woman's voice chimed through the comm.

"Our depot is full," Gresher replied. "We don't have good air quality. The oxygen in the drop masks is bad too. We've got the individual masks, but one is defective."

"Noted," the woman said. "Other depots are having the same issue. We're doing our best to get this done quickly, but our current ETA is forty-five minutes."

"Our supply only holds thirty minutes."

"We're hurrying, Sir. I'll keep you apprised." She ended the communication.

"Scheisse," Gresher muttered.

Jori's chest tightened. If others suffered the same plight, the people here weren't the only ones at risk.

"When she said other depots are having the same problem, did she mean with these masks, too?" an officer asked.

"I think so," Gresher said.

"What happened?" Singh's tone rose. "What exploded? How did all these air tanks break down? Anyone else thinking sabotage?"

Some eyes fell on Jori. He scowled. *I was imprisoned, idiots.*

"The Tredon emperor is coming for him," an officer with a private's rank said.

"Doubtful." Gresher shook his head. "He probably doesn't know he's alive."

"Yeah right. Maybe we should let him go without a mask."

Jori gut churned but he didn't argue. He'd already given up his mask. And what if the man was right? What if Father had done this somehow? It made no sense, but it didn't stop him from thinking it.

Lieutenant Gresher's expression firmed. "Jori has nothing to do with any of this, so save your breath. We ration air and take turns."

"How long can we survive that?"

Gresher studied the holographic display. Jori did, too. He didn't know much about medical stuff but made a mental note to learn it—assuming he survived.

"I'm not sure, but we're all strong," the lieutenant finally replied. His optimism wavered as he took off his mask and handed it to Jori.

Jori swallowed the dryness from his throat. He looked down at it but didn't touch it.

"Put it on," Gresher said.

"Go ahead," Singh added. "Taking turns is a good idea."

Jori obeyed.

"No way." The officer shot Jori a dirty look. "I'm not risking my life for him."

Gresher raised an eyebrow. "You'll do as you're told, Private."

The man scowled but dipped his head.

Twenty minutes passed. Jori took several turns without a mask. Nausea made his mouth water. His vision faltered as dizziness set in. He sensed others weren't feeling well either.

"SD-fifty-six," the woman through the comm said. "We're still thirty minutes from completion. Sorry we had a complication. Ration as best you can."

Curses spewed. Jori would've too but kept to himself.

Gresher motioned downward with his hands. "We can get through this." He swept his arm at one half of the room. "We'll all take our masks off in intervals, conserve our tanks."

Two officers glared at Jori as he took another turn with a mask. The fresh oxygen entered his lungs, but his stomach roiled—partly from his bouts with the foul air and partly from guilt. This wasn't his fault, though. His father couldn't be doing this, could he?

The first person to throw up had done it just before their next air session. A sickly, tangy scent further polluted the room. Others soon followed suit. Jori managed two more turns without vomiting, but he heaved the third time he removed the mask. His head swam and an ache swelled in his skull.

Singh passed out. Jori's heart skipped a beat. He didn't sense the pain of death from her, but this was a different death. The brain was shutting down so slowly that it didn't know it was dying.

Jori took off his mask and handed it to Ortega. "Here. She needs this more than me."

She put it on her friend and shook her. "Singh. Wake up."

Singh's eyes fluttered. "My turn already?" she said groggily.

"Yes," the other woman replied.

She was too disoriented to realize the lie. Though she sucked in the air, she swayed in her seat.

Jori closed his eyes and breathed evenly to keep the dizziness from overwhelming him. A rancidness rose from his throat. He swallowed it down and almost threw up again. His heart picked up its pace in a struggle to get what little oxygen there was in his blood to his body. His lips turned cold, then tingled.

Someone dropped a mask on his lap. He kept his eyes close and lifted it to his head. He filled his lungs, but it wasn't enough. The next inhale gave him tunnel vision.

"I'm out," the private said in a weary tone.

Jori swallowed as the tingling spread. He would have panicked if he wasn't so tired. Maybe this was for the best. The thought of sweet oblivion drifted behind his eyes just before blackness fell.

41
Aftermath

Something snapped—not audibly. Maybe not even physically. Jori's eyes popped open, revealing a blur of colors. He blinked, each action sharpening his vision.

A woman with kind hazel eyes held a mask over his nose and mouth. He took in the sweet, fresh air and relished the coolness revitalizing his lungs.

"Just a few more breaths," she said.

He breathed until tingling pinpricks of energy spread over him. The woman pulled the mask away and moved on to the next person. After Gresher received his dose of oxygen, he rested his forearms on his knees and bowed his head. Jori mimicked his position, his body too weak to do much else. His mind shifted from bewilderment to sharpness with each beat of his heart.

Once he felt more himself, he stretched out his senses. Hapker was still alright, thank goodness—and on his way here. He scanned the crowded infirmary next. Everyone he'd shared the safety depot with sat or lay on gurneys nearby. No one had died because of him. Nor did they need medical attention beyond receiving oxygen. The tension left his shoulders.

Sergeant Ortega rose to a sitting position. She still wore her sunglasses, so he couldn't see the clearness of her eyes, but her lifeforce blazed brighter than everyone else's. If she'd come from a race of subterranean-dwelling people like he suspected, perhaps that heritage had also strengthened her resilience to bad air quality.

Her emotions warmed when she faced Jori. "Are you alright?"

He moved his head to say yes.

"Good. I'm glad." She glanced at Singh, who pressed the oxygen mask to her face, then back to Jori. "You saved her. You saved my best friend."

Jori soaked in her gratitude. He should've replied but was too sluggish to think of a response.

"Why did you do it?" she asked.

Jori considered all the things he'd observed, including his own emotions. "I didn't want her to suffer."

"But she's a stranger to you. Why put her life above yours?"

"She's a good person." Jori looked away. "Better than me."

Guilt emanated from Ortega, though Jori didn't understand why since she agreed.

Gresher rubbed his eyes with his palms.

"Sir?" Jori said. "Are you alright?"

The man's smile lifted some of the fatigue hanging on his face. "Much better. Everyone in our group made it."

Jori smiled in return. Although a heavy grief punctuated the room, there was also relief.

Ortega touched his shoulder. "Jori, that's your familiar name, right?"

He nodded.

"Thank you, Jori." Her sincerity brushed against his senses like a warm breeze. "You can call me Letta." She chewed her lip. "I owe you an apology. I was wrong about you and I'm sorry for being hard on you."

Jori swallowed the extra liquid building in his throat.

"In our prejudice, we prejudged you," she said. "We should know better. That's what the Cooperative is supposed to be about—giving people a fair chance. You deserve that too."

Jori swallowed. "Thank you."

Maybe she was right. Perhaps that sentimental weakness Father kept criticizing him for was a good thing. His core radiated a warmth that shifted his feelings of unworthiness to the pride and honor Sensei Jeruko used to impart. For the first time since his arrival on the *Defender*, he believed he might fit in here. If only he could convince the Prontaean Council.

The woman with hazel eyes finished scanning everyone in their group. "You're all clear to go."

They hopped off their beds, Jori the least enthusiastic since he'd be going back to his prison. He changed his mind when he sensed Hapker waiting for him there.

"Does anyone know what happened?" Ortega asked as she grasped Singh's hand.

Gresher shrugged apologetically. "I haven't heard anything."

Ortega accepted his response without emotion. Before exiting sick bay, she took stock of all the people. "It's just you and I, Lieutenant," she said to Gresher, then turned to Jori. "Can I trust you to not make trouble?"

"Yes. You have my word."

A few hours ago, she would've questioned his honesty. Jori appreciated how easily she accepted it now.

After entering the corridor, Singh separated from them. "I'm probably needed in engineering."

"Wait," Ortega said, stopping her before she turned around. She straightened into a formal post and addressed Gresher. "Something is going on here, Sir. Normally I'd speak to my command officer about it, but I doubt he'll listen to me." Her chest expanded. "We, meaning me and the chief engineer here, need your and the commander's guidance." She glanced at Singh who dipped her head in agreement.

"I'm happy to help, Sergeant. Please join us—just for a moment. I don't want to keep you from your duties."

"Thank you, Lieutenant. What I have to say is too important to wait."

Jori reined in his nervous curiosity. If she had information about what happened here, why talk to Gresher and Hapker about it?

They passed several more people in the corridor. Some sat along the walls with their heads cradled in their arms. Others with harried expressions bustled by with med-scanners, oxygen masks, or first aid kits. The few who noticed Jori emitted dark, ugly emotions. He wore Ortega's words like armor and kept his posture firm.

The conveyor opened. Officers rushed out, either carrying or assisting the injured. The pain of death reverberated through Jori's senses. One of them wouldn't make it. He expected it to be the light-haired woman with half her face congealed in blood, but the internal struggle to hold on to life came from the man being supported by two officers. It sent a tremor down Jori's spine. A wave of blackness rolled in around his vision, making him flounder.

Gresher grabbed his arm to keep him from falling. “Hey! You alright?”

The knot of rescuers disappeared into sick bay, taking the victims far enough away for Jori to block their emotions.

“Yes,” he replied, not wanting to explain.

“You sure?”

Jori straightened and entered the conveyor with mock confidence. “I’m sure.”

“Maybe we should go back,” Gresher said even though he followed him into the car.

“It’s nothing.”

After some hesitation, Ortega ordered the computer to take them to the brig. The conveyor door closed, then lurched into motion. She tilted her head toward Jori. “You can sense things, right?”

“Yes.”

“So do all these scared and hurt people affect you?”

“Yes.” Jori averted his eyes. Talking about the pain of death might break down his imaginary wall.

Gresher’s emotions sparked in a way that signified he understood. Thankfully, no one pressed the issue.

The conveyor stopped and the doors slid open to the secure holding area. The only occupant halted his pacing and faced them with barely contained relief. Jori’s heart leapt as Hapker rushed to him and pulled him into a hug. The strength of their shared regard penetrated his mental barrier and he allowed himself to sink into the warmth.

Hapker let go and a collective sigh filled the room. Gresher’s wide but tired smile infected the others, even Ortega. Jori soaked in the comfort of their fellowship.

“Do you know what happened?” Gresher asked, putting the pressure back on.

“An energy conduit from the long-range communications array exploded.”

Jori’s emotions turned to ice.

“Woah,” Gresher said. “That’s unheard of.”

Singh gasped. "It's impossible. There are a ton of warning alerts that should have gone out before it got to this point."

Everyone's darting eyes signified they suspected sabotage.

"The explosion triggered a smaller event elsewhere," Hapker continued, "which contaminated the air on five decks."

"How many dead?" Gresher asked.

Hapker's throat bobbed. "At least twenty, possibly including Commander Ramgarhia."

"Oh, shit," Ortega said while Gresher's jaw dropped.

Jori swallowed. "Could my father have done this?"

"No," both Gresher and Hapker said at the same time.

"This is something else," Gresher added.

They'd told the truth, yet Jori detected their rising suspicion. "What do you think happened?"

Hapker shot a wary glance at Ortega.

"You can trust her," Jori said.

Hapker accepted his word as easily as Ortega had done earlier. He leaned in and told them about the bot that may have killed someone named Vavich. Ortega and Singh confirmed that something was odd but had no evidence.

Ortega elbowed her friend. "Did you tell him about Glastra and Lieutenant Krause?"

"Yes. That in itself isn't suspicious, but…" She rubbed her brow. "I don't know. I just have a bad feeling about them."

"Wait." Jori pulled back, his face twisted. "You think Gottfried had something to do with this?"

Hapker shook his head, though agreement emanated from him. "Lieutenant Krause is helping us, more so than anyone else, but something about him doesn't sit right."

Ortega and Singh concurred. Jori swallowed the lump in his throat. The correlation between the man's cybernetics and the robots made his hair stand on end. He hadn't told Hapker the MEGA secret, but perhaps he should. What if it was just a coincidence, though? What if Hapker confronted him and he had nothing to do with it? Besides, Jori had made a promise.

"I'd say we take this up the chain of command," Gresher said, "but I'm not sure we can trust that now."

"Fuck the chain." Ortega radiated earnestness, but it faltered when Hapker's eyebrows rose. She cleared her throat. "Sorry, Sirs. I meant we should go straight to the admiral."

"I doubt the admiral will take us seriously," Hapker said, brow wrinkled. "Anyone who sides with Jori seems to be on the outs with him."

Singh raised her hand. "I can do it."

"I still don't understand," Jori said. "Why do you suspect Gottfried? Just because he's strange?"

Hapker hesitated, then locked eyes with Jori. "Yes, he's trying to help you, but perhaps he has more than one agenda. He's already shown that he'll go behind the admiral's back to do something he shouldn't." Gresher interrupted with a question, but Hapker waved it away and continued speaking to Jori. "Plus, you still haven't told me what he said to you to upset you so much."

Jori glanced down. "I told you, it wasn't anything he said or did." Hapker looked like he wanted to ask about it, but Jori kept talking. "I still don't understand why you suspect Gottfried. What's his motive?"

Gresher crossed his arms. "The database."

"The one the soldiers from the space station are guarding." Ortega's jaw tightened. "I don't trust them."

"My friend Korbin works closely with them," Gresher said. "Told me there's something odd about them."

"Sergeant Carter and Creston said the same thing," Hapker added.

Jori frowned, not following the conversation. "What's so important about this database?"

"It's best if we don't tell you," Hapker replied. "I'm not even supposed to know about it."

A strange foreboding raised the hairs on Jori's arms. "Is it dangerous?"

"No," Hapker said. "But it holds dangerous information."

Database. Dangerous information. Something that has to be guarded. Jori followed the clues. Realization practically slapped him in the face. The perantium emitter. After his father had stolen it, the *Defender* undoubtedly assisted the Thendians with securing the specs so they could build another. Even if it had nothing to do with the emitter, the Cooperative felt it required protection. "Are you sure it's not my father causing this?"

Hapker shook his head. "I highly doubt he'd be able to reprogram our robots or damage the ship from the inside."

Jori sensed the truth of his words and accepted it. Father didn't have the means or the resources to send someone with enough skill to alter a bot's primary function. But Gottfried did. And he might have a motive as well. The way he'd been talking about the Cooperative made him sound rebellious. But would he go that far? A cold perspiration fell over him as he considered the possibility.

He opened his mouth to divulge what he knew about the man but snapped it shut again. If Gottfried wanted the emitter, how did Jori fit into it?

"There's something else," Gresher said to Hapker. He went on to explain about the problems in the safety depots.

Hapker's misgivings swelled. "Chief Singh. Do you have anything you can go to the admiral about?"

"Nothing yet, but I'll do more digging."

"Send him an anonymous message in the meantime so he's at least considering the possibility," Gresher said.

"That's a good idea." Hapker tapped his chin, then addressed Gresher. "Lieutenant, see what else your friend can tell us about those soldiers." He refocused on Ortega. "Is there anyone who could tell us more about Lieutenant Krause? Or monitor him?"

Ortega's emotions turned glum, though she didn't show it. "I'm afraid I'm in the hot seat for ratting out Sergeant Banks. The only one who will talk to me now is Corporal Harley, and..." She shrugged. "You know."

The weight of distress made Jori's bearing slump. Everyone who'd stood up for him seemed to suffer.

"Hey, Jori," Ortega said. "You can sense emotions, right?"

"Yes."

"So can you tell if someone is lying to you, too?"

"Usually, but I can't always sense Gottfried."

"Even when he takes out the inhibitor?"

"Even then," Jori said.

"Well," Ortega drawled. "If that's not suspicious, I don't know what is."

Jori agreed, but only to a point. Now would be a good time to tell them the secret, but he remained hesitant and offered something else instead. "I can still read him in a way. People have tells. Gottfried too. And he may be more forthcoming with me than he would with any of you."

Hapker pulled back. "You mean speak to him alone? I don't think so."

Jori made a face. "I can handle him."

"In the short term, yes. But what if he has other allies?"

Jori took a formal stance to signify his determination to take on the task. "I won't ask him outright. It will be as simple as talking to him about all these events and seeing how he reacts." *Hopefully, he's innocent.*

"Even if you think he's responsible," Ortega said, "the admiral won't accept your word."

"But *we* will know," Jori replied. *And I will have something more definitive to tell you.*

"And if we know with greater certainty…" Gresher added.

"We'll have a better idea of where to find evidence," Singh finished.

The group shared glances until Hapker relented. "As much as I don't like this, we must figure out what's happening and keep more people from dying."

"Agreed," Jori said loudly. He'd speak to Gottfried whether Hapker liked it or not.

As they discussed more options, a chill seeped into Jori's bones and threatened to claw at him until he succumbed. Despite Hapker and Gresher's reassurances, he couldn't help but suspect his father had something to do with this. And if that was the case, all these deaths were his fault.

*****

Gottfried Krause waited in stillness as people teemed about. Medics and officers tended the wounded, wheeled out the injured, or carted away the dead. Dozens of wounded still sat against the wall or lay sprawled on the floor. Though soft weeping sounds brushed through the air, a hefty silence pressed around them.

Despite the oppressive heat, Gottfried's spirit was light. The lingering odor of burnt metal, plastic, and flesh added to the thrill of success swelling inside him.

There'd been just one hitch. Jori shouldn't have been in the gymnasium. Fortunately, he'd survived with no long-lasting effects. His insides itched with the desire to check on the boy, but Admiral Belmont had sent him here to investigate.

The light above the door shifted from flashing yellow to flashing green. The hatch clicked and the light turned solid. With a hydraulic hiss and a few clanks, it slid open to reveal a clump of officers wearing their vacuum-safe and radiation-protective armor.

The one with the lieutenant symbol emblazoned on his shoulder approached Gottfried. A mist of decontamination fluid still clung to his suit. He flipped up his visor, revealing the hard and chiseled face of a super-soldier. "Lieutenant Krause," Lieutenant Buckeye said as he jolted into a stiff stance. "Everyone beyond this point is dead, including Commander Ramgarhia and Major Kozlov. That's nineteen people."

Gottfried refrained from bouncing on his toes. Nineteen plus the others who'd died from the tainted air brought the total to thirty-seven. "Doctor Fritz and the MEGA Inspection Officers as well?"

"Yes, Sir."

Too bad Major Esekielu wasn't one. That would come soon enough, though. "So they didn't make it to a safety depot?"

"I doubt there was time, Sir. It happened too quickly."

"Such a shame." Gottfried put on a mask of regret while his insides jumped for joy. Not only were these MEGA-hating fanatics dead, Glastra reported that his mini bot had successfully infiltrated the inspector's systems and deleted Jori's falsified test results.

"Any explanation?" Gottfried asked.

"Not yet, Sir. As soon as the decon is complete, another team will investigate."

"Thank you, Lieutenant. Join the other teams in patrolling the ship. I want you to check the more populated areas and do a little PR. Check on our young guest as well."

"Yes, Sir."

Gottfried suppressed a smile. Getting rid of certain personnel while also exacting revenge on the MEGA hunters hadn't cost him a thing. He entered Buckeye's report on his MM tablet, then added a recommendation that the entire ship go on lockdown. No doubt, the admiral would jump on the idea and Gottfried could initiate the next stage of his plan.

42
Lockdown

Carletta Ortega perched on the edge of Jori's bed and removed her sunglasses. Even though they'd dimmed the room, she put her hand over the yellow light source. An odd sensation wormed its way through her gut, but with more of a nervousness than a queasiness.

Jori leaned in, studying her with obvious fascination. "They're beautiful."

She blinked. "Thank you."

"So if I turn the lights off, you'll still be able to see me?"

"Definitely." She smiled. "Better than I can see you now."

She usually felt vulnerable when people looked at her eyes. It was different with children, though. Their genuine curiosity made her feel special rather than singled out.

The boy slid off the bed and took a stiff posture. "Someone's coming. I think it's Lieutenant Buckeye."

Ortega's heart jumped. She imitated Jori's pose and waited with fluttering anticipation until Bryce appeared.

His handsome face broke into a smile, but it wasn't for her. "Jori! I'm so glad you're alright."

Jori stiffened into a formal stance. "Yes, Sir."

"You wouldn't have been hurt if you'd visited the gym on your normal schedule."

Jori's eyes narrowed, catching Ortega off guard. She had no trouble believing Lieutenant Krause had something to do with this, but surely Bryce wasn't involved. *Was he?* He had argued more than once in Krause's favor.

"What happened, Sir?" she asked him.

He waved his hand, seemingly disregarding both her question and her at the same time. "We don't know yet."

"Could it have been sabotage?"

Bryce faced her with eyes the cut into her soul. "I said, we don't know yet. What are you doing in here anyway? Aren't you supposed to guard from *outside* the cell?"

Ortega stepped back. "I-I was just talking to Jori, Sir. He's been through a lot. He nearly suffocated. Me too."

Bryce smiled, but something about it seemed insincere. "So you're friends with the boy now?"

"He saved Singh."

Bryce's brows rose and he gave Jori an appraising look. Again, his manner looked off—almost like he'd made an accusation.

Jori cocked his head, adding to the skepticism in his eyes. For a moment, Ortega thought he might've picked up on his veiled criticism, but a glance at the inhibitor behind his left ear indicated not.

She rubbed the back of her neck. Maybe she was imagining things. It made no sense for Bryce to be upset that Jori saved someone's life. Still, her insides roiled.

"Good for you, Jori," Bryce said, eliciting no change in the boy's expression. "Lieutenant Krause has spoken well of you. I'm beginning to see why."

This time, his words sounded sincere. In that one moment, he was the man she'd fallen in love with.

But then he turned to her with a critical mien. "Sergeant, as happy as I am that Jori has a new friend, don't let that friendship interfere with your duty. You will keep guard from the outside." He thumbed at the corridor. "Is that understood?"

Ortega's throat tightened. "Yes, Sir."

She removed herself from the cell with her face scalding as though sunburned. Bryce stayed behind, giving the commander and the lieutenant a brief rundown on the recent events. She wanted to listen in but couldn't hear anything beyond her own churning thoughts.

A grating beep sounded in her ear, making her flinch.

The message played without her having to tap her comm. "Security personnel. Report to the briefing room."

Admiral Belmont's order repeated itself two more times. That she'd received this meant she should obey, but who would be left to guard the boy? She glanced at Bryce, her superior officer. He jerked his head toward the exit, telling her to go.

She didn't see anyone else until she got off the conveyor. Even then, she didn't come across many people. Those she did wore expressions tight with anxiety. Although she felt something similar, there was a relief in getting the commander's support.

All her angst returned when she entered the briefing room. The sight of all the officers sitting restlessly at the rows of tables didn't bother her. Not even the way the admiral stood at the podium with a crinkled brow troubled her.

The things that made her hair stand on end were twofold. Lieutenant Krause practically hugged the admiral's side as he waited for the room to quiet. And lined up behind them were the blank-faced soldiers they'd picked up from the space station.

*****

A nervous energy vibrated through J.D. Hapker's body as the viewscreen outside the cell flickered on, revealing a typical-looking military briefing room. The words, *Emergency Security Announcement*, scrolled across the bottom in a red bar. Acid rose to his throat as Lieutenant Krause stepped beside the admiral. The aide's stupid smile flashed for a second, then disappeared under a false mask of seriousness.

"You'll want to hear this," Lieutenant Buckeye said as he left the cell. After closing the plasti-glass door, he tapped the keypad. The sound fed through, just a rustling as the admiral waited at the podium for everyone to settle.

After a few moments, the admiral puffed out his chest. "We lost thirty-seven people today." His forehead wrinkled, giving the illusion that this upset him. Hapker doubted he cared beyond the fact that it had occurred on his watch. "Although we don't yet have many details on what happened or why, rest assured that we are utilizing every resource to solve this. In the meantime, I declare an emergency lockdown. Everyone who is not involved in the investigation or on security detail is to remain in their quarters."

Hapker approved the strict measures. Unfortunately, if Gottfried had done this, it was meaningless.

"The damage to the *Defender* itself is minimal," the admiral continued. "Therefore, we will head to our destination with all due haste. If we haven't found the culprit—or culprits—by that time, no one will leave the ship."

At least he's acknowledging sabotage.

"Dragon spawn!" someone in the crowd yelled.

The murmurs that followed sent a chill down Hapker's spine. Even those who remained silent showed a flicker of malevolence.

"All possibilities are being explored!" the admiral said, talking over the disgruntled officers.

A sourness rose from Hapker's throat. *All except the one that matters.*

He shared a look with Jori. Rather than be offended about the hateful reactions, the furrow of the boy's brow showed his hurt and worry.

The admiral droned on about all the security measures, including armed and armored guards. Even though he never explicitly implicated Jori, his words seemed directed at him. The boy paled. Hapker touched his upper arm, offering reassurance.

Belmont finished and the screen flickered off.

Hapker, Gresher, and Jori drowned in silent thought until Gresher released a heavy sigh. "We're on your side," he said to Jori. "We won't let anything happen to you."

Hapker matched his earnestness. He squeezed Jori's forearm and offered his conviction. Jori seemed to turn inward with worry.

The cell door opened with a hiss. Lieutenant Buckeye reentered and stood before them with a solid posture. The formality of his stance conflicted with the resigned breath escaping from his lips. "Lieutenant Gresher, someone will be here to escort you to your quarters shortly."

Hapker's veins turned to ice. "You saw how those officers reacted. Jori needs protection."

"He'll have it," Buckeye replied. "I won't let anything happen to him."

Hapker believed the man's sincerity, but an unsettling sensation lingered in the back of his brain. "Then see if you can allow Lieutenant Gresher to remain here."

Lieutenant Buckeye dipped his head. "I'll do what I can. In the meantime—"

The cellblock door opened. Hapker and Gresher stepped to either side of Jori, both protecting him with an arm over his shoulders.

Sergeant Carter and Corporal Lengen appeared. Legen's mouth had a subtle twist to it while Carter wore a softer, almost apologetic, expression. "Lieutenant Gresher, come with us, please."

Gresher smiled tightly. "Of course."

"Does the lockdown include communications?" Hapker asked.

"They're open but restricted to emergencies only," Carter said.

And monitored, no doubt.

"Sir, what about the Commander?" Lengen asked. "Shouldn't we escort him to his quarters?"

"His quarters are here, as he requested."

"So he's in on it then," Lengen mumbled.

Hapker pressed his lips together and glowered.

Carter snapped his attention to the corporal. "Commander Hapker may be a bit misguided when it comes to this boy, but he wouldn't do anything to get anyone killed."

"Thanks," Hapker replied with half-sarcasm. "I wouldn't support Jori if he was the type of person to commit murder. Whoever did this did it for another reason. Sergeant, I'm sure you can guess what that is."

"Yes. They want something," Carter said with an edge in his tone. "Something that the boy's father wants as well."

"The Dragon Emperor must be behind this, Sir," Lengen said.

Indignation contorted Jori's face. "If my father wants something, he'll just attack and take it."

Lengen harrumphed. "Because he's a murderous bastard who—"

"Enough!" Carter snapped hand up. "This is not for us to debate, Corporal. We're here to escort Lieutenant Gresher and that is all."

Lengen clamped his mouth shut and stared down at Jori with withering hatred. Jori tensed but Hapker admired how not a trace of fear showed in his defiance.

Hapker pulled him closer and matched his severity. "Haven't any of you noticed how all the high-ranking officers on this ship are dying? Who does that leave in charge?"

Carter scoffed. "You can't possibly be implying the admiral has something to do with this."

"No, not the admiral." Hapker refrained from naming Gottfried since he didn't have proof. "Someone else with influence, though."

"You mean Lieutenant Krause?" Lengen barked a laugh. "The one who also sides with that little monster?"

Hapker flinched inwardly, realizing how implicating Gottfried meant implicating Jori. "Whoever is doing this is doing it for their own reasons. Jori's not involved."

"Again, it's not up to us to discuss this." Carter shot Hapker a disappointing look. "We're done here. Lieutenant Gresher, let's go."

Gresher clapped Jori's back. "Call me if you need me."

The boy made a single nod.

As Lieutenant Gresher left with the two officers, a twitch in Jori's shoulder captured Hapker's attention. At first, he assumed Lengen had caused it. But in following his gaze, he noticed Lieutenant Buckeye and how they assessed one another.

The hairs on Hapker's arms prickled. Since Buckeye served Gottfried, he could be in on it too, and now he knew his suspicions.

43
Friend or Foe

Jori stared beyond the plasti-glass at Lieutenant Buckeye, trying to get a read on the man since the inhibitor prevented him from gleaning more. When Buckeye smiled at him, it looked genuine. But when Hapker had hinted at Gottfried, a flicker of disdain seemed to cross his features.

Was Buckeye a MEGA as well? Gottfried hadn't mentioned anyone else, but if he was behind all these incidents, then he probably had allies. Jori mentally shook his head, still not sure if Gottfried was involved.

"Want to play schemster?" Hapker asked, taking a seat at the game table.

Jori plopped onto the chair beside him and folded his arms. "I'm beginning to hate that game."

"We can try a new game," Hapker said, radiating a dull resignation.

Jori leaned back and sighed. "Sure. You pick." The level of his boredom paled compared to all the recent deaths—deaths that might be his fault. If only he could do something about it.

After about thirty minutes of mind-numbing dullness, Jori's senses caught someone familiar. He pushed away from the table and stood with a stretch. "My lawyer is coming. I bet Gottfried is with him.

Hapker's eyes widened, and his emotions lurched. "You shouldn't speak to him alone."

"It's necessary."

"We'll figure out another way."

Jori shoved his own internal nervousness away. "The sooner we know, the better. If it's him, it's probably not my father, and maybe we'll have a chance of stopping it."

Hapker rose with defeated slowness. “Let’s see if they’ll even let me out of here.”

Shortly after the main door hissed open, they faccd thc newcomers. Hapker’s relaxed stance contradicted his nervousness. Jori fell into his formal, and more familiar, posture.

Gottfried wore his usual empty smile. Bilsby didn’t have an expression and his emotions were dull.

Jori clenched his fists. *People died. Don’t they care?*

“Good to see you, Jori,” Bilsby said.

“I’m so glad you’re alright,” Gottfried added. His brows tilted with what seemed like genuine concern. “This shouldn’t have happened.”

“What *did* happen?” Hapker asked.

Gottfried shook his head. “We’re still not sure, but we’re investigating.”

Jori chafed at not being able to sense whether he told the truth—or if he felt sad about it. “Who died? Anyone I’ve met?”

“Corporal Sahim, one of your guards.” Gottfried’s eyes turned down as though sad, but it seemed simulated.

Jori remembered the man. Quiet. Dutiful. Suspicious but never hateful toward him. Sadness slipped through his mental wall.

Gottfried frowned. “You’re upset.” He said it like a statement, but Jori suspected he didn’t understand why.

“We’re all upset.” Hapker’s tone carried a hint of accusation. “People died.”

“Yes, so tragic.”

This time, Jori was certain the man faked his sympathy. Misgiving settled in the pit of his stomach. “Who else?”

“Commander Ramgarhia and Major Kozlov, I’m afraid.”

Hapker radiated a distrust that was directed at Gottfried.

If the aide sensed it, he didn’t show it. He folded his hands and hung his head in mock sorrow. “Sadly, Doctor Fritz, Doctor Menger and his assistants were killed as well.”

Jori almost choked. The MEGA hunters that Gottfried hated so much were dead?

“They didn’t find evidence of augmentations,” Gottfried continued, “but I’m afraid you’ll get tested again in Asteria.”

So caught up in Gottfried’s possible motive, it took a moment for Jori to register what he’d said. “Why?”

Gottfried leaned toward him with a soft expression. "Because the results didn't come out as expected."

Hapker tensed. "That's not a good reason."

The aide exhaled. "Agreed, but too many people higher up believe there should've been MEGA indicators." He faced Jori. "Even if you're exonerated, they'll never leave you alone. Every new update the MEGA Inspectors get, every time they discover a new MEGA technology, whenever some jealous rival whispers in their ear, they'll retest you."

Jori worked his tongue, trying to wet the dryness from his throat.

Hapker turned purple. "He's just a child." He glared at Bilsby. "Is there something we can do to put a stop to this?"

Bilsby raised his hands as though in apology. "The MEGA Inspections Office has a lot of leeway. I will certainly try, but the lieutenant is right. If they want to test him again, they can."

Hapker exhaled noisily. "This is wrong."

"There's another problem," Gottfried said.

"What?" Jori and Hapker asked at the same time.

"You're being investigated, Commander. Lieutenant Gresher, too. Everyone who's sympathized with this boy."

Indignation swelled in Hapker's emotions. "For this recent disaster?"

The aide dipped his head.

"You're kidding! Why in the hell would I do something like that?"

Gottfried put up his hands. "I'm not accusing you, Commander. I'm merely telling you what's happening. People are questioning your loyalty. Some are even saying you're conspiring with the emperor against the Cooperative."

Hapker barked a laugh. "This is ridiculous. This prejudice has gotten way out of hand."

"Again, I'm not accusing you. I'm sorry you have to go through this. I'm sorry for both of you."

"All I've ever wanted was to do the right thing," Hapker replied in an almost beseeching tone.

Jori swayed as the commander's outrage shifted to shame. He shared the same emotions, plus some self-criticism. "Do you think my father has had something to do with what's happened?"

Gottfried's brows drew in. "I don't see how, young one."

"Can I…" Jori hesitated. "Can I speak to you privately?"

Hapker squeezed his shoulder. "That's not necessary, Jori. I'm worried this might actually go up further."

"There's more I want to ask him."

Resignation wafted from Hapker like a smoke.

"Would you like me to stay?" Bilsby asked.

"No," Jori replied.

Hapker stepped forward. "Am I allowed to leave?"

"Lieutenant Buckeye," Gottfried called. "Escort these two out. Commander Hapker is to wait in the holding area."

"Yes, Sir."

Jori remained in his formal pose despite the jitters revving up inside him. How would he do this? How would he find out if Gottfried was up to something if his sensing ability didn't work? If this man was responsible for the deaths, would asking get him an honest answer? If Gottfried wasn't to blame, what was the best way to ask without offending him?

He'd had no training for this. *What would Sensei Jeruko do? or Hapker?* No ideas came.

"What do you wish to speak to me about, young one?"

Jori startled and snapped back to the moment. "Um…" He hesitated, still not sure how to proceed. "Um, did someone cause that explosion on purpose?"

Gottfried's smile dropped, but it might've been because of the seriousness of the question. "Admiral Belmont believes so."

"Do you?"

Gottfried didn't answer right away. Jori maintained eye contact despite his unease. He tried to read the man's flat expression to no avail.

"It certainly seems that way," the aide finally said. "I'm told we haven't had this kind of trouble for a few decades. That signifies either complete incompetence of the crew or sabotage." He leaned in and Jori resisted the urge to pull back. "Why do you ask?"

Jori's heart thudded wildly. "Um…" He unintentionally licked his lips as Gottfried studied him. His mental wall held, but he suspected his trepidation showed on his face. "Corporal Lengen and others say my father is doing this."

"Your father doesn't know you're alive."

"But…" Jori faltered. He wasn't supposed to know about the database, so if he brought it up, Gottfried would assume Hapker had told him. He didn't want to get the commander into trouble. How could he word this without lying and without implicating his friends? "I've heard hints that this ship is transporting something, and I've sensed a cluster of guards in another area. Considering this ship's past mission, could it be something my father wants?"

Gottfried's smile returned. "Aren't you just a clever boy."

Goosebumps formed on Jori's arms and ran up to the side of his neck.

"I highly doubt your father knows of it," Gottfried continued.

"So what, then? Why would anyone sabotage the ship?"

"That's a good question, but I don't know the answer."

Jori was unable to determine whether Gottfried had spoken the truth, but the split-second shift of his eyes kindled his suspicions. He needed something more convincing, though. Could he use Gottfried's supposed friendship to get answers? If so, how?

This man had told him his secrets before. Surely, he wouldn't risk telling more, especially since Jori hadn't reciprocated.

Maybe that was it. He could share something personal and hope for more in return. *No. If he murdered those people, I won't keep quiet.* Which meant Gottfried would have ammunition to retaliate with.

Perhaps if he pretended to agree with the sabotage—say he hated the Cooperative and was glad they'd died. *No, I won't lie.* He probably couldn't pull it off anyway.

Maybe a half-truth? "You mentioned places I could go where I'll be accepted. It's obvious too many people here hate me so much that they're willing to lie or believe lies. Can you help me escape before we get to Asteria?"

He held his breath as Gottfried scrutinized him with a wooden expression. Although his mind twitched with nervousness, he kept his mental wall up.

"Why are you hiding your emotions?"

Jori's chest constricted. He maintained an outward calm. "You hide yours."

"Touché," Gottfried replied with a smile. "If you truly wish to escape, don't block me when you tell me."

Jori reluctantly dropped his shield. "Of course," he replied truthfully. "I don't want to be locked up."

"Surely the commander has already offered to help you get out of this?"

"Yes, he has. But I don't want his career to suffer because of me." That was one hundred percent true. Seeing how many people here looked down on Hapker made his throat ache with guilt.

"What about *my* career and the risk *I'll* be taking?"

"I have a feeling you can make things happen without anyone knowing you've done it." Jori allowed the truth of his words to flow but slammed his wall back in place after, lest the man sense the accusation behind them.

"Indeed." Gottfried nodded. His smile seemed empty. "I need to think about this, though. Helping you escape when there's so much else going on will be risky."

"I understand."

Gottfried's flat smile remained. Jori resisted the urge to fidget and hoped he hadn't raised the man's suspicions. Uncertainty coursed through him. He still didn't know whether the man had anything to do with those deaths.

The aide exited and turned back to Jori with a fake smile. "Be careful, young one. I don't want something to happen to you."

Jori's body prickled ominously. *Chusho.*

44
Analysis

Gottfried Krause entered the conveyor with a strange feeling. He analyzed his physiological functions, not an easy task since the six basic emotions combined, twisted, and turned into a multilayered complexity so deep that not even a psychology implant could identify them all.

Once he compared his internal sensations to his thoughts, he realized what it was—misgiving. He'd been so sure that Jori would see the flaws of the Cooperative and side with him, yet he remained aloof.

The conveyor jerked to a halt. Gottfried exited to a hall with no passing traffic. It would've been completely empty if not for the officers further down guarding Belmont's office.

Good. He's keeping the same schedule. He didn't need Admiral Belmont nosing around the bridge right now. The next part of his plan depended on everyone being where they should be, including himself.

He tapped a quick message to the admiral, informing him the boy was secure, then entered his own tiny working space. A faint odor of heated metal made his nose twitch. He endured it, though. The air was deemed safe, so replacing the filters was a low priority.

He sat at his small workspace and used the biometric scanner to turn on the monitor that took up most of the desk. Gottfried sighed at the number of unread messages. Several repair reports dominated the list. Since his processors made it easy to reorganize and reprioritize everything, he didn't bother with them right now. He ignored the most likely superfluous ones from Belmont as well.

One caught his eye—a flag from his monitoring program. Someone had sent the admiral a private message. A mixture of anger and worry bubbled inside him as he read it. Somebody suspected him of the sabotage. They didn't have conclusive evidence, but it might be enough to make Belmont suspicious.

Good thing the man hadn't seen it yet. Gottfried traced it back to its source, wiped it from the system, then considered what to do about the chief engineer. Too many plans were already in motion for him to eliminate her now. He must keep her busy on ship repairs and intercept future messages. With a quick thought, he activated his internal comm and told his soldiers not to allow anyone to visit the admiral without express permission.

Then he leaned back and reassessed his conversation with the commander and the boy. Commander Hapker's suspicions had been obvious. It wouldn't have concerned him if Jori hadn't hidden his emotions. The only sensation that came through was his sadness about the death of a guard.

Why, though? They hadn't treated him well, so why would he care so much when one died? Even the demise of the MEGA hunters had bothered him. It didn't make sense.

Gottfried accessed his memories and replayed the events, paying special attention to the boy's physiology. For some reason, the private conversation had triggered Gottfried's wariness. What his subconscious picked up at the time became apparent now. Although Jori had erected a mental wall, the hesitance of his questions and the way he shifted his eyes indicated his nervousness. When he'd asked for help in escaping, Gottfried should have been elated. But the boy posing the question didn't mean he had an interest in the answer.

Was he testing Gottfried's commitment? He hoped so, but Jori's recent heroic act and his sadness at the deaths showed otherwise. He couldn't shake the feeling that he'd asked because he wanted to know if Gottfried was the killer.

Those people served an evil system. They deserved to die. Jori should understand that more than anyone, but Gottfried didn't trust him to appreciate it. Commander Hapker's influence, no doubt.

Perhaps MEGA-Man could do without the boy. Gottfried sat up and accessed a secure section on his workstation. A prompt appeared several minutes later.

<MM> _

<716Krause> Everything is going as planned, but I'm worried I'm not winning Prince Mizuki over to our cause. Should I bring him to you by force?
<MM> Negative. His cooperation is imperative.
<716Krause> I don't mean to question you, but I'd like to understand why.
<MM> We need the alliance of the last Mizuki heir. Without him, forecasting shows an 87.845% chance of the Tredon empire succumbing to civil war, resulting in our victory being delayed by over three decades.

Gottfried paused. Thirty years was too long. He'd be an old man by then.

<716Krause> I understand. If he doesn't cooperate, what should I do?
<MM> Upload recent data for analysis.

Gottfried sent him all the new information, then studied his reply. The results surprised him. He wasn't to push the guards further. Nor was he to eliminate Commander Hapker.

Interesting. The initial prediction had been that turning the officers against Jori was the best way. Now it was the worst. According to MEGA-Man's analysis report, pushing them to be more hateful could result in him getting maimed or killed. It might also cause more officers to decide to support him. Natural antagonism toward the boy was likely to continue without Gottfried's influence, and without the risk of going too far.

Gottfried skimmed the next part of the report. Sure enough, the best way to secure Jori's alliance was to keep the commander alive. He should also try to win the man over, even if his chance of success was low.

How, though? He replayed his recent conversation. Although the man had distrusted him, he got upset when Gottfried told him that the Cooperative would never leave Jori alone. So Commander Hapker's weakness was Jori and Jori's was the commander. He could use that.

<MM> Recommended course of action – Remove Sergeant Ortega and Corporal Harley from security detail. When tensions rise, take Prince Mizuki and Commander Hapker into protective custody. Do not divulge that you are involved with the deaths. Let them escape the ship as soon as it becomes necessary. I will arrange for their retrieval.

<716Krause> Who will I blame the attack on?

<MM> The Tredon Emperor, but make sure Prince Mizuki is not implicated.

Gottfried reveled in MEGA-Man's brilliance. He ended the conversation, deleted all evidence of it, then dropped against the back of his chair. A smile spread across his face. This would be easier than he thought.

45
Evidence

Now in standard issue battle armor, Carletta Ortega stifled a yawn. This was her third time in three days patrolling the corridor with this silent companion, and she yearned for oblivion. Sergeant First Class Niel Novak was as exciting as watching a stalagmite grow. The weak-chinned man had spoken less than ten words over the course of their shift. He hadn't even grunted when Ortega attempted to goad him into conversation. All she got was a withering look that would have intimidated her if not for his ridiculously boyish face.

Had she met him without the black, stronger-than-steel combat armor, she never would've pegged him for a soldier. He had the build—tall and broad shouldered. The mannerisms—unflappable and serious. Just not in the face. Even the faint wrinkles around his eyes didn't take away from the childlike roundness of his features.

His silence both unsettled and irritated her. Why did he unnerve her? She'd met several soldiers who took their job too seriously, so not that. Was it because everyone on his team had similar closed-off attitudes? Was it how he seemed to look down on her, like she was a mere worm? Or was it because Bryce had gotten along so well with him and the rest of his squad, and he probably worked for Lieutenant Krause?

A shroud of gloom fell over her. She couldn't get over how quickly he'd changed. Or maybe he hadn't, and she only now saw his true colors. It was best that he'd cast her aside, but it still hurt.

She and her current teammate made another mindless trek through the corridor. *Three more hours of this.* She would have groaned if it would've done any good.

The conveyor beeped, signaling its arrival. She and Novak swung around at the same time as its doors hissed open.

She flipped down her visor and snapped her phaser rifle to the low-ready position while Novak went into the high one. "Halt!"

Singh threw her hands up and froze. "Whoa. I just want to speak to the admiral." She motioned with the tablet in her grip. "I have something important to show him."

Ortega reopened her faceplate and relaxed. Novak maintained his aggressiveness and advanced. "You shouldn't be here. Back to your quarters!"

Ortega's heart leapt to her throat. She lowered her weapon and put a restraining hand on his arm. "She's on the investigation team."

Novak ignored her. "You have no business here. Leave now!"

Singh kept her palms up and maintained an open posture that seemed remarkably calm considering the situation. "I must report to the admiral."

"Send a message," Novak barked. "You're not allowed here."

"It's important," Singh said in a softly defiant tone.

"Unless you have express permission, you can't be here." Novak leveled his rifle. "Leave now."

Ortega tensed and planted herself in the man's way without getting in front of the barrel. "Sergeant! We don't have orders to shoot anyone unless there's a threat. Put down your weapon."

His hard expression turned to her. "Her being here is a threat. We're charged with protecting the admiral."

"She's not armed!"

"Listen!" Singh said. "It's important. If it was something I could say in a message, I would. You must hear me out. We're all in danger."

Novak refocused on the woman. "Report through the proper channels."

"The channels are compromised."

Ortega almost gasped. "You have evidence?"

"On Glastra only, but you know who—"

A deafening boom paralyzed everyone. Novak moved first, wheeling into motion without a word. Ortega clicked her visor closed and followed a split second later, racing down the hall toward the bridge. Only it hadn't come from there. She raced past Novak, who'd halted at the admiral's office and yanked off the panel.

A flip of the emergency switch opened the door. Smoke billowed out. Novak ran in. Ortega rushed to follow, only to bump into the soldier.

She squinted, trying to see through the haze and spraying foam of the automatic fire extinguishers. Her eyes stung and filled with liquid. The odor scorched her throat. Novak shouldered her aside and charged by with somebody flung over his shoulder. If the smog bothered him, he didn't show it.

A figure silhouetted through the smoke and grabbed her arm. She flinched, then turned cold when she realized it was Lieutenant Gottfried Krause.

The man doubled over and croaked. "Esekielu." Ortega held him up. He pushed her off. "Esekielu."

She followed the angle of his finger and noted the dark blob in the corner. Leaving the admiral's aide to find his own way out, she hauled the form onto her shoulder. The weight put pressure on her knees, and she ambled out with a hunch. Novak eased the admiral to the floor. Ortega knelt and laid Major Esekielu next to him. Gottfried rushed over with an oxygen mask and placed it over Admiral Belmont's face. When his chest rose and fell with a wheeze, Ortega slumped with relief.

Singh tapped her comm. "We need medics here now. We have three injured on the command deck." She paused, probably listening to the reply from sick bay. "My guess is smoke inhalation. I see no external injuries."

Ortega placed another mask over the major and nothing happened. She pulled off her armored glove and touched her fingers against his neck. Nothing. *Shit*. She tried again. Still nothing. "Get me a med-scanner!"

Lieutenant Krause scampered to the first aid kit, coughing all the way, and returned with the hand-held device. "Is he alive?"

Ortega turned on the scanner and ran it over the man. The small screen displayed a flat line. Red text popped up, stating no heartbeat detected. "Shit"

With a bland expression of someone checking the charge on their gun, Novak took the device from her and tried again. "He's dead."

"Get the AED!"

"Don't bother." Novak showed her the scanner.

Ortega studied it. “What am I seeing here?”

“Severe cerebral hemorrhage.”

A chill crackled through Ortega’s spine. There was no coming back from that kind of damage. She glanced at Krause who was more lucid. *Did he plan it this way?* She exhaled as thoughts spun through her head faster than a pulsar. The major was dead, but the admiral was alive. Someone had tried to kill him as well. They failed. Novak saved him. *Geezus, Admiral Belmont almost died!*

Too many deaths, and most were key people. Singh had said Glastrabot was involved. She’d hinted that she had no evidence against Lieutenant Krause, but they’d been speaking in private. Either the admiral’s aide was blameless, or he was very good at covering his tracks. And this might all be a ruse to make him seem innocent.

A tremble quaked through the wall. Ortega’s heart seized as alarms blared. “Shit!” She sprang to her feet and glanced around.

Whatever had happened didn’t happen here, though. The smokey air remained the same. Her instincts told her to bolt into action. Before she acted, the conveyor opened and medics rushed in. Shouts for this and that rang through the corridor as they hoisted the admiral onto a gurney.

Someone attempted to shove an oxygen mask over Lieutenant Krause’s face, but he pushed it away. “I’m alright.”

A medic with a shaved head scanned her.

“I’m okay too,” she said. To prove it, she pulled in a deep breath.

Krause froze. For a split second, she wondered what was wrong. But then he tapped the comm behind his ear. “There’s been another explosion. I must get to the bridge.”

The iciness still in her spine radiated out like a plasma ball. She wanted to stop him but couldn’t think of a good reason in time.

Lieutenant Krause rushed down the hall, holding his hand to his comm. “People might accuse our guest. I want you to go—”

The bridge doors shut behind him. Ortega remained glued to the entrance, trapped with confusion and indecision. *Why’s he worried about the boy at a time like this?* Certainly, there were bigger concerns.

Singh nudged her. “Are you alright?”

Ortega blinked, then shook her head. “Yes.”

"You should go with the admiral to the medical bay," Singh said.

"Him." Ortega reorganized her thoughts and pointed at the bridge where Krause had gone. "What about him?"

"The admiral needs us," Singh said with intense concern in her eyes. "Someone just tried to kill him."

Ortega watched as four medics rolled Admiral Belmont to the conveyor. As much as she wanted to keep an eye on the aide, Singh was right. Whoever did this might come back to finish the job.

"Okay," she said. "What will you do?"

"I'll find Harley and meet you at the medical bay. We need a plan."

She nodded, then gathered her resolve. With a sudden focus, she took in her surroundings. Two things stood out and made her spine tingle—the pair of medics she'd never seen before and Novak standing out of the way with an empty expression.

She followed the medics as they got into the conveyor. They were undoubtedly planning on taking the admiral to sick bay, but she couldn't help but wonder whether they were conveying him to his death.

As she stepped inside, Singh stopped her with a pinch to her forearm. Her penetrating stare was both stern and concerned. "Tell everyone," she whispered in a tone so powerful that it made Ortega's bones tremble.

Before Ortega could ask more, Novak grabbed Singh by her upper arm and hauled her back.

Ortega's mouth dropped in helpless dismay. *Tell everyone what?* That it was Glastrabot? That was easy enough. But did Singh mean about Lieutenant Krause?

Damn it. Who would even listen to her?

46
Blame

Jori lay on his bed, front down and elbows propping him up. Although his eyes ached from reading the MDS for so long, he kept at it. One section in the PG-Force's code of conduct made his heart caper. Even though the lighting remained the same, the room seemed to brighten.

He jolted up and swung his feet to the floor. "Hapker! I think I found something that can help."

Hapker leaned over and peered at the tablet.

Jori pointed at the line and read it out loud. "If captured by the enemy, make every effort to resist and escape."

"Yeah, that's part of our code of conduct. It's what I meant when you mentioned Sergeant Davis."

Jori reflected on that conversation from long ago when they'd taken the shuttle from the *Odyssey* to the *Defender*. "But I didn't know it was an *official* rule. Since the Cooperative considers it so important, why am I being condemned for doing the same thing?"

"Because you're a murderous little sh—kid," Corporal Lengen said.

Jori clenched his teeth. Hapker's emotions turned up further. He approached the plasti-glass door with his shoulders squared. "I've had enough of your attitude, Corporal. As soon as this mess is over, I'm writing you up for conduct unbecoming."

Lengen smirked. Jori bit his tongue. The threat was empty, and they all knew it. Hapker had already filed a report. "*We're short-handed*," the security officer had stated when Hapker called him from the comm in Jori's cell. "*I don't have the resources to remove someone every time they say something to hurt his feelings*," the officer added.

A simmering anger had festered in the commander's emotions ever since. That was two days ago, one day after all those people had died. Jori's guards, now down to a detail of three with Sergeant Ortega—Letta—and Corporal Harley assigned elsewhere, had blamed him. Most shot him dirty looks. Some muttered slurs with their fellow officers. And some, like Lengen, were brazen enough to speak out openly.

After an ineffective stare-down, Hapker sat. Jori gave him a thankful look, then dived back into his reading. Nothing as interesting as what he'd just found came up, and soon his eyelids drooped as though weighted. The words on the tablet blurred. Even when he saw them clearly, his brain didn't fully grasp them.

A vibration wriggled his bed. A ship maneuver could've caused it, so he continued to drift off. An alarm rang out and jolted him awake. A powerful sensation struck his senses. No, not just one—many, and all in dire panic. Jori concentrated. Terror ticked up with each passing second.

He slid off the mattress and immediately regretted it as his disorientation made the room spin. "Something's happening."

Hapker grabbed his arm before he teetered over. "What is it? What's going on?" His confusion seemed divided—one part probably wondering about the alarms and the other concerned about Jori's sudden condition.

Jori steadied. "People are hurting."

Hapker paled. Nausea rolled in Jori's stomach as the intensity of the emotions jacked up to the full-blown pain of death.

"What the fuck did you do?" Lengen yelled.

"It's not him!" Hapker bellowed.

"The hell it isn't!" Lengen jabbed at the door panel.

Hapker tightened his fists and planted himself at the entrance. "Don't you dare come in here, Corporal. I will take you down faster than you can blink an eye."

Adrenaline kicked in and Jori stood at the ready beside him. Lengen had a solid grip on his rifle, but it wouldn't do him any good in close-quarter fighting. Despite his armor, Hapker could handle him. There were still the other two officers to contend with, though.

The woman exuded dismay at Lengen's unauthorized action. She'd be the easiest for him to take by surprise, but the other officer was too much of a threat to ignore. His emotions emitted a hatred almost as dark as Lengen's. Jori scrutinized the man's bearing, looking for a weakness. He was short and stocky, meaning he wouldn't be easy to stop. Based on his current stance, he'd probably charge head-on, allowing Jori to sidestep out of the way.

The plasti-glass door clicked. Hapker leapt for Lengen before the opening reached the width of his shoulders. Jori dove in low, sliding between Lengen and the stocky man and swiping out with his arm at the back of their legs.

While they concentrated on keeping their balance, Jori focused on the woman. He lunged for her before she took aim, her eyes widening just before he headbutted her in the lower abdomen. Unfortunately, it hurt him more than her since she wore armor. The stocky man exploited his momentary disorientation and thrust the butt of his rifle toward Jori's head. It whiffed by his ear but missed and struck the woman's thigh instead.

Her leg buckled. "Argh! You son-of-a-bitch! Get the kid!"

Jori rolled away, landing on his feet. The stocky man rushed at him. Jori tried to dodge, but there wasn't enough space. The man grabbed his arm with a snarl that was cut short by a reverberating smack to his temple. Hapker swung the phaser rifle back toward the woman but halted when she threw up her hands.

"Drop your weapon!" Hapker roared.

She tore the strap over her head and set it down. Jori remained readily tense but still and let Hapker handle the situation. The commander kept his eyes trained on her as he knelt and groped for the stocky man's rifle. Once it was away and the man had risen to his hands and knees, Hapker yanked his arm, brought him to his feet, and threw him beside the woman. The rifle he'd confiscated from Lengen hung uselessly by the strap in his hand. Jori suspected the biometrics wouldn't let him use it. He had the only weapon, so all three officers stayed put.

Blood flowed from Lengen's long, sloped nose. He stood with a slight hunch and held his abdomen. Murder blazed in his eyes. The stocky man glanced away with guilt. He shot a look at Jori, perhaps expecting him to take advantage of their lessened state and escape.

Jori took a formal pose with his feet planted at shoulder width and his hands clasped behind his back. He jutted his chin and dared them to try something again.

"Sir," the woman said. "I didn't have anything to do with this. My actions were reactions only. I had no intention of breaking the rules and coming in there to hurt anyone."

Jori sensed her honesty. "She's telling the truth."

"I don't care what your intentions were." A purple vein pulsed on Hapker's forehead. "I don't know what the hell you all think you're doing, but this is pure insubordination. Even if Jori—"

The main cellblock door opened. Hapker dropped the rifle and put up his hands as a half-dozen soldiers wearing opaque helmets and carrying phaser rifles entered. A moment of confusion snapped into an overwhelming threat. Jori followed Hapker's lead and surrendered.

Surprisingly, not all the soldiers pointed at him.

"What do we have here?" the lieutenant asked. "I was sent here to make sure you all didn't do anything stupid, and it looks like I'm too late."

"Sir! They escaped."

"Liar!" Hapker barked. "You barged into the cell, intent on attacking Jori."

"No, that's not true!"

"How else did the door get open, dumbass?" Jori replied.

Lengen glared at him. He glanced at the two other officers for help. The woman returned the glower while the man looked away. Lengen's face turned purple at their lack of support.

"You three, inside," Buckeye said to the guards as he pointed to an empty cell next to Jori's. "We'll sort this out later."

"Sir?" they replied simultaneously, Lengen with an angry curl to his brows and the others with wrinkled foreheads.

"I have orders to take these two somewhere safer."

"What's safer than a cell?" Lengen asked with a sneer in his tone.

"It's not safe if assholes like you can go in and make trouble," Buckeye said. "Now get your asses in there."

Buckeye's soldiers prodded them inside with the muzzles of their rifles. The corporal stumbled, consternation replacing the twist in his expression.

After the lieutenant shut and locked the plasti-glass door, Hapker tensed even more. "What happened?"

"There were several localized explosions. A lot of people are hurt."

"What caused it?"

Buckeye shrugged. "That's for others to piece together."

Jori shot him a narrow glance. He opened his mouth to ask for more information, but Hapker spoke up first. "Where are you taking us?"

"Until we figure out what's going on, we're keeping you close at hand."

Jori's sensing ability focused on the admiral. His lifeforce was still there, but didn't carry any emotions, which meant he was unconscious. Thankfully, no beginnings of the pain of death tainted him.

"What does *close at hand* mean?" Hapker asked.

"To the command deck where most of our force is concentrated."

"Don't you get it?" Lengen's face twisted in incredulity. "That's what he wants. You might as well put a lion in a cage with lambs and tell it not to eat them."

Buckeye ignored him and faced Jori and Hapker with genuine sincerity etched in his features. "You'll be safe with us."

Jori narrowed his eyes. "Take off that inhibitor and say it."

Buckeye gave a perfunctory smile. "Of course. I forgot." He removed the device and his even-tempered emotions drifted into Jori's awareness. "You'll be safe with us."

His words rang true, but also ambiguous. What was his definition of safe? And what about the battle-ready soldiers with him? They carried themselves as well as a senshi with the same intent focus and rigidity. The difference was, he couldn't see their faces or even sense them. "Them too," he said.

Buckeye wagged his head and held up the inhibitor. "I only removed this as a courtesy. You'll just have to trust these soldiers are with me and won't hurt you."

Jori's suspicion coincided with Hapker's, but he didn't see a way to argue out of it. "He's speaking the truth—*on all counts*."

Hapker's emotions stung with dread, indicating he'd probably caught on regarding the soldiers being with the lieutenant. He didn't voice his concern, though. "Corporal Lengen has a point. Why would you take a criminal to the command deck?"

Jori agreed. His father would never allow someone he distrusted there.

Buckeye shrugged. "I'm just following orders, but I assume it allows us to keep a closer eye on you as well as keeps you safe from those who think you have something to do with this."

It made sense, but it didn't. Jori considered this situation from two angles. Either Gottfried was responsible for all this, or he was innocent and someone else did it. *But what does any of this have to do with me?* Surely Lieutenant Buckeye could alter the prison's door code so this wouldn't happen again. Why not do that now? Why bring an enemy anywhere near the command center?

His suspicion of Gottfried grew by the minute. He'd promised to keep the man's secret so long as he and Hapker weren't hurt, but what about the others? Breaking an oath didn't sit well, but this was important. He should do it when all these soldiers weren't around.

As they exited the cellblock, Jori halted. His mother's necklace was still under the mattress. Although he'd intended to separate himself from it, the thought of leaving it increased the rapidity of his pulse. Before he decided whether to retrieve it, a soldier grasped his shoulder and prodded him forward. He swallowed down the hardness in his throat and complied.

The main door hissed shut, cutting him off from the last vestiges of his past life and prompting him to pay heed to the current crisis. The intensity of the soldiers' demeanors made them seem like the type of warriors who followed orders without question. None frowned or even smiled. Since most wore inhibitors, walking with them felt like going through a minefield blindfolded.

Jori held his mental wall in place and asked, "If the admiral's injured, who's in command?"

"Lieutenant Krause."

Iciness flushed through his veins. Hapker's increased anxiety augmented his own. There was no evidence, though. Just because Gottfried was in charge didn't mean he had something to do with this. Could the type of man who wanted to protect him be the same type to kill a bunch of innocent people? Besides, the admiral wasn't dead.

He darted a questioning look at Hapker who shook his head. They had no choice but to let this play out. Jori forced himself to breathe though his body constricted as the emotionless soldiers surrounded him.

47
Commandeer

Gottfried Krause infused despondency into his heavy sigh. He clasped his hands behind his back and faced the bridge crew with his brows drawn down in a way he hoped displayed distress.

"My friends. With the admiral injured, I am obligated by the chain of command to take charge of this ship. Please bear with my inexperience. With your help, we will find out what's going on and get this situation resolved before it gets worse."

Three officers remained stone-faced. He couldn't sense their emotions but didn't need to. They were like him—MEGAs who'd infiltrated the Cooperative and waited for their moment to serve the cause. If they had an emotion right now, it was elation.

The other crew members expressed a mix of fury, disbelief, and fear. One also exuded suspicion and this purple-haired woman with matching lavender eyes directed it at him. With a mental prompt, Gottfried sent a private message to his three friends, telling them to keep an eye on Corporal Kramer.

"Several more people are dead or severely injured. We can no longer assume these are accidents."

"No shit," an officer with a clean-cut blond beard said. "We all know who's responsible."

This one didn't look at Gottfried with mistrust, which meant he blamed Jori.

"We're investigating all possibilities," he said diplomatically, hoping to allay Kramer's suspicions. "I've considered calling in another PG-Force ship, but unfortunately the long-range communications array is damaged. Sending people off in a shuttle is a possibility to consider, but until we figure out who is doing this and how, I'm afraid to risk it. We will maintain our current heading while continuing with the lockdown, and our investigation will take place from the security of the command deck."

A woman with curly black hair raised her hand. "How do we know no one here is responsible?"

Corporal Kramer agreed and narrowed her gaze at Gottfried. He expected her to see right through his next statement but didn't have another option. "I can sense emotions and determine whether someone is lying. I will speak to everyone here privately."

The corporal's jaw dropped. She glanced around, probably checking if her crewmates saw the problem. Her mouth snapped shut when no one seemed to have a clue.

Gottfried took in a savoring breath. With the plan running smoothly, this current state of confusion would allow him to proceed with the next phase.

When Kramer's emotions spiked, he realized his expression was smug and shifted it back to despondency. *I must be careful. My authority here is tenuous.*

Kramer jutted her chin. "Procedure states that all command center personnel are to be armed in a situation like this."

Gottfried blinked. "Does it?"

"Yes." She nodded and the other officers heartily concurred.

Clever. "Of course. After I verify none of you are a part of this." He considered interviewing her first and reporting her as suspicious, but needed all the bridge staff until more of his own people arrived.

He mentally sent a message to his pilot, telling him to covertly locate the aptly named *Deus Ex Machina* and intercept. As soon as the *Defender*'s sensors detected that ship, the soldiers and his other allies would begin their hostile takeover. Kramer and other witnesses would be eliminated. He'd allow some people, including Admiral Belmont, Jori, and a handful of others to leave in escape pods. With them out of the way, he could point a finger at whoever he wanted.

Once MEGA-Man's other followers had control of the *Defender*, they'd download the specifications for the perantium emitter. MEGA-Man would then build the planet killing device and begin the revolt that would revolutionize mankind.

Gottfried swelled with pride but tried not to show it. "To maintain command security," he continued, "I will conduct interviews from the nearby conference room. Since security is a priority, I'll start with our guards. You all will be next. In the meantime, continue coordinating ship repairs and keep me apprised of the investigation. Thank you."

The bridge crew jumped back to work.

After putting his pilot in charge, he exited the room and headed to the conference room down the hall where Jori and Commander Hapker waited. The commander's emotions oscillated between nervousness and suspicion while the boy kept his wall up. Gottfried suppressed his own anxiety at not knowing where the boy stood.

Something else occurred to him. Technically, the commander had the rank to take charge. Since he couldn't let that happen, he had to project the confidence that he had everything under control.

He met Lieutenant Buckeye at the door. "Any trouble?"

"Corporal Lengen entered the boy's cell without permission, intending to do violence."

"Where is he now?"

"I locked him up," Buckeye said.

"Is the boy alright?"

"Yes, Sir. He handled himself well. He'll make a great soldier someday."

Gottfried smiled. "Good. Now go back out on patrol. I have reasons to suspect some people may question my authority here, so I need you to enforce it."

"Will do, Sir. Do you want me to leave more men here?" Buckeye indicated the five soldiers behind him.

Gottfried cocked his head to the side and considered. "No. I have enough."

"Not all of them are ours," Buckeye said in a low tone.

"The sergeants won't be a problem."

The lieutenant accepted his reply without question and left. Gottfried clasped his hands and entered the conference room with his head held high. Inside, Jori and the commander stood side-by-side in a strict military posture.

Gottfried stifled his emotions and put on a mask of mock concern. "I understand you had some trouble."

"People are blaming him… Or his father, rather," Hapker said.

"I have no doubt this young man isn't responsible, but I must consider the possibility that the emperor is involved somehow."

Commander Hapker narrowed his eyes. "But how would he get saboteurs on this ship?"

"That's a good question," Gottfried said.

"What happened?" Jori asked. "I sensed more deaths."

"Several bombs detonated."

Hapker paled. "Bombs? How is that possible? Explosive detection devices should have alerted us."

Gottfried shrugged. "Either someone sabotaged them, or used new tech."

Jori and the commander exchanged looks. "Why are we here?"

Gottfried expected the question and supplied his ready answer. "I brought you here to keep you safe."

"People are questioning your reasons for doing that," Hapker said with uncertainty emanating from him but not showing on his face.

"I'm not sure why. It's not unreasonable for me to want to interrogate you with my reading ability. Of course, I already know that isn't necessary." Gottfried waved to the food and water dispenser. "Please, be comfortable. I'll have someone bring you two cots. If you need anything else, don't hesitate to ask."

"I'd like to see Lieutenant Gresher," Jori said.

The boy's eyes reflected a challenge and Gottfried got the sense that he should tread with care. On the one hand, he didn't want to give him access to allies who weren't also Gottfried's allies. On the other, saying no without a good reason might turn the boy against him.

"You can use your ability to determine he's not involved in this," Hapker said.

Gottfried dipped his head. "Of course. I'll send someone to bring him over."

"That would be appreciated." Hapker's suspicions wavered. "What's your plan for rooting out this sabotage?"

"I will interview everyone individually. If I'm certain they are not to blame, they'll help me maintain order. Anyone I'm skeptical of will remain in their quarters until reinforcements arrive."

"Are communications still down?" the commander asked.

"Internal comms and short-range communications are operational, but we still haven't repaired the hub transponder for long-range transmissions."

Hapker's suspicion flared brighter. Jori's emotions remained as blank as his expression. Gottfried smiled, hiding his jealousy of their closeness and hoping to remind them he was also their friend. He couldn't afford to have either turn against him, which made getting rid of Lieutenant Gresher and the boy's other friends a challenge.

A quick assessment of the situation gave him an inspiring idea. People like Corporal Lengen who blamed Jori for these events presented the perfect scapegoats since they'd suspect his friends were involved as well.

Gottfried left the room with the smile still on his face.

48
Allies

Carletta Ortega hugged the wall of the conveyor as the medics assessed their patient. The entire left side of Admiral Belmont's body had been singed, but not terribly so. He probably wouldn't have any scarring. That he was unconscious worried her, but his chest moved in a rhythm expected from someone sleeping. *That's good, right?*

She closed her helmet shield and activated the medical diagnostic application. Its limited capabilities gave little information, but the yellow light indicator put her at ease.

Flipping her visor back up, she studied the medic who seemed in control and strained her brain with trying to remember him. There was nothing unique in his features. His medium-toned skin, brown hair and eyes, and contours of his face—all as nondescript as a river rock.

Ortega nudged the familiar blond-haired medic who'd just finished her assessment of the admiral's left side. "Who's that?"

"Doctor Schmitt."

"I've never seen him before. Where's he from?"

"He came aboard after the battle at Thendi."

Ortega nodded. It made sense, but all these new crew members piqued her suspicion.

The conveyor stopped. She followed the medics out and halted at the swarms of people. They dashed about, tending to the wounded. Apparently, more incidents had occurred elsewhere. Her eyes roved across the multitudes of conscious and unconscious, the burned and the broken, the scared and defeated.

An empty chill settled over her. *Someone wants us all dead.*

She shook off her unease and lurched to follow the admiral. A soldier with his faceplate open halted her. Her heart clenched at his square-jaw and fierce blue eyes.

"Authorized personnel only."

She fought against the instinct to back away from this man and took a stiff stance. "I'm tasked with guarding the admiral."

"Not anymore. We've got it from here."

"Nobody told me anything. Unless someone says otherwise, my job is to look after him."

The man stared at her with a frosty expression that froze her to the core. She kept eye contact, even after it remained fixated on her to the point that she wanted to blink.

Her comm beeped, making her jump in her skin. "Ortega here."

"Report to deck five, guest quarters," Bryce said. "I need you to escort Lieutenant Gresher to the command deck."

A hollow feeling swelled in her gut like a balloon. Hearing Bryce's voice did that to her lately, but this time it was blotched with angst. "I'm supposed to guard the admiral, Sir."

"I've already got people there to monitor him, now go."

Her spine tingled at the coincidence of Bryce reassigning her right after her debate with the eerily intense soldier. "May I ask why we need Lieutenant—"

"Do as you're told, Sergeant."

He cut the connection, leaving her with her mouth hanging open.

She stood frozen until the blue-eyed soldier shifted. She startled at how intensely he still glowered at her. *This isn't right.* She shouldn't leave, but what choice did she have?

She stumbled backward. His eyes followed. Either defiance or fear kept her from turning away, even as she reached the closed conveyor. She spun on her heel and smacked the door button… Or tried to. She missed and struck again, plus three more times for good measure.

The door opened, slower than she would've liked. She slid in and turned about only to find the blue-eyed soldier still staring at her. "Deck five!" she called out in a rush. *Get me the hell out of here.*

When the doors shut her inside, she broke out into a cold sweat. "What in the fuck!"

Her frazzled nerves made it hard to piece together what'd happened, but she was almost certain that Bryce was in on it. A part of her suspected she was seeing false shadows, but this situation was too fucked up to not have powerful people behind it.

Damn him! She couldn't believe she'd once thought he was so wonderful.

The conveyor opened to an empty hall. It was a stark difference from the chaos she'd just left. It took a moment for her to adjust. With a huff, she stepped out and tapped the MM on her wrist. Room five-twenty-seven, to the right.

As she rounded the curved hallway, a murmur of voices reached her ears. A few steps later, four friendly faces appeared.

Her shoulders fell. "Oh, thank goodness." She rushed to them, almost grabbing the nearest one and pulling him into a hug. "Are you alright?"

Corporal Harley's eyes brightened as though he was just as relieved to see her. "Yeah. I was nowhere near the trouble."

She examined the other three. Singh looked no worse for wear. Korbin and Warszawski—or Warsaw, as everyone called him—didn't appear injured. They both seemed tense, but nothing about their faces or clothes indicated they'd been in a situation. That might change soon, though.

"What happened with the admiral?" Singh asked.

"I wanted to stay with him, but they sent me away."

Singh's eyes widened.

Warsaw's short but thick brows tilting inward. "Who's they?"

"To be honest, I'm not completely sure." Ortega thumbed behind her. "Let's get Lieutenant Gresher and I'll fill you in." She hit the buzzer and announced herself.

The door swished open, revealing the darker skinned man who usually wore a bright, white smile. However, he didn't wear one now. His wide mouth had a downward arc that matched the rest of his face. "Do you all know what's happening?"

"We're to take you to the command deck," Ortega replied.

"What for?"

"Orders. No idea why. No one's telling us anything, though I can tell you more people have been killed."

Gresher's face fell.

"And Lieutenant Krause is in charge," she added.

"Scheisse," he cursed. "Is it him, then?"

Singh stepped in. “One of my engineers, Glastra, is involved. I’ve seen him. We’ve seen him—” She glanced at Ortega. “—working with Lieutenant Krause. And Krause has been approving some of his work, namely the things that have gone wrong.”

The lieutenant’s countenance sank further. “Did you find any proof?”

“Yes,” Singh said. “I had to act fast, though. I noticed workorders disappearing from my list, so I’ve been taking snapshots. There’s evidence of three occasions where Glastra completed a job, Gottfried approved it, and it disappeared afterward.”

Korbin edged in, his tall frame hovering over them. “How can he do that? Make information disappear, I mean. Doesn’t our system have securities in place to keep that from happening?”

“Yes,” Singh replied. “But every system can be defeated, given enough time and skill.”

“If your evidence is on that tablet,” Gresher said as he pointed at the object in her hand, “it may already be gone.”

Singh lifted it. “This is my personal tablet. It’s not connected to the network. Plus…” She pulled out several small data transfer devices from her side pocket. “I downloaded the information onto these.”

“DTDs,” Gresher said.

“Everyone take one.” Singh held them out. “Hide it. Don’t let anyone else know you have it until we are off this damned ship.”

Ortega took one and stuffed it in a utility pouch on her vest. “If we ever make it off.” A heaviness fell over her.

Singh licked her lips with tentative hopefulness. “One of us will, surely.” She returned the remaining three to her pocket. “But only if we can find a way to fix the long-range array.”

“Wait,” Harley said. “I thought the damage was minimal.”

Singh’s posture sagged as all eyes fell on her. “Gottfried assigned me to work on something else. Glastra and others I don’t trust are supposed to be doing it and suspicious issues keep arising.”

Warsaw cleared his throat. “Everyone is saying it’s the Tredon boy doing this. If it’s the admiral’s aide, what’s his angle? Is the boy helping him?”

"Jori almost died in that first explosion," Ortega replied defensively. "And he almost died because he saved our lives." She pointed her finger back and forth between her and Singh. "If he's behind it, why would he put himself in danger? And why would he help us if he wanted us dead?"

Warsaw took on a thoughtful expression, then cocked his head sideways. "Something's got to be up between the boy and the lieutenant, though. Why else would he they take him to the command deck?"

"Who? Jori?" Ortega asked.

"Yeah, I saw Lieutenant Buckeye escorting him and the commander and asked what was going on. He said that recent events have put them in danger, so he's taking them to a more secure location. Out of curiosity, I had my friend check the conveyor's last destination and it was the command deck."

"And that's where we're taking you now," Korbin said to the lieutenant.

The way he spoke wasn't an accusation, but it still roused Ortega's suspicion. "Why would he do that?"

Gresher shrugged. "To interrogate me? If others think Jori's involved, then they'll want to interview him and all his friends, right? After all, the lieutenant has extraho abilities."

All the blood drained from Ortega's body. "Does it seem odd that all Jori's friends are being called to the bridge?" Warsaw wasn't a friend, exactly, but he'd never harassed the boy.

She massaged at the ache in her forehead. This made little sense. If Krause was behind it, what did Jori have to do with it? Was calling in the boy's allies a ruse to hide his own involvement? No better way to get rid of the people who suspected him than to accuse them of siding with a Tredon.

She turned to Gresher since he was the highest-ranking officer here. "So what do we do?"

"Shouldn't we start by heading to the command center, like we've been ordered?" Warsaw asked.

Gresher pointed down the hall with his chin. "Let's go. We can talk on the way."

Ortega could practically taste the tension as they headed to the conveyor. When Singh shared a worried look, she took her hand and squeezed.

"Do we have more information about those soldiers?" Gresher asked Korbin.

"All I can say is there's something off about them. It wouldn't be such a big deal if it was just one or two, but it's all of them."

"The blue-eyed one with the square jaw," Ortega said as she suppressed a shudder. "What do you know about him?"

"Not a damned thing. He doesn't talk to us. None of them do. Whenever we try to start up conversations, they give us these cold-ass looks that make you wanna crawl up inside yourself."

Ortega nodded, glad to not be the only one to feel that way. "They speak to Lieutenant Buckeye easily enough." Sadness swept over her. When Bryce spoke to them so amicably in that first encounter, she'd thought it was his winning personality. Now she knew better, and anger resurfaced.

After entering the conveyor, she filled the lieutenant in on the explosion that killed Major Esekielu, and how Sergeant Novak had saved Admiral Belmont.

Gresher rubbed his jaw. "This isn't adding up."

"Maybe killing the admiral isn't his objective," Singh said.

Ortega shifted her feet. "Then what is?"

"The database," Korbin replied.

Warshaw made an apologetic noise. "Maybe he wants it for the Dragon Emperor. Maybe the boy isn't involved, but who else would want it so badly?"

Singh nodded. "The emperor could've put a reward out for it, let others do the underhanded work."

"And it fits if he doesn't know Jori is alive." Ortega straightened as something else occurred to her. "We should tell the commander. He's now the highest-ranking officer on this ship. He can take command from Lieutenant Krause."

Singh folded her arms. "Oh, Krause won't let that happen. That's for sure."

"I doubt Commander Hapker will get much support," Gresher said. "Not with everyone believing this is Jori's doing."

"We should at least warn him about Krause," Ortega said. "He might have some ideas we don't."

Gresher's eyes turned distant. After a heavy sigh, he spoke. "Alright. If he's also on the command deck, let's get going and hope we'll have a chance to talk to him."

Ortega swallowed. Hopeless was more like it.

49
Revelations

J.D. Hapker paced the room. One hand cupped his elbow, the other stroked his chin. If Lieutenant Krause was behind all this, he and Jori were in big trouble. But if that was the case, why were they here? What did he want from them? He had to do something but couldn't map out a trail if he couldn't see the terrain.

He rounded the conference table and stopped in front of Jori. "You can't read him? Not even a little bit?"

"His emotions come through once in a while, but he's completely blank most of the time."

"Is that normal?" Hapker asked. Although he and Jori had discussed this before, he hoped to glean something new.

"No, but it's not impossible either. My mother can block hers, but she has to concentrate."

Questions ran through Hapker's head but trying to find answers was like trying to see through the fog. Only shadows lurked, nothing substantial enough to determine their nature. "So she did it intentionally. Does that mean Gottfried is blocking you on purpose?"

Jori opened his mouth, then closed it again. Something about his hesitance seemed off. "I don't know. He says he does it out of habit, and I believe that's possible. But if he's lying, I don't understand his motive."

The boy looked troubled, so Hapker bent low and placed both hands on his shoulders. "Something's bothering you. Let me help."

Jori exhaled slowly. "There are some things I haven't told you. Things Gottfried asked me to keep secret."

The ominous weight in Hapker's stomach intensified. "This secret is probably troubling you for a reason. Sometimes when someone asks you to not to tell, it's to protect themselves when they've done something wrong." Jori looked down. "Listen. A lot of people are dead. If his secret is related to what's happening here, then you must speak up."

Jori's throat bobbed as he glanced around. "Could this room be bugged?"

Hapker blinked, then searched as well. "It shouldn't be. Private meetings are held here."

"Gottfried is a MEGA," Jori said.

Hapker jumped to his feet. "What?!"

Jori flinched backward, then resumed his stance. "I think he wanted me to admit it too, so he shared his secret. He says we're the same because we're both being suppressed for being different."

The thudding of Hapker's heart hurt his eardrums. A MEGA being this high in power was unheard of, frightening even.

"It's probably the real reason I can't sense him," Jori said, his words hitting Hapker's ears but his mind not registering them. "I've met cyborgs before, and they were the same way. It's like their cerebral implants do something to them."

Hapker's face tingled as though all his blood drained from his head. A MEGA working for the admiral. Was Belmont a MEGA too? Or was it just Gottfried reaching for power despite the injunction?

"Remember how Gottfried mentioned places I could go where people would accept me?" Jori's eyes glittered with guilt, but he faced it. "He brought up a specific place. He said the MEGA Injunction doesn't apply there. I don't have to worry about MEGA Inspectors or others watching me or trying to suppress me."

"Where?"

"Have you ever heard of the Parvati system in the Kanivian sector?"

Hapker knew it. It was located well outside of Cooperative territory.

"What about a planet known as Cybernation?"

Hapker cocked his head. He was aware of it, but never gave it much thought since it was far away and not part of the Cooperative. Its government was free to run their world however they chose. Why would a MEGA from that world want to join the Cooperative?

Realization struck him like a blast of cold water. Gottfried might belong to an organization that wanted to spread its ideology beyond its borders. It wouldn't be the first time in history this had happened. "He wants the emitter specs. He wants to take it to people like him so they can use it against the Cooperative."

Jori paled. "So that *is* the secret cargo. I suspected, but it didn't occur to me he'd do all this to steal it." He shook his head. "I should have known. I should have made the connection. Of course that's what he wants. He hates how their rules about being a MEGA work against him. He believes it's unfair and… Well, I can understand why."

"Murdering people isn't fair," Hapker said harshly.

"No. I agree. It's not," Jori said. "So what do we do?"

Hapker stroked his chin. Jori's belief that the Cooperative behaved discriminately resonated, but he wasn't sure what to think about MEGAs. History pointed at how those with enhancements had once corrupted governments and kept certain segments of society down, but didn't the injunction do the same thing?

That was a debate for another day, though. Regardless of whether Lieutenant Krause might have a point, taking innocent lives made him the bad guy.

He sat and rested his elbows on his knees. "I have no idea."

"And what does he want with me?" Jori's throat bobbed.

"It sounds like he's been trying to recruit you. Even if you're not a MEGA, you're special. And I bet you being the emperor's son doesn't hurt either. He might be planning to use that somehow."

Jori's face turned ashen. "I didn't think about that."

"The good news is he doesn't want to harm you. We can use this against him."

"You mean pretend he's still our friend?" Jori's nostrils flared. "I'm not sure I can do that. I felt the deaths of all those people he killed."

They remained silent, letting the implications of this new revelation take hold.

"There's one more thing," Jori said, another twist of guilt marring his features. "Gottfried has been hiding imperium-animi abilities."

Hapker sucked in a breath and froze.

"I doubt he's used it on us," Jori continued as though reading Hapker's mind. "It probably wouldn't have worked on you anyway."

"How can you be so sure?"

"Because my mom has that ability too, remember? She says it doesn't work on strong minds, and you're one of the strongest people I know."

Hapker racked his brain with trying to decide whether Lieutenant Krause might have used his ability on him. If he had, how would he tell?

What about others like Chesa? She'd always had the personality of a storm, but had he pushed her into a hurricane? Or Banks? And why would Gottfried do that if he considered Jori an ally?

Oh crap. Had Gottfried been manipulating the admiral?

He ran his hand through his prickling scalp. "I wish you would've told me all this earlier. We might have been able to stop him before it was too late."

Jori hung his head. "I thought he was my friend, and I didn't want to get him in trouble."

Hapker didn't mean to make him feel guilty. Jori probably wasn't the only who'd been manipulated by Gottfried. "He still believes he's your friend, otherwise we wouldn't be here. I know you don't like him, but we should use this to our advantage."

Jori looked up in earnestness. "I'll try."

Hapker swallowed the guilt of using a boy to take down a monster, but they had no other options. "Let's wait for Lieutenant Gresher and see if he comes up with any other ideas."

Jori nodded. Hapker leaned back in the chair and considered everything that had happened. It all made sense now. Not just the people dying, but how people behaved toward Jori. Gottfried might not have the power to manipulate strong minds, but perhaps he'd enhanced their negativity. Maybe Banks and Chesa weren't entirely to blame. It didn't change his discontented feelings about her, but it somewhat redeemed her.

He broke out into a cold sweat at the realization that Gottfried could turn more crew members against him. And if that happened, he'd have no idea who the real enemies were.

*****

Gottfried Krause's chest burned like an ember. Jori, the commander, and all his friends reeked of suspicion. It hardly mattered since he had plans for them, but he couldn't afford to lose the boy's allegiance.

He wished he'd had the foresight to bug the conference room. Not knowing the details of their misgivings presented uncertainties, so he must be careful.

"Sir," one of his people said right on schedule. "You should see this."

Gottfried made a show of looking over the man's screen, then rose with mock horror on his face. "Oh, no. Keep monitoring them and let me know what else you find."

"What is it, Lieutenant?" Corporal Kramer asked, suspicion blazing from her.

"Communications between Sergeant Ortega and Corporal Harley are very suspicious," Gottfried replied. "It almost looks like they have plans to rescue our prisoner."

A collective gasp resounded through the bridge. Kramer straightened. The wideness of her purple eyes highlighted both her shock and disbelief. "I don't believe it. Why would they do that?"

Gottfried shrugged. "Maybe he promised them something."

Kramer harrumphed. "Being easy on a child, especially one who's saved some of our people, is one thing. Turning against us is another."

"*Someone* is committing the sabotage on this ship."

Her face twisted as though to say, *Maybe it's you.* "So what did you find?"

Gottfried had their false messages ready to share but waited. "Nothing conclusive at the moment, which is why I asked him to keep monitoring them."

Her eyes narrowed, but she turned back to her workstation. Gottfried pretended to review the readouts on another workstation while communicating with his soldiers. They were to allow Lieutenant Gresher and the others to reach the command deck. The attack should wait until they exited and moved away from the conveyor. Sergeants Creston and Carter, who also patrolled the area but not near the conveyor, would rush in. Thanks to their prejudice, they'd probably assume they were allied with the boy.

Commander Hapker would undoubtedly hear the skirmish and want to help. His soldiers would keep that from happening, though. Since those men either wore inhibitors or couldn't be sensed, Jori wouldn't be able to determine who started it or why.

The plan was perfect. The boy's allies had too much influence. Eliminating them without implicating himself meant he'd succeed in both objectives. If he could give himself a congratulatory pat on the back without looking like an idiot, he would. For now, he imagined MEGA-Man's praise when he brought in both the emitter specs and the last Dragon Heir.

50
Command Deck

Carletta Ortega held her phaser rifle in the low ready position as she peeked out of the open conveyor. A glance to the right revealed an empty hall. Two soldiers from the space station stood a few yards down on the left. They made eye contact, and although they didn't make a move against her, she couldn't shake the feeling that she was walking into a trap.

She stepped out, rifle still low, and faced them. "We're here with Lieutenant Gresher, as ordered."

The dark-skinned soldier with coal irises and yellow sclera made a sharp nod. It was undoubtedly meant to tell her to go ahead, but the way he watched her reminded her of a spider perched on a web.

She motioned the others out. Korbin came first, peering to the left before exiting. Harley next, taking the right. Lieutenant Gresher followed, his bearing presenting calm but the flicking of his eyes giving away his wariness. Singh came after. A strained expression crossed her features. Warsaw was last. His gaze shifted even more, but his training kept him steady.

"Where do we take him?" she asked the soldiers.

"Room F," the one with the short toffee hair said.

She peered down the left hall, which curved in a large oval and had several support, supply, and conference rooms along the way. The bridge lay at the other end, out of sight from the conveyor, giving guards the space to head off any incursions. It also allowed the soldiers to converge on her and her team from both sides.

She couldn't say why this situation unsettled her, but the others seemed to share her unease. They faced soldiers who were too stiff, their eyes too penetrating, and their expressions lacking even a hint of friendliness. *Damn it. I wish I had a body energy shield.*

"Is that where Jori is?" Lieutenant Gresher smiled disarmingly, though Ortega doubted the soldiers appreciated it.

"You're not here to see the boy."

Gresher stepped forward with his hands loose at his sides. "Then why am I here?"

The toffee-haired soldier squared up into a position that was as tight as his haircut. "Lieutenant Krause has some questions."

"Ah, so he's in Room F?"

"He'll be there shortly."

"Hey," Ortega said, both stalling and because something occurred to her. "Where's Sergeant Novak? I thought he was on duty here."

"That's not your concern. Your concern is taking this man to Room F."

Ortega leaned in toward Gresher's ear. "This doesn't feel right, does it, Sir?"

"It doesn't," he whispered while still smiling.

"We should leave, come back better prepared," she murmured.

Gresher jerked his head down in an almost imperceptible assent.

"Singh," Ortega said in a normal tone. "You should go."

Singh's face crinkled as if to ask if she was crazy. "I'm not leaving you."

"*Get* in the conveyor," she replied with a drawl that she hoped communicated her true intent.

"Oh. Yes. I've got work to do." She smacked the panel, reopening their only way out of here if things went sideways.

"Hey!" both soldiers yelled at the same time. "Where do you think you're going?"

Ortega winced. *Damn it.* The soldier with the tight haircut leveled his weapon with a snap. The one with black hair and yellow sclera followed suit. Ortega reflexively did the same and her team copied her.

"Woah, woah, woah!" Gresher put his hands up and palms out. "Chief Singh is the only—"

"Incoming!" Warsaw yelled.

The man took a step back, then collapsed. The zing of phaser shots zipped through the air from both sides.

"Scheisse!" Gresher protected Singh as they stumbled to the rear of the car.

Two space-station soldiers converged on them from either side. Ortega laid down cover fire, hitting one opponent with an energy blast only to have his armored vest neutralize it. "Get inside!"

Korbin jumped in next with Harley backing in after him with a limp. A hole had torn through the armor of his thigh, indicating a soldier had used the projectile ammo of his Power-K rifle. An energy blast struck Ortega's own armor but diffused in a dissipating vibration. She dived into the conveyor last, returning fire as she went. The chlorine-like smell of the phased air switched her from caution-mode to an outright defensive one.

Ortega and her team crowded around the inside edge of the doors. She and Harley fired to the right while Korbin took the left. Warsaw lay in a heap on the floor in the hall. A rupture to his visor and the red gore beneath denoted yet another injury by gunfire—only Warsaw was likely dead. *Oh, hell.* The pang of regret piercing Ortega's chest evaporated as more pressing concerns dominated her attention.

"Emergency Lockdown!" a soldier barked, stopping the car doors from closing. "Confirm. All deck functions locked down."

"Deck functions locked," an automated voice responded.

"Shit!" Ortega said, though she appreciated the protection of the partial opening.

"We're sitting ducks in here!" Harley called out.

"Keep firing! Don't let them get close," she ordered. "Singh, can you override the controls?"

"Yeah, I-I can do that." A clunk indicated she opened the emergency toolbox.

"Cover me," Ortega told Harley.

He took the high position while she dropped low and reached for Warsaw. The air sizzled above her as she grasped his shoulder and pulled.

Lieutenant Gresher helped. "Got him."

She left him to check on the man and fired down the hall.

"He's dead," the lieutenant said.

Ortega held back her remorse and concentrated on defending the others. "Can anyone disable the biometrics of his weapon?" She yelled. No one answered.

As suddenly as the enemy had started, they stopped. The lull wasn't a reprieve, so she waited for them to charge in at any moment.

"Sergeant Ortega!" a voice rang out from the left. It sounded like Sergeant Carter. "What are you doing?"

"Lieutenant Krause is the saboteur!" she replied.

"You expect me to believe that?"

"It's true!" Singh said. "I have evidence."

"Then why not present it? Why come in here with weapons blazing?"

"Those soldiers fired first, Lieutenant," Ortega said. "They killed Warsaw."

A whispered curse carried from down the corridor.

"They report to Lieutenant Buckeye," Gresher added, "who reports to Lieutenant Krause."

"Stop trying to shift blame," a woman shouted. "Everyone knows that little Tredon monster and his father are behind this. That's the real reason you came in here shooting. You're helping him take over the ship!"

Ortega clenched her teeth. She'd never cared for Sergeant Chesa Creston, but now she liked her even less. The woman was relentless in her scathing attitude. Everyone called her Firestorm because of it. Ortega preferred Firebitch. "I'm telling you guys, it's not Jori. It's the admiral's aide."

Sergeant Carter's tone remained firm. "Stand down. Let's talk about this."

"Sir?" Korbin said. "Haven't you noticed the strangeness of those soldiers you're standing with?"

"That they're highly trained professionals? Nothing unusual about that," Carter replied. "Now stand down. You have 'til the count of five."

Ortega gritted her teeth in frustration. "No way! If we come out, they'll kill us. Then they'll kill you and say we did it."

"Five… Four."

She glanced at her friends, who all looked to her. Sergeant Carter and Creston probably weren't in on it, but they believed they were in the right. She wanted to surrender and tell them everything but didn't want to put the others at risk.

Gresher saved her from deciding by shaking his head. "If you get an opening for Carter or Creston, don't take it. Focus on the soldiers. We'll surrender once they're out of the picture."

"If we survive," Harley muttered.

"One." Carter paused. "Damn it, Ortega." He hesitated again. "Open fire!"

A series of blasts erupted. Ortega and the others returned the gesture.

"This won't last," Harley said. "We'll run out of ammo soon."

Ortega pulled behind the doorjamb and checked the energy level of her phaser rifle. The bar was yellow and about halfway down. "Shit," she muttered.

Singh stood just inside, somewhat safe from the incoming blasts. She rummaged inside the panel, her face twisting into a focused determination.

"How close are you?" Ortega asked.

"Not close at all. They make this difficult on purpose and all I have are these shitty emergency tools."

Shit. Ortega pointed her rifle back around the corner and fired.

Her weapon dropped from her hand with a shock. *What the hell?* She glanced stupidly at the damned thing, then realization struck her. "I've been hit!"

A projectile had penetrated her armor and lodged in her forearm. She attempted to move her fingers but received a surge of pain in reply. She switched the rifle to her other side. "Korbin, change sides with me."

He did. She hunched in her new position and propped the butt on her knee. *Tricky but doable.*

Did we take any of them down? She doubted it. Working for Lieutenant Krause meant they were probably better prepared, which meant body energy shields and a stockpile of ammunition.

Despair ran through her like a crashing wave that took her under and threatened to drown her. If Singh didn't get that door open soon, they'd be done for.

51
Rescue

Jori sat at the conference table with his head resting on his forearms. Taking in the swarms of varying emotions of the ship's occupants made him woozy, but it was necessary. He got an idea of their locations and moods, which told him who to avoid should he get out of here and who might be easier to convince of Gottfried's treachery.

He almost laughed. Unless someone had outstandingly obvious evidence, no one would believe him and Hapker over the admiral's aide. Not even the two nearby sergeants, Carter and Chesa.

Damn. Why does it have to be Gottfried behind all these deaths? Going against him meant remaining the Cooperative's prisoner.

Patting his chest where his mother's necklace should hang made his heart ache but also hardened his resolve. No way would he side with a murderer.

He focused his senses on a group of six people. Gresher, Ortega, Harley, the woman from the safety depot, and two others—all with agreeable essences—zoomed closer.

He sat up when they reached this deck. His skin itched in anticipation as their emotions burst into wariness. A shiver ran down his spine. Gottfried wanted *him* for something, but he didn't need his friends. He sprang out of his chair. "They're in trouble."

Hapker, who'd been pacing again, froze in his tracks. "Who? What sort of trouble?"

"Gresher. Others. They're here and something—"

The pain of death pierced him, followed by a surge of their panic. He rushed to the exit, evading Hapker when he grabbed for him. The conference door slid open. Distinctive zaps and yells resounded through the hallway.

A soldier whose clear faceplate revealed a man with a weak chin stepped in Jori's way. "Stay inside!"

Jori attempted to dart around him, but the man grabbed his arm and shoved him back in.

"What's going on?" Hapker asked too late as the door shut. He pressed the open button, but nothing happened. A few more jabs didn't change the situation. His emotions flipped from consternation to dread.

"They're in trouble!" Jori ripped off the control panel cover. "We've got to help them."

Hapker gripped Jori's shoulder. "Hold on. We need a plan."

Jori jerked away in a flicker of annoyance. Rampant thoughts spun in his head. His chest heaved as he attempted to rein in his panic. *Weapons. We must have weapons*. He glanced about.

An emergency box almost as big as him hung on the far wall. He rushed over and yanked it open. Bandages. Oxygen masks. Flashlights. Blankets. *Useless*.

He tossed them aside and continued rummaging. Hammer. Wrench. Electric screwdriver. Utility knife. Better, but only in close-quarter fighting. Some of the smaller heavy items would be good for throwing so he dropped them into the pile.

The box also held military-grade enviro-suits. Like all vacuum-rated wear, they protected against extreme temperatures and high-speed particles. Because he was on a battleship, they had some defense against phaser fire as well.

He grabbed two, tossing one back to Hapker. With a flick, he unrolled his. It was too big but didn't need to fit to provide protection.

"What are you doing?" Hapker asked as Jori slid his foot into the suit leg. "You're staying here."

"They need our help."

"You're *staying* here," Hapker repeated.

"Where Gottfried can get to me? I'm going."

"Jori—"

"*I'm going*." He defiantly slipped on the rest of the gear.

Hapker's shoulders slumped in resignation. He finished putting on his suit, including the helmet, then grabbed several of the implements Jori had set out.

Jori tested his mobility. The material bunched up in uncomfortable places, making it pinch his skin, but he maneuvered his throwing arm well enough. He snatched the remaining items, plus the utility knife.

Hapker winced. "We don't know for sure if they're voluntarily aiding Gottfried, so don't use that on anyone unless you absolutely have to."

Jori's heart stung. Even Hapker expected the worst from him.

The heaviness of everything he carried on his utility belt pulled the waistline down past his hip. He walked like a lumbering blob but managed a swift pace.

"How many are there?" Hapker asked.

"I don't know. I can't sense them."

"Not a single person?"

"Sergeant Carter and your friend Chesa, but no one else in the corridors. Either those soldiers are wearing inhibitors or they're like Gottfried."

Hapker paled. "Alright. Let's see what we're up against."

Jori returned to the control panel. Glancing at its innards, he used his tools and experience to trigger the manual override. The door didn't slide open as usual, but the crack was enough. He and Hapker threw their weight on either side and widened it.

When they stepped out, nobody stopped them. Two soldiers hugged the wall and faced the opposite direction. One with a sergeant's epaulette took the high position while the other knelt. Both remained poised to fire but waited for their opponents to show themselves.

Hapker charged in. Jori raced after him as fast as the cumbrous and chafing suit allowed. Stopping midway, he yanked the heavy wrench from his belt and flung it with swift precision.

It hit the kneeling soldier's helmeted head at the same time as Hapker tackled the other one. Both soldiers toppled. Hapker too, but with the advantage of expectation. While he wrestled the man and attempted to disable his weapon by stabbing it with the electric screwdriver, Jori hurled more tools at the brown-eyed man storming toward him.

The make-shift weapons bounced off the armor with no effect. Jori flung the hammer, aiming for the gap between the thigh guard and knee plate. The crack of metal on dense composite material caused the man to stagger, but not fall. He pounced after Jori, whose suit inhibited his ability to evade. The soldier struck Jori in the middle, knocking the air out of him. Despite the discomfort, he snagged another tool from his belt and stabbed it into the unprotected side of the man's gluteus.

The soldier remained stoic. He grabbed the folds of Jori's suit and yanked him close enough that their helmets bonked.

Jori reacted with a trained instinct, but his smallness did little against the soldier's size and armor. Battle induced time distortion allowed him to see the man's fist coming in slow motion but gave him no chance to deflect it. Just before it hit, the soldier collapsed.

Hapker poised the butt of the phaser rifle, ready to strike again if the soldier moved. "See if you can unlock this weapon, then set it on stun and give it to me."

"Stun won't penetrate their armor, but there's a setting that will jam the electronics in their suits and weapons."

"Do it."

Jori dipped his head and set to work. The same buzzing tension that he'd experienced back when he'd helped Hapker escape Father's ship vibrated through him. The comfort of the man's presence aided his focus but didn't allay his fear that this situation would end just as badly.

Hapker glanced down both sides of the corridor, likely considering whether to join their friends and fight together or go around and take the enemy from the back.

Jori unlocked the weapon and reset it at the same moment as a tromp of footsteps echoed from the opposite direction. He handed Hapker the rifle and darted for cover.

Hapker dropped to a knee and fired. Jori grabbed a fallen rifle and gripped it like a club, then hunched behind him. Blasts from both sides zipped toward them. One glanced off Hapker's helmet. Another struck the puffy material around Jori's arm, producing only a whispering sensation of heat. An icon on his visor display flashed, indicating the integrity of the suit was compromised. Had he been in a vacuum, it would have been a problem for only a moment as the augmented fabric automatically repaired itself.

Repeated bursts from Hapker's Power-K rifle struck the soldier until his shield failed and blue sparks sizzled around his weapon.

The man tossed it aside and continued his advance. Return fire zapped Hapker, making him yell but not stopping him.

The soldier dodged sideways while the other with a corporal's epaulette dove forward and tackled Hapker. Jori wielded his still locked weapon like a baton at the weak-chinned man's rifle, hoping to disable its energy flow. It worked. A glitter of electric blue discharged as the man's heavy hand struck the side of Jori's helmet hard enough to make him lose his balance.

The soldier came for him. Jori rolled out of the way, sprang to his feet, and swung his rifle. He missed, but it kept the man back while the corporal manipulated Hapker into a chokehold. The weak-chinned man pivoted to take on the adult threat. He punched Hapker in the gut with the speed of a piston.

Jori charged into the foray and bashed at the back of the corporal's leg. The man buckled. Hapker thrust out with the flat of his foot. The soldier bowled over backward. Jori slammed his weapon across the front of his helmet. The soldier's head snapped sideways. Jori struck twice more. The soldier rolled to his hands and knees. Another mighty swing to the top of the spine and he collapsed.

Jori panted as he rushed in to help stop the remaining soldier. Hapker twisted out of the chokehold. He confronted his opponent with a face as red as the planet Laalgahana.

The corporal wore an expression with less personality than a stone as he lunged. He grappled Hapker to the floor and pressed his hands into his throat. Jori jabbed the butt of his rifle in the vulnerable spot where the helmet and suit met as Hapker's skin took on a purple tinge. Not getting much reaction, he clouted the side of the corporal's head. The soldier pitched over. Hapker twisted and maneuvered him into a prone position.

Jori used the opportunity to snag the unlocked rifle. As Hapker kept the corporal pinned, Jori aimed it at the energy mechanism of the suit and fired. Blue sparks erupted.

Jori's chest heaved. He stared down at the unconscious soldier. It was over. They'd won.

A whizzing sound brought him back to the moment. *His* fight was over, but not the one against his friends. His instincts were to rush in, but he looked to Hapker for direction.

Hapker held out his hand for the rifle in Jori's hands. Jori gave it to him, and they sped like rockets until they came to the backs of two more soldiers. Hapker fired. Jori clutched a torque multiplier over his head and leapt into a dive for the second soldier.

52
Frustration

Gottfried Krause gripped the arms of his chair as an internal notification of Jori and Commander Hapker's actions came in. He knew the commander would want to help, but he didn't think he'd leave the boy, let alone involve him. Granted, Jori was a warrior, but he was also a child.

<716Krause> Report this to the C-deck channel so everyone can hear.
<M185Y2> Roger.

"M-Striker to Command," the soldier's voice rang through the bridge. "The prisoners have broken out and are assisting the attackers."

Gottfried feigned disbelief by widening his eyes and lurching forward. "M-Striker, confirm. The Tredon boy and the commander have left the conference room and are attacking you?"

"Correct. Should we take lethal force?"

"Negative." Gottfried pulled his finger out of his mouth, then looked at his hand in askance. He hadn't bitten his nails since he was a teenager. This situation had him so discombobulated, not even his cybernetic chip could hamper his flawed human tendencies.

"Stun only," he added with unintended panic in his voice. When he glanced at Kramer, her head tilt prompted him to explain. "We must capture them alive and discover the depth of their treachery."

Kramer's shoulders fell. Gottfried refrained from allowing his to do the same.

"Roger. M-Striker out."

Gottfried accessed the feeds from his soldiers and cringed inwardly at finding two dark. His stomach churned with an intensity he hadn't felt since before his cybernetic surgery. Everything had gone smoothly until this point. Why was Jori messing it up?

"Kurti. Stein. Secure the command deck."

Two of the six soldiers here left their posts without question and headed out. As the echo of the battle intensified through the open door, Corporal Kramer's eyes widened. A wavering confusion emanated from her. Gottfried used his reading ability to graze her thoughts.

Good. Her opinion that Gottfried was behind it had waned. It was still there, but not as strong. Having his soldiers initiate the attack, then telling everyone that Jori's allies had started it helped him with people like Kramer but might not work with Jori now that he'd left the room and seen the soldiers.

He must be careful. Notifying all the security officers on the ship must be done—or Kramer would re-question his motives—but if he openly blamed Jori, his chances of turning him to his side dropped to zero.

He compromised and depressed a select channel. "Don't let anyone escape the command deck."

An officer not allied with him emitted a sense of doubt and Gottfried realized how unnecessary the order had been. That the attackers had to be stopped here and now was obvious. Superfluous commands took up radio space that was better served for military actions. That he wasn't a soldier made him look weak, so he jutted his chin and projected confidence.

If only my imperium ability worked on these louts. Unfortunately, his earlier attempt when he'd interviewed them had failed—especially on the strong-willed purple-haired woman.

The feed of another soldier stopped transmitting. Gottfried received an alert from his own personal internal sensors telling him his blood pressure had gone up. He forced his heartrate to slow and considered his options.

Continuing with lethal force risked Jori but leaving his friends alive would create problems. He had to get them separated again.

He opened the comm link to Lieutenant Buckeye. Since the man didn't have an implant, he had no choice but to speak out loud where the other bridge crew could hear. "Lieutenant. Do you still have a relationship with Sergeant Ortega?"

"No, Sir," Buckeye replied.

Gottfried gritted his teeth. "If you contact her, do you think she will listen to you anyway?"

"Possibly, Sir."

"Do it. See if you can convince her to surrender."

"Yes, Sir."

Gottfried's augmented processors worked in overdrive to figure out his next move. Chances that his soldiers would win were in his favor, but he'd likely lose Jori's alliance in the process. That meant he'd win one objective but fail in the other.

MEGA-Man had said there would be future opportunities regarding the boy, but where would that leave their cause? Only half succeeding at this mission held unpleasant repercussions. Although Gottfried shared MEGA-Man's desire for the ultimate goal, his own personal goal of being exalted in his superior's eyes seemed less likely with each passing moment.

This was Commander Hapker's doing. Gottfried clutched his chest at the spreading inferno of jealousy. He hated that man with an unreasonable fervor, but he couldn't bring himself to care about the potential pitfalls that came with it. *Hapker must die*.

"Sir?" Corporal Kramer called out. The way her eyebrows cinched together made him suspect that she'd been trying to get his attention for some time. "I haven't heard about the admiral's status lately. I'm beginning to worry."

Gottfried's mouth almost spread into a smile, but he held it back. He opened a channel to the medical bay. "Doctor Schmitt."

The man left in charge after Doctor Fritz's death answered. "Yes, Lieutenant."

"Please update the crew on the admiral."

"Will do," the doctor said.

The ship-wide channel opened. "We are pleased to report Admiral Belmont's condition is stabilized. We expect a full recovery."

Gottfried held back his satisfaction. MEGA-Man had operatives all over the galaxy. Getting some on this ship after the battle at Thendi had been easy. It helped that Schmitt had spoken the truth. Since the admiral would be the easiest to fool after this was all over, keeping him alive did nothing but bolster MEGA-Man's cause.

At least something was going right.

53
Trapped

Carletta Ortega peered intently at the curved edge of the corridor, trying to anticipate when a soldier would pop out enough for her to take a shot. She tried not to think about her aching hand or the limited energy of her phaser rifle. There wasn't anything she could do about them so she might as well keep firing and hope to peg one of those bastards.

"Nothing from this side," Korbin called out.

"Not much from over here either," she replied.

Lieutenant Gresher, standing behind and over her as she held the low position, poked his head out. "They're probably planning a charge, so brace yourselves."

"Sergeant Ortega," a stern voice chimed in her earpiece, making her flinch.

A mass hardened in her chest "Yes, Lieutenant."

"What the hell are you doing?"

"Your friends—" She halted, unsure whether these assholes were really his friends. "These soldiers from the space station… They attacked us."

"Do you know why?" he asked like a patronizing parent.

She moved her mouth, not sure how to answer. If Bryce was allied with Gottfried, then telling him wouldn't do any good. And if he wasn't… Well, somehow that prospect seemed unlikely despite her wish otherwise.

"People are saying you're in league with that Tredon boy," Bryce said. "Perhaps he's not behind this, but his father undoubtedly is. That makes you on the wrong side of this."

His softened tone tugged at her but didn't hide the condescension of his words. She tightened her grip on her weapon. "Those soldiers fired on me. I had no choice but to defend myself."

"Letta." The compassion in his voice might've melted steel. "You have a choice now. Stand down. We'll work things out. I can get you exonerated. After all, you didn't realize the boy's father arranged all this."

She blinked as doubt surfaced but held onto her resolve. "What about Lieutenant Krause? There's evidence he's behind the attacks."

"Fabricated by the enemy," Bryce replied. "He was with the admiral during the attack, right? How could he have been in the middle of that if he was a part of it?"

To divert suspicions, she wanted to say. But the warmth in his voice made her second-guess. What if Jori's father had a hand in this? Maybe the boy wasn't at fault, but he might still be the cause.

Gresher's knee nudged her shoulder. "Hey. You alright? Who's that?"

"It's Bryce."

As if in reply, Bryce spoke again. "Did you hear me, Letta?"

"Who?" Lieutenant Gresher asked.

She ignored her ex and responded to Gresher. "Lieutenant Buckeye. He says Jori's father is behind this, not Krause, but also not Jori."

"If that's the case, it doesn't change that they shot at us first."

"Perhaps the emperor hired them, Sir," she said.

"The evidence—"

She cut him off. "They altered it to point to Krause."

Gresher's mouth quirked dubiously.

Ortega still wavered. Before she pulled together a coherent thought, a yell sounded from beyond Harley and Korbin's side.

"It's us!"

It took her a moment to register who the voice belonged to. "Commander?" she called out at the same time as Lieutenant Gresher.

"It's me, Commander Hapker," the man said. "Jori is with me. We've escaped and incapacitated some soldiers."

"Ortega!" Bryce barked.

"I'll get back to you." She turned off her comm. While keeping her eyes to her side, she waited as the two people approach—the commander with heavier steps and the boy's softer than cat paws.

Although she agreed with what Bryce had said about Jori's noninvolvement, she couldn't shake the uncertainty crawling through her insides. *Great. Trapped in a car and trapped with indecision.* Who do you trust when lovers cast you aside and enemies become friends?

*****

J.D. Hapker raised his hands and trod with caution toward the conveyor. Corporal Harley and Gresher's friend Korbin kept their weapons level. He accepted the threat, knowing he and Jori had to prove themselves.

"Jori sensed you all were in danger. We came to help."

"Let them in," Gresher said.

Harley and Korbin lowered their rifles.

"What happened?" Hapker asked as he ducked with Jori into the conveyor, passing an officer with the dead eyes lying on the floor.

"They opened fire on us, Sir." Gresher slanted his head to Hapker. "Your weapon work?"

"Yeah. Jori unlocked it."

If Gresher was surprised, he didn't show it. Instead, he handed the boy another rifle. "Can you unlock this one for me?"

Jori took it and popped open the controls.

Harley's dark brows twisted into a pained expression. "I think they lured us all here to eliminate us. Their weapons are set to kill."

The shock of the situation struck Hapker like a bolt of lightning. Commandeering a Cooperative ship was almost unheard of nowadays, but now he'd experienced it twice in less than a year.

He and Jori hugged the wall opposite of where Chief Singh fiddled with components inside the car's operations panel. Before he had a chance to reveal Gottfried's secrets, she blurted, "I have evidence against Krause."

"Tell them about Gottfried," Hapker said to Jori.

Jori nodded and handed the rifle to Gresher. "I modified the setting so you can shoot through their armor without killing them. Also, Gottfried is—"

"Commander Hapker!" a familiar voice called out. "You're all in enough trouble already. Everyone stand down before someone gets hurt."

Hapker's shoulders dropped in relief. If anyone was likely to listen, it was Carter.

"I don't trust those soldiers with you not to kill us all, including you, once we surrender," Gresher said.

Hapker reconsidered his own response. Gresher was right. If they were allied with Gottfried, they wouldn't just let them all go. He had to convince his friend. Before he spoke, another familiar voice rang out.

"That's what happens when you side with that *boy*." The disdain in Chesa's tone made Hapker grit his teeth. "You are the ones who attacked, not us."

"Are you sure about that?" Gresher replied. "Where were you when we came out of the conveyor?"

Neither Chesa nor Carter answered, which meant they hadn't seen who fired the first shot.

"Listen, please," Hapker said. "This isn't our doing. It's Lieutenant Krause."

"You seriously expect us to believe that?" Chesa shouted. "You're so gullible, J.D. Only a fool would trust that little monster over an admiral's aide."

Hapker groaned inwardly.

"Gottfried is a MEGA," Jori yelled.

Curses and gasps hissed through the corridor. Sergeant Ortega choked. Her rifle lowered and a subtle wobble threatened to topple her. She jerked her weapon in place and shook her head as though to snap herself back into focus.

"Bullshit," Chesa said. "MEGAs can't work for the Cooperative."

"He told me himself," Jori continued in a strong tone. "Confessed it because he thinks I'm like him. He also admitted he's an imperium-animi."

Chesa cackled. "That's the stupidest thing I've ever heard. What evidence do *you* have?"

"He's been manipulating us." Hapker gritted his teeth. How could he get through to someone under that man's influence?

"Look at how much Banks and Lengen have deviated from their duties. You too. Someone's been manipulating you."

"Bullshit," she said. "That little brat is the one manipulating all of you."

Jori darkened but didn't respond.

"It's Gottfried," Hapker said. "Think about it. He's after two things. The database and—"

"How do you know about that?" Carter yelled.

"Deductive reasoning. This ship came from Thendi and there are people guarding something somewhere in the lower levels."

"You're only making your case against that boy," Chesa said. "The emperor went after the emitter once. It stands to reason he'd want the database too."

Singh stopped her work. "Listen you guys! Gottfried is behind this." She leaned out of the conveyor. "I have evidence. Let me give it to you." She pulled something from her pocket. With a low swing of her arm, she slid it along the corridor. It hit the wall, then ricocheted out of view.

If Carter retrieved it, he didn't say. "Whatever the case, this must stop," he said, his tone conveying both resignation and frustration. "I have no doubt it's what you believe, J.D. But you've always had a tendency to believe in the wrong things."

Hapker ran his hand down his face and sighed. He had no time to defend himself from Carter's judgment. And trying to get him and Chesa to understand his perspective was like talking to a deaf dog from the other side of a meter-thick wall. "Just check out Chief Singh's evidence for yourself."

"I will. You have my word," Carter said. "But first, consider your position. You're trapped. Unless you plan on shooting your way out and getting more innocent people killed, you must surrender."

Hapker winced. He didn't want to hurt anyone but the enemy, but this situation made it difficult. He glanced at Jori. "Can you read him?"

"His emotions are a mix. He wants to trust you, but he's also unhappy with you."

"Unhappy enough to shoot me?"

"Yes, but I doubt he'll use the lethal settings. I can't sense Gottfried's soldiers, though. I don't know how many there are or what they'll do."

Chief Singh grunted as she fiddled with the conveyor's internal controls. "I have a pretty good idea," she mumbled.

"We can't risk it, Sir," Gresher said. "Those soldiers shot at us first. They're part of this. Let's get away from here. Sergeant Carter has the DTD. Hopefully, he'll check it out."

Hapker reluctantly agreed. He had no way of proving anything. All he had was his trust in these people. It was enough for him, but he understood why it might not be for Carter.

"Alright. Let's get out of here."

54
On the Run

Carletta Ortega's gut did a series of tumbling exercises. She didn't like this—not one bit. She'd been on the verge of accepting Bryce might be right about it being a setup to being confused all over again. Lieutenant Krause was a MEGA? Really? How was that even possible? And how did that make it more likely that he was the saboteur?

Something niggled in her mind, but she didn't have a chance to grasp it. Her ears caught faint rustling sounds that the others probably couldn't hear.

"They're coming!" she yelled.

She tightened her focus in time to see the point of a rifle. She pulled the trigger, then edged back as they returned fire. "Singh! Where the hell are you with that damned door?"

"I'm trying!" Singh's tone held both frustration and fear.

Ortega had always admired the woman's strong personality. However, without practical experience, the stress of a real battle rattled Singh's nerves.

"Let me try," Jori said. "I know a trick."

Sergeant Carter and a soldier appeared in her view, releasing a barrage of firepower. *Damn it.* Those soldiers acted too quickly for him to check the evidence.

"Aw, shit!" Korbin shook his arm. "That fucking burns. I'm hit."

"Pull back!" Jori shouted. "I've got it."

"Get inside, now!" Commander Hapker echoed.

Ortega skittered backward as fast as her lowered position allowed. More blasts whizzed by. True to the boy's word, the doors closed and the car jolted into motion.

"Where are we going?" she asked him.

Jori pressed something within the panel. His forehead wrinkled in concentration, but he answered. “Away from here. They’ll regain control soon, so we must get somewhere before they trap us.”

Oh shit. “What next? What do we do after that?” Ortega gave everyone a questioning look, but nobody responded. *Right. Where the fuck do we go when everyone’s either a terrorist or assumes we’re the enemy?*

*****

Gottfried Krause sprang from his chair. When Corporal Kramer looked at him like he was crazy, he remembered that no one else sensed what he had. Before he sat back down, the report came in through the command channel.

“They’ve escaped.”

Gottfried stayed on his feet. “How?”

“Unknown, Sir. The conveyor doors shut and now they’re gone. The Tredon boy included.”

“Sir,” the woman with curly black hair said. “Somehow they overrode the lock and got the car moving.”

“Well, stop it.”

“We’re trying, Sir.”

Gottfried retook his chair and ground his teeth. He should’ve anticipated this. Chief Singh was a competent engineer and Jori was too smart for his own good.

A tepid heat rose in his chest as he pressed the ship-wide comm. “The Tredon prisoner has escaped, assisted by Commander Hapker and his allies.” He named them all with assistance from the bridge crew. “Use whatever force is necessary, but we must capture the Tredon boy alive so we can determine the extent of his involvement.”

“But, Sir,” Corporal Kramer said. “The others might have information, too. Shouldn’t we capture them *all*? It’s not like we can’t stun them.”

Gottfried forced a smile. The plan had been to kill them, but he couldn’t risk alienating anyone until he had complete control.

“Of course. You’re right.” He pressed the comm once more. “I changed my mind. Use stun weapons only. I want them all alive.”

"Say again, Lieutenant," Sergeant Carter replied.

"Stun only and bring them all to me alive."

"Sir," the sergeant said in an annoyed tone. "This is an open channel. Are you saying *everyone* should go after them?"

Kramer made an exasperated sound. "Great," she muttered. "He doesn't know what the fuck he's doing. Doesn't even know radio communication protocol."

Gottfried's face burned as an emotion he hadn't experienced in a long time surfaced. *So much for being a brilliant strategist.* He glowered at her back, hating that he performed so inadequately in an actual situation.

"Hold on a moment." Gathering his thoughts, he evaluated every angle. How many people could he spare from here or the database and send to kill those troublemakers? He was stretched too thin, at least for a few more hours. But something must be done now, before this got too out of control.

"Sir," an officer said. "We stopped the conveyor at deck eight."

Gottfried opened the channel. "Everyone is to continue with their current duties unless ordered otherwise, but keep an eye out for the traitors." He pressed the direct link to Carter. "Sergeant, I need you and Sergeant Creston on deck eight aft. Find the terrorists and capture them alive, if possible."

"Roger."

Next, he called his ally. "Lieutenant Buckeye. Coordinate the patrol teams to locate the terrorists while also maintaining order on the decks. Start with deck eight aft."

"Roger. Which has priority, Sir?"

"The boy."

"Roger that. Out."

Gottfried mentally connected to a few of his soldiers and gave them explicit orders—separate the others from the Tredon child and use lethal force.

After they all confirmed, he eased back into his chair. Now to figure out what the boy was up to and why. What did he hope to achieve? What did any of them hope to achieve? And could he stop them before they ruined his plans?

55
Flight and Fight

Jori held his breath as the car carried them to another part of the ship. Every second that passed without the authorities regaining control only brought them closer to the inevitable.

"Everyone check in," Hapker said.

Korbin tapped the cracked armor on his forearm. "Just a graze."

Hapker peered at it. "They're using projectiles." He patted the rifle he'd taken from a soldier. "We should've grabbed more of these."

"Yeah," Harley said. "I got hit in the leg but it's not bad."

Ortega nodded down at her hand. "I can't move it."

Jori felt their pain, but it wasn't as strong as their willpower. Even Ortega seemed determined despite her bouts of doubt.

"But it coulda been worse," she added.

"Like Warsaw." Harley shared a look, then lowered his head.

The inside of the car quieted. Everyone's expressions folded in with despair. Something hard settled into the pit of Jori's stomach. If he'd told everyone about Gottfried sooner, he could've prevented these deaths.

The conveyor screeched to a halt before arriving at a proper destination. *Chusho.* Jori looked up at the emergency hatch, hoping they wouldn't have to use it, then reached into the control panel. With a press of a small metal piece, a click sounded. "Try pulling the doors open."

Hapker and Gresher moved in from either side and dug their fingers into the middle crack. A gritting of teeth and a few grunts later, the door pulled apart just enough for them to get their hands in. At the sight of the light coming from the lower half of the gap, some of Jori's trepidation subsided. The chances of getting this close to an exit after a forced stop were small, but they must've had a little cosmic luck on their side.

"I don't sense anyone out there," he said as the opening grew wide enough to let them out, "but that doesn't mean it's clear."

"I can't hear anything either," Ortega replied.

"She has exceptional hearing," Harley said, "so it's a good bet there's nobody out there."

Jori appraised the sergeant. Having both keen eyesight and acute hearing were handy talents. *Maybe we have a chance against Gottfried's enhanced abilities.*

Lieutenant Gresher and Corporal Harley poked their rifles and heads out to be sure. "Clear," one called out after the other.

They guarded the exit while Korbin's thin frame slipped through. Ortega followed, but a little more awkwardly because of her injured arm. The others went next, with Gresher and Harley taking up the rear.

An eerily silent hall made Jori's arms prickle. The white walls and tiled floor created a painful brightness. He envied Ortega her sunglasses.

"We're on deck eight," Gresher said as he guarded the left with Korbin.

"Research section," Singh added. "It should be quiet here since there's a lockdown."

"Not very defensible, though." Ortega grimaced as she struggled to keep her rifle steady.

Hapker took on a low-ready position while scanning the corridor on his side. "The enemy can tell we got off here, so let's get moving. There's an emergency shaft this way."

"They might expect us to use those." Jori pointed the opposite direction. "There's a maintenance tunnel over here. It's a tighter fit, but they may not consider it right away."

Ortega's brows shot up. "Is there anything you *don't* know?"

"Good idea," Hapker said without the same surprise that everyone else had. "Get to it."

"Wait." Singh stopped. "I can disable this car so they'll have to take the long way here."

"Do it," Hapker said. "That'll slow them down, at least."

Singh ducked in. When she was done, she, Jori, and Ortega followed Gresher and Korbin while Hapker and Harley guarded their backs.

"Oh, shit." Dread tumbled through Harley's emotions as he held his finger to his comm. "Did you all get that?"

"What is it?" Hapker asked.

"Gottfried just told everyone that we're the saboteurs."

Everyone's alarm combined with Jori's own, causing a shiver that penetrated him to the marrow. Evading Gottfried and his allies would be difficult enough. Now they had to contend with the entire ship.

Jori regarded his friends but let his gaze slip away whenever they looked back at him. Was Gottfried trying to kill them because they allied with him? Or was this his plan for everyone here? The man had tried so hard to convince him the Cooperative was evil, so it was likely the former.

An image of the dead soldier in front of the conveyor flashed through his mind. He'd been killed because of him.

Jori wrapped his arms around his middle.

*****

Fire roared through Carletta Ortega's veins. All she ever wanted was to do the right thing. Standing up for Jori was right, yet very few people appreciated that. Her fellow officers sneered at her. Those she thought were her friends avoided her. And Bryce's cohorts were trying to kill her.

Like a splash of cold water, she was struck with the realization that he hadn't saved her from that attack. He'd probably intended to finish the job.

"Here," Singh said. She opened the toolbox and grabbed a small driver, then ducked down to a wide panel.

Ortega took in those around her. Two were good friends. One was a nice guy she considered a friend, although they didn't hang out often. She barely knew the other three. It surprised her how much she trusted them. Trusting had never come easy for her, which only made the sting of Bryce's actions worse. She only hoped she hadn't misplaced her trust in these people.

Thinking of him reminded her of something. She turned her comm on while waiting for Singh and Jori to remove the panel. Sure enough, Bryce had pinged her half a dozen times. With a tap on her earpiece, she called him back.

"Letta! What the hell are you doing? You're making things worse."

She clenched her jaw at his tone. When had he become such an asshole? "Making it worse for who? For you? Did I mess up your plans?"

"Don't be like that," he replied patronizingly.

Commander Hapker threw her a questioning look. She lifted her shoulder to the comm in her ear, then responded to Bryce. "You're one too, aren't you?"

"What are you talking about?"

"A MEGA. You're a MEGA, too." She had no proof, but it made sense. Him being so damned perfect and good at everything was only part of the reason she had suspicions. Add that to the way he kept making excuses for Lieutenant Krause and how he got along so well with those robot-like soldiers, and the pieces fit.

"Don't be ridiculous," Bryce said. "Why would you say such a stupid thing?"

She suppressed a growl. Had he always talked down to her like this and she just didn't notice because she was so in love? Well, she wasn't anymore. She was done pining over this jerk. "Tell me the truth. You're a MEGA and your soldier buddies are too, right?"

Bryce made an exasperated noise. "Are you really stupid enough to fall for the lies of the emperor's son? He's your enemy, or did you forget that?"

"Ha! Who says it was him that told me? I figured it out after your friends tried to kill me."

He laughed without humor. "Oh, Letta. You and I could have been great together, but you're too damned stubborn."

"It's not stubbornness. I just finally see you for what you really are, asshole." She cut off her comm with finality.

A weight lifted from her shoulders as certainty replaced doubt. She glanced at her friends, both old and new, and bolstered her determination to stop Gottfried and his allies.

56
One Step at a Time

The panel to the maintenance tunnel came loose. Jori slipped the screwdriver onto his belt, wishing it was a knife or a phaser but still glad he had some kind of weapon. He felt guilty about these people doing all the fighting while he just tagged along—but also grateful for their help.

Singh set the cover to the side of the gaping hole lined with electrical conduits and other components. Jori flashed a light inside, making sure it was empty. Of course it was, but his training required him to check.

Ortega pointed at the panel. "How will we put that back on after we're in?"

Jori touched a corner screw. "Singh can use her magnetic driver from the inside."

"How do you know all this stuff?" Ortega's tone almost sounded accusatory but the emotion she projected carried more awe.

"Toradon is a dangerous place. Sensei Jeruko taught me several tricks." Saying the man's name out loud made his gut pinch. He pushed the feeling aside and stepped back to let someone else enter first.

Hapker ducked down, then dropped to his elbows and shimmied inside. "If they find out we're in here, we're sitting ducks," he said, his voice echoing.

Jori would have laughed at the ridiculous analogy if the other part of the commander's words hadn't put him on edge. It'd be his fault if they got caught.

After Harley was in, Ortega indicated for Jori to go next. Despite the bulkiness of his suit, he wriggled in easily. Ortega came after. She struggled a bit more because of her arm but didn't make a single noise of complaint.

The others were inside and encased in darkness by the time Hapker reached the ladder and climbed down the shaft. Everyone followed him into another horizontal tunnel. Singh opened this panel, then moved out of the way so Gresher could check the corridor. Jori didn't sense anyone but kept his breaths shallow while the man cautiously peered out.

Gresher aimed his rifle first one direction, then the other. When he waved an all-clear, Jori exhaled. The sounds of others doing the same hissed through the tunnel.

This hall was drearier than the other—the lights more yellow and the tan walls scraped and gouged. Singh pointed at the doors that branched off from the corridor. "Supplies."

"I don't like the looks of it," Ortega said, "but I bet there's a lot of places to hide."

"Hiding isn't a good idea." When everyone gave Jori a questioning look, he explained. "If those soldiers work for Gottfried, they might be MEGAs too." They still seemed confused. "They may have sentio abilities too."

"Shit," Harley said. "I didn't think of that."

"So what's the plan, then?" Korbin asked.

"This way, for now." Hapker led. "We can talk as we go."

Ortega swiveled her head as she stalked forward with her rifle at the ready. "Even staying on the move, they'll eventually corner us."

"We've got to convince everyone we come across that Lieutenant Krause is doing this," Singh said.

That'll be hard with me here. Jori swallowed the lump in his throat. If he'd stayed behind with Gottfried, his friends wouldn't have looked like they were conspiring with the enemy.

"That's not gonna be easy if they're shooting at us first," Ortega replied.

Harley took point at the cross corridor. "Yeah, but we gotta try."

Korbin covered the other edge. "There's not enough of us to do anything by ourselves."

"Especially since we're getting low on ammo," Ortega said.

"Is there any place here we can get more?" Hapker asked. "And perhaps a suit for Gresher and the chief?"

Singh stopped at a door. "Through here." The group halted while she turned an old-fashioned knob. "There's a weapon locker on the other side of this room. A maintenance tunnel is near there too. If we keep going down the levels, we can reach the communications array—fix it and call for help."

"Is that possible?" Ortega asked. "Fixing the array?"

"I think so," Singh said. Jori detected her elevated stress compared to the officers, but she handled herself well. "It's damaged on the inside of the bulkhead, so at least we don't have to go outside."

They entered a dark, musty room. Automatic lights came on but did little to light the murky space. Rows of boxed goods were stacked up and strapped in place on either side.

Ortega stepped over a rat bot as it scrolled by in search of humanity's oldest stowaways. "Two problems. Only a lieutenant or higher are authorized to open those lockers and I doubt the commander and lieutenant here have access."

"I can break into it," Jori said.

Ortega's jaw dropped, but she didn't question it. "Okay, next problem. How damaged is the array? Singh is the only one here with the skill to fix it, but only if it's not blown to hell."

Jori held back the offer to help. It was an odd time to worry about sounding like a braggart, but he'd assist when necessary. The prospect of getting it working again led to the memory of him putting together the perantium emitter. He loved problem-solving, whether it was with equipment or strategic games.

Jori spoke up before Singh explained the condition of the array. "Gottfried will expect that. He'll try to stop us."

They came to the exit and Ortega hesitated. "Are we sure that's the plan? What about protecting the database? Hell, what about protecting Admiral Belmont?"

Jori locked up. Normally, the idea of tactical planning filled him with an eager energy. But this was Gottfried he was going against—the only person who'd consistently beat him at strategic games. And those were just games. This was real. His life wasn't at stake, but the lives of his friends were.

Despite being outmatched, he clenched his fists and gathered his resolve. One way or another, he'd defeat this cybernetic monster.

*****

J.D. Hapker struggled for a solution, but nothing came to mind. What does a leader do when they don't have the answers? He maintained a false confidence as he met the eyes of the others. "Let's discuss our options."

Trying to come up with a plan while taking point and being ready for anything wasn't easy. All his focus was on the dimly lit corridor and the shadows that lay beyond. Fortunately, they came across an emergency box and stopped for Singh and Gresher to get a suit. That didn't take his mind off the daunting tasks ahead, but it gave them a little room for discussion.

He noted how the six people before him carried their tension in their bodies. Harley and Korbin waited in tight defensive positions that were much like his own. He couldn't see Ortega's eyes, but the swivel of her head indicated that she, too, kept a lookout. Jori also seemed attentive but showed no other signs of anxiety.

Hapker shattered the tense silence by clearing his throat. "We know Lieutenant Krause is a MEGA and we know he's after the database."

"He wants me as well," Jori said, his words apologetic. "He's been trying to recruit me."

"For what?" Gresher asked without shifting from his position.

"I'm the last Dragon Heir."

"The last?" Harley replied. "Your brother was still alive when we escaped."

"When I sabotaged the emitter…" Jori's voice hitched. "I accidentally went too far. Something happened. My brother is dead."

Singh halted midway through putting on her suit. "Oh, no. I'm so sorry, Jori."

Hapker's heart would have gone out to him as well, except the dozens of questions running around in his head pushed that emotion to the side. "What? When did this happen? And how do you know about it?"

Jori's brows folded. "Gottfried let me send a message to Sensei Jeruko. Only he didn't receive it because he's also dead. One of my men found it and replied. He said the perantium emitter blew up and killed them."

Korbin scoffed. "Not to downplay your grief, but if the admiral's aide let you do this, I bet he had his reasons. I wouldn't trust that crap if I were you."

Jori seemed to struggle with wanting to believe him, but not. "It came from someone I know. I doubt he's in league with Gottfried."

Hapker yearned to pull him into a hug, but they had more pressing matters at hand.

Gresher finished putting on the enviro-suit and tilted his eyes in a soft expression. "Whether it's true about his brother, Jori's still connected to a race of warriors. It makes sense for Lieutenant Krause to align with our young friend here."

"Are we sure Krause isn't working for the emperor?" Harley asked.

"Pretty sure," Jori said. "Gottfried said a lot of things that makes me suspect he's part of some larger MEGA organization."

"But I'm still not getting how it ties to you being the last Dragon Heir," Harley replied.

"Here's my guess." Hapker glanced at them and turned his attention back to the corridor. "Gottfried is a MEGA. He and others like him have somehow infiltrated our ranks. Think about it. What better way to make changes for a race of MEGAs? But perhaps things are moving too slowly and it's time for an insurrection. They have MEGA soldiers on their side but not enough. They need a weapon of mass destruction. Maybe they also need to recruit someone they suspect is like them and just so happens to be the heir to a powerful military force."

Singh sealed the neck of the suit. "If that's the case, then this is big. *Really* big."

"But why keep the admiral alive?" Korbin took point and the group followed.

Hapker kept an eye out behind them. "Belmont is under Gottfried's influence. Plus, he's not seeing all that's going on now. If Gottfried does this right, he can make himself the hero."

"But we messed that up," Singh said, her voice carrying her trepidation.

"He won't let us live," Ortega added.

And where does that put Jori? Hapker sent a worried look Jori's way. The boy responded with the same expression.

"So what's the plan?" Harley asked.

"Ammo." Hapker's brain still hadn't come up with an idea, but that was a good place to start. *One step at a time.* "We'll switch out these rifles as well. I want the TR7s. They have better stunners."

"That won't stop the soldiers," Ortega said.

"No," Hapker replied. "But they can penetrate most armor, and they won't harm our friends. Everyone thinks we're the enemy, so they're only doing what they believe is right. We must try to convince them, and if we can't, we'll protect ourselves without killing them."

They all responded with a yes, sir—even Jori. Hapker maintained a hawkish watch at their backs. Now and then, he looked behind him to make sure he stayed with the team.

Before Gresher reached the next corner, Jori called out. "I sense people ahead. At least five."

Ortega cocked her head. "I hear them but can't verify the number."

"Can you tell who?" Hapker asked Jori.

"I don't recognize them."

Gresher halted at the edge. "Shoot or talk?"

"Talk," Hapker said. "You do it. No one here trusts me."

"Hey!" Gresher yelled. "I wanna talk."

A tromp of footsteps echoed. "It's them! Call it in!"

"Before you come charging in," Gresher called out, "we're armed but we don't want to hurt anyone."

The stomp of boots silenced and the rustling of people getting in place for cover followed. Hapker held his breath, hoping they'd listen. Sweat tripped down his nose, tickling his skin and adding to his overwhelming unease.

Please hear us out.

57
Difficult Position

Carletta Ortega hugged the wall and prayed. Religion had never been her thing, but she hoped there might be a benevolent deity out there listening. Lieutenant Krause's announcement had rattled her more than anything else had thus far. People already hated her for telling the truth about Banks. Now it would be worse.

"Before you come charging in," Gresher said, "we're armed but we don't want to hurt anyone."

"Yeah, right," a woman responded. "That's why you attacked the bridge."

Ortega's heart skipped a beat. It was Sergeant Fenyvesi. If anybody was likely to listen, it'd be her. "We were ordered to be there, then they attacked us."

"You really expect me to believe that? I always took you for a softie, Ortega. Even a fool at times. But you've gone too far. Surrender and we'll work it out."

Ortega despaired at how much Feny sounded like her mother whenever she'd scolded her. Yes, sometimes she was lenient, but it wasn't foolish to do the right thing.

Singh cupped her hand by her mouth. "I have evidence that Lieutenant Krause is behind this."

"If Krause is in on it, then so is that boy," someone else said. The anger in his voice made it hard for Ortega to tell who it was.

"Listen," she pleaded. "I don't know if the boy's father has something to do with this or not, but I'm sure Jori doesn't. He's saved my life twice now."

"Both our lives," Singh added.

"I can't trust somebody who turns against their own," the same man said.

Ortega bit her tongue. She remembered him now. Paldino. He wasn't a thug like Banks but could be just as hard-headed about his opinions.

Gresher spoke in a rational calm she envied. "We need to use our heads here. This is obviously much bigger than Jori. Singh has evidence against Krause, so check it out." He dipped his head to Singh, who removed a DTD from her pocket. "She's sliding something over to you. Take a look. It shows him deleting work orders from the system—work orders on equipment that eventually malfunctioned."

"Alright," Feny said. "Send it over."

Ortega relaxed her knotted fists. *Thank goodness for level-headed people.*

Singh flung the DTD across the floor and Gresher nudged it so it rounded the corner. The sharp hiss cut short as someone caught it. Feny, she hoped.

The following silence was punctuated with occasional protests.

"The evidence is right here," Feny told her team.

"Doctored up, no doubt," Paldino said. "They attacked the bridge, for fuck's sake. You can't believe anything they tell you."

"We didn't," Ortega protested. "I'm telling you, Krause's soldiers attacked us. They killed Warsaw."

"Warsaw's dead?" another officer said.

"What do you mean Krause's soldiers?" Feny asked.

"The ones from the space station," Ortega said. "The weird ones who act like robots."

"We suspect they're MEGAs, like Krause," Gresher added.

Feny barked a laugh. "First you tell me the admiral's aide is behind all this—and I'll admit this evidence is somewhat convincing—but now you're telling me we have MEGAs on this ship and the aide is one of them? Impossible. What proof do you have?"

"Nothing conclusive," Gresher said. "But let me ask you something… Feny, right?"

"*Sergeant* Fenyvesi to you."

"Sergeant Fenyvesi, are you aware that it's mostly those soldiers from the space station who are guarding the emitter? They're also protecting Krause on the bridge. Why them and not our own people?"

"And they're with the admiral in sick bay," Ortega added. "I tried to stay with him after the attack, but they wouldn't let me. Also, remember when you found me after I was assaulted?"

"Yeah?"

"You probably saved my life. I'm almost positive it was those soldiers who did it. I got away and ran into Bryce. If you didn't come along, he might've killed me."

"You think he's in on it too?" Feny's voice pitched upward in disbelief.

Ortega's insides hardened. "I'm certain of it."

Feny huffed. "I don't know, Ortega. This is a lot to swallow."

"How in the hell does that make sense?" Paldino asked. "MEGAs can't join the Cooperative."

Feny and the group argued. Their discussion switched from heated to reasonable, and back again.

"Hey, Zambarda. You're from that space station," someone said, then chuckled. "Are you a MEGA?"

Ortega didn't catch the reply—if there was one. Her skin prickled. She'd heard all five voices and guessed who they belonged to. But there must be a sixth person who hadn't spoken yet. "Oh shit," she told Hapker and the others who probably couldn't hear the conversation. "A soldier is with them."

"We'll work that out later," Feny said to her team. "For now, I think the lieutenant is right. There's more to this that we've got to consider."

"There's nothing to consider," the sixth voice said. It was deep and carried a serrated edge. "You have your orders, Sergeant. They are to be captured."

"You're not in charge here, soldier," Feny snapped. "I am. And if they're willing to talk peacefully, I'm good with that."

"You'll do as ordered, Sergeant," the man replied in the same hard tone. "Or I will relieve you of duty."

"The fuck you will."

The hair on the back of Ortega's neck stood on end. She didn't see the soldier's reaction, but practically tasted the coming fight. Uniforms rustled, a sound like a crackling bonfire.

Zips ripped through the air, making Ortega flinch. A man yelled out. Feny roared. Ortega raced around the corner. Hapker and the others joined her, even Jori, though Singh attempted to hold him back.

Ortega bolted onto the scene and found three people down. Feny attempted to wrestle the phaser rifle away from a soldier. The man wasn't as tall or heavy as her, but he flung her aside like rotten meat. Energy blasts struck him, but not before he shot her.

"No!" Ortega yelled at the same time Feny cried out with a roar filled with agony.

*****

Jori darted after Gresher and the others. Someone grabbed him by the arm. He reflexively twisted out of the hold and kept going. When he reached the fray, the pain of death blinded him. Then another stabbed through him, making him stumble.

The person seized him again. They were frantic but not aggressive, so he let them pull him back. Their arms wrapped around him and they panted. He puffed along with them, but in a controlled way so he could get a hold of himself and help.

The pain of death subsided, meaning the two people it had come from were dead. He didn't dwell on that now. His friends were still in trouble.

He blinked his eyes and regained all his senses. It was Singh who held him, and she was terrified. The others radiated a powerful but focused sense of alarm. A pained outcry coupled with intense emotions indicated someone else was hurt.

He pushed his hands under Singh's arms and flung them out. Released from her embrace, he rushed round the corner. Hapker tackled a soldier, driving him to the floor. Jori halted, wondering whether he should intervene. Before he decided, Gresher, Harley, and Korbin shot the man. Three stun shots probably killed him, but the inhibitor blocked the pain of death.

The agony came from the officer Ortega had called Feny. Jori busted through his indecision and dropped to her side. She hugged her abdomen and grunted. Blood spilled, indicating someone had shot her with an armor-piercing projectile. If she didn't get treated soon, she'd die too.

"I'll get you something," he said in a rush before jumping to his feet and sprinting down the hall.

"Hey!" Feny yelled, then yelped in pain. "Get back here."

Jori darted around the corner and found an emergency box. He yanked it open and grabbed an armful of items.

"Someone grab him!" Feny called out. "He's running away."

"He's not," Ortega said in a calm voice that belied her worry.

"How do you—" Feny cut off when Jori returned.

He knelt beside her and dropped the supplies. Feny's jaw dropped. Jori ignored her confusion and pressed a hypospray to her neck. She flinched, but her fear dissipated as the medicine kept her from going into shock.

Jori compressed gauze against her wound and analyzed her lifeforce. She was in pain, but it wasn't the pain of death. He sighed in relief. He didn't know Feny, but he was glad she was alive.

That relief was short-lived as guilt crept in. Three people had died now. Although Gottfried would have done this regardless, he couldn't help but feel responsible.

"So it's true," she said. "Those soldiers want to kill us."

"Yeah." Ortega grasped Feny's hand.

"And you're really not a part of this?" Feny asked, mouth agape.

Jori blinked, realizing she was asking him. "No." He looked down. "I've also suspected my father might be behind it. But Gottfried has given me the impression that this is about the Cooperative and their rules against MEGAs."

"He said that?"

"Not exactly. But he told me he's a MEGA."

She made a sound, but no words came out. Jori wanted to say something, too. He wanted to tell her he was sorry for not telling anyone about Gottfried sooner. But like her, he couldn't speak.

"We've got to get you to sick bay." Ortega turned to Feny's two surviving team members. "Can you take her there?"

The men nodded. Jori pointed down the hall. "There's a gurney in the emergency box over there."

They jogged off to retrieve it.

"We must go," Hapker said. His brows rolled up in an apology. "More soldiers will be coming."

Jori's heart clenched, but not for him. For Feny and the two officers. "But they'll go after them, too."

"It's possible," Hapker replied, "but Gottfried hasn't been killing anyone else yet. I think he still needs them." He looked at Feny and her remaining team as they returned with the stretcher. "Call this in. Say we did it to you."

Ortega pulled back. Then her eyes glinted in understanding. As Feny shook her head, Ortega gripped her hand harder. "You're gonna have to lie about what happened here—at least for now. It's the only way they'll let you go."

"I'm not an idiot, girl. I know what I've gotta do, but I don't like it. You're not the enemy. We've got to stop this madman."

"If you see our crew members face-to face," Hapker said, "tell them the truth. But lie to Lieutenant Buckeye and the soldiers."

Recalling the possibility that some might have sentio abilities, Jori pulled off the soldier's inhibitor. "This," he said, holding it up then putting it in Feny's hand. "This is an inhibitor, for in case they can read you."

Her face paled but understanding crossed her features. "Thank you." She faced Ortega. "I owe you an apology."

Ortega cocked her head. "For what?"

"For criticizing you for standing up for this boy. I get it now. We were wrong."

The warmth coming from Ortega and the woman fell over Jori like a warm blanket. He blinked away the wetness in his eyes and stood. Without meaning to, he went into his formal attentive stance and suppressed his emotions. Hapker rose and placed his hand on his shoulder, reminding him that emotion wasn't always a weakness. Jori cleared his throat and gave the women and the two soldiers a small smile.

58
Plan of Action

After the officers helped Sergeant Fenyvesi onto the gurney and carried her off, J.D. Hapker and the others hurried to the weapon locker. The black storage box took up a meter of space along the wall. It had at least a four-centimeter thickness of metal. One look at the biometric scanner, and he was certain they wouldn't get into it.

Jori used a tool to loosen and remove the panel. With frightening confidence, he went to work on the interior. Hapker crouched and watched everyone's backs. His heart galloped. Since Feny and her team had called in their presence on this floor, more officers would arrive soon.

"Got it," Jori said.

Hapker did a doubletake. "Already?"

Jori didn't answer. He had a pinkish tinge to his cheeks as he stepped away and let the others pull open the heavy door. Was he embarrassed or just ashamed since skills like this had enabled him to commandeer the *Odyssey*?

Gresher handed Hapker a TR7 rifle and several ammo packs.

"Should we grab some grenades, Sir?" Ortega stuffed cartridges in her vest.

Hapker didn't want crew members hurt, but explosives had other uses. "Yeah, take as many as you can. We'll use them to block our retreat—disable a conveyor car or two."

"Get some flash bombs and energy shields too," Gresher said.

"What about me?" Jori asked.

"Sorry, champ," Gresher replied. "A shield only."

Jori scowled. "They'll also be shooting at me. And I can help."

"No," Hapker said firmly.

"Why not?"

Because I hate the idea of a child having a weapon. But that wasn't a good reason. "Because if we run across more people, convincing them Gottfried is the bad guy will be easier if they see you're not armed."

Jori made a face but didn't protest.

This all took less than two minutes, but it felt like an eternity. Their luck wouldn't hold out for long.

They closed the locker and headed for the next maintenance tunnel. Fortunately, several of these lay at intervals. The enemy would have a tough time searching them all.

Singh and Jori took longer to open this one—or maybe that was Hapker's imagination. Sweat trickled down his brow. He flipped his visor up and wiped it with his gloved hands.

They slid inside with Hapker taking the rear.

"I sense people coming," Jori said just after Singh pulled the panel in behind her.

"Hurry," Ortega replied needlessly.

Hapker hastened back. The others followed with pants and grunts. They entered a shaft and headed into the darkness without incident.

Sergeant Ortega climbed down the ladder with ease despite her injured arm. "So our plan. We convinced Feny that Krause is behind this. Instead of running away, we can find others and convince them too."

"I agree," Hapker said, "except about the part where we *look* for other people. We lost two officers in that fight, so let's only do it as a last resort."

"Can we broadcast Singh's evidence somehow?" Harley asked. "Put it on all the info consoles?"

Hapker reached a safety grate that blocked the shaft and opened it. After passing through and to the next passageway, he waited for the others so Singh could crawl in first. "They're controlled from the bridge during emergency lockdowns."

"He's right." Singh entered the tunnel, carrying a sidearm in one hand and the tool in the other.

"Jori, you can hack them, can't you?" Harley asked.

"Yes, but only one at a time."

Hapker took up the rear again. Perspiration slicked his face despite the cool ventilation in his suit. "And we don't have time."

"I still think we should fix the communications array," Singh said from ahead. "That's why we're going down, isn't it?"

A drop of sweat slid to the tip of Hapker's nose as he considered the most prominent options—save the admiral or fix the array. Making those repairs would allow them to call for help, expose Gottfried, and keep him from getting his hands on the emitter database. The choice seemed obvious, but could Singh do it?

"It makes little sense to go to the admiral since he might be under Gottfried's influence," he said. "Besides, if he wanted him dead, he would've—."

"Hush!" Jori whispered. "Someone is out there."

Hapker tapped Korbin's leg and motioned for him to follow him. Korbin did the same to Ortega, and the group crept backward.

A bang echoed. Singh squeaked in surprise. The smack that followed indicated she probably clapped her hand over her mouth. She scurried into the shaft and froze with the others.

They waited in total silence. If anyone breathed, they did it so silently that all Hapker heard was the thumping of his own heart.

A metallic screech denoted someone had removed the panel. A light flashed above them.

"See anything?" a woman's voice echoed.

"Nothing," a man replied.

"Alright. Close it back up and check the next one."

Hapker let out a long but quiet exhale. He and the others remained in utter silence.

"They're far enough away now," Jori said.

"You sure?" Harley asked.

"Unless one is wearing an inhibitor, yes."

"Ortega," Hapker whispered. "You hear anything?"

"Nothing."

Singh returned to the horizontal tunnel.

"Back to our next step," Hapker said. "I doubt the admiral is in immediate danger, so we fix the communications array." He'd probably be criticized for not rescuing Belmont first, but it wasn't like the authorities were ever happy with his decisions anyway. *To hell with them.*

After Singh opened the panel, she and the others squeezed out. Hapker exited last and stood against the wall beside Korbin while Singh and Jori worked to replace the cover.

Hapker watched the corridor. "How long will repairs take?"

"If it's just me," Singh said, "half a day."

Hapker groaned inwardly. They couldn't defend against Gottfried's soldiers for that long.

"I can help you," Jori said.

"I have at least one helper." A smile resided in Singh's voice, making Jori's eyes light up. "And perhaps one or two of you can assist with mundane stuff."

Hapker shifted, attempting to relieve the tickle of sweat running down his spine. "How long with their assistance?"

Singh rubbed her forehead. "Four hours."

That was better but still too much. "It'll do."

"We have explosives," Ortega said. "Let's disable doors so not even a good hacker like Jori can get in."

Hapker agreed. After Jori and Singh finished and stood, he tilted his head. "This way."

"So we're going to fix the array?" Ortega asked.

"That's the plan, unless we come up with a better one," Hapker said.

His heart took on a steadier rhythm now that they'd decided on what to do. He still didn't know how Gottfried expected to pull this off without anyone finding out he was the cause. Blaming Jori was a good tactic, but surely contrary evidence would arise. The only way he could succeed was if he downloaded the database and destroyed the proof.

Realization struck him with such a force that he stumbled. *Oh no.* All Gottfried would have to do was organize an evacuation and get everyone he wanted off the ship before blowing it up.

Crap.

59
Chances

A high priority internal message made Gottfried Krause blink out of his thought process. With a mental nudge, the transmitted recording played in his head. The accompanying text showed it to be a one-to-one conversation between two privates. Normally, he'd have no interest in the discussions of insignificant officers, but this one sent his blood boiling.

"Oh. And Sergeant Feny says he's a MEGA," the young officer in the recording said. "Can you believe that shit?"

Gottfried slammed his hand onto the arm of his chair. Corporal Kramer side-eyed him. He told himself that he didn't care what that bitch thought and reined in his fury. As much as he wanted to kill her, he must wait for his reinforcements.

That traitorous boy was an immediate problem. Why did he leave his protection? And why was he helping everyone? Didn't he understand they were his enemies?

But maybe the reports were wrong. Perhaps Commander Hapker had guilted him into it. He had some sort of hold over him. What, though? The commander was just a man, and not a very good one at that. He was a disgraced officer that almost no one respected. What did he have to offer that made Jori want to follow him?

Gottfried must understand this. He rose from his chair with a sense of purpose. Although he didn't feel happy, he smiled at them. "Excuse me. I have a quick matter to attend to."

Nobody responded. He wasn't surprised. Most likely, Corporal Kramer would use his absence as another opportunity to gossip about him. He gave her a dirty look, but she studiously kept working.

As he stormed off to the captain's ready room, he vowed to kill her as soon as the situation allowed.

*****

Jori pumped his arms, determined not to slow down his friends as they ran. Four officers pursued them, all yelling and cursing, none in the mood to check Singh's evidence. After Sergeant Feny, Jori had hoped convincing others would be easy, but it wasn't. The hate people continued to spew because of him frightened him more than anything his father had ever done.

The hallway shrank as various-sized tubes roped the ceiling and walls. Just like on his father's ship, aesthetics were no longer a concern on the lower decks. Pipes carried water, sewer, or fuel—a different color for a different function. Conduits containing communication wires, electricity, or other cables ran alongside them. Ventilation ducts dominated most of the space, especially the boxy air cleaners that hung low enough that Hapker and Korbin had to duck. If Jori wasn't in his suit, he imagined it would smell and feel damp.

Despite the tighter fit, these corridors had one benefit—a crisscross of aisles that only those who traversed here regularly could navigate. Singh turned left, then right. After passing two other narrow halls, she turned left again. Their pursuers fell behind from having to stop and consider every direction.

Singh frantically waved them into a tight opening. Everyone squeezed through, Jori with ease and Hapker with more trouble. They went around the giant water recycler, ducking or stepping over pipes of various sizes. Once out of sight in a corner, Hapker signaled for a halt.

Jori panted, and he wasn't the only one. Singh held her abdomen and hunched over, her face redder than anyone else's. Hapker removed his helmet and wiped the sweat from his forehead. Harley eased to a knee with a wince and did the same.

Hapker tapped his lips and everyone quieted. A man's voice carried, but he couldn't make out his words.

"Jori?" Hapker whispered.

Jori pointed in two directions about thirty degrees apart. "A pair that way and over there. Neither are headed our direction and both far enough that they won't hear us if we talk low."

"Which way are they going?"

Jori closed his eyes and focused. “They’ve stopped.”

Hapker frowned, then he nodded. “They’re probably deploying drones.”

“Scheisse,” Gresher said.

Incredulity crossed Hapker’s features and he tapped his comm. “Gottfried. How can I help you?” he asked in a flat tone.

Everyone tensed and looked to Hapker expectantly.

“I have a better idea,” Hapker replied with confident authority. “As the highest-ranking officer fit for duty, I hereby take command of this ship.”

Jori wished he could see Gottfried’s reaction. Although the man seldom showed emotion, a picture of him turning red blossomed in Jori’s imagination.

“You murdered a lot of people,” Hapker said.

Whatever Gottfried said next made a vein on Hapker’s forehead pulsed menacingly. “That’s not happening.”

Silence ensued. Jori realized Hapker’s emotions had diverted his attention away from their pursuers and so he forced himself to focus again. They were still in the same place. Ortega tilted her head, probably listening for the low whine of drones.

“Fine. See for yourself.” Hapker removed his comm and handed it to Jori.

Jori grimaced. He didn’t want to talk to the man, but curiosity compelled him to open the faceplate of his helmet and stick the device behind his ear.

“Yes, S—,” he said, stopping himself from saying *sir*.

“Jori, my dear boy. What are you doing with these people?”

“They’re my friends.”

Gottfried tsked. “But for how long? They don’t understand you the way I do.”

Jori’s chest flared with indignation. “You don’t understand me. You know nothing about me.”

“I know what you’re going through. Everyone is afraid of you because you’re better than them. And you know what people do when they’re afraid? They lash out. You’ve seen it.”

“Not everybody is like that.”

“I’m your friend,” Gottfried said. “You must see that. All I want to do is help you.”

“I won’t ally myself with a murderer.”

"Me? These people are our oppressors. What I'm doing here is necessary to protect my kind. I'm only acting in defense."

"Ha! I didn't believe that kind of bullshit when it came from my father's mouth. I certainly don't believe it from yours. You're killing people out of spite, nothing more."

Gottfried wasn't *exactly* like his father, but murdering to gain supremacy was the same. Before Jori met Hapker, he'd assumed there was something wrong with him for not agreeing with Father's justifications. But the commander had helped him see things differently—and in a way that didn't look skewed with sharp angles and shady corners. His father was wrong, and so was Gottfried.

"The Cooperative will lock you up just for doing what they would've done in the same situation. They're trying to hold you back. Don't you see that?"

After everything Jori had been through so far, he admitted that part was true. Sensing the hatred from the waiting pursuers validated Gottfried's argument.

"They hate you because you're different," Gottfried continued. "And they'll never stop hating you. Even if they don't convict you, they'll always be watching you and looking for ways to suppress you."

Glimpses of an imagined future flashed through Jori's head. Him imprisoned. People like Sergeant Banks harassing him. The MEGA Inspectors testing him. Admiral Belmont glaring down at him with a hate.

Hapker clasped Jori's shoulder. He didn't say anything, but the understanding in his eyes and the sympathy wafting off him bolstered his confidence. Peering at his new friends solidified it.

Gottfried had valid points, but they had nothing to do with the current situation. "Even if you're right about the Cooperative, this is wrong. You're condemning innocent people in order to force your selfish beliefs onto others. You think you're better than them?" Jori huffed. "You're worse."

"You're just parroting what the commander told you," Gottfried replied in a nasty tone.

"No. These are my words." Something profound warmed him as he realized he'd spoken what he'd known deep down all along. The Cooperative's unfair treatment of him didn't matter. The admiral, the council, everyone who had mistreated him and would likely continue to mistreat him, they didn't either. What he did here and now had more value than anything.

"Jori, please," Gottfried said with a whine. "You're like me. You belong with my kind."

"No. I'm not siding with you. And if you harm my friends, I'll *never* side with you and your kind."

He clicked off the comm and tossed it back at Hapker. His insides blistered with anger. Everyone gazing at him with varying degrees of admiration smothered his temper.

After a few deep breaths, he regained his composure. "That pissed him off. We should get out of here."

They unfroze. Korbin clapped Jori on the shoulder. "I'm with you, kid."

"Let's stop that asshole," Ortega added.

*****

Gottfried Krause banged the desk with his fists until a sharp twinge snapped him out of his irrational behavior. His anger was so deep, it shocked him. He had to get a hold of himself. The need to control his temper was the main reason he'd gotten implants to begin with.

He forced himself to calm down, using several calming techniques. Logic returned, so he accessed his analytical program. It took a minute to input all the data, and only a few more for the analysis to be completed.

His emotions ignited once again as he read it. The level of disappointment it contained made him sick. Some of it lay with himself, but most with the boy. His analytic capabilities weren't as good as MEGA-Man's, but with a ninety-six-point-three percent probability that Jori had meant what he said, it left little room for error.

He couldn't allow the boy's friends to live but killing them would prevent him from reaching his second objective. The more people those troublemakers convinced, the greater the chance they had of thwarting him. That mustn't happen. When comparing his two objectives—the database or Jori—attaining the database for MEGA-Man was the most important.

It was decided then. Stay the course. Kill the commander and the others. Take Jori by force and hope MEGA-Man could still turn him.

60
Separated

Jori's hand slipped inside the oversized suit, also making him lose his grip on the ladder. His breath caught as he grasped the rung in the nick of time. Gottfried must've suspected they'd been using the maintenance tunnels since all the safety gates were now open. If anyone fell, it'd be a long way down. That the narrow shaft emergency handholds might still save them didn't calm the pattering of his heart.

After descending a few more rungs without incident, the surge of adrenaline flittered away. That relief brought a new worry. The sensation of other people getting close fired off another burst of panic. "Chusho," he muttered. "Someone's coming!" he called out.

"From which way and how far?" Hapker asked from below.

"They're above us, about halfway to the shaft." The fluster of everyone else drowned out Jori's own.

"Anyone below?"

Jori concentrated. "Not that I can tell."

"Alright, we double-check our energy shields and keep going."

Jori inspected his device while keeping his senses open. The officers above felt like predators on a hunt where vigilance mixed with eagerness and purpose.

Jori's friends radiated trepidation and varying levels of determination as they moved faster. Singh almost stepped on his hand as he struggled to keep pace. His sweaty hands kept slipping because of the gloves, then catching at the last moment. Getting to the next opening in time seemed impossible, but he maintained a battle-focus.

The officers reached the shaft. He stayed quiet and hoped they wouldn't see them in the darkness—except they probably used infrared. *Chusho.*

Shouts of predator and prey alike drowned out the sound of phaser fire. Jori wanted to move faster, but the bulky gloves forced him to go slow.

A scream followed by a conk to the top of his head lost him his grip. Singh fell on him and sent him down. He flailed his arms, hitting her legs and the wall. He crashed into Sergeant Ortega, who screamed and also let go. Crashing into her halted him enough that he found a handhold. Singh's weight still pushed on him, but he clutched the rung with everything he had.

She kicked him in the gut as she flailed, making him grunt, then pulled off him. He maneuvered back to the ladder and moved with both more speed and care.

Everyone panted as more shots rained down. Gresher took the brunt of the hits. Unlike the soldiers, these crew member opponents used stun-fire. This setting meant their energy shields would last longer, but they'd eventually penetrate. Getting stunned here would be deadly.

They reached the next level tunnel. Singh hyperventilated, too terrified to move. Jori snatched the tool from her and clambered in.

"Jori!" Hapker said, too late.

He didn't stop. Time was of the essence. He kept his sensing focused outward. If people waited for him there, they were soldiers. If Gottfried wasn't too pissed and still intended to keep him alive, he only needed to worry about getting captured.

Everyone scrambled inside the horizontal passageway. Jori reached the panel and immediately went to work on opening it. Moments later, he pushed it and it fell to the floor with a clatter. He made sure his energy shield stayed in front and poked his head out.

Blink. Nothing happened. Maybe it was safe.

Blink. A zing of firepower struck his shield, making it shimmer a transparent blue. "Soldiers!" he cried out.

They couldn't go back, but they shouldn't wait here either. Getting out and finding cover was their only option. The shots only came from one direction. Perhaps they had a chance. He scooted out of the tunnel, keeping his depleting shield in front.

Gresher exited next, shooting the entire time. At least four soldiers fired from an intersection a short distance away. They blocked the way to the communications array, so Gottfried had guessed they were coming here. The man could've kept them out by closing the emergency doors, but probably left them open to lure them into a trap.

Chusho. Jori had no chance against this man's cunning.

His friends came out, keeping low while Hapker protected their backs. Several blasts struck shields, making a dazzling show of blue light.

Gresher pulled back behind Ortega and the others. "My shields are drained!"

Jori glimpsed Hapker's shield device as they switched places. A seventy-five percent strength, which made sense considering his rear position. That level wouldn't last long, though.

"Scheisse!" Gresher dodged to the middle of their group as phaser discharges erupted from behind them.

A cold sweat broke out over Jori's body. This was a battle—a real battle. And he was stuck in it with little defense.

"Cover your eyes. Get ready to move," Hapker said in a harsh whisper as he drew his hand back.

Jori squeezed his eyes shut. Even with the auto-tinting of his visor, the flash bomb burned red light through his eyelids. Although everyone, including the enemy, wore this same type of headgear, the distraction gave Jori and his friends a chance to move.

Someone grabbed his arm and hauled him. When he opened his eyes again, they were at the lip of a door jamb. Too bad the door was closed.

Korbin hugged the wall. "We can't stay here, Sir."

Hapker continued to fire. "Alright. Prepare to charge. Keep Jori and Singh in the center."

Jori tensed. He hated the idea, but they had no choice. It was either wait here until their energy shields died and them along with it, or take a chance and get to where they needed to go.

"Move!" Hapker yelled.

Jori hustled with his friends, wishing for a weapon. Their attackers pulled back. "It might be a trap!" he called out.

Hapker tossed a second flash bomb and rushed forward on the same trajectory. Jori and the others did too. Hapker roared as he fired at soldiers down the hall on the other side of the intersection.

Like repelling magnets, the two forces withdrew from each other until they reached the cover of another junction.

Gresher backed into the next corridor and fell with a curse. More phaser fire erupted. Jori dived over him to keep him from getting hit again. Fortunately, Gresher was still conscious. He stayed low, making him less likely to get caught in the crossfire.

Jori forced his panicked thoughts aside and analyzed the situation. Hapker's energy shield had to be low, as did Harley's and the others. Without a weapon, Jori was useless in a fight, but he could do something else.

Gottfried wanted him. Usually, dividing forces wasn't a good idea, but since Jori wasn't part of the force, he might as well be a distraction. Although not able to sense the soldiers, the sounds of their blasts allowed him to guess their numbers and locations. One direction possibly lay open. If there were soldiers there, he'd be caught. It was his only chance, though.

He lunged from the cover of his friends and ran to the intersection. He kept his head low, noting the blue flickers of his shield and the light of its falling strength.

"Jori, no!" Hapker and Ortega called out.

The soldiers stopped shooting, but not the attacking crew members. He darted around the corner and broke out into a full sprint. The tromp of heavy boots reverberating at his back told him they gave chase. Perfect. Now Hapker and the others had fewer people to fight. Just what he wanted. Except… *Chusho. Now what?*

Jori gritted his teeth. It unnerved him that he couldn't sense his pursuers. All he had to go on was the sound of their pounding feet.

His hearing and vision heightened as adrenaline coursed through him. The soldiers weren't shooting at him, so his life wasn't in danger. He still didn't want to get caught, though. They'd take him to Gottfried. Even if his friends got a communication out, that cybernetic freak would abandon ship and escape, taking Jori with him.

He rounded a corner and was confronted by two soldiers. He pivoted back around and smacked the panel to the stairwell. The door ripped open. Jori dove in and bounded down the winding steps.

His heart thumped in rhythm with his pursuers' footsteps. They gained on him. Their longer strides gave them the advantage of covering more distance. Jori's smallness and agility training granted him an edge too. Just as he neared the bottom of the next turnaround, he grasped the railing and vaulted over it and to the other set of stairs like a tree monkey.

Using the handrails and his lighter weight, he leapt three or more steps at a time, and flipped over the rails at every opportunity. The gap between him and the soldiers widened. After four flights, he shouldered through the exit and into darkness.

Motion sensor lights flickered on, revealing a danker space than before. He recognized the similarity to the lower decks of his father's ship and assumed the atmosphere here was heavy with heat and moisture. His suit compensated with a burst of cold air, making it harder for him to catch his breath. He raced to the left. The door behind him clanked open just as he took his first turn.

With his mind shielded, he hoped the soldiers couldn't sense him. However, he'd only mastered shielding his emotions. Blocking his lifeforce was difficult under duress.

His fear of the soldiers being able to track him seemed to be unfounded since he didn't hear the clomp of their boots behind him. Turn after turn brought him closer to calmness. He considered hiding, but without knowing his foes' abilities, he wouldn't risk it. Laying low meant being in a place with no way out. It was best to stay on the move.

He peeked around a corner. Nothing. As he crept onward, a rustling noise fractured the silence. Jori halted, then tiptoed backward. At the intersection, he considered his options. The time he'd spent in flight mode had him disoriented. Was he closer to the bow or the stern, port or starboard?

One direction was as good—or bad—as any other, so he took the left side. A few random turns later and he found himself back at the same door. Before he turned away, it burst open, revealing a red-faced Sergeant Banks.

Chusho!

Banks snarled. His inhibitor prevented Jori from sensing him, but he didn't need his ability to know the man intended to kill him. He spun around and sprinted off.

"Get over here, you little shit!"

Fear propelled Jori onward. So did the blasts of phaser fire. One struck the wall as he turned the corner. His peripheral vision caught the black mark it left. That meant Banks had his weapon set to max. The shock of it sent so much adrenaline through Jori's body that his fright transformed into a blind drive to escape.

It shouldn't surprise him that Sergeant Banks was here. The man had been reprimanded and ordered to remain in his quarters, but with the situation the way it was and many people thinking Jori was responsible, he'd likely taken it upon himself to come out and hunt.

Jori felt like a scared rabbit as he fled. His agility skills didn't help him in these halls. He must get somewhere with more options.

A patch of dingy yellow caught his eye. As he ran past, the faded paint revealed a number and letter. He knew where he was now and the best direction to go.

"You're dead!" Banks bellowed.

A phaser blast struck Jori's shield. The way the blue cut out told him his protection was gone. The next shot would penetrate his suit. Jori's chest tightened. Sweat poured down his face as he gasped.

He swept around another turn then dodged through the open entrance to the water recycling center. More blasts zipped by as he ducked under a sizeable pipe.

A few jumps, dips, and rolls later, a bunch of machinery blocked Banks' line of sight. Jori panted so hard his lungs hurt. Banks undoubtedly heard him.

"There's no escape," the man said, his voice dripping with menace. "I'm gonna slay me a dragon."

Jori dropped to his stomach and squirmed under a pipe too big around for Banks to climb over. It was too low to the ground for Jori to get under, and his suit kept bunching up in the wrong places. He turned head sideways and let all the air out of his lungs and pulled. The pressure of the floor below and the pipe above snared him like a trap. Panic welled up as he struggled to get through. If Banks caught him there, he'd be dead.

Taking a breath was torture, but his blood screamed for oxygen. His sight narrowed to tunnel vision. He clawed the hard floor, unable to find any purchase. The bulky suit caused his elbows to slide rather than dig. He pressed his toes to the ground and pushed, but his oversized boots didn't cooperate.

Damn it. This is a stupid way to die.

"I'm coming for you."

Banks' chuckle made Jori's skin crawl. Perhaps that dread caused him to shrink because he wrenched through. With a frantic slither, he hauled himself the rest of the way under. He stumbled to his feet and bounded away. The zap of phaser fire erupted, but the snaps that followed denoted they only struck objects behind him.

"Damn you!" Banks roared. "You won't get—" A resounding zip cut him off.

Swishes and clops indicated more people in here. Jori peeked through a gap in the recycler components. A soldier stood over Banks' body. Jori's blood turned to ice. Although he couldn't tell because of the inhibitor, he suspected the man was dead.

Those soldiers did that, and they did it with weapons set to kill. Jori swallowed. What if Gottfried had changed his mind about wanting him alive?

He dropped low and huddled in a nook between a tank and a pipe. If one soldier was here hunting for him, then there'd be more. With no energy shield and only a suit to protect him, he didn't have a chance. His eyes darted about, looking for a way to escape. None of his prospects were good.

This real-life crap wasn't as easy as it had been in all those practice simulations Sensei Jeruko had him do. Losing here meant losing forever—just like his brother. He clutched his chest and remembered his mother's necklace wasn't there.

Chusho.

61
Plans Revealed

Phaser fire erupted from both sides. Carletta Ortega stayed low and returned the gesture with her one good hand on the grip of her sidearm. An opposing blast struck her energy shield, overlaying the surrounding scene in a diaphanous azure.

Thanks to Jori's diversion, half their opposition had pulled out to give chase. Her shield remained strong, and their chances of success had risen from zero. Concern for the boy dwelled in the back of her mind as she fought on, determined not to let his sacrifice be in vain.

They'd found cover just within reach of the array but were blocked by soldiers lying in wait. Now they were surrounded.

On the plus side, they'd interrupted those ambushers before they set their bombs. While Singh checked a beetle-shaped one to deactivate the remote trigger, Ortega pinpointed the locations of all their attackers and waited for an opportunity to stun their asses.

"Got it!" Singh said. "No one's getting blown up."

"Should we go help Jori?" Harley asked.

"No," the commander answered. The pain in his voice signified he wanted to. "We must get that array fixed."

"Or we're all screwed." Ortega took a shot at a head that poked from around the corner. *Damn it. Missed.*

"What if we take cover over there?" Gresher pointed. "It would force them to move back."

An enemy's weapon stuck out. She fired and hit the hand holding it. The man she'd struck cursed, indicating the stun didn't knock him out. It likely only made his arm go numb, which was enough.

The discussion about their next strategy continued. Since she had no unique ideas, she tuned them out.

Another head poked out. The familiarity of this one startled her, and she froze at the intensity of his blue eyes. He fired twice, hitting her shield both times.

"Shit!" She fled back behind her cover. The speed of her heart stirred her panic. She inhaled and exhaled like a fish out of water. What was it about that man that terrified her so much?

"You alright?" Korbin asked her.

Her lips quivered but she couldn't get a word out. Korbin took her place, getting off a few shots. He pulled back with a yelp.

Ortega blinked, her fear forgotten. "What's wrong?"

"That man…" Korbin shivered, then shook his head.

Ortega related, but why were they so unnerved by that soldier? She could picture his stone-cold face and the piercing of his eyes without it bothering her, but seeing him in person was different. "He must have some kind of ability."

"An imperium?"

"We've got to take him out," Ortega said.

"Listen up everyone," Commander Hapker interrupted. "We're moving over there." He pointed. "Ortega, Korbin, you cover us."

Ortega dipped her head. The further she could get from the blue-eyed man, the better.

"Singh, can you close and disable that door?"

"Um." Her widened eyes darted as though looking for an answer. "I can shut it, but I don't know how to make it stay closed."

"Can you do something so that even the emergency override malfunctions?"

"I-I… I don't know."

"That's alright," the commander said. "Do what you can."

Singh clenched her fists in determination, then bounded to her feet and pulled the red-handled emergency lock button. The hatch slammed down with frightening swiftness, sending a loud clunk that resounded throughout the different sections of the enclosed area. Ortega puffed, thankful that a half-meter of metal separated her from the blue-eyed man.

Singh opened the panel beside it and fired inside. "Maybe this will melt the electronics and keep anyone from overriding it."

"Good. Now, go!" The commander charged from his cover.

As Harley and Gresher followed, weapons firing, Ortega and Korbin laid cover fire.

"Singh," Hapker called to her. "Reactivate the bomb. Set it for fifteen seconds, then shove it over here."

"I thought we didn't want to hurt our people," she replied.

"Those aren't our people," the commander said in a severe tone.

Singh hunched near Ortega. Her hands shook as she fiddled with the insectile thing. "Shit." With a huff, she slid it away from her as though it were on fire.

Ortega and Korbin grasped her arm and moved out. Ortega's shield flickered four times along the way. She dived behind a machine encased in a huge metal box. It worked. The soldiers in the array room pulled back to another area.

Commander Hapker sprang up, chucked the bomb, and dropped low. Ortega hunkered down. She waited in tense silence for what seemed like ages before a boom blasted her eardrums. A hard repercussion followed, pitching her to the floor.

The commander's voice rang out. "Everyone alright?"

Ortega wagged her head to ease the ringing and assessed herself. Singh perched onto her elbow and patted her body. The others did the same.

While Ortega kept a sharp eye out, Commander Hapker held his phaser in a low position as he stalked forward. He reached the edge of the enemy cover and glanced behind it. Then did it again more slowly. "They're down. Ortega…" He waved her over.

She kept her sidearm level and dashed in and around the machine. Two soldiers lay sprawled on the floor. The cracked helmets and horrific gouges in their suits suggested they were probably dead, but she checked anyway. After removing one helmet, she pressed her fingers to the man's neck. Nothing. She did the same for the next soldier. Nothing there either. She exhaled noisily and stood. "Clear!"

"Clear here, too," Korbin called out.

"Clear," Gresher repeated.

Ortega left the corpses. Gresher and Korbin returned from their sweep, and everyone met in the most open space of the vast but machine-crowded room.

"Alright," the commander said. "Singh, let's get working on the array. Tell us what to do."

"There's a problem, Sir." Singh's brow creased and her shoulders appeared as though they carried a heavy weight. "I fired inside the panel of that door, but I doubt it'll work. There's a manual unlock I might be able to disable but need to remove the wall covering to get to it."

"I'll take care of it," the commander said. "Which part?"

She pointed and explained what to do.

"Got it," he replied. "You work on the array." After she disappeared behind the other machinery, he met everyone's eyes. "Report energy shield status."

Ortega looked down. "About one-eighth."

"Same," Korbin said.

"A little more than that," Harley added.

"No shield," Gresher said, "and I've only got two flash bombs left."

Commander Hapker's lips pressed together, making the natural crookedness of his mouth more pronounced. "Ortega, Harley. You two guard the door. That's your priority. Gresher, give Harley the bombs. If that hatch opens, he'll toss them out. Then you and Korbin, take cover here and here." He pointed to two places. "Unless Singh has something for you to do."

"Yes, Sir," they all snapped.

"I'll take care of the wall covering and see if I can figure it out."

"We could really use a certain little genius right now," Harley said.

An agonizing flicker crossed the commander's face. "He'll be alright."

A pang wiggled through Ortega's insides as she hoped it was true.

The commander exposed the wall's innards. Before he did any work, the hatch rose, making him jump back and grab his weapon. "Incoming!"

"Shit!" Ortega took the high position while he took the low. The sizzle of enemy fire made the hair on her arms stand on end.

"Flash out!" Harley flung a flash bomb out the door.

Ortega turned away in time to avoid the flare, then followed up with phaser blasts.

"Letta!" a man's voice roared.

Chills ripped down Ortega's spine. *What's he doing here*? "Don't you get it, asshole? We're done!"

"Come on, Letta," Bryce said. "We can work this out."

"I want nothing to do with you, you lying piece of shit."

"I lied for a good reason. You know how the Cooperative treats people like me."

"So you *are* a MEGA."

"No mechanical enhancements. I'm genetically altered—from birth—which means it's not by choice. Does the Cooperative care? No. If they found out, they would have slapped a label on me with no concern for the life I'd be forced to live because of their stupid restrictions."

Ortega readjusted her grip on the phaser. "Sorry to hear that, but it's not a good reason to murder a bunch of people."

"History is full of fights against unjust governments. My cause is just as worthy."

"There are other ways to fight."

Bryce laughed. "You don't think that's already been tried? We've had enough. It's time for us to take our proper place in society."

It was Ortega's turn to laugh. "And where is your proper place? At the top with that fucking weirdo, Lieutenant Krause?"

"You could have been a part of it, you know. You're something special. Unique. Talented. You don't belong with these losers."

Ortega squirmed with discomfort. She wasn't sure how to reply to that. He'd said such sweet things before but that was when they'd been together. Now that they were broken up, what reason did he have?

"Hey." Commander Hapker frowned at her, but in a way that showed concern. "Are you alright?"

She shook off her unease. "Yeah…" She shrugged. "He threw me off, is all. But I don't have any problem shooting his ass if it comes to it."

He gave her an apologetic look, then refocused his attention outside.

"Letta, come on," Bryce called. "You can't win this. But if you surrender, I'll see that you live. You *and* your friends."

Ortega had no intention of surrendering but responded anyway. "What about everyone else on this ship?"

Bryce didn't reply right away. "That's not my call."

"Didn't think so," she muttered.

"Hey," Harley whispered. "See if you can get information out of him. Find out what this is all about."

Good idea. "Alright. You want us to surrender. Tell us what we're surrendering for. Explain why it was necessary for you to commit murder."

"Like I said, it's time for us to take our proper place in society."

"Let me guess. You're here to steal the database so you can make a planet killing weapon—force the issue by committing genocide."

"It doesn't have to be that way. Perhaps taking the database will be enough to show your government our resolve."

Commander Hapker whispered in her ear. "Ask him about Jori."

"What about Jori?" she asked Bryce. "What do you want with him?"

"He may or may not be a MEGA, but like you, he's got remarkable abilities. I don't know all the ins and outs of it—I'm just a soldier—but I imagine there's a use for his genetic information."

"So it's not about him being the Dragon Emperor's son?"

"That's possibly part of it. My boss also wants to replicate his talents."

"Why do you want him, though? All you need is his DNA. You can find that in a hair, right?"

Bryce laughed. "You're smart in some ways, Letta, but you don't have a clue about anything scientific. Living and naturally regenerative samples are required. Sure, we can get it from his blood, but there's a risk that it will degrade. So we need him—alive and well."

"I don't think he wants to go with you."

"He doesn't have to be willing."

Commander Hapker's jaw twitched. Ortega took strength from his anger and pushed away her unease. "You'd do that to him? Kidnap him? Hasn't he been through enough already?"

"He'll be better off with people who don't hurt him because of who he is."

He had a point. "Not everyone is like Banks and Lengen," she said.

"You sure about that?"

She considered the way those two always spewed their hatred. Then she glanced at her friends. She glanced at Commander Hapker too, the man who risked both his career and his life to help Jori. "Pretty sure."

"Come on. Let's not argue."

"No. Let's not," she snapped. "You're free to shut the fuck up at any time."

"Letta…"

"Don't *Letta* me, asshole. You've made some good points, but your lack of human decency shows me who you really are."

"You're making a mistake."

"My mistake was in liking you."

"Fine. If that's the way you're gonna be," Bryce replied ominously. "Don't say I didn't warn you."

Foreboding crawled up Ortega's throat. She swallowed it back and hardened her resolve. She probably wouldn't win this, but she'd be damned if she'd let him win either. Bryce was going down.

62
Capture

Jori deftly climbed onto a filtration unit. The panoramic view up here gave him a better vantage, but it also made him vulnerable. The broad, rectangular space provided some cover with its multiple valves, hoses, compressors, and other protruding parts. If anyone saw him, they'd have a hard time shooting him. But with his means of escape limited, they still had the advantage.

His heart pattered. Staying low, he used his eyes and sensing ability to locate his opponents and evaluate his options. The soldiers who'd killed Banks held their rifles level and searched every nook and cranny. So far, they only did a cursory search above. Two additional soldiers appeared between units before moving out of sight again.

If he didn't get out of here soon, they'd find him. But how? The exit behind him had too many twists and turns for him to reach it without being noticed. However, his smallness allowed him to fit between places the soldiers couldn't. A shiver ran through him as he recalled nearly getting stuck.

The exit to his left was too open. Their weapons would strike him down before he made it halfway. The right was more promising, but tricky. His agility would allow him to hop from the top of one unit to another. Even with this bulky suit on, he was confident of his sense of balance. He might make too much noise, though.

His shoulders dropped in resignation. It was his best option. With the four soldiers currently out of sight, he stepped onto a pipe and crept across with swift nimbleness. This new unit was about the same size and had multiple cylindrical parts on top.

The sensation of two intruding lifeforces made him duck between them. Chesa and Sergeant Carter appeared at the exit he'd planned on taking.

Chusho! He pulled in tighter, trying to make himself as small as possible. This room was vast, but the more people that came in here, the harder it was to remain unseen.

What now? He considered the unit he was on. He had the tools to take pieces off it. This pipe along the side held a gas. If he loosened a joint, pressurized air would escape and a minor explosion would follow.

He caught another glimpse of Carter getting closer. If Hapker's friend was nearby when it happened, he'd get hurt. Jori cringed at the thought, but Gresher's changdu training also came to mind. Carter wasn't trying to kill him so doing something that might cause his death would be wrong.

Chusho. He glanced around, hoping another idea would come to him. Instead, the sight of Banks' body made him realize another danger. Would the soldiers who'd murdered him do away with Carter and Chesa, too?

The obligation of saving both himself and them made his chest tighten. If being discovered was inevitable, perhaps getting caught by these two would get them all out of here alive.

He moved from his hiding spot before his decision solidified. Remaining low, he snuck over a wider pipe to a shorter unit and eased down onto the crook of a tube.

Carter and Creston stalked closer as he waited on his haunches. She went one way and he another, but still in his general direction.

Sergeant Carter neared. Jori gritted his teeth in resolve and dropped to the floor. The clop of his boots brought the man rushing from around a broad column with his rifle at the ready. Jori threw up his hands and swallowed as Carter's eyes glowered from above the point of his weapon.

"Got him!" Carter called out.

Chesa darted in from his other side. "There you are, you brat. We've been looking all over for you."

"We've got to get out of here," Jori said with urgency.

"Why? So you can blow up this place, too?"

"What? No. I had nothing to do with that. It's those soldiers. They killed Sergeant Banks. They might try to kill you, too."

Chesa's lip curled. "Pfft. You expect us to believe that?"

"It's true." Jori tilted his head over his shoulder. "He's over there. Shot. And I don't have a weapon."

With a look from Carter, Chesa lowered her rifle and pulled out a set of handcuffs. "You figured out a way, just like you did on the *Odyssey*."

Jori ground his teeth at her obstinance. "If I had a weapon, why don't I have it now?"

She put her a hand on her hip. "Either you hid it, or you still have it. Remove your suit."

Jori fumed but unlatched his helmet and slipped it off his suit. If Gottfried did something drastic to kill everyone on this ship, he'd be vulnerable.

Chesa frisked him, then grabbed his arm. After slapping the metal clamps onto his wrists, she twisted him around. "Get going, you little—"

"Enough, Sergeant," Carter said. "Let's get him to Lieutenant Krause."

"What!" Jori jerked away but Chesa held him too tightly. "You can't take me back to him. He's the one who wants to kill us all."

"I'm not arguing with you, kid," Carter replied. "We have our orders."

"If I'm to be detained, why not return me to my prison cell?"

"We're to bring you to the bridge."

A pang burst in Jori's chest. Going into the den of the blackbeast was a terrible idea. Gottfried would murder them, for sure. "Does that make sense to you? Why would he want me there?"

Carter exhaled noisily. "I said I'm not arguing with you. Now let's go."

Chesa yanked Jori into a walk. He didn't resist as they propelled him between them.

Two soldiers stepped in front, making Jori's breath hitch. The stone-faced men carried their rifles across their chests, but a simple shift would have them aimed and firing in less than a second.

Jori twisted from Chesa's grip and tramped forward. A cold sweat fell over him as the soldiers' flinty stares shifted to him. "Don't kill them."

They didn't reply. Carter made a sound of annoyance and pulled Jori back. "We've got this, Sirs."

"We will accompany you," the soldier with a wide nose said.

"No." Jori struggled but his captors clutched his arms like industrial vice-grips.

"Knock it off, kid," Carter said.

Jori's chest constricted as the soldiers fell in behind him. He glowered over his shoulder as Carter and Chesa dragged him. "Tell Gottfried that if he kills these two or my friends, I won't cooperate."

Their stark silence made his skin crawl. Surrendering had seemed like a good idea at the time. Now he wasn't so sure.

*****

The alert of an internal message startled Gottfried Krause. He opened and read it, then blinked to make sure it was real. They'd captured Jori and were bringing him here.

He laughed out loud and beamed, not caring what Corporal Kramer thought.

<0HGQ-7> Should we kill the sergeants?

Gottfried's smile snapped away as he realized there was more to the message. Sergeant Carter and Sergeant Creston had been the ones to find him. That shouldn't have been a problem except now the boy insisted they not be killed either.

What would it take to get this ungrateful brat to understand who his real friends were? With that monster Sergeant Banks dead, Jori should be happy, not pleading for the life of two more officers—one who'd mistreated him. Commander Hapker had too much influence on that boy.

If he eliminated those officers, it might convince everyone that the boy was behind it. But he didn't need their support, especially since they'd die anyway. Jori was the one he had to persuade. Speaking to him face-to-face might have better results if he permitted Carter and Creston to live a little longer.

<716Krause> No. Allow them to come to the bridge. We will handle them later.
<0HGQ-7> Roger.

"Lieutenant Buckeye to command," the general comm rang out.

"Command here," Gottfried replied.

"The enemy has reached the array."

Gottfried inhaled sharply. They'd reached the communications array. He slammed his fist down on the arm of the chair. "Kill them."

"But, Sir!" Kramer swiveled in her chair and faced him with wide eyes. "Chief Singh can fix it and we can call for help."

"She's with the enemy. She probably intends to sabotage it for good."

"But why would she do that if it's already broken?"

"Because she's a traitor, Corporal! Who knows what's going through her head?" Gottfried glowered at her until she turned back to her station.

He took in a deep breath, but instead of his anger dissipating, irritation replaced it. He'd expected them to go there, but not to succeed. Apparently, his strategizing skills failed him when under pressure. He wrung his hands with uncertainty.

"Sir?" The curly black-haired woman tilted her head. "What's your reply?"

It was Gottfried's turn to be confused. He must've had a questioning look on his face because the officer explained.

"Lieutenant Buckeye said it's a standoff."

"What happened…" He wanted to ask why they didn't use the bombs, but doing so out loud wouldn't be smart.

"The lieutenant reported two men down and the enemy has secured the area. He's awaiting your instructions."

Two men down? Gottfried accessed his comm connections and noted the two highlighted in red. Asking about the bombs was impossible.

His face heated. Once again, his ability to strategize failed him. He needed to spend at least five minutes analyzing the situation. Looking inward for that long would draw unwanted attention, though. Not that he had the time to begin with.

Gottfried pulled the mobile workstation of his chair in front of him. "Lieutenant, I'm shutting off the lights and air in that section. We'll flush our enemy out." He deactivated both with a perfunctory jab of his finger.

"Sir." Buckeye's tone sounded tired. "That won't work. The officers are in full battle gear and the others are wearing enviro-suits. Plus, Sergeant Ortega can see in the dark."

"How did they get those?"

"They're in emergency lockers all over the ship, Sir."

"Why didn't anyone tell me about this?"

"It's in the text update, Sir."

Gottfried gnashed his teeth. Of course. Buckeye didn't have implants, so he had to communicate using normal channels.

"Well, maybe turning off the air and lights will slow them."

"No more than it'll slow us, Sir."

Gottfried slammed his fist onto the chair's arm. "But the chief will have a harder time fi—sabotaging the array."

Damn it. He'd almost slipped up there. His emotions were getting the best of him. He better get a grip soon.

A twinge of perplexity emanated from Corporal Kramer. Did she catch his misstep? He patted the weapon at his side. If she called him out on it, he'd kill her. It would make it harder to coordinate the docking of his allies, but he could always disable the transport-blocker and allow them to beam aboard.

"Yes, Sir," Buckeye said. "What do you want me to do in the meantime?"

Gottfried couldn't think and it frustrated him, and that made it hard for him to regain control. It was a vicious cycle. *Damn them all.* "What's your recommendation, Lieutenant?"

"Charge in. We must end this before they do any more damage."

"Agreed." Gottfried regretted that this was likely to lose him Jori's allegiance, but the way things were going indicated he was irredeemable. MEGA-Man would be disappointed, but getting the database was the priority. "Do it."

"Yes, Sir." Lieutenant Buckeye cut out.

This had better work. His allies would be within short-range communication soon, but it was still a while before they reached transport range.

Damn that boy and his companions.

63
Duty

Jori studied the sensations from Sergeant Carter as they marched down the corridor. The man didn't have Chesa's prejudice or Banks' darkness. His aura was a little like Hapker's—reasonable, even-tempered, and generally optimistic. However, there was something about the mix that suggested an uncompromising nature.

Carter seemed disgruntled when it came to Hapker, but not malevolent. Perhaps using their old camaraderie would help him see he was on the wrong side of this.

"I'm aware you don't agree with Hapker on some things," he said. A flash of disappointment streaked through the sergeant's emotions, but his face didn't change. Jori pushed on. "But he saved my life."

A trickle of doubt leaked through, but Carter didn't respond.

Jori filled his lungs, hoping to tip the scale. "He has a good heart. He's not like anyone I've ever met."

"If he's such a good person, why is he trying to sabotage the array?" Chesa demanded.

"He's not. He wants Chief Singh to repair it."

"It's already being fixed," Chesa said. "The only reason to go there is to stop it from happening."

"So who's working on it?" Jori asked with a challenging tone. "There's a lockdown, remember?"

Carter slowed but didn't meet Jori's eye. "Yeah, he's a good guy. I can't deny that. But he's not right for this job. This isn't the first time he's put other things above his duty to the Cooperative."

A twang of irritation made Jori want to retort, but he kept his tone calm and logical, the way Hapker or Gresher would've done. "Is duty more important than doing the right thing?"

"We have to trust our leaders to know what the right thing is."

"Where would your crewmates be if I had made that choice? Those officers my father kidnapped and tortured would be dead if I had decided to put duty above morality."

Carter's emotions wavered. "Hapker didn't face the same thing you did."

"Didn't he? Following orders would've cost innocent people their lives."

"They died anyway—and in a more horrific way—because he didn't do as he was told."

Jori held in his frustration. "But he didn't know that would happen." He took the twitch in Carter's brows as a sign that he was getting through. "The orders were unlawful. Even the Cooperative courts decided that."

Carter's chest expanded as he inhaled. "It's not that simple, kid."

"Neither is this situation." Jori's heart clenched as they marched toward disaster.

"You've corrupted them," Chesa said. "J.D., Ortega, Korbin, and Singh. They were all good officers before you came along. Now look at them. They're betraying their own people—all because of *you*."

Jori swallowed the acid that rose to his mouth. She was right. This was his fault. If it wasn't for him, they wouldn't treat Hapker and Ortega like outcasts. Carter and Chesa wouldn't assume they were a part of a conspiracy, and they'd probably suspect Gottfried.

How could he fix this? Despair wrenched his gut. He had no hope of convincing Carter *or* of outsmarting Gottfried. Everyone here would die because trusting an admiral's aide was more logical than accepting the word of a mass murderer's son.

They reached the conveyor. Jori didn't want to go in but had no escape. His eyes burned as not just his fate, but the fate of Hapker and the others neared the end.

Chesa pulled him inside the car and Jori didn't resist. Even though he doubted he'd persuade them, he took another chance. "Did you check the DTD Singh gave you?"

"No," Carter replied. "I'm sure she believes she has proof, but it might've been doctored."

"What if it's not? What if Gottfried is behind this? You're delivering us to the enemy."

Chesa harrumphed. "The only one who has sent anyone to their deaths is you."

Jori lowered his head. Convincing them he had nothing to do with this was impossible. He had no way of showing them Gottfried's true colors.

"Knock it off, Sergeant," Carter said. "This boy might not be a part of whatever his father is doing here."

"You seriously believe him, Sir?"

Carter sighed, giving Jori a little hope. "Hapker can be naïve at times, but that doesn't mean… Hell. I don't know what it means. Just conduct yourself appropriately."

Her mouth twisted. "Yes, Sir."

Jori's insides rolled. Hapker wasn't naïve. He was just the type of man who wanted to do the right thing no matter the consequences. Why couldn't people see that? Instead of blaming him for the actions of others, they should look deeper.

Hapker was in the right. Jori had to prove it, or all would be lost. But how?

Then it hit him. "Have you ever entered a query into a computer and had it cease all other functions while figuring it out?"

"Yeah," Carter said. "Who hasn't?"

"Gottfried does that. He freezes whenever he has a complex problem to solve."

"Everyone needs to stop and think," Carter replied dismissively, though a hint of uncertainty spotted his emotions.

"This is different. He freezes like a computer. He doesn't see or hear what you say. I doubt he even breathes. And I suspect it's because his brain has been augmented."

"There's no way a MEGA could be an admiral's aide."

"You think I'm a MEGA, right?"

"Duh," Chesa responded.

"Then why didn't they find proof? If it's possible for me to be a MEGA despite the lack of proof, then why is it so hard to believe an admiral's aide is a MEGA?"

"Because he's not a homicidal maniac like you are."

It was Jori's turn to harrumph. "*Yes. He. Is.* He's the one killing your crew, not me. Think about it, Sergeant," he said to Carter. "You have your doubts that I'm not directly causing this.

So that means someone else is. It's not Hapker." Carter's expression changed. Jori pressed the issue. "Even if he's naïve to trust me, he's not a murderer. He would *never* be a part of something like this."

Carter didn't reply. His mixture of emotions made reading him difficult. *Chusho! How can I convince him?*

They exited to the command deck. A blast of coldness washed over Jori that had nothing to do with the temperature. He'd reached the end of the line. If he didn't prove Gottfried was a MEGA soon, more people would die. Probably not him, but Carter and Chesa for sure. Hapker and his other friends too.

Jori detected others on the bridge, which meant they were regular crew members and hopefully not Gottfried's lackeys. At least one harbored misgiving. Jori needed to tip the scales and get these people to realize what Gottfried was.

Carter nudged him forward. Jori evaluated his options. Fighting his four captors and escaping the command deck would be damn near impossible. But that didn't mean he couldn't escape. The bridge wasn't the only place located here. Several control and conference rooms went all around this circular hallway.

That's it. A control room. The lessons Sensei Jeruko had given on ship layouts came to him.

He glanced up and down the hall. The bridge was ahead, and a control room back the other way. It would have a secure lock, but Jori could open it if he had enough time.

Fighting and possibly hurting Carter or Chesa was out of the question. Besides, he had the skill but not the strength. His only chance was to outmaneuver and outthink them.

He glanced at the soldiers following silently behind. One had a flash bomb in his vest. Unlike phasers, this device didn't need biometric authentication. And even though everyone except him wore a helmet with an auto-tinting feature, they all had their faceplates open.

Jori would be vulnerable too, but this was one of many scenarios he'd practiced with Sensei Jeruko. He knew where to go, what to do, and he could do it blind.

Carter prodded him again. Jori exaggerated a fall. He slipped between Carter and Chesa and collided with a soldier. With his wrists secured behind him, he snapped a pocket open and grasped the device. The thickness of the vest and Jori's impact hopefully meant the soldier didn't realize what he'd done.

The other soldier seized Jori by the upper arm. A drop at the right angle caused him to let go. Jori rolled away, tucking his hands under him at the same time and switching the cuffs to the front.

He darted off. Yells followed him, curses from Chesa and demands from Carter. The soldier-freaks were as silent as the dead.

As he raced full speed around the curved corridor, he fiddled with the flash bomb until he found the trigger. Then he set it off and dropped it.

It bounced at his feet and rolled behind him. A blazing light erupted. Even with his back turned and his eyes closed, a painful brightness still penetrated. The yells of his captors indicated it had affected them too.

Jori opened his eyes, seeing just enough to tell him he was where he'd expected to be. He unlatched the toolbox. After a half-second of fumbling, he found the flathead screwdriver.

He felt along the wall until arriving at the door panel and flicked it open. His vision was still blurred, but he made out where to stick the tool next. Reaching it was difficult and his haste didn't help.

He sensed the disorientation of Carter and Chesa. If the soldiers didn't have cybernetic defenses against flash bombs, he had a few more seconds.

The control room door slid open. Jori rushed in. His eyesight cleared enough to see two crew members and no soldiers. Their lifeforces didn't name them warriors, so he hoped to complete his task without too much interference.

"Lieutenant Krause is a MEGA and so are the soldiers from the station," he said in a rush. "We must stop them before they kill more people."

The woman's eyes grew while the balding, older man glanced around with his mouth opening and closing with indecision. He stood as though to confront him, but stepped back when Jori darted toward him.

With a plop, Jori dropped into his seat and tapped the monitor. Finding the encryption program took more time than he liked, but still only a few seconds. He removed the DTD from his pocket and inserted it into a port on the side. A window popped up. Jori clicked the appropriate option, and the program went to work. The data changed.

"What the hell are you doing?" The balding man asked, fear quivering through his voice.

Jori didn't reply. So long as the two people wavered with uncertainty, they didn't concern him.

The control room door hissed open. Sergeant Carter entered with a dark expression. "Here!" he called out to someone behind him. He didn't wait for them, though. He stormed in, grabbed Jori's arm, and yanked him out of the chair.

Jori resisted, but only as an act. "No! I need that!" He reached for the DTD with his handcuffed hands.

Carter snatched the device out of the workstation. "Are you crazy, stealing information at a time like this? Where the hell did you expect to go after this?"

The sternness of his tone made Jori flinch. He'd expected to piss off his captors, but not so much that a purple vein throbbed on Carter's forehead.

"It's not what you think," Jori replied, barely keeping himself from stammering. "Don't let Gottfried see it."

Carter shot him an incredulous look and hauled him out. "You're out of your mind, boy."

A jackhammer pounded in Jori's chest, but he didn't resist. Would Carter give it to Gottfried anyway? The man's emotions were too livid for him to guess.

The plan was weak, but it was all he had. His only other hope was that Hapker and the others would get the communications array working and call for assistance. That would be good for them, but not much for Jori. If help came, Gottfried could still take him and leave in an escape pod or shuttle.

I'm doomed.

64
Lights Out

Losing the lights and air was annoying but hardly concerning. Carletta Ortega didn't need the night vision feature of her helmet. Infrared would work better whenever a soldier stuck his hand or something out from behind their cover, but she didn't need her headgear for that either. Why Lieutenant Krause thought this would help him was beyond her.

Shit. He might have a surprise for them.

She'd removed her sunglasses, disabled the auto-night vision of her visor, and now waited in darkness like a Similean tawny owl. Unlike an owl, she had a wider field of view. And unlike an owl, she perceived infrared. Not the red and orange blobs other people claimed to see, either. Every feature around her was sharp and distinct. If a soldier stuck out a thumb, a warm glow would overlay it, but she'd still be able to make out the dirt under his fingernail.

Ortega's exceptional hearing allowed her to catch Bryce's words despite his helmet and despite the recyclers working to remove the air. So long as the big room held a little atmosphere, she could detect the beat of his heart.

"Yes, Sir." The thinning air made Bryce's voice tinny. "What do you want me to do in the meantime?"

Ortega waited on the edge of anxiety and listened intently.

"Charge in," Bryce said, but in a conversational way rather than as an order. "We must end…"

Without a medium to carry sound waves, his words flittered away. Ortega signaled with a wave to let the others know their opponents were about to attack.

Gresher returned from helping Singh just as the soldiers stormed in. Ortega fired in rapid succession at the closest one. She used the kill rather than stun setting, so the soldier's energy shield failed. Her next shot hit between his torso and thigh armor, and he dropped like a heavy stone.

They'd all agreed the soldiers were a threat. Since Ortega saw well enough to distinguish them from their crew members, Commander Hapker had ordered her to focus on those bastards. His vehemence had surprised her. The way his normally amiable demeanor had switched into a full-blown warrior when it mattered solidified her own determination.

She kept her courage as more soldiers rushed forth. She shot another one in rapid bursts. He hit the floor with a smack that would have been louder had there been more air.

She aimed at the next soldier. His silhouette sparked something within her that made her freeze. The blue-eyed man. She shouldn't be able to see his eyes through the activated mechanisms of his visor, but two blue orbs glowed menacingly and sent a pang of fear through her chest.

Fuck! How is that possible? She pulled the trigger and scampered back at the same time. Either her aim was off or he had other defenses against kill-fire, because he kept coming. She struck his weapon in the right spot, making it spark.

He flung it to the side, the shoulder strap keeping it on his person but out of his way. Like a Spearhead-class spaceship on a collision course, he came at her too swiftly for her to think, let alone move.

He whammed into her. His rock-hard head struck her chest and knocked the wind from her. When she pitched backward, his skull bashed under her chin. Her teeth rattled and stars burst through her vision.

Before she knew it, he had her pinned. His weight pressed down on her torso and his hands drove her shoulders to the ground. Being trapped didn't scare her as much as the blue glow of his eyes that bored like drills. The piercing sensation intensified her fear to where she thought her heart would explode.

She couldn't move. She couldn't breathe. She couldn't even scream.

*****

Despite the swarm of soldiers rushing in, J.D. Hapker maintained a hyper-focus. Sergeant Ortega had taken down two, but many more came. They were like locusts coming to raze crops. Nothing stopped them. Certainly not his stun weapon.

As much as he wanted to save his own life and the lives of his new friends, he didn't want to kill misguided crew members.

The infrared blob of a soldier bolted through the wide hatch, and like a lion on a mission it lunged and tackled Ortega. Hapker shot at his back but was forced to return his attention to the charging army. A longer burst from his phaser finally penetrated an energy shield and armor. His target collapsed. Another jumped over the body and came at Hapker like a cannonball. He fired, to no avail. Several more enemies breached the room.

"Fall back!" he yelled into the comm. Then to Singh, "Take cover!"

Keeping low, he skittered backward. A kill-blast struck his shield, disabling it for good. He ducked behind a bulky machine. Another shot hit a spot beside him, making a white spark. It had come from a different direction, so now he was pinned. Panic blasted through him like fireworks. If he didn't think of something soon, he'd die.

"Switch to kill!" he reluctantly told his friends.

A red blob appeared in his line of sight. Someone with a rifle pointed right at him. He fired and dropped to the floor at the same time they did. Did they shoot each other? That Hapker wondered made him realize he was still alive.

"I got your back, Commander," Harley announced through the comm. Another infrared form popped up at his side, only this person didn't shoot at him. Hapker blinked and his visor display labeled it as Corporal Harley. The soldier who'd fallen didn't have a label, which meant either the crew members had masked their identifications, or it was a soldier. Hapker hoped it was the latter.

"Thanks," he said to Harley. "Now we've got to help Ortega."

Despite no longer having an energy shield, he darted from his hiding spot, keeping low, and hustled. Harley followed until they reached a rectangular unit. Hapker peeked over. The larger of two red bulks dominated the smaller one on the floor. He aimed and fired. At that same moment, a blinding agony seared through his arm.

*****

Carletta Ortega spiraled into a vat of pure terror. It was as though those blue eyes seared into her soul and frazzled her mind. Phaser fire erupted and shimmered behind him. His azure orbs turned away from her. Her fear remained, but no longer suffocated her. She gulped in air like she'd been under water and just broke the surface.

Now that she was partially free, she thrust out her elbow and bashed it into the more flexible armor of his neck. The jarring made her wound burn like a thousand spider bites, and she cried out.

The man's head snapped sideways and back again with those blue orbs practically stabbing her. Despite her escalating fear, she pulled her eyes away. Her phaser lay near her uninjured hand. She lurched for it. His weight kept her down. When more blasts struck him, he eased off. She swiveled her hips and grabbed the weapon.

In one swift movement, she jammed the barrel between the neck of his armor and fired. His blue eyes blinked to black, and he dropped lifelessly to the side.

She lay in shock for who knew how long before someone's voice zapped her back to the present.

"I'm hit!"

Ortega expanded her attention. A brief scan of the room revealed several bodies sprawled on the floor in various poses. None were her friends. A glance to her left proved her wrong. Corporal Harley knelt over Commander Hapker.

Ortega jumped to her feet and rushed through enemy fire as fast as her wobbly legs could carry her. Blood gushed from Hapker's mangled arm. He was still conscious, but her sensitive eyes noted his pale skin.

"He's going into shock!" She frantically scanned the walls of the room for a first aid box.

"Shit. Projectiles," Harley said.

Ortega concurred. Armor piercing bullets were terribly inhumane. She swallowed back the bile rising from her throat. "Fuckers."

65
Freeze

Agony exploded through Jori's brain. "No!" Still cuffed, he threw his arms over his head and crumpled to the floor. Someone, either Carter or Chesa, tried to pull him up but his feet couldn't stand.

Chesa spoke with a nasty tone. Carter's stern retort followed. Jori heard them, but the overwhelming sensation of Hapker's agony muted their words. It dominated every function of his body, making it difficult to breathe.

Someone shook him. The urgency of it pierced through his senses. "Hapker's been hurt," he choked out.

"Well, duh," Chesa replied. "That's what happens when you commit mutiny."

Carter's emotions signified he agreed. Jori's anger flared, helping him to think beyond the pain. He managed to take in air. His discomfort abated but persisted in the back of his mind like a giant blood-sucking insect.

Once he got a hold of himself, he studied the sensation like an outsider looking in. Though hurt, Hapker wasn't on the cusp of death but could be if he didn't get medical help soon.

Carter brought him to his feet. A feverish fury possessed him. He clenched his fists while his captors escorted him onto the bridge.

Gottfried turned around wearing that stupid smile of his, and Jori's ire erupted like a volcano. "You chima! Your men shot Hapker!" He lurched forward to attack, but Carter restrained him. Jori kicked and wriggled. "I'll never side with you or your kind now. Never!"

Gottfried's smile dropped. A shadow crossed his features. "This is your fault, boy. Your friends are the ones trying to take over the ship."

"Liar!" Jori wrested his hands under Carter's hold and slipped out. He charged toward Gottfried only to get yanked back and held even tighter. "Gottfried is a MEGA! He's the one behind this. He's the one killing your people."

Gottfried's emotions gushed forth like the acidic geysers of Tymneria. He jabbed his finger to the exit. "Get him out of here!"

Jori didn't shy from the man's outrage despite the malevolence infused in it. He'd faced far more dangerous people before and would be damned if he'd go down easy. He considered biting Carter's arm but didn't want to hurt Hapker's friend. As the man hauled him back, Jori's feet found purchase on the top of a chair. He pushed out, making Carter stumble and lose his grip. Jori broke free once again, but instead of going after Gottfried, he spun away from Chesa's grasp and bounded over a workstation.

Chesa gave chase, with her face twisted like a furious blackbeast. Gottfried's soldiers joined in. Carter kept guard at the door. Jori dodged, leapt, and ducked. Bellows and curses followed him, but he remained out of reach.

"Get him!" Gottfried screamed uselessly. His expression nearly matched Chesa's, though she had more emotional control.

A soldier almost snatched the loose material of Jori's clothes. He foundered right into another soldier who snared him like a bola weapon, making it impossible for him to do more than squirm.

Gottfried huffed. Jori sensed the wheels of his brain turning with indecision. The man's emotions called for blood, but he reined in just enough anger to refrain from lashing out. "Get him out of here."

Jori growled, unable to stop the soldier from lifting and carrying him.

Less than halfway to the exit, Carter pulled Jori's DTD out of his pocket and handed it to Gottfried. "I caught him in a workroom downloading something onto this."

Gottfried snatched it. "This won't help you now, boy."

Jori's heart skipped a beat. "No! You shouldn't look at that!"

Gottfried narrowed his eyes. It was just the reaction Jori had hoped for. He swallowed and allowed his nervousness and fear to spill out. A mental nudge poked inside his head, but he pushed it back so Gottfried wouldn't know why he was on edge.

"Wait," Gottfried told the soldier. A broad and sly smile spread over his face. He turned to the nearest workstation and slipped the DTD into the port. "We'll see what you're hiding, boy."

Jori held his breath as Gottfried clicked open the folder. A box opened, revealing lines of gibberish text.

"What's this?" Gottfried asked.

"It's encrypted," Jori said while holding back his elation. "It needs a decryption code."

Gottfried's smile broadened. He leaned in and studied the information.

Jori's heart fluttered. *Is it working?* Did Gottfried freeze or was he just staying very still? He waited for five agonizing seconds before speaking. "Gottfried is a MEGA. He told me so when he thought I was one. And I've seen the evidence."

"What evidence?" a purple-haired woman asked.

"Look at him." Jori pointed with his chin. "He's not moving because the chip in his brain is processing."

The woman's eyes widened. Jori pressed the issue. "These soldiers work for him. Haven't you noticed how emotionless they are? I don't know for sure, but I think it's because they have chips in their brains too."

Carter scowled. "That's impossible."

"Tap him on the shoulder," Jori challenged. "Yell in his ear. See if he responds."

Carter strolled up to the man. Uncertainty radiated from him, but he jostled the admiral's aide. No response. He shook harder. Nothing. His emotions spiked. He glanced back and forth between Jori and Gottfried with his brow wrinkled in dismay. "Lieutenant." Gottfried remained as still as a statue. "Lieutenant!"

The realization struck everyone at once. The purple-haired woman's jaw dropped. Another officer on the bridge gasped. Chesa cursed.

Jori didn't sense the soldiers. Nothing changed in their faces, but their bodies went taut. Two yanked weapons from their holsters at the same time as Carter and the purple-haired woman—with Carter also taking away Gottfried's phaser.

Rapid energy fire erupted. The soldier holding Jori let go. A blast struck the nearby workstation. Jori didn't know if it had come from a crew member or soldier, or whether they had aimed at him or the enemy. He ducked, taking cover behind the backrest of a chair. A sharp odor of ozone tweaked his nostrils.

One person cried out and the pain of death seared through Jori's senses. He held his gut and willed it and the guilt-infused bile to stay down. A part of him wanted to retaliate, but common sense told him to remain where he was.

"No. No. No!" Gottfried roared.

The sounds of scrambling created such a ruckus that Jori couldn't tell who did what.

He flinched when someone crashed next to him.

"You little shit!" Gottfried's white knuckles contrasted with the purple of his face. "I don't care if MEGA-Man wants you alive. I've had enough of you!"

Jori had no time to consider who MEGA-Man was as Gottfried seized his throat and squeezed. Jori jammed his hands between Gottfried's wrists and thrust upward. The man should have involuntarily released him, but his grip held. Jori fought for air. He tried again to no avail. With the cuffs still on, he kicked out instead. Gottfried grunted but didn't let go. His weight fell on him, pinning him so he couldn't move. The force on his neck tightened. Heat crept up into his face as his blood pressure increased.

No! I can't die. I have to save Hapker!

66
End of the Line

J.D. Hapker felt like a fish out of water. He sucked air in and out in rapid succession, never getting enough. His surroundings swirled and shifted in a disorienting muddle. Fish didn't sweat, but he bet they experienced the same uncomfortable half-wet-half-dry sensation.

His pulse beat like a crazed woodpecker. Someone connected a cylindrical object to the side of his helmet. The resulting sweet burst of pure oxygen triggered alertness. The room still spun, but he grasped onto enough reality to recognize he was going into shock. He forced his breath to even out. The cold sweat that had coated his body warmed, either by the reaction of his own bodily defenses or the temperature of his suit adjusting.

The figure over him sharpened. Their helmet light brightened their face. The moment he recognized Chief Singh, a new and agonizing sensation spilled over him. The increased pressure on his injured arm made the world turn white and hot.

"Sorry. I must stop the bleeding," Singh said.

Hapker's abdomen lurched. Something acidic seared his throat.

"Try not to throw up." She touched the side of his helmet. "We can't take these off."

Hapker sputtered but managed to swallow most of the biting liquid down. He took in labored breaths. "Status?"

"Korbin got the hatch closed again."

"The others?"

"Were all fine… So far."

"We've got to get the commander to sick bay," Ortega said.

Hapker raised his good hand and attempted to wave off Ortega's distress. "No." His voice came out too faint for his helmet comm to activate. "No!" he said more forcefully. He swallowed. "Fix the array. That's our priority."

"We must help you," Ortega said. "You're injured badly."

"Shock," Hapker croaked. "My legs." He tried to point but the weakness in his body only allowed his good arm to rise a short distance before falling back to his side. He fought the dizziness by keeping his breathing steady. "Prop my legs up. Someone else—argh—stop the bleeding. Singh… Fix array."

A hulking figure dropped a hand on Singh's shoulder, making her jump. Her reaction sent a twang through Hapker's arm, triggering a cry.

"Sorry," Lieutenant Gresher said. "But he's right. Our best chance is to fix the array and call for help."

Ortega took her place. The change elicited more excruciating bursts of pain. Someone put something under his feet.

"So I'm the only dummy who got shot?"

Ortega almost laughed.

Hapker smiled. "I'll be alright."

Her eyes turned sad. "Yeah."

The uncertainty of her tone resigned him to his fate. Although he didn't want to die, he couldn't afford to be a burden. Gottfried would undoubtedly send more troops. But if his friends got the word out, they had a chance to win this.

A pang of regret clenched his insides as he thought of Jori. What was he doing right now? Did he escape or had they captured him?

A powerful determination crashed into him like a bull. If he didn't know any better, he'd say it came from an outside source. That made no sense, but the sensation of dwelling in despair one moment to imagining himself in a mighty fight the next was real. Jori needed him and he needed Jori. Together, they'd pull through, even if they were far apart.

*****

After what seemed like hours but was probably only a minute, Carletta Ortega sighed with relief when color returned to the commander' face. The clearness of his eyes gave her hope that he could make it.

The hatch opened and a gust of air plowed in, dashing any optimism she had left.

"Letta!" an enraged yet frantic voice carried.

She growled. When would she finally be done with that asshole?

Beyond her cover and on the opposite side of the entry, an illuminated face poked from behind a wall. Bryce glowered at her like an angry bull. She practically saw him pawing at the ground, getting ready to charge.

"You bitch!" His voice sounded tinny yet still carried a sizzling malice.

She embraced the fury that exploded inside her. First, he used her. Next, he betrayed her just because she'd spoken the truth. Then he'd tried to kill her and pretended it was her own fault. She could almost taste the fire she wanted to spit at him.

He aimed at her. She didn't wait to see if he'd shoot. She released her pressure on the commander and pulled back from his line of sight. Bullets struck the area she'd just left. She peeked from her cover and fired at his swiftly approaching form.

Others charged with him, but the ferocity in his eyes seized all her attention. She kept shooting, but his defenses held. The new type of mech suit he wore had armor plating so bulky that he shouldn't be able to move so fast. It also had mini cannons on its arms and shoulders and a utility belt loaded with grenades and ammo.

Damn it! Every one of her shots glanced off him like rain from a raincoat. Before she knew it, he breached her personal space. She shot him point blank, but nothing happened. His armored fist plunged down and smashed into her helmet. Her head rattled as her body pitched backward. Like the blue-eyed man, he fell on top of her. Unlike that freak, he pummeled her, never giving her a single respite.

"No easy death for you, bitch." His voice trembled with violence. "I want you to suffer."

The power of his mech suit cracked her faceplate. She flailed her arms and legs, only succeeding in increasing the agony in her injured hand. The adrenaline coursing through her heightened her panic. Despite the rattling of her brain, she didn't feel pain. However, the darkening of her vision warned her of the danger she was in.

"You'll pay for what you've done," Bryce said venomously.

The absurdity of his words gave her a second wind. How dare he make this about her when he was the one murdering people.

With a mighty effort, she pushed out from under him and thrust out her arms with such force that he tumbled back. The bulk of his suit made his fall awkward. She took advantage of his momentary disorientation and leapt on top of him. She instinctively pulled in air, filled her lungs to their maximum capacity, and let out a pitch too high for most people to hear.

The plasti-glass of her helmet shattered further. A crackling crunch followed, indicating his had probably done the same. Her ability surprised her but she didn't let up.

He shrieked. "Stop!"

Wrath spewed from her throat in what others would consider a soundless yell. Without understanding how, she focused it in one direction.

Bryce screamed and thrashed but more out of pain than in any attempt to dislodge her. Then his cries ceased, and his body crumpled beneath her.

Her cry tapered off. She panted and removed her helmet. Whether the dizziness that fell over her was from the thin air or from her exertion, she wasn't sure. However, she was certain that Bryce was dead. The man lay sprawled, his bloody eyes locked in eternal death.

She blinked, surprised at her newfound skill. Was this how supersonic yells worked, only arising out of extreme need?

She swallowed at the scratchiness of her throat and rose on wobbly legs. "That's what you get, you fucking asshole."

Ending him brought a relief in the heat of the moment, but regret threatened to rear its ugly head like the Medusa from ancient stories. She kept flinching from its gaze, knowing it would turn her to stone if she stared too long.

A groan from the commander shoved her out of her stupor. She returned to his side and pressed down on the super-absorbent gauze. He grunted, but clarity came back to his eyes.

Seeing him fight for consciousness kept her going. Maybe they had a chance after all.

67
Hostile Takeover

Blackness crept into the periphery of Jori's vision as iron hands squeezed his throat. He forced his mind to function. Gottfried had weight and strength in his favor, but Jori had experience. If jabbing at his attacker's wrists didn't do anything, there were still the nerves in the forearms. The technique would work better if he chopped both arms at once, but his handcuffs hindered him.

He struggled into position, then swung. Gottfried's right arm twitched just enough to allow blood to flow back into Jori's head. The onrush blotted his vision with black and red, but he didn't let that stop him.

A chop to the bend of Gottfried's other arm followed by a jab upward into the man's face broke the hold. Jori struck again, this time with a satisfying crack of teeth.

Gottfried bellowed. Jori scrambled backward and kicked. His heel connected with Gottfried's nose, sending out a spray of blood.

Jori rolled away and to his feet. With the firefight still going on around him, he kept low and took cover behind a chair.

Another soldier with his attention focused outward fired slugs instead of phased energy. Outrage kindled through Jori's veins. Using ballistic weapons was barbaric, even by Toradon standards. Phasers were far more effective at ending an opponent while bullets ripped and tore into flesh, causing a long and tortuous death.

Is this what they did to Hapker?

He snarled, then lunged at the man like an enraged blackbeast. He was small, but the fury in his attack impacted the soldier like a meteor, sending them both tumbling. Jori used the momentum to somersault away.

The soldier sat up, preparing to reorient himself when a series of phaser blasts struck him at once. The man jerked before sinking to the ground in a slowness that suggested his body knew it was dead while his brain did not. Thanks to the inhibitor, Jori didn't sense the pain of his demise.

An abrupt silence blanketed the room. Jori held his breath. *Is it over?* His ability told him at least four people lived. He rose from his hiding place with his hands up. Faces turned to him. None were soldiers. All emitted suspicion, but no one pointed their weapons at him.

Chesa doubled over and clutched her thigh. Pain flittered through her emotions, but it wasn't severe. "Well, I'll be damned."

She threw Jori a bewildered look, which prompted his own bafflement as her hatefulness dampened and a touch of guilt crept in. The way she blinked and shook her head reminded him of how it felt to come out of the shade and into the sun.

Gottfried's voice detonated—a sound like a roar crossed with a pained yowl. He lunged at Jori with hands out like talons, ready to rip. The muzzle of Carter's weapon to his temple stopped him short. His eyes widened, then narrowed. "You little brat!"

Jori pulled his shoulders back and jutted his chin. He considered making a clever retort, but Sensei Jeruko's training came to mind. "*Sometimes you don't need to say anything to make your point.*"

Gottfried bared his teeth and stepped toward him but halted when the purple-haired woman blocked his way. She aimed a phaser between his eyes. "I've been waiting all day for an excuse to shoot your ass."

"She sounds like she means it." Carter spoke with a remarkable calm. "I'd sit if I were you."

Gottfried eyed them with uncertainty, reserving his more hateful glower for Jori. But he eased to the floor and pulled his knees to his chest. Fresh blood still dribbled from his nose but with the slowness of cooling magma.

"Kramer," Carter said to the purple-haired woman who held her weapon with barely constrained self-control.

"Yes, Sir?" she replied without taking her fierce eyes off Gottfried.

"If he so much as moves his mouth the wrong way, shoot him."

"Yes, Sir," she said in a gleeful drawl.

Carter faced Jori. “You. What do you say we remove those cuffs?”

Jori’s knees almost gave out with relief. He approached Carter with his hands out. With the tap of an electronic key, the manacles fell away, making Jori sigh.

His reprieve was short-lived as an officer with a blond beard knelt beside the woman with curly black hair. Jori detected nothing from her, which meant she was dead. Blood and gore plastered the side of what was left of her face. He hadn’t sensed her pain of death during the firefight, so it must’ve been quick. He didn’t want to think about the suffering she would’ve endured if that shot had been but a centimeter off.

His gut ached, but he turned that distress into hostility and glowered at Gottfried. “For someone who thinks he’s superior, you’re worse than a pile of ape shit.”

Gottfried sputtered, then his face darkened with a withering heat. “You’ve made a huge mistake, boy. These are the apes.” He gestured to the purple-haired woman. “Look at them, how they wallow in their primordial soup. You’re so much better than they are, so why are you siding with them?”

“You’re not superior,” Jori said. “Killing people just so you can have things your way makes you less than an animal.”

Gottfried threw up his hands, making Kramer tighten her grip on her phaser. “They’re holding us back! My actions have been no different from any other suppressed member of society.”

The logic made Jori pause.

Sergeant Carter’s emotions flared. “So stage protests! Go to the Prontaean Cooperative headquarters, to governing offices all over the system. If you’re so damned intelligent, figure out how to change the laws without committing murder.”

“You won’t listen!” Gottfried shifted into a crouch and snarled.

Kramer fired, the blast seizing Gottfried’s body. But the man didn’t fall. He merely hunched over and hung his head.

Carter looked at her with wide eyes. Kramer shrugged. “A low-level stun.”

“Good,” Carter said. “As much as I hate this bastard, he has a lot to answer for.”

Chesa grunted in agreement. Jori noted the copious amount of blood on her thigh and admired how she remained standing.

Her brows quirked, likely from both pain and emotion. "What now, Sir?"

Carter responded by tapping his comm. "Attention everyone. This is Sergeant Andres Carter. I have taken command of this ship after discovering Lieutenant Gottfried Krause is a MEGA. The soldiers from Indore station are his allies. Shoot on sight. Kill authorization delta-niner-zulu-five-kilo. I repeat—"

The floor beneath Jori's feet shook violently.

"You're too late," Gottfried sneered.

Kramer shot another stun-fire into the man's chest. This time, he collapsed. She darted to her workstation at the same moment Jori dropped low to avoid falling as the ship rattled.

Carter dashed to the tactical station and strapped in. "What's happening?"

"A ship just appeared on our sensors, Sir!" Kramer called out. "They're firing at us."

"Evasive maneuvers!" Carter gripped the edge of an operations workstation.

"We need a pilot, Sir!"

Sure enough. The man at the helm slumped lifelessly in his chair.

"I can help!" Jori scrambled over, unbuckled him, then took his place.

"Sir?" Chesa said. "Should—"

"We don't have a choice, Sergeant." Carter activated the ship-wide alert and opened the main channel. "Everyone to a safety depot!"

Jori glanced at the stats, understanding the situation in an instant. With a few taps, he put up the shields and navigated the vessel using the first tactic that came to his mind.

"Report, Kramer!" Carter yelled while Jori focused on putting some distance between him and the attacker.

"It's an old Carpathian-class… Has a renovated hull and…" She studied the readouts. "Possibly weapon upgrades, too."

"Any communication?"

The blond bearded man scrambled to the comm station. "Nothing, Sir! Not even on the short-range channel."

The ship quaked again, rattling Jori's teeth. Close combat situations didn't leave much room for maneuverability, but he could try a little trick he'd seen his brother use in a desperate—yet simulated—attack. If only his brother were still alive. He ignored the aching pit in his stomach and focused on his task. "The fore-ventral of the Carpathian-class is vulnerable. I can push the engines and get closer if you can hit between the gravity wheel and arc drive."

"Won't work," Chesa said. "They're shielded."

"I'll get close," Jori repeated. "Inside their shields."

She scoffed. "That'll leave us open to attack."

Jori remained fixated on the helm display and made a slight adjustment. "The *Defender* is a tough ship."

Carter gritted his teeth. "Can you do it without running into them?"

"Yes, Sir," Jori said.

"Do it."

Jori entered a navigation sequence, then revved up the drive. When the red warning light flashed, he smacked the activator. His head snapped back, the inertial dampeners keeping his neck from breaking.

The chair responded to the acceleration by applying pressure to certain parts of his body. His training in high-G maneuvers kicked in too, triggering the proper breathing response. Blackness plunged from the edges of his vision, but he remained conscious.

The ship shuddered as it flanked the enemy. Jori's moment of exultation cut short with a thought. *What will this do to Hapker?*

*****

J.D. Hapker hobbled with the gait of an injured deer pursued by wolves. Gresher and Ortega dragged him to a safety depot while the emergency alarm shrieked and flashed. Each step, whether it was his own or theirs, sent excruciating stabs up to his shoulder and through his entire body. He clenched his teeth, determined to remain conscious.

After what seemed like an agonizing eternity, he found himself in a chair. Sergeant Ortega pulled the straps over him and tightened. With all the pain from a moment before, the belt cinched over his injured side barely fazed him.

Before his awareness slipped, hard-hitting G-force wrenched him back to alertness. Not long after, the floor, walls, and seatbelt quaked with the violence of an erupting volcano. He felt like a rabbit being shaken to death in the jaws of a wolf.

The quaking stopped only to be replaced by opposing G-forces. The ship rumbled again. It took him a moment to realize it was from the release of the *Defender*'s weapons.

"Who the hell are we fighting?" Ortega called out, her voice juddering from the ship's movements.

Hapker couldn't think. His head wobbled as consciousness blinked in and out. The next time he woke, everything seemed normal. No more G-forces or vibrations. His chest heaved with a gritting willpower to find stability. Dizziness, pain, and every other uncomfortable stew of sensations ebbed. He swallowed the bile that sprang to his throat and hoped this was over.

*****

Jori shook the disorientation from his head. The ache in his skull abated but didn't go away. With a snap, he remembered where he was. He glanced at the readouts. Most gauges had gone into the red, but a few dropped to orange. He pulled up the sensor array and located the enemy vessel.

"Sergeant Carter!" he called out. No response. "Carter! The enemy's fleeing. Should I pursue?"

"Sir!" Chesa shouted. "You must stop them."

A groan sounded from behind him. For a moment, it seemed Carter was out of it. But he shook his head and released more cannon fire. Lines marking their trajectory illuminated Jori's screen. A few seconds later, they hit their mark.

"Sir, should I pursue?" Jori asked as the distance between the *Defender* and their opponent increased.

"No," Sergeant Carter said, reluctance in his tone.

When the enemy disappeared in a flash of gamma rays, Jori exhaled. They did it. They'd survived. And his senses told him that Hapker did too.

68
Isolated

Time stood still. With his elbow propped on the edge of the bed, Jori cradled his head in the crook of his arm. An oxygen machine hissed and wheezed at regular intervals. The diagnostic monitor emitted low beeps, indicating the patient remained stable.

Jori clutched his mother's necklace, glad to have it back and sure he'd never part from it again. He kept his sensing ability trained on Hapker's lifeforce. It was strong, thank goodness, but flat because of the medically induced coma. The tissue regeneration machine did its work in deathly silence. The doctors decided that Hapker's arm was too damaged to repair, so they'd cut it off and prepped the amputation site for the regrowth.

Jori swallowed at the guilt tightening the back of his throat. It didn't matter that the Cooperative put all the blame at Gottfried's feet, Hapker wouldn't be in this situation if he'd stayed on the *Odyssey*.

At least he was alive. With time and a specialized machine, Hapker would be whole again. The process was a little different from how Jori got his new heart. Getting a new arm had to take place on the host, rather than grow separately.

Jori's chest ached. It wasn't fair. If anyone should have been hurt in this mess, it was him.

Chesa leaned over Hapker and swept a stray hair from his forehead. Concern emanated from her. It seemed genuine, but Jori bit the inside of his cheek to keep from lashing out at her contradictory behavior.

Although Gottfried had manipulated her—Sergeant Banks and Corporal Lengen too—she still disliked him.

"You'll be as good as new," she cooed as she brushed her fingers down Hapker's face.

Then she smiled at Jori, but he detected the falseness of it. He smiled back, trying to keep his expression casual instead of tight. Neither spoke to one another. He didn't trust her enough and her feelings were probably mutual. Maybe she still blamed him even though they'd cleared him of any culpability in Gottfried's crimes.

The tense silence broke when Sergeant Ortega, Chief Singh, and Corporal Harley arrived. They'd been healed and looked well rested.

Ortega grinned. Singh's face radiated the same warmheartedness that her emotions did. Harley smiled too. A sense of guilt lurked behind it. Jori couldn't tell whether it was because he blamed himself for Hapker's injury or felt bad at how Jori had been treated. It didn't matter. Either way, Jori held no grudges against him.

Sergeant Ortega grasped Jori's hand. "He'll be alright."

Jori nodded. She'd spoken the same truth as the doctor but seeing Hapker like this still made his heart hurt.

Ortega took Hapker's hand as well. Chesa's emotions ignited and Jori saw a flash in her eyes, but she said nothing.

Singh put her arm over Jori's shoulder. "You should get some rest. We can watch over him for a while."

"I want to stay." He almost added, *until he wakes*, but that wasn't likely to happen for several more days.

Ortega squeezed his hand. "Feny's alright, too. I just saw her. She'll be released soon."

Jori gave a small smile, thankful someone else who'd suffered because of him would return to health.

Admiral Belmont had recovered physically but was in a hard place. Jori caught a bit of the man's lifeforce and found him sulking. Finding out a MEGA had manipulated him for years had demoralized him.

A quiver ran down his spine. Gottfried and his soldiers hadn't been the only MEGAs on the *Defender*. This prompted an investigation, which uncovered them throughout the Cooperative ranks. This MEGA-Man's ideals had spread like a stealth virus. Once discovered, it created a frenzy of panic that disrupted nearly every government in the known galaxy.

"She wanted me to thank you," Ortega added.

Jori blinked until he remembered she was talking about Sergeant Fenyvesi. He wasn't sure how to respond so said nothing.

After everyone left, Lieutenant Gresher and his friend Korbin came to visit. Gresher wore his usual wide grin. Despite everything, his emotions remained balanced.

Korbin leaned against a wall and crossed his arms and feet. "Help will arrive soon. The *Adventurer* has a great medical team."

An alarm sounded inside Jori's head, a whisper at first, then more insistent as he considered the consequences. "Is that where they'll finish treating him?"

Korbin opened his mouth, then he and Gresher shared a look. "I don't know."

Jori's insides clenched at their uncertainty. "If they take him over there, will I be allowed to go with him?"

Neither responded, but their disquiet said it all. Jori's heart hammered. "Is the *Adventurer* also heading to Asteria?"

Gresher's mouth turned down with a curve almost as deep as his smiles usually were. His hand pressed on Jori's shoulder with doubtful assurance. "Don't worry. No matter what happens, we'll make sure you're okay."

Jori wanted to believe him, but his previous experience with the Cooperative left him feeling uncertain.

*****

Jori snapped awake. Sleeping in this chair caused the muscles in his neck to twinge, but he rose and went into his formal at-ease stance and met the new visitor.

Sergeant Carter wore a weak smile. Although it was sincere, something about the reluctance tainting his emotions made Jori's insides writhe.

"Good morning," the man said.

Jori hesitated, knowing he was being nice for a reason beyond friendliness.

Carter cleared his throat. "I never did thank you for helping us."

No, you didn't. Jori kept this to himself. After all, Carter's tone and demeanor suggested he wanted to make peace.

"Well," Carter continued. "Thank you. In risking yourself to expose Lieutenant Krause, you saved a lot of lives. I see why Hapker likes you."

Guilt peppered the man's emotions, causing Jori to break into a sweat. "But that's not why you're here, is it?"

Carter hung his head. "Mostly. I truly owe you, which is why this next part pains me so much."

Jori's mouth dried. "And what part is that?"

"I need to transfer you to another ship."

Jori's heart leapt to his throat. "The *Adventurer*?"

Carter didn't answer right away, which told him volumes. A burning sensation filled his sinuses.

"To the *Fortitude*," Carter said in a tone that hinted how unfair this was.

"A military ship," Jori croaked. "Where I'll go back into a prison."

"I'm afraid so. There's still the trial in Asteria."

Despair lodged in Jori's throat. "Who's going with me since Hapker can't?"

"Your lawyer."

"The one who works for *Gottfried*?"

Carter put up his palms. "He doesn't work for him. We've checked him out and he doesn't seem to have any connection to him prior to this."

"How can you be so sure?" The rapid thumping in Jori's chest threatened to unnerve him.

"I didn't make the call, but those who did hadn't made it lightly. I promise you that."

Jori sensed his honesty, but that didn't settle his panic. "What about Lieutenant Gresher or Sergeant Ortega? Can one of them accompany me?"

"I'm afraid not. They're being held until this is all sorted." Carter shifted his feet. "I argued on your behalf—even offered to go with you myself. The authorities wouldn't have it. I'm sorry. There's nothing I can do."

A hailstorm of emotions swirled in Jori's head. A part of him needed to bawl like a baby and the other wanted to fight like he'd done to escape the *Odyssey*. Where would he go, though? He had nowhere and no one. Although he didn't trust Gottfried, he had no reason to distrust the senshi warrior in the video. His brother and Sensei Jeruko were most likely dead.

He had his mother but couldn't bear to face her. Nor would he want to put her in danger. If Father discovered he still lived… He shuddered. She was better off without him—and safer.

"Look," Carter said. "Your lawyer is certain you'll get exonerated. And I know Hapker. He'll go to you as soon as he's healed."

Despite the man's conviction, liquid welled in Jori's eyes. He dipped his head, mostly to hide his quivering chin.

"I'm sorry you can't stay long enough to say goodbye." Carter's tone conveyed his regret. "But we have to go now."

Jori glanced over his shoulder, wanting to believe he'd see Hapker again but suspecting otherwise. He stepped away to follow Carter, the movement tearing something inside him. Every footfall ripped further until a hollowness remained.

69
The End?

Jori held his head high as Bilsby strutted before the council and jury members with the confidence of a zealot. That same conviction eluded him, however. Councilor Greymore's hateful emotions were almost as bad as Sergeant Banks' had been. Several others harbored the same feelings—not as intense but just as poisonous.

Hapker not being here diminished his self-assurance further. It was as though someone stabbed his heart anew. He was completely and utterly alone as he faced this council of hateful blackbeasts.

"Yes, he kept the knowledge about Lieutenant Krause to himself," Bilsby said while gesturing animatedly. "But he did that out of fear and uncertainty, not malice. Once he realized the seriousness of the situation and who was at fault, he spoke up. And he didn't just speak up, folks. He did something about it. He'd been part of the efforts to stop the man. Indeed, without his actions, we might not have won this. He's a hero. He deserves a medal, not imprisonment."

"We can't ignore the fact that he commandeered one of our ships," Greymore said, disdain littering his tone.

"What would you have done if you'd been told you couldn't leave the ship of your enemy?"

The councilor twisted his mouth as though he'd eaten a lemon but didn't answer.

"No, please. Tell me what you would've done, Councilor," Bilsby pushed. Still not getting a reply, he directed his question to someone else. "You, Sir. What would you do?" Councilor Pham fidgeted in his seat. He didn't reply either. "How about you, ma'am?" Bilsby asked Councilor Alvia.

Alvia folded her hands. Her eyebrows drew in. "I would've tried to escape."

Jori's heart skipped. Bilsby smiled and jerked his index finger in the air. "Exactly. You would have tried to escape. Why? Because you don't want to stay on an enemy ship. And also because our code of conduct says you must."

Greymore froze. Bilsby directed his next argument to him. "So why are we *required by law* to attempt escape, but Jori isn't?"

Bilsby paused as though waiting for a reply to his rhetorical question. "That's correct, ladies and gentlemen. He did exactly what we would've and should've done had our situations been reversed." Greymore opened his mouth to speak, but Bilsby cut him off. "And get this. He did it without killing anyone. Let's face it. We had no right to hold him since he'd broken no laws."

"He doesn't belong here," Greymore said.

Bilsby smiled at the weak argument. "Several people say differently."

Jori recalled the recorded testimonies given earlier by crew members of the *Defender*. Sergeant Ortega, Corporal Harley, Chief Singh, everyone he'd been on the run with after escaping Gottfried. Even Sergeant Fenyvesi and Sergeant Carter had testified on his behalf. The day Bilsby had played all those was the only day he'd believed he might have a chance at a decent life here.

Greymore's hate surged, bringing Jori back down to the brink of loneliness. Even if the council decided in his favor, he would always be a warrior outcast.

If only Hapker was here. He swallowed the glob of saliva that had built up in his mouth and blinked away the welling tears.

*****

Councilor Alvia rested her chin on her knuckles and considered the debate. It amazed her how Councilor Greymore clung to his increasingly weakened arguments like a petulant child. They were supposed to be an open-minded organization that accepted all cultures and lifestyles, yet people like him still cluttered their society. It was sad, really.

Fortunately, his obstinacy had turned his supporters. They all agreed the young prince was to be exonerated. The next hard part was deciding his fate. The council remained divided in that respect. Nobody wanted him to become a Cooperative citizen but no one—

other than Greymore—wanted to send him home to his death either. A compromise was in order.

She filled her lungs, then exhaled quietly. "I understand all of your misgivings." She looked everyone in the eye to convey her sincerity, including Greymore's. "Having him here under our protection is dangerous, even if the danger doesn't come from him directly."

Greymore harrumphed, but she ignored him. "But I have an idea."

Councilor Bjorn tapped his chin in curious anticipation. Pham tilted his head. Greymore glowered, but he waited for her to speak.

"We'll send him to Marvdacht. It's within our territory, but more isolated and the laws there are stricter than on other planets. He will enter their childcare program for orphaned children under a new name—a name that only we will know so we can monitor him. We won't permit him to contact anyone on the *Odyssey*, nor anyone in the Cooperative except for a liaison that we'll designate."

Pham nodded his pointed head. Bjorn seemed thoughtful. Greymore harrumphed. "What makes you think either the commander or the boy won't figure out how to reconnect?"

Alvia gave her ready answer. "Marvdacht doesn't allow citizens to communicate beyond the planet without special permission, and I'll speak to him—explain this is for the best."

"So you say," Greymore said, but stroked his chin as though considering it.

Alvia sighed inwardly. At least he didn't insist Jori tell them about his father's assets. Even though several sources claimed the elder prince had been killed, the boy refused to put his mother in danger. And it wasn't like the Cooperative could do anything with the information—not with the chaos this MEGA-Man had created.

"Isn't giving him a new identity a bit risky?" Pham asked. "Shouldn't people know who he is?"

"The more who do, the greater the chance the Dragon Emperor will find out," Alvia said. "We can't risk it."

"Alright," Greymore said. "I'll go along with this, but on one condition."

Alvia raised an eyebrow but dipped her head to indicate for him to go on.

Greymore jutted his chin. “The boy’s history of violence needs to remain on his record. We must make sure Marvdacht is aware of how dangerous he can be. His martial skills, his tendency toward violent reactions, his many and possibly MEGA-induced skills—and that he’s killed people.”

Alvia hesitated since the boy had only ever acted in defense, but the inclusion wasn’t outrageous. At the very least, it would get him some much-needed counseling and cognitive therapy. “Agreed. So it’s decided then?”

A few more questions arose, but no one opposed the idea. With this issue settled, they could now focus on more important matters—the infiltration of MEGAs into the highest echelons of society.

*****

MEGA-Man processed the data with no emotion. He’d lost the perantium database. Several of his key people had been compromised. And Prince Mizuki helped it happen. If MEGA-Man hadn’t rid himself of inefficient and illogical emotions, he’d be furious.

While tubes carried nutrients into his body and waste out, wires transferred data into his CPU and instructions out. Old plans fell apart now that the Cooperative had discovered concealed augmentations in a majority of his operatives. New plans revealed themselves, allowing some timetables to be extended and others to speed up.

Despite all the possibilities, situations involving Prince Mizuki still cropped up. And they continued to have an enormous potential to either help or hinder MEGA-Man’s primary objective. Retrieving him and convincing him to be an ally remained a top priority.

The boy wasn’t beyond reach. Getting to him wouldn’t be easy, but it wasn’t impossible. Where one agent had failed to gain his cooperation, another would succeed.

*****

At first, Jori refused to sit. Standing in the stiff way he'd always done when facing his father seemed more appropriate to the situation. However, Councilor Alvia's pleasant demeanor changed his mind. He eased into the plush chair across from her and tried to relax.

She crossed her ankles and folded her hands. A warm smile stretched across her face. "Thank you for agreeing to meet me. I'm hoping we can have a heart-to-heart away from the official proceedings."

Jori didn't reply. He sensed her sincerity but wasn't sure whether he trusted her.

"Although I'm sure you're not happy with our decision," she continued, "I want you to know why I agreed to it."

Jori's eyes and nose burned at the reminder that he'd never see Hapker again. He squeezed the necklace hidden in his hand and forced his emotions back.

She took in a deep breath. "Councilor Greymore and others aren't comfortable with you on a Cooperative ship. If Commander Hapker adopts you, he'll have to give up his career."

Jori lowered his head.

She leaned forward. "Have you considered what that means for you both?"

Tears filled Jori's eyes. He blinked, hoping to keep any from spilling, but a small drop leaked out. He'd thought about it. Banks had disrespected Hapker. Carter distrusted him, Chesa criticized him, and the admiral and the council had threatened his career—all because of him.

Hapker could avoid it if he resigned, but where would they go? To Hapker's homeworld? Probably not. If the diversity of the Cooperative wouldn't accept him, no one else would either. Could they travel the universe together, just the two of them? That sounded good on the surface, but it was riddled with uncertainties.

Empathy emanated from her. "He thinks we don't appreciate him, but we do. *I* do. His values and my values are much the same. We both want a galaxy where everyone accepts everyone else, regardless of their differences. I'd hate to lose him."

The truth of her words instigated more tears. Although Hapker had said he would do whatever it took to help him, Jori tagging along would muck up his life.

She stood and made her way over, her blue robe flowing like water. Despite her old age, she knelt with a grace that reminded him of his mother. Then she grasped his hand and enclosed it in hers. “I promise, we’re sending you somewhere safe. No one will know you’re the emperor’s son. You can have a fresh start where you won’t be hated for being a Tredon because we’ll give you a new identity.”

Jori wiped his eyes. “Who will my new guardian be?”

“A childcare facility where other children without parents reside. But that’s only temporary. Marvdacht is full of good people who’d love to have you in their home.”

Although she’d spoken truthfully, he felt manipulated. There was more she wasn’t saying. This was for the best, though. At least he wouldn’t be in jail. And he wouldn’t have his father’s evils hanging over his head either.

Jori lifted his chin. “Can I tell the commander goodbye?” When she hesitated, he squeezed her hand. “He won’t believe you when you tell him I’ll be alright. But he’ll believe me. He knows I don’t lie.”

She patted his hand. “You’re right. That’s a good idea. I’ll arrange it.”

Jori considered asking whether he could contact his mother as well, but the risk was too great. Not only was he too ashamed to face her with his brother’s death hanging over his head, but he also didn’t want to put her life in danger. So long as Father ruled Toradon, Mother was safer if she didn’t know he was alive. Like Hapker, she was better off without him.

A lump formed in Jori’s throat as he struggled to hold back his anguish. It hurt like hell to let them go, but he must move on. This was his chance to start over, leave the warrior life behind, and become someone else—someone better. If he could do that, then maybe—after Father passed on and Hapker’s career was secure—maybe he’d seek them out.

Did you enjoy this novel? Leave a review. Authors love reviews!

Next:
Orphaned Warrior: Book Five – Jori meets a cyborg far worse than Gottfried Krause.

And:
Isle of Hogs: A Dragon Spawn Novella – After escaping the madness of his father, Prince Terkeshi must adjust to his new life as a farmer. The worst part isn't the smelly livestock or the lack of respect that comes with being a mere peasant, but the ghastly injuries that have diminished his fighting ability. When cyber-pirates kidnap people from his village, can the once-promising warrior overcome his disabilities and fight to save his new friends?

Sign up for my newsletter by visiting my website, DawnRossAuthor.com, and get great deals!

The first thing you'll receive is an exclusive Prequel to Book One. You'll also get access to the first few chapters of the current books plus upcoming books. There may also be more free short stories related to the main story.

Connect with Dawn Ross online:
DawnRossAuthor.com
Twitter.com/DawnRossAuthor
Goodreads.com/author/Dawn_Ross

Glossary

Adventurer – A PCC ship.

AED – An automated external defibrillator that is used to help those experiencing sudden cardiac arrest.

Aeneas – A planet mentioned by Hapker where a famous sport reminiscent of football (aka soccer) is played.

Andres – Lieutenant Andres Carter serves as a PG-force on the *Defender*. He is also an old friend of Hapker's.

Andulan – A proper adjective defining people or things from Andul, in this case, sausage.

Arc drive or Arc reactor – This is one of the largest components of a spaceship. It is the engine that allows a ship to travel many light years away without violating the speed of light by bending space-time.

Arden – Captain Silas Arden is the captain of the *Odyssey* and Hapker's commanding officer.

Asteria – The planet and city namesake that the Prontaean Cooperative calls its headquarters.

AV sensors – A sensor that alerts engineering of problems within certain types of conduits.

Banks – Sergeant Banks is a PG-Force officer on the *Defender* who hates Jori.

Barker test – A type of test used to detect signs of whether someone is biometrically enhanced.

Belmont – Vice Admiral Belmont of the Prontaean Cooperative is largely an administrative officer, but he occasionally partakes in important missions.

Biometric authentication – A security measure that uses retina scans, fingerprint identification, voice recognition or other unique biological characteristics to keep anyone but the authorized persons from using certain devices.

Blackbeast – An animal that Jori often refers to. It is never described but it is hinted that it might be dog or wolf-like.

B-Lounge – A small, quiet lounging area that doesn't have all the amenities of the main lounge.

Bryce – Lieutenant Bryce Buckeye is a PG-Force officer who serves under Admiral Belmont.

Buckeye – Lieutenant Bryce Buckeye is a PG-Force officer who serves under Admiral Belmont.

Bunmi – Master Bunmi was Jori's Jintal teacher.

Cambiner puzzle – A complex three-dimensional puzzle.

Carletta – Sergeant Carletta Ortega, aka Letta, serves as a PG-Force officer on the *Defender*.

Carpathian-class – An outdated battleship from Carpath, but no longer used by the Carpathians.

Carter – Sergeant First Class Andres Carter serves as a PG-Force officer on the *Defender*. He is also an old friend of Hapker's.

Chance – An engineer serving on the *Defender* briefly greeted by Ortega.

Changdu – A martial art that focuses more on preventing or deescalating fights while still teaching self-defense. Aka the Art of Least Force, the Art of Not Fighting or the Art of Control.

Chesa – Sergeant Chesa Creston, aka Firestorm, serves as a PG-Force officer on the *Defender*. She used to have a romantic relationship with Hapker.

Chima – Means vile one or hated enemy in Jori and Terk's language.

Chusho – Means shit in Jori and Terk's language.

Comm – A communication device.

Communication hub – A form of communication that uses quantum entanglement technology for an instantaneous exchange.

Conveyor – An elevator-like car on a spaceship that moves vertically and horizontally.

Cooperative – The agency that governs space. It has numerous treaties with various worlds that provides its charter to keep space safe, ensure peace, regulate fair trade, and colonize new worlds. Its powers are granted by several planets, and the number of planets that are part of the Cooperative continues to grow. The Prontaean Cooperative has two aspects to it. The first is the Prontaean Colonial Cooperative (PCC). This sub-organization handles intergalactic relations, conducts space exploration, performs space-based scientific endeavors, assists travelers, and sometimes provides transportation. The second aspect is the Prontaean Galactic Force (PG-Force). This sub-organization polices space.

Corners – A same similar to checkers or draughts, but slightly more complicated.

Councilor Alvia – Chairperson of the Prontaean Cooperative Council.

Councilor Bjorn – One of the nine most prominent council members of the Prontaean Cooperative Council.

Councilor Greymore – One of the nine most prominent council members of the Prontaean Cooperative Council.

Councilor Pham – One of the nine most prominent council members of the Prontaean Cooperative Council.

Creston – Sergeant Chesa Creston, aka Firestorm, serves as a PG-Force officer on the *Defender*. She used to have a romantic relationship with Hapker.

Cybernation – The planet Gottfried wants to take Jori where he'll be accepted.

Davis – Sergeant Davis had been a prisoner on Jori's Father's ship. He attacked Jori and so Jori's father killed him.

Decon – Decontamination process.

Defender - The name of a PG-Force battleship captained by Richforth. This vessel is the largest type of vessel in the PG-Force. The ship houses hundreds of people but no families (unlike the PCC vessels). It comprises mostly military personnel, but also engineers and technicians.

Deus Ex Machina – The name of a Carpathian-class spaceship that plans on helping Lieutenant Gottfried Krause.

Donnel – Doctor Mazie Donnel psychiatric doctor who serves on the *Defender*.

Dragon Emperor - Emperor Mizuki, Jori's father, is the ruthless ruler of the Toradon Nohibito/Dragon People, aka Tredons. He is often referred to as the Dragon Emperor.

Dragon Prince – Another term for Prince Jori Mizuki since his father is known as the Dragon Emperor.

DTD – Data transfer device that plugs into most Cooperative computer stations and electronic devices.

Edenshire – An imaginary force in the Galactic Dominions game.

Enviro-suit – A form-fitting spacesuit that uses nanites to regulate body temperature and protect the wearer from just about any environment, including the void of space.

Esekielu – Major Esekielu is a PG-Force officer who serves directly under Admiral Belmont.

Expedition-class – The largest of the Prontaean Colonial Cooperative (PCC) spaceships. Though the officers who run this ship are formal personnel of the Cooperative, they are sometimes considered civilians because they are mostly doctors, engineers, and technicians. This ship has a small presence of Prontaean Galactic Force (PG-Force) officers for security. Expedition-class starships have the broadest scope of responsibilities. They are the ships most often used for exploration and scientific endeavors, but they also provide transport, medical and mechanical assistance, and are used for diplomatic missions.

Extraho-animi – A reader who can pull thoughts from others. It is the second level of a reader. The Cooperative requires any of their personnel with this ability to register it.

Fabricor – A replicating machine. There are various types such as a food fabricor, a clothing fabricor, and a parts fabricor. Fabricors work much like our digital printers of today but the types of things that can be made has expanded greatly.

Fenyvesi – Sergeant Fenyvesi, aka Feny, serves as a PG-Force officer on the *Defender*.

Firestorm – The nickname of Sergeant Chesa Creston.

Football – A sport revived from ancient Earth soccer.

Fortitude – A PG-Force cruiser.

Fritz – Doctor Fritz is one of the primary doctors on the *Defender*. He is currently researching ways to detect MEGAs.

Galactic Dominions – A highly complicated strategic game that utilizes a holo-table and a myriad of pieces that follow one of many storylines.

Gideon space station – A space station in Cooperative territory. This is the space station the *Defender* was initially going to visit and drop off Admiral Belmont, but the admiral changed his mind.

Glastra – Glastra, aka Glastrabot, is an engineer who serves under Chief Singh on the *Defender*.

Gonoro – A small outpost attacked by Jori's father. Jori helped and feels guilty for the resulting deaths since most people on that station were civilians.

Gottfried – Lieutenant Gottfried Krause serves as Admiral Belmont's personal aide.

Gramosh – An imaginary force in the Galactic Dominions game.

Grapnes – A race of people known for being scavengers. They tried to abduct Jori at one time, but he defended himself.

Gravity wheel – The device that gives the ship artificial gravity.

Gregson – Doctor Gregson is one of the primary doctors on the *Odyssey*.

Gresher – Second Lieutenant Rik Gresher is one of two lieutenants serving under Captain Arden on the *Odyssey*.

Gretchen – Lady Gretchen is a Cooperative dignitary mentioned by Hapker.

Guiding Principles – The written principles that the Prontaean Cooperative claims to follow.

Hapker – Vice Executive Commander J.D. Hapker is second-in-command of the *Odyssey* under Captain Arden.

H.A.R.K. testing – A type of test used to detect whether someone is genetically altered.

Harley – Corporal Harley is a PG-Force officer who serves as a PG-Force officer on the *Defender*. Sergeant Ortega and Chief Singh are his friends. He had also been a prisoner on Jori's father's ship.

Henthian – A proper adjective defining people or things from Henth, in this case, brandy.

Holo-man – A projected image of a person. This projection uses haptic technology that allows it to be touched and felt. It is used for various functions including as a visual instructor for dancing, exercise, and martial arts. It isn't always a man. It can be programmed to look like just about anything, including animals and objects. There is a more technical term for this, but it is not mentioned in this story.

Hyena – The Hyena is the nickname of Doctor Menger, a MEGA hunter.

Hypospray – Used by medics to inject medicine or nanites.

IM – Instant message.

Imperium-animi – The strongest and most dangerous type of reader. They can wipe memories or implant thoughts into another person. The Cooperative strongly regulates people with this ability.

Indore space station – A space station in Cooperative territory. This space station is where fresh squads of special forces soldiers are picked up.

Inertial dampener – A device on starships that keeps inertia from throwing and smashing the crew when the starship is being maneuvered or when it is struck.

Inhibitor – A new technology worn behind the ear that can block the abilities of sentio, extraho, and imperium-animis.

Jahara – A province on one of the Toradon worlds, known for its white sand dunes.

Jakes – An officer mentioned by Ortega.

Janelle – A MEGA Inspection Officer and assistant to Doctor Menger.

J.D. – Vice Executive Commander J.D. Hapker is second-in-command of the *Odyssey* under Captain Arden.

Jerom – Doctor Beck Jerom is one of the primary doctors on the *Odyssey*.

Jeruko – Sensei Jeruko, aka Colonel Jeruko, is Jori's mentor and primary martial instructor.

Jintal – A Jintal master is a master that teaches people how to endure pain.

Jori – Prince Jori Mizuki is a ten-year-old warrior from a race of people the Cooperative calls Tredons. Jori refers to his people as Toradon or Toradon Nohibito/Dragon People.

Kanivian sector – An area of space well outside of Cooperative territory.

Karina Klaspil – A well-known news reporter that reports on galactic news.

Kimurian – A proper adjective defining people or things from Kimuria.

Kishimir outpost – A space-based outpost in Cooperative territory where a MEGA Inspections Office is located.

Korbin – Korbin is a PG-Force officer on the *Defender*. He's also a good friend of Lieutenant Gresher. His rank is never given.

Kramer – Corporal Kramer serves on the bridge of the *Defender* and is suspicious of Gottfried.

Kozlov – Major Kozlov serves as a PG-Force officer under Captain Richforth on the *Defender*.

Krause – Lieutenant Gottfried Krause serves as Admiral Belmont's personal aide.

Kraykians – A race of people mentioned by Major Esekielu.

Laalgahana – An uninhabitable red planet in the same system of Hapker's homeworld.

Lamprey – The Lamprey is the nickname given to a powerful extraho who works for the MEGA Inspections Office.

Leisure deck – The deck on the Defender where one can relax or participate in recreational activities. It doesn't actually take up the entire deck.

Lengen – Corporal Lengen serves as a PG-Force officer on the *Defender* who hates Jori.

Letta – Sergeant Carletta Ortega, aka Letta, serves as a PG-Force officer on the *Defender*.

Liangpi – Wide flat noodles usually served cold and spicy with bits of seaweed mixed in.

Loushian – A proper adjective defining people or things from Loushi, in this case, a cat.

Marvdacht – The planet that Jori will be sent to. They have strict laws about MEGAs.

Matro – Sergeant Ortega's pet lemur.

Mazie – Doctor Mazie Donnel psychiatric doctor who serves on the *Defender*.

MDS – This is a read-only device used to access the Main Data Stream, which is a digital public library. Media can only be accessed via a direct-connection port and must be uploaded onto it.

Mech suit – A military enviro-suit with strength enhancers, additional protection against weapons, and embedded weaponry.

Med-scanner – A medical scanning device that can detect heartbeats and a range of other physiological functions.

MEGA – Stands for mechanically enhanced genetically altered.

MEGA hunter – A slang word for a MEGA Inspection Officer.

MEGA Injunction – Some decades ago, it was popular for rich people to get genetic and biometric enhancements. Common people felt such enhancements were unfair, especially since these enhanced people considered themselves superior and tended to seek positions of power. Protests became violent. As such, governments all over the galaxy stepped up. People with unnatural abilities were ejected from positions of power and strict laws were made to protect future generations.

MEGA Inspection Officer – Aka MEGA Inspector or MEGA hunter. This officer works for an organization that roots out MEGAs and makes sure they get filed in the intergalactic database. Many officers are fanatic about their work as they strongly believe that alterations to the human body is immoral.

MEGA Inspections Office – The formal name of the organization that roots out MEGAs.

MEGA-Man – A cybernetic man who has made himself into the most advanced man-machine in the galaxy. He is the leader of a race of cyborgs.

Menger – Doctor Menger, aka the Hyena, is a MEGA Inspections Officer, aka MEGA hunter.

Mizuki – Mizuki is Jori's family name. His father is Emperor Mizuki and is the ruthless ruler of the Toradon Nohibito/Dragon People, aka Tredons.

MM – Stands for Mini Machine. It is a computer that is most often worn around the wrist like a brace but can be flattened and held like a tablet.

Nanites – Microscopic machines with various capabilities. The Cooperative uses them in their healing beds, enviro-suits, and more. The nanites that were in Jori's body could replicate into various properties. Some specialized in helping him heal while others created electronic functions that record, emit signals, or send out pulses. His nanites had a short shelf-life and so he no longer has them. The Cooperative highly regulates the use of nanites since they can be used as weapons and can be dangerous if there is a flaw in their programming.

Nedell – Specialist Nedell serves as a technician on the *Defender*.

New Bristol – A city on the planet Aeneas where a famous sport reminiscent of football (aka soccer) is played.

New Croatia – A planet in Cooperative territory where the news reports a plague of locusts.

Nohibito – Means people in Jori and Terk's language. It is often used together with Toradon Nohibito, as in Dragon People.

Novak – Sergeant First Class Niel Novak is a special forces PG-Force officer temporarily assigned to the *Defender*.

Odyssey – The name of a PCC Expedition-class vessel captained by Silas Arden. This vessel is the largest type of vessel in the PCC. It has some firepower for protection, but it is a non-military ship. The ship houses hundreds of people and their families. Families are permitted on this vessel because of its non-military nature. There are military personnel serving on this type of ship, but they act more as security than as a military force.

Ortega – Sergeant Carletta Ortega, aka Letta, serves as a PG-Force officer on the *Defender*.

Paldino – A PG-Force officer serving on the *Defender*.

Parvati – A distant star system in the Kanivian sector that the cyborg race inhabits.

PCC – The Prontaean Colonial Cooperative is the sub-organization that handles intergalactic relations, conducts space exploration, performs space-based scientific endeavors, assists travelers, and sometimes provides transportation.

Perantium – A hardy type of crystal. It was used to create a powerful emitter intended to quell the tectonic activity of the planet Thendi but was stolen by Jori's father. The emperor planned to convert it into a planet killing weapon.

PG-Force – The Prontaean Galactic Force is the sub-organization that polices Cooperative space.

PG Institute – The Prontaean Galactic Institute is a training facility for anyone who wants to work for the Prontaean Cooperative. The institute trains both PCC and PG-Force officers.

Pholatian Protector – A service-oriented military force from the planet Pholatia, Hapker's homeworld.

Plasti-glass – See-through panes that are more flexible than glass.

Polemos station – A space station in Cooperative territory briefly mentioned by Hapker.

Potaway flute – A musical instrument that is made of wood.

Power-K – A sidearm that uses both projectiles and energy-based firepower.

Primitivo – A type of wine.

Prontaean – It is a word that describes the known galaxy. It is believed the word derived from an ancient Earth Indo-European language where the prefix pro- means advanced or forward and the suffix -anean means relating to.

Prontaean Colonial Cooperative – The PCC is the sub-organization that handles intergalactic relations, conducts space exploration, performs space-based scientific endeavors, assists travelers, and sometimes provides transportation.

Prontaean Cooperative – The agency that governs space. It has numerous treaties with various worlds that provides its charter to keep space safe, ensure peace, regulate fair trade, and colonize new worlds. Its powers are granted by several planets, and the number of planets that are part of the Cooperative continues to grow. The Prontaean Cooperative has two aspects to it. The first is the Prontaean Colonial Cooperative (PCC). This sub-organization handles intergalactic relations, conducts space exploration, performs space-based scientific endeavors, assists travelers, and sometimes provides transportation. The second aspect is the Prontaean Galactic Force (PG-Force). This sub-organization polices space.

Prontaean Cooperative Council – The Prontaean Cooperative is ruled by an elected council.

Prontaean Galactic Force – The PG-Force is the sub-organization that polices Cooperative space.

Prontaean Games – Similar to the Olympics from ancient Earth.

Ramgarhia – Commander Ramgarhia serves as the second-in-command under Captain Richforth on the *Defender*.

Reader – The generic term for someone who uses the power of their mind to sense emotions or to read or manipulate thoughts.

Rhinian – A proper adjective defining people or things from Rhinus, in this case, mercenaries.

Richforth – Captain Richforth is the captain of the *Defender*, a PG-Force ship. Hapker used to serve under him when he was a PG-Force officer.

Rik – Second Lieutenant Rik Gresher is one of two lieutenants serving under Captain Arden on the *Odyssey*.

RR-5 rifle – A phaser rifle with multiple settings and functionalities.

Sadalge – An officer mentioned by Ortega.

Safety Depot – When a ship is in danger, non-essential personnel go to one of these many designated areas to strap in. Many safety depots double as escape pods when needed.

Sahim – Corporal Sahim is a PG-Force officer who serves as security on the *Defender*.

Santerian – A proper adjective defining people or things from Santera, in this case, a space fighter.

Scheisse – A curse word that means shit in Gresher's language.

Schemster – A game based off chess, but more complicated, has more pieces, and several layers of difficulty built into the moves the pieces can make.

Schmitt – Doctor Schmitt is a doctor recently transferred to the *Defender*.

Senshi – Means warrior in Jori and Terk's language.

Sentio-animi – The lowest level of reader. They can sense emotions only. Their ability does not force anything out or in and so people with this ability are not required to register with the Cooperative.

Shashti station – A space station in Cooperative territory mentioned by Gottfried.

Shokukin – Means worker in Jori's language. In the caste-based society, shokukins are barely considered better than slaves.

Shuku – The name for a particular nebula that Jori is familiar with.

Similean – A proper adjective defining people or things from Simil, in this case, a tawny owl.

Singh – Chief Singh serves as the chief engineer on the *Defender*. She is also a friend to Ortega and Harley.

Shimla sette wine – A red spiced wine reminiscent of once famous wines from ancient Earth.

Spearhead-class – A spaceship used in battles known for its speed.

SSHIN scanner – A scanner that scans for biometric implants and nanites.

Suarana – First Lieutenant Suarana serves as a PG-Force officer on the *Defender*.

Tablet – A small hand-held computer device much like the tablets of the 21st century, but with more functionality. Some tablets can be folded around the wrist, and are then called an MM.

Tavandish – A proper adjective defining people or things from Tavandier.

Thendi – A planet that is having trouble with plate tectonics.

Thera-pen – A medical device used to heal minor-wounds.

Toradon – Means dragon in Jori and Terk's language. It is often spoken as Toradon Nohibito, which means Dragon People.

Torque multiplier – A powerful wrench.

TR7 – A phaser rifle that specializes in stunning its targets.

Transport – One way to transport uses a device that teleports people or objects from a ship to another or to a planet's surface. The person or object transported must have a bio-reader.

Transport-blocker – A device that keeps the transport from working. Since the shields on a ship work the same way, transport-blockers are usually used on planets or other bodies.

Tredon – This is what everyone outside Toradon calls this race of people. It sounds like the words tread on, which is what the Toradons are known to do to people.

Triptolemos – A newly settled planet in Cooperative territory.

Tymneria – A location on Gottfried's homeworld known for geysers.

Vadomese – A proper adjective defining people or things from Vadomere.

Varma – An extraho-animi who works for Doctor Menger in the MEGA Inspections Office.

Vavich – A technician who serves on the *Defender*.

Venezuela – An officer mentioned by Ortega.

Viewport – A large screen that shows the view from outside. Ships don't have windows, but a viewport simulates a window.

Viewscreen – A large computer screen.

Wall ball – A game played by two people where they hit the ball against a wall with racquets.

Warszawski – Warszawski, aka Warsaw, serves as a PG-Force officer on the *Defender*. His rank is never given.

Wood – Doctor Wood is a MEGA Inspections Officer and assistant to Doctor Menger.

Xandu delegation – A body of representatives formed to solve a dispute between two worlds. The admiral was supposed to meet with them.

Zambarda – A special forces PG-Force officer temporarily assigned to the *Defender*.

Zimmer – Rear Admiral Zimmer presides over both the PCC and PG-Force. He commanded directly over Hapker at one time.

Books by Dawn Ross:

<u>**The Dragon Spawn Chronicles**</u>

StarFire Dragons
Dragon Emperor
Dragon's Fall
Isle of Hogs (a novella)
Warrior Outcast

Connect with Dawn Ross online:
DawnRossAuthor.com
Twitter.com/DawnRossAuthor
Goodreads.com/author/Dawn_Ross

About the Author

Dawn Ross currently resides in the wonderful state of Kansas where sunflowers abound. She has also lived in the beautiful Willamette Valley of Oregon and the scenic Hill Country of Texas. Dawn completed her bachelor's degree in 2017. Although the degree is in finance, most of her electives were in fine art and creative writing. Dawn is married to a wonderful man and adopted two children in 2017. Her current occupation is part time at the Meals on Wheels division of a senior service nonprofit organization. She is also a mom, homemaker, volunteer, wildlife artist, and a sci-fi/fantasy writer. Her first novel was written in 2001 and she's published several others since. She participates in the NaNoWriMo event every year and is a part of her local writers' group.

About the Author

[illegible]

Made in the USA
Monee, IL
02 December 2024

70406891R00233